JAMAICA
BREAKDOWN

JAMAICA
BREAKDOWN

The story of love in a time of sickness

A ROMANTIC THRILLER

C. JEAN BAKER

AND

GARY P. BAKER

A Novel

Cover design by: C. Jean Baker
Published in the United States of America

ISBN 979-8-9986066-1-8

To Jeffrey, Keshia, Mary Jo, and Jane for giving optimism and love on our journey to write this work of fiction.

"You know people exaggerate that all is wild in Jamaica. I think that sometimes people fire a shot to try to make you nervous. They are not trying to hurt you."

MICHAEL MANLEY (B. 1924, D. 1997), JAMAICAN POLITICIAN, FORMER PRIME MINISTER. DAILY TELEGRAPH, (LONDON, FEB. 8, 1989).

TABLE OF CONTENTS

CHAPTER ONE

Thursday, Sept. 20, 1984 — Returning to the U.S.A.

Streaking like a silver arrow high across the nighttime sky, a darkened Boeing 727 carried Barry Wright and his wife Mae home from a horrific vacation cut short. Amid the passengers flying in coach, the rumpled couple sat strapped in bulkhead seats and trapped in their own labyrinth of terror. Both wanted to end their awful nightmare that was not a dream.

High on adrenaline and feeling jacked up like a clown, Barry sat wedged in a tiny aisle seat for a big guy like himself. He gave a weary, worried sigh, shaking his head to dispel his fury about what had happened. Their getaway to the terrific Caribbean — a pricey vacation in paradise that his wife had cooked up, shape-shifted into an inescapable nightmare. And the ordeal was not over. To top it off, he had endured two time-consuming layovers to get home with Mae alive. He desperately wanted to come down from what felt like a bad psychedelic trip.

Mae slept in the window seat with her fears, which made him glad. As long as she was asleep, he could rest. If only he could sleep, but he was afraid to even close his eyes. His massive body leaned in the direction of her bantam body, ready to control her like a guard rail.

Eager to see something familiar, Barry glanced out the porthole next to Mae. He tensed up as he watched thunderheads blooming and growing with the rapidity of malignant midnight fungi, edge-lit with electrical activity and towering higher and higher. Suddenly turbulence bucked the big jet. He felt sick with dread when he heard the engines shriek in the blackness, straining to reach their destination as the storm gathered in dark promise, threatening to close the busy airport.

"Ladies and gentlemen," the captain's voice came crackling over the PA system. "We are beginning our final approach to Chicago O'Hare International Airport... "

Barry irritably blurted out, "'Bout time we catch a break!"

Their flight had received permission to land, possibly the last one for a time that night due to the increasingly foul weather. As the jetliner banked and began its descent, a ripple of activity ran through the dimly lit second-class cabin. The smattering of passengers on the late-night flight gathered their belongings, returned their seats to the upright position, fastened any still unfastened seat belts, laughed nervously joking about the weather, and generally prepared for landing.

Not Barry Wright, he remained still, fixed in his seat. His sweaty palm rubbed against his wife's softer skin as he resolutely held onto her hand. Worn out from being up for 28 hours straight, 12 of them trying to get to this point, Barry lacked the strength to scratch an itch. He never had been so tired, not even from working at his crummy demanding job, which up until this time was his definition of hell. But, inside his mind, thoughts whirled like a blender chugging away at too much head-throbbing rage mixed with too much gut-wrenching worry.

Struggling with exhaustion, Barry tried to keep his mind focused on the problem at hand, literally *at hand*. He stared at the pale, clammy fingers of his right hand tightly entwined with the small, slender digits of his wife's left hand. The dull gleam of Mae's simple wedding band triggered a familiar pang of regret that he had been unable to give the woman he loved the simplest diamond engagement ring. There just never seemed to be enough money to cover all the necessities of life. The Florentine piece of metal, warm from his grip, ground into the tender flesh between his fingers. He welcomed the dull pain. It helped to keep him awake; helped to remind him that this nightmare was real and that he and Mae were still trapped in it.

Although Barry hoped Mae would remain unconscious for as long as possible, his hand had held her hand in the same position for so long it felt numb. So slowly, minutely, he moved each finger to get blood circulating while trying not to wake her or relax his clutch.

Clutch, like a nickname, he thought. It suddenly rang like an echo amid the turmoil in his mind where a voice that sounded like himself gibbered whenever he was conscious, and even when he was asleep and dreaming. So much of what the voice had to say was trivial snatches of doggerel, advertising jingles from his childhood, and small mean thoughts. Under more normal circumstances, Barry frequently considered that if only he could silence the gibberer he might be able to better focus his mind, cultivate his talents, achieve higher consciousness — an enigmatic goal of his hippie college years. Still, he had a penchant for naming things like native American tribe members and possessed a vivid imagination (though not a plus in his present state).

My good pal *Clutch*, Barry fondly considered his grip on his wife. Clutch gripped her hand, sometimes her upper-arm for greater control, while great-big-Barry tussled with his tiny resisting wife through hotel lobbies, in and out of ground transports, what passed for a hospital in the Third World, through U. S. Customs in Miami, and on and off too many planes while strangers pretended there was nothing at all odd about the sight until they had passed, and then they came to life, whispering, gaping and pointing, agreeing amongst themselves that maybe someone should call a cop or something. Now, Clutch maintained a grip on Mae's hand while she slept, so she could not escape if she suddenly sprang up into a fight or flight mode. In his weariness, Barry thought Clutch took on a life all its own. Clutch reacted involuntarily like a knee-jerk reaction whenever the wild and crazy spirit that possessed his wife emerged. When the irrational Mae was conscious, Barry wished he had more pals to control her.

Lightning tore a jagged "Y" in the sky. Barry lifted his gaze to see it and watched as the prolonged flash reflected a scary figure on the windowpane. Instinctively he flinched at the sight, even as he realized it was his own distorted image. He smirked. Thunder like a sonic boom ensued. The noise must have penetrated to wherever Mae had retreated in her drug-induced sleep because she mumbled and stirred. His heart pounded loudly in his ears for a few long seconds, eyeing Mae closely to see if she came awake with that frantic look in her eyes. When she settled back to sleep, he realized he was holding his breath and exhaled, relaxing a couple of notches but still wound up dangerously tight.

Once more Barry Wright turned and stared back into the night, searching the thunderous clouds for a glimpse of his hometown's glittery skyscrapers. He often griped about how the buildings cluttered and ruined the natural beauty of Lake Michigan's shoreline. But he yearned to see Chicago's skyline tonight, a desperate glimpse of his salvation. Instead, cumulonimbus clouds prevailed.

Lightning flashed again followed by a prolonged roll of thunder that gradually rumbled off into the distance. Undaunted, Barry watched the storm intensify. The growing disturbance outside the aircraft paled in comparison to the tempest in his mind. He had endured more pure concentrated "bull" since he left Chicago five days ago than ever before in his life. He would rather eat glass than have a confrontation, yet he had faced one after another and then another on his vacation!

"Come-back-to-Jah-may-kah, yah mon."

Barry realized with shock that in a mockingly, singsongy Jamaican lilt, he had been moving his lips and speaking aloud. He glanced around the shadowy cabin to see who might be watching and revolved his head just in time to catch the male flight attendant staring at him. Their eyes made the briefest contact. Obviously startled, the slender, fussy man ducked back into the galley, moving like he had just been stung.

Barry sensed that the prim flight attendant was going into the galley to talk about him.

*   *   *

Relatively few passengers boarded the late-night flight from Atlanta, which the Wrights changed over to from a flight out of Miami. Those passengers who looked at Barry steered clear of the big, ghastly traveler. Even the flight attendants tried to avoid him.

In the galley, the male flight attendant, Scott Lodge, gestured his head in the direction of Barry and whispered to the two female attendants.

"You know that boorish, splotchy guy looks like a real psycho."

They knew which passenger he meant. Beth Kaminski, who dabbed at one of her false eyelashes, allowed the mousy blonde attendant to squeeze past her as that woman scurried back into the first-class section. Scott, a two-year airline veteran, returned to assisting Beth with the disposal of empty plastic cups, napkins, stir-sticks, and assorted beverage service trash.

He continued, "When that psycho boarded, I gave him my best Pan AM smile and politely asked, 'How are you doing this evening?' Do you know what he said to me?"

Scott hesitated for effect. "That barrel-chested weirdo hovered over me like a schoolyard bully, stuck his raggedy walrus mustache and two-day-old beard right in my face, and said, 'I feel like hammered shit!'"

"How rude! I should've told that drunk with his bloodshot eyes, 'Sir, you look like it!'"

"I know exactly what you mean," Beth agreed. "He looks mad and smells bad, but I didn't smell alcohol. He stinks, especially his wet stringy hair. And did you see his shirt pocket? It's torn and just dangling there! He might as well tear it off. And the way he pushes around that pitiful, petite woman... ugh! How can she stay with that brute? He told me that she is his wife. He wanted me to hold her when they first came on board, some fishy story about her being sick."

Beth, who lapsed into a momentary silence, felt a slight twinge of guilt at having been so ready to dismiss the troubled passenger's plea. Then she remembered the man's abusive manner when, shortly after take-off, he pushed a pill down his wife's throat, forcing her to swallow it without water. She congratulated herself on her intuition to steer clear of the whole affair.

"The guy was practically raving at me." Scott added, "I've been watching them."

Both attendants braced as the plane gave a sudden lurch.

"But his wife does look like she might be sick or something." Again, the twinge of guilt troubled Beth. "Scott, maybe we should see if the guy really might need our help."

Scott straightened up to his full five-foot-five inches with alarm evident on his pale face. "I distrust burly, unsightly people. Let's just mind our own business, shall we?" He said firmly, "If you ask me, that big ape is the one who's sick!"

The plane gave another lurch. Scott grabbed Beth's shoulders to avoid colliding with her.

"So, *you* be careful, Beth, when *you* go tell him they aren't prepared for landing. She's still reclined, and his seatbelt isn't fastened."

A little speck of Scott's spit hit Beth's cheek. Beth stared at him until he realized he was still holding on to her shoulders rather tightly. He swallowed hard, releasing his grip on her, fussed with his tie, and straightened his jacket. Then he pointedly went to strap himself in for the impending landing. Beth watched Scott's retreat, unconsciously dabbing her cheek with the back of her hand, wondering why anything he said or did could still have the power to astonish her.

Somebody had to act like a professional, Beth thought, and, steeling herself, she marched around to the opposite side of the cabin and over to the bulkhead to do her duty. She confronted the imposing passenger, at first intending to be authoritative about his compliance. But the haunted look on his face when he turned his hollow brown eyes to meet her gaze, replaced by such ferocity at recognizing her, made her waver in her resolve. She took a respectful approach.

"Sir, you'll have to put your wife's seat upright," she whispered, as if concerned for the sleeper. "As you can see, the captain has turned on the fasten seatbelts light, so…"

The scary passenger turned a hostile gaze upon her, staring her down and looking resentful of anything that might disturb him and his wife.

"Please fasten *your* seatbelt," she added more sternly, voice quivering a tad. "We're about to land."

His unforgiving expression never softened as the angry-looking passenger slowly released the hand he held and rocked the smaller figure into a position for landing, watching to see if she would wake up. When she did not, he twisted forward and fastened his own seatbelt. Then he took his wife's hand once again, looking up defiantly at Beth as if daring her to find anything else to complain about.

Refusing to be intimidated, Beth maintained eye contact. She could feel a potential for violence radiating off his dead-white complexion like heat. Neither spoke a word, but volumes passed between them. Satisfied that she had proven her point, Beth turned and, with a practiced grace, quickly made her way back down the aisle of the swaying plane to take her position beside the almost-smirking, self-congratulating Scott. He jabbed her conspiratorially with his elbow as she fastened her harness. Beth kept an expressionless face.

* * *

Barry glowered at Beth until she had secured herself in her jump seat, thinking she should go bother someone else and just leave him and Mae alone! He had given that ditzy bimbo a chance to be part of the solution. She had chosen to be a part of the problem.

Barry leaned back, trying to ease the muscle spasm in his back. He reminded himself not to get too comfortable because he had to stay in control of Mae.

The plane dropped free of the obscuring clouds as Barry looked out the porthole again. It was drizzling rain. The lower atmosphere was more of a dark and dirty green than black. Below, the gridwork of lights that was the greater Chicago metropolitan area feebly asserted itself. Even with the assistance of the frequent strokes of lightning, Barry was unable to recognize any familiar landmarks or tell from which direction they approached O'Hare.

Instinctively he glanced at his wrist for the time. Startled briefly, he found himself looking at an untanned circle of skin where his Seiko diver's watch used to be. He shook his head and softly gave a bitter chuckle, remembering one of the "highlights" of his stay in Jamaica. He twisted to better read the watch of a young woman sitting across the aisle. It was 10:47 p.m. Noticing his eyes fixed on her, the young woman was unbearably squirming in her seat. He looked back at Mae, thinking they must make quite a spectacle.

He even wondered who that woman was next to him. He could hardly believe that the puffy moon-shaped face beside him belonged to his wife. Once he was able to *get* Mae to what passed for a hospital and to *see* a doctor in

Jamaica, the physician said, "There's nothing I can do for her here." *Unbelievable*, he thought, considering her altered state.

Just a few days before, he had traveled with a different woman. He remembered how beautiful and poised she looked, so vibrant and lively, joking and laughing with her dimpled smile. He missed her sweet voice, sparkly brown eyes, and stirring kiss. He did not fully understand what had happened or why, but he had to get *his* Mae back.

Their trail of trouble boggled his mind. They took a vacation that they could not afford. They got robbed. The police were "in on it." And the only way he could get his wife home alive was to hand out money like he was the Sultan of Brunei!

Barry wanted to rant and rave and rip somebody apart! An entire island of people had tap-danced on his last nerve. It took all his willpower to control his boiling rage. He seriously contemplated thermonuclear warheads and tactical air strikes. If he had found himself possessed of the power at that point in time, Barry Moore Wright would have called down Armageddon on the island of Jamaica.

Thinking of a Nina Simone song, he spat out two words as if they tasted like the whites of lemons, "Jamaica Goddam!"

Barry held tight to the hand of his stirring wife as the plane began to drop through the clouds and the rain, down, through the dark, for its landing. Suddenly he *felt* more than *heard* the landing gear come down. When the plane touched down, Barry felt an immense sense of relief. The thought of being home again — home, where he knew the rules; home, where he understood the language and the culture; and home, where he and Mae were citizens not tourists and they could go back to their simple lives once more — brought a Handel chorus to mind.

As they taxed to the gate, the captain announced, "Ladies and gentlemen, the time in Chicago is..." Blah, blah, blah, he went on about the weather, baggage pickups and connecting flights. His voice and the cacophony of passengers' noises caused Barry to test his endurance more. A bespectacled 5-foot 3-inch woman of African descent, his wife Mae, opened her eyes.

*   *   *

Outside O'Hare, the sodium vapor lights held the darkness at bay and combined with the storm gave an eerie, unnatural quality to the airport. Barry and Mae Bea Wright came out of the doors of Terminal 2 still dressed for the tropics as rain slashed down, driven by a chilly wind. With Mae pulling and tugging to get away from him, Barry, who was overloaded with their luggage, forced her to the curbside shelter of a bus kiosk in the open air.

"Mae, we need to wait here for a shuttle bus to take us to the remote parking lot where we parked our car," Barry harshly explained.

Mae, who had awoke trapped in an overwhelming onset of fear, could not shake off a feeling of impending doom, triggering a desire to jump out of her skin and run away. But her husband clutched her tightly. She could feel that her eyeglasses were askew and knew her Afro looked unkempt, but there was nothing she could do. Her hands were full of a stuffed, extra-large multicolored straw tote that Barry had stuffed in her hands. She hugged it like a teddy bear.

When they reached the kiosk, they stood in the shadow of the main building, wet and shivering, waiting for a shuttle bus. Scared and jittery, weeping and quivering, Mae kept trying to break free from Barry. She pulled and tugged harder, struggling to get away. But Barry, holding onto their luggage, held her like a prisoner, wrangling her in the outdoor kiosk. A hard, windy downpour ensued. Barry clutched her even tighter. Looking up, she examined his frowning face and peered into his hardened brown eyes, hoping to discover a way to escape. Yet, she welcomed his warmth as rain dripped down from her short, coily Afro onto her tear-streaked cheeks. The deluge gradually became a steady downpour as they waited for half an hour.

With each passing minute, Mae's world got swallowed by a bigger and bigger wave of primal fear. When it became extremely great, she pleaded with her husband to let her go.

"Barry, it's not safe. Why won't you listen to me?" Overcome with panic about the safety of their only child, she begged, "Please, we can't go home. We'll lead them to Zac, and they'll kill him, too!" Bobbing up and down, she cried, "Why won't you *listen* to me!"

Holding her forcibly against her will, Barry barked out, "Stop it, Mae! Now, you listen to me. Home is where we are going. It's *exactly* where you belong." She shivered from the cold. He gave a big sigh, "Guess we weren't prepared for this weather, but it's the least of our problems."

Mae thought Barry was naive about the danger they were in, but she was exhausted from fighting him. So, she stopped struggling and collapsed against his damp chest. She closed her eyes and heard a familiar soft, even tone say, "Awe, Honey." *Honey,* the magic word. The sweet sound of Barry saying the magic word rang like Pavlov's bell, awakening an unconditional love for him deep in her heart. Mae breathed in his body musk, which became so intoxicating her fear dissipated in his strong embrace. Right then, she felt normal: loved, protected and safe.

But then Mae opened her eyes. She saw a stranger approaching. Instantly she tensed up.

The solitary figure, who exited the airport terminal, headed rapidly in their direction, head ducked beneath a newspaper, sheltering from the slashing rain. As the slender Black man ran, he started to put his hand inside the breast of his jacket. Mae stiffened. The strange man's approach triggered an overwhelming wave of terror. She started to jerk away from Barry, resisting as he held her tightly to him. Like a wild horse she bucked, trying to get away from the threat while Barry fought to hold onto her. Mae kept bucking in his grip, helplessly watching the onrushing stranger get closer and closer. Despite the rain and her state of terror, Mae could not help seeing him in detail. Although she quickly shut her eyes tight, what she had seen already burned an indelible memory in her mind. An ugly, brutish Jamaican with a scarred face, leering at her with an evil grin filled with teeth filed to sharp, shark-like points came towards her. Dreadlocks dripping rain waved around his head like live snakes. As he rushed straight at her, he reached inside his coat and drew out a big, flat-black, automatic pistol with a silencer jutting from the end of the barrel. He pointed it at her.

Mae yelled, "He's going to kill me!" The thought blazed through her overloaded brain, already seething on the verge of meltdown. She begged, "Barry, please let me go!"

Barry bellowed, "No! Stop it!"

Like a motion picture in reverse, images flashed across Mae's racked and tortured mind. She gradually stopped struggling to get loose from Barry's clutch as she accepted that her violent ending was her own fault. She had devised the plan months earlier that led to this fatal blow. She was going to die for one reason only, and she squeezed it out of her fear-constricted throat.

"I just wanted a *real* vacation."

CHAPTER TWO

Thursday, Feb. 2, 1984 — Beginning with an itch

An Alberta Clipper moved across Northern Illinois that early morning and smacked Mae Wright in the face when she stepped outside her back door, arms full of papers. From the thick rubber tread of her boots to her premium arctic parka with a merino wool scarf wrapped tightly around her neck and covering her mouth, Mae had tried to avoid suffering from frostbite. But outside, where it was as dark as midnight, there was no way to avoid the tingling pain in her eyebrows. She persevered, trudging along like Boris Karloff in "The Mummy" as her boots' traction-ensured soles gripped the packed snow and crushed in her footprints. She guessed at the path of the hidden red-brick walkway, which led to the detached garage at the end of the long backyard. By the time she reached the garage's side door, Mae had goosebumps and chattering pearly whites. The mercury had to be zero in that crisp pre-dawn hour, and, with the wind chill factor, even colder than that. Still, Mae carried on, thinking there was nothing more torturous than a mild, colorful autumn followed by a brutally cold winter. She squeezed her eyes shut and pushed open the side door. A gust of freezer-locker wind assaulted her.

Mae whispered her desire, "I wish I were somewhere warm and sunny."

When she opened the squeaky car door, the little dome light winked at her like a fellow conspirator. She flung manila file folders and a faded old book, Mammals of the Great Lakes Region by William H. Burt, onto the passenger bucket seat. Then she went and pulled up the stiff tilt-up garage door. Returning to the driver's side of the car, Mae squeezed her heavily clad body behind the steering wheel of the VW Rabbit, feeling like the Michelin Man — the fat mascot of a tire company. With the door closed, she pulled her scarf down and her warm breath fogged up the windows and her tortoise shell-framed eyeglasses. She ignored it, feeling around adjusting the car seat and mirrors from her husband's position to suit her. Finally, Mae's bright blue hooded parka began to warm her body. But whenever she wore that goose down jacket, she felt overstuffed like Monty Python's Mr. Creosote, just before he exploded from that one last mint.

Playfully Mae puffed out her cheeks and said, "Ka-boom!"

Breath sputtered from her clear glossy lips like air escaping from an untied balloon. Amused, she giggled and began using her strong, rabbit-like front teeth to pull the ragg wool mitten off her right hand. Mae sorted out the ignition key from a big bunch of keys on a jumbo key ring. Making sure the transmission was "in neutral," she put the correct key in the switch, pushed in the clutch, and turned over the key. The cold engine started. The instruments lit up, but she could barely make out 4:58 a.m. on the dashboard clock.

Her eyeglasses had defogged, so Mae wondered for a second why the numbers looked fuzzy to her even with her prescription eyeglasses on. But she soon forgot about it, quickly congratulating herself for meeting her first goal of the day: leaving the house by 5 a.m. While waiting for the engine to warm up before beginning the 35-mile trip to her job, Mae felt an itch. She reached up her left sleeve and aggressively scratched the dime-sized rash on her left forearm, just below the elbow. That did the trick.

Mae carefully pulled down her coat's hood, uncovering her short Afro. She patted down her strands of short, coily hair, then fastened her seatbelt and switched on the headlights. Mae glanced over her shoulder to make sure the coast was clear. Upon seeing a foggy empty alley, she let out the clutch slowly until she found the pressure point, fed the engine a little more gas, released the clutch completely, and then backed out slowly behind the frame bungalow she and her husband rented on the 2300 block of Grey Avenue in Evanston, Illinois.

"Thank you, Barry," Mae said lovingly.

Barry, her sweet husband, had promised to close the heavy garage door when he left to take the elevated train or "L" to downtown Chicago for his job. That meant Mae did not have to go back out into the cold. Also, her caring husband had taught her to drive.

Growing up on Chicago's South Side, Mae's family was poor and did not own a car. Her White husband was shocked to learn that, at 21 years old, she had never driven a car. Astonished, he immediately taught her how to drive, and a manual transmission at that.

Mae carefully proceeded to cruise in first gear to the end of the bumpy, crusty alley.

She found no easy escape from a couple of familiar potholes that Barry would not be happy about. Finally, she got onto the plowed pavement of Grant Street and headed West. Using the stick shift to change gears, she put a heavy foot down on the gas pedal and sped off in the yellow Rabbit like a bat out of a cave, heading for another long, exciting day at the Chicago Zoo.

Although Mae had arrived home from work about 9 p.m. the previous night, she had to leave extra early this morning for a special event. The previous day, Mae arrived at work about eight o'clock with a long to-do list, including writing and reproducing a news release for the next day's special event. First thing, as usual, she went to the office of the zoo police to sign out a walkie-talkie for the day, the zoo's method of rapid communications.

"Looks like Brook's about to pop," Jack, the nasally sounding guard on duty said, proudly spreading a newsworthy announcement.

Mae, trying to act nonchalant, replied, "Really?" Still, grateful that he had told her the breaking news, she smiled, "Thanks for letting me know."

She calmly took the walkie-talkie and slowly walked out the door, pretending not to be excited. Then she practically sprinted across the snow-cleared plaza, through Admin — the administration building, and back to her PR/Marketing office. So afraid of missing the delivery, she grabbed a notebook off her desk and moved quickly out the back door, rushing on the snow-cleared path to get to the Pachyderm House, making a beeline to the secluded off-exhibit area.

Shima, a 60-pound black rhinoceros, finally had been born in the Pachyderm House just minutes before she arrived. The birth of a healthy black rhino, an endangered species, was a happy occasion for the zoo staff, who were as proud as the parents Embu and Brook.

They had been recording for more than a week for scientific purposes since no one could predict the exact time of birth. As planned, Mae quickly worked with the zoo photographer, Jake, to edit the footage for distribution to the news media. Then, while Jake dubbed the videotape, Mae called editor Paul Zimm to announce the birth and provide other facts over the telephone, information he would distribute via the City Newswire Service.

Simultaneously Mae's secretary, Callie, typed up the final news release, which Mae had drafted days earlier. Without a delivery service nearby because the zoo was in the suburbs, Mae hopped in her yellow Rabbit and drove to Chicago. She walked freely into the offices of the four major television stations, WBBM, WMAQ, WLS, and WGN, and handed B-roll footage and a copy of the news release to the news editors. The black rhino story and segments of the B-roll aired as the feel-good story at the end of the local news on those channels. But Mae saw none of the coverage that evening. She worked well into the evening to meet a copy deadline for the second quarterly zoo membership newsletter — what she was supposed to be doing instead of delivering rhino footage to Chicago broadcast stations.

Mae knocked herself out trying to get media coverage of the zoo. In those days, the news media had no beat reporters for zoology, ecology, or conservation. As the zoo's newly appointed PR/Marketing manager, she had to beat the bushes and blaze the trail. But, as a woman of African descent, Mae was used to putting in long hours and going above and beyond the call of duty. In fact, she expected nothing less. Mae had grown up listening to sermons about how she was going to have to be smarter and work harder and longer than anyone else to get ahead in this world because she had African blood.

Mae came from a long line of American slaves who endured biases in the United States. In college, she had gone to the Newberry Library and, scrolling through microfiche, traced her lineage back to the 1800s in North Carolina, one of the original 13 colonies. It gave her a little pride to know that her family tree consisted of more than three generations born in the U.S.A.

Still, her mother drilled in one fact while she was growing up, "White folks ain't gonna *give* you nothin'!" Mae had *heard that.* During her 35 years on this earth, she found it to be true. Mae had worked like a dog since she was 12 years old, trying to prove that she was highly competent. And she had shaken the chip off her shoulder once she discovered everyone carried their own bag of rocks. Black or White, rich or poor, everyone lived with some kind of prejudice or misery. If you were Black, you were not White. If you were White, you were not White enough as either peasant, gentry, or nobility. Even the noblest, Whitest family in England felt they had to change their name because of German ancestry.

So, Mae met her challenges with a genuine smile, which lifted the corners of her mouth and created a dimple in each cheek that brightened her face. She stayed optimistic in the face of most obstacles as Mae spent every day trying to show she was worthy of the rare management position she held as the only African American employed by the Chicago Zoo, a quality that endeared her to her family, friends, and co-workers.

On this day, driving to work, Mae flicked on the radio, stabbing the pre-set button for her favorite station. She hoped for some good music or at least the most recent weather and traffic report. The time Mae spent alone in the car each working day was about the only time she had to call her own. She rarely saw her best friends, Emjay and Veejay. She glanced at the stack of papers beside her. An avid reader who had majored in English lit, Mae spent her time nowadays reading to absorb knowledge of zoology and conservation. She needed to learn so much more than she knew. She told herself, "Stop with these scattered thoughts and focus on driving." Too often she found it difficult to clear her mind. The commute had become so familiar after five months that she frequently drove most of the way on automatic pilot, arriving with little memory of the details of that day's drive. Heading west on Golf Road, Mae zoomed along the western outskirts of the City of Chicago at a fast clip. Tiny lake-effect snowflakes whirled in the beams of her headlights. She pushed the button on the turn signal wand. The readout indicated she had gone exactly 5 miles.

"Only 30 miles to go," she murmured to herself, and a hearty, unanticipated yawn surprised her. She tittered, "I could've used a little more sleep this morning."

No matter which route Mae chose to travel between home and the zoo, the distance was about the same: a helluva long way. Still, she felt living in Evanston, so far from work, was worth the trouble. This morning, which appeared hazy to her spectacled eyes, she chose to take her favorite route. She would drive west down Golf Road to the Tri-State Tollway, then onto I-294 south to the Eisenhower Expressway, and then drive back east to exit in Maywood, Illinois, at First Avenue. This route meant more miles, but driving the expressways made it the fastest. The peppy little 4-cylinder Rabbit had warmed up nicely. She sped along with everyone else.

Mae cut back on the heat, took off her gloves and unsnapped the top of her parka. She considered stopping for "a cup of joe" to-go but decided against it. She did not enjoy coffee anyway; never developed the habit of drinking it. Besides, caffeine jangled her nerves too much. Barry called her a cheap date because a little coffee or alcohol went a long way with Mae. A love song playing on the radio caught her attention. She sang along. When it came to its sentimental conclusion, Mae switched from easy listening to an all-news station. She tried to listen to as many stations as possible because her efforts usually resulted in news reports on most of them.

Again, her forearm itched. Mae tried to scratch it through the thick parka but that did not work. To be safe, she would have to live with the itch until the car stopped. Mae set her mind to ignore the irritation. What nagged at her that morning was having missed time with her 11-year-old son, Zachery. Zac went to bed at 8 p.m., so she had not spent time with him the night before. This day, she left before he got up. As a working mom, Mae could give Zac material things that he needed and wanted, but it saddened her heart to miss irretrievable moments of his growth. She let out a heavy sigh.

Next, she started to worry about finishing her to-do list so she could leave on time that evening to pick up Barry. Then, she worried about her weight. In the winter, it was so easy to gain a few pounds. Luckily, she weighed in at a tolerable 125 pounds that morning. She was losing weight without any effort. She wondered why. Still, putting on the blue parka, which she thought added the appearance of another 20 pounds, was very disheartening. But she had to wear that coat often during the record-breaking cold temperatures of the Chicago winter of 1983-1984.

Mae looked up at a highway billboard with a White model advertising sunscreen. She wondered what it would be like to lounge in the sun on a vacation — the type of vacation she had never experienced or even knew she could dream of for herself. Mae's experience with vacations as a youngster consisted of 8-hour drives down Interstate 55 (I-55) to visit relatives in Memphis, Tennessee, staying in their homes for a three-day weekend. Since marrying Barry, she had dragged him on an airplane trip to stay a week with friends in Colorado. Another time, they drove to Roanoke, Virginia, to spend a week in the home of friends. Otherwise, vacation meant camping out in Wisconsin, in early spring or late fall because Barry wanted to avoid the crowds.

She admonished herself to get serious, now was not the time to think about that stuff.

Mae stabbed another radio pre-set, this time finding a loud-mouthed, opinionated rock jock and his affable buffoon of a sidekick. Rock music did not soothe her nerves, but Neil Young's "Cinnamon Girl," a song her husband often played for her, came on. Soon the duo's empty-headed chatter entertained her for the remainder of her trip until she realized she was driving along First Avenue with barely a mile left to go. As soon as Mae turned onto Zoo Avenue, she slowed to a safety-conscious crawl, honoring the zoo's regulations. She switched off the radio and rolled down her window, pushing in the clutch and coasting the rest of the way to the guard post at South Gate. The cold air rushed in and carried the crunching sound that her tires made rolling over the newly spread crystals of salt.

There were three small, heated sheds where the public paid their admission fee. Mae pulled up to the only staffed booth at that hour. She cheerfully greeted the old guard inside who slid back the glass.

"Good morning, Harve." She pushed up her tortoise shell-framed eyeglasses and flashed him her brightest dimpled smile, "Happy Groundhog Day!"

"Mornin'," the perpetually taciturn security guard responded with great effort, ignoring her reference to the quasi-holiday. The old guard near retirement wore his usual dour expression — as if he were sucking on something unpleasant that would never quite melt in his mouth. It was a game they played every working morning: Mae trying to spread a little sunshine his way, and Harve remaining unmoved by her attempts to be charming. After a pause, Harve finally worked up the steam to add, "We didn't get the papers."

Along with most of the other long-time security guards, Harvester Pissant, called Harve, did not like the fact that soon after starting as the PR/Marketing manager, Mae inadvertently caused what he believed to be an extra burden of responsibility on his shoulders: the back-breaking task of receiving two daily newspapers from a delivery service around 6 a.m. and then turning them over to Mae upon her arrival at 9 a.m. On Mondays, the stack was very bulky since it contained the weekend editions, unless Mae had worked the weekend and picked them up.

This day was Thursday and only a few minutes past 6 a.m.

Although Harve endeavored to be difficult, Mae responded with a relaxed lack of concern, "Really? It's still early. Please give them to Callie when she comes in."

Mae's secretary, Calandra Lark, called Callie, was a very attractive young woman in full flower, blessed with a voluptuous figure. Most males were happy to see Callie coming their way and stared after her when she departed. Even Harve, Mae amused herself with the secret thought.

Harve pointed to the junction and said, "Channel 2 is waiting down there."

Sure enough, Mae spotted the WBBM-TV news van at the junction where it sat idling, red taillights tinting the plume of its exhaust. It was about 50 yards down the hill from the guard post, where the street dead-ended into the South Gate's main entrance.

"Already? They're early."

Despite her best efforts, Mae had missed her goal of arriving before the TV crew. She did not want to be known for operating on CP Time, you know, Colored People's Time.

"Thank you, Harve."

Mae suspected that Harve knew she felt disappointed and was hiding his mirth at her discomfiture. She could not imagine what his laugh would sound like, but she was certain it would be a scrawny undernourished thing, entering the world with little hope of flourishing. She smiled but knew better than to wait for any further acknowledgment of her existence from the guard, who had already closed the glass and returned to sitting on his stool, practicing the high art of lacking all facial expression while maintaining a thousand-yard stare.

Rolling up her window, Mae pulled forward to the stop sign at the top of the hill. From there, she could see over the wall and take in a good portion of the zoological park. In the crisp, early morning silence, with the air so frigid, the many smoking chimneys gave evidence that the zoo's denizens were snug in their various habitats. Warm light leaked from the windows of many buildings. The snow-encrusted zoo reminded her of a magical castle or some fortified self-sufficient medieval town where magic happened.

Normally, after proceeding down the hill, Mae would turn left at the crossroad and drive across the parking lot to where she could gain access to a private driveway in the southwest quadrant of the park. This morning, however, she would lead the TV crew over the freshly cleared pavement to the right, leading to the southeast quadrant.

* * *

Feb. 2, mid-morning — Smoldering a desire for a vacation

Groundhog Day was a customary celebration at the zoo. Winter-weary Chicagoans waited to know whether the North American marmot (*Marmota monax*), also called woodchuck, would see its shadow. The legend ran that if it did, the sight would frighten it back into its warm burrow, predicting six more weeks of winter, and, if it did not, spring would arrive soon.

Mae's organized event for the annual observance was to be held at 10 a.m. That prior Friday, she had issued a media advisory announcing the photo opportunity. However, because of the brutally cold weather, she expected only a few hardy souls from the nearby news weeklies who were interested in obtaining "Chi-town" coverage. But the preceding day, just after she returned from delivering black rhino footage, WBBM-Channel 2's weather forecaster Harry Sutherland called to request an exclusive daybreak location shoot for his morning segment. Mae depended on news media coverage to generate zoo visitors, and broadcast reached a far larger audience than print. Not to mention, she genuinely liked Harry. So, she decided to be obliging. It meant more hours of her time but guaranteed that the Chicago Zoo, 20 miles from the media hub in Chicago, would get TV coverage that day.

As she approached the van, Harry Sutherland slid open the side door and stepped down, waving a gloved hand in greeting. She pulled her car over, leaving the headlights on to illuminate the scene of the impromptu meeting. She struggled briefly with the seatbelt and her overstuffed coat, recovering sufficiently to make a graceful exit from the yellow Rabbit.

"Good morning, and welcome to the zoo!"

Mae extended her hand, her frosty breath illustrating her words in the chilled air as her eyeglasses fogged up a bit. Harry, a trim, attractive man, with qualities of elegance and style, tipped his fedora as he shook her outstretched ungloved hand.

"Hello, Mae, always a pleasure to see you. Thanks for meeting me so early to do this."

"My pleasure," she said respectfully.

Harry had a down-to-earth, folksy demeanor, which had stood him well and kept him popular during a long, distinguished career as an on-air personality. Mae felt proud to have him there, anytime, because he was pleasant, modest, and not too pushy.

"Well, let's get going before we freeze," laughed Mae. "Just follow me down this private access road around to the back entrance to the Children's Zoo." She had to add, "One more thing, please don't honk your horn. It scares the animals. Okay?"

Harry laughed, "Sure, no problem,"

He snugged his hat and glove back on and climbed back into the van. Mae hurried into the warmth of her car. She proceeded along the road, heading for the Big Red Barn in the Children's Zoo, as the van stayed close to her tail.

The Chicago Zoo sprawled over 315 acres of county-owned forest preserves. Not only did the zoological park have large ground squirrels like the groundhog, but species of lions, tigers, bears, apes, and monkeys. It also had double-wattled cassowaries, cuscus, kiwis, okapis, Tasmanian devils, and a great many other species, both wild and exotic. Even marine mammals were represented in the form of dolphins, sea lions, a seal and an incredibly popular walrus named Olga. The zoo ranked among the top five in the nation, with more than 2,100 specimens of 485 species from around the world. It was among the first in the U.S. to begin exhibiting animals in spacious naturalistic outdoor enclosures. A whole community all by itself, the sprawling Chicago Zoo operated its very own water tower, fire brigade, ambulance, sanitation and police force, animal hospital and commissary, a library and bookstore, and a gift shop.

Mae was responsible for promoting all of it, quite an unexpected environment for the daughter of sharecroppers from the Mississippi Delta. While growing up in a Chicago ghetto, part of the legendary South Side, the only wild animals she knew about walked on two legs.

Mae counted herself fortunate to have been taken while barely in grade school under the wing of an educated, socially active African American woman of roughly her mother's age, named Mrs. Robbie Shields Terry. Mrs. Terry had courageously taken on a group of African American children whom she chaperoned to youth concerts at Orchestra Hall during the winter, shepherded once a week to the 63rd Street beach in Jackson Park during the summer, and taught many of them, including Mae, at her Saturday morning music education workshop, which each year culminated in a staged performance of an operetta like the ones composed by Gilbert and Sullivan, Offenbach, and Lehár.

This wonderful woman was the one who trained Mae to speak English properly. She explained the art of enunciating. Mrs. Terry said, "Take your tongue off the roof of your mouth to pronounce 't' or 'k'. Don't say 'axe.' Say 'ass-k'. It's not lie-berry. It's pronounced lie-brair-ree." Mae received 12 years of private piano lessons from Mrs. Terry and served as her companion at a wide variety of events, which exposed Mae to scholarly Black and White people, civic issues, and cultural differences. It also practiced Mae in proper etiquette and social norms. Due to this heroic woman's interest in coaching, coaxing, and mentoring neighborhood kids, Mae turned out the way she did: articulate, gregarious, and ambitious.

Mae now realized how lucky she was growing up in the time of Mrs. Terry, an educated woman whose husband worked as a Pullman porter, which left her with free time on her hands. This early exposure had been a head start extended to only a very few underprivileged children like Mae. Mae was grateful for the poise, polish, and confidence she had gained, and she was grateful for the ways in which it had paid off in an enhanced sense of self-esteem that recognized no color boundaries. In many ways, it was as if Mae had had two mothers: one who showed her how to work hard as a poor member of a subjugated people in the United States of America and the other one who taught her to be fearless of social barriers and reach for limitless dreams.

Mae's dreams had included working her way through college, marriage, parenthood, and a career in public relations and advertising. She had worked through her personal identity issues, too. Now, here she was a self-made PR/Marketing manager for one of the largest and finest zoos in the world — not bad for a female specimen bred from a poor family in the class of people of African descent, at one time politely called Negroes instead of niggers.

So, on this freezing winter morning in 1984, Mae Bea Wright came to be leading a TV news van onto a restricted access road that dead-ended at the horse stables in the Children's Zoo. Bright electric light streamed out through the opened top half of a Dutch door in the rear of the Big Red Barn. A hooded face peered out into the cold. She recognized Philomachus Pugnax, the assistant curator of the Children's Zoo, leaning over the closed lower half, watching for their arrival. Phil left the warm confines of the barn, closing the door to conserve the heat for the animals sheltering within. He hurried to meet Mae where she had finished parking her car. Phil carried a two-way radio — used at the zoo to facilitate quick communication among employees liable to be anywhere in the park. He proffered the device to Mae. Having not been to her office yet that morning, she had none and took it gratefully. The PR lady, as she was familiarly known around the zoo, needed to be able to stay in touch, especially on the day of a special event.

Even at that early hour, the Children's Zoo was coming alive with activity. Zookeepers attended to their charges, and the pungent aroma of livestock in the freezing air was nearly overwhelming. Mae no longer cared. These were the normal odors of healthy animals, their food, and their waste. She had grown accustomed to the smells of the zoo.

The technicians from the TV station got busy raising the mast of the antenna that would send the live signal from the zoo to an orbiting satellite. The satellite, in turn, would bounce the signal back to Earth to be received at the station downtown. From there, it then would broadcast to the station's two million viewers across the greater Chicago metropolitan area, resulting in a near-simultaneous transmission of that morning's pivotal event. It was then slightly less than an hour before sunrise. The crew, seasoned professionals, needed most of that time to prepare. In addition to raising the antenna, there was a cable to be strung to the location itself, a camera and tripod to be readied and the actual live feed to be established. They did all their work quickly.

Mae recognized Julio, who set down a bucket, wiped his hand on his coat, and hurried over to stand beside Phil. If Harry Sutherland had been any of several other on-air personalities Mae could mention, he might have remained inside the heated van or demanded to be led to a warm office to await his moment. But, with his usual gentility, Harry strode over in the cold to be introduced to Phil. Phil in turn introduced Julio, the zookeeper for Eddie the groundhog.

Julio, who was a character, looked forward to Groundhog Day every year when his charge attained celebrity status for a few brief minutes. He had only one arm, and the other keepers were prone to tease him good-naturedly, calling him "*Hook*-io," after the prosthetic device he occasionally wore. Julio had found that he got along so well without the device in the general performance of his duties that he seldom strapped it on. Mae had no idea of how or when he had lost the limb, but she had heard several stories, each purporting to be true. Her favorite version of the "absolute truth" had Julio formerly working in the Reptile House where it had been his responsibility to feed the American alligator (*Alligator mississippiensis*).

Dawn glimmered in the eastern sky as Phil led the party from the Big Red Barn to Groundhog Hollow where Mae could see what Julio must have been doing prior to their arrival. The concrete apron in front of the naturalistic habitat had been carefully cleared of snow and ice. The exhibit itself was gaily festooned with the red, white, and blue bunting that mysteriously disappeared from the restaurant the previous summer, shortly after the Fourth of July celebration.

Mae flashed a look at Julio, who winked at her and smiled broadly. Nice touch, Hook-io, Mae thought, wishing he had checked with her before putting his plan into action. She noticed how pleased Harry looked, though; it meant more color for his live feed. So, Mae quickly determined that no harm had been done and admitted to herself that it was a pretty good idea. Still, she made a mental note to discuss protocol with Julio later.

Mae never knew what the animals would do. It was not like she could coach them or ask them to be there at a certain time, stand on a certain mark, and be upbeat for the cameras. She had to consider their natural behaviors, as well as the concerns of their curator and keepers. Then she would organize an event that accommodated all.

Phil led Mae and Harry back to his office in the barn where they kept warm. The crew completed the set-up. Harry declined a cup of hot coffee, preferring not to tarnish his expensive smile, asking instead for a cup of plain hot water. Mae accepted a cup of coffee she would never finish, trying to be courteous since Phil had offered it. After a little small talk, Phil left to attend to his routine duties.

Mae led Harry back to the exhibit, where they found the crew ready, Julio waiting and the sun rising in a dazzling blaze of winter brilliance. Shielding her eyes against the mounting glare, Mae watched where she placed her feet to be sure she did not lose her way or balance. Harry squinted a little, but not nearly close to the debilitating way in which she shielded herself. When she faced the rising sun, Mae thought her eyeglasses were filmed over with petroleum jelly. She wondered briefly what was causing the problem. The next moment, the thought went out of her head as she returned her focus to the impending live feed.

The camera was ready. The crew was all set, and Harry was in position, awaiting the critical moment. Indeed, everyone involved was ready except Eddie the groundhog. The star of the show was still sound asleep in his snug little burrow. With the clock ticking down to the last minute before showtime, Harry looked a little bit worried. Mae, experienced enough to know better than to leave anything to chance, had spoken to Julio the previous day, before assenting to Harry's request. Julio had promised her that Eddie would be up to the task and would not muff his big chance. He assured Mae that in the seven years since he had taken over the care and feeding of the groundhog, Eddie had never failed to appear at dawn to perform his prognosticator function. Thus reassured, she had returned Harry's call and answered in the affirmative.

So, with no time left to lose, Mae wondered, in mounting alarm, where was Eddie? And, for that matter, where was Julio?

"Live in 10 seconds," came the announcement from the cameraman. Harry, the consummate professional that he was, squared his shoulders and faced the camera.

"Nine...eight..." continued the countdown — still no sign of the groundhog.

Mae was beginning to wish she had said "no" to Harry's request and followed Eddie's example by staying home in her warm, cozy bed.

"...Seven...six...five..."

Something was going on. A clatter sounded from behind Groundhog Hollow.

"...Four..."

A trap door in the exhibit banged open, and Julio appeared. With the sound technician mouthing the finish of the countdown, and little beads of perspiration beginning to show on Harry's upper lip — despite the cold, Julio sprang to the wooden box that served Eddie as a burrow. He seized up the heavy box with his one good arm and unceremoniously dumped the large, reddish-brown rodent out into the springy cedar shavings scattered on the bottom of the exhibit. There was an angry squawk from Eddie. Julio dropped the box, tossed something to his rudely awakened charge, and left through the trap door, which slammed shut behind him as the feed went live. Mae stared in absolute astonishment as Harry went into action.

"Good morning, ladies and gentlemen, and Happy Groundhog Day to you all! We're coming to you live at sunrise from the Chicago Zoo, where Eddie the Groundhog is about to show us whether or not Spring is right around the corner."

Eddie finished devouring what looked to Mae like a contraband *French fry* and stood up on his hind legs, an even bigger "ham" than Harry. With the bright, rising sun shining from behind, Eddie cast a perfect shadow, squawked once more, spun about, and disappeared back into its snug burrow. The illusion came off without a hitch.

Harry took it from there, as the cameraman zoomed in for a tighter shot. "And there you have it. I'm sorry, folks, but, as you saw for yourselves, Eddie clearly looked at his shadow, and it scared him right back into his den. So, don't put away those woolens yet..."

Mae heaved a huge sigh of relief. Everything dovetailed into position perfectly. She thought, wherever Julio is right now, he is laughing up his sleeve. Nevertheless, she was going to have that talk with Julio and *before* the scheduled event at 10 a.m.

Mae had no real idea what Julio had tossed to Eddie. She realized she did not want to know. She knew too much already. She thanked her lucky star that zoo director/CEO Dr. George Buffalo had not witnessed Julio's bizarre choreography of Eddie's movements. Mae could well imagine his reaction if Dr. Buffalo had seen what occurred there. He probably would have fired everybody, including Harry and the TV crew, before having an apoplectic fit and collapsing into a coma. In all fairness, she acknowledged it was not that Dr. Buffalo was excitable. He truly had the deepest concern for the welfare of his charges, especially providing healthy diets and not permitting any display of anthropomorphism.

Afterwards, Mae walked the apparently pleased Harry back in the direction of the barn where the vehicles waited. As they walked along the winding path, she kept bumping into the barnyard fences that bordered and separated different species. She thought it was because her toes felt nearly frozen, despite her insulated winter boots. Also, she had to field a tissue from her coat pocket to wipe a drip from her nose.

Sniffling and dabbing at her nose, Mae said, "I don't know about you, Harry, but I can't take much more of this cold weather."

"I know what you mean." He continued, "This 1983-84 winter season has been one of the worst in our history. So far we've had three record-breaking snowfalls and 10 straight days of sub-zero degree temperatures."

Mae half expected Harry to launch into a detailed explanation involving high-pressure and low-pressure zones, prevailing winds, global warming and probably El Niño thrown in for good measure. But he appeared finished, evidently sure that he had made his point.

Mae nodded her sage agreement. As they hurried along past the Walk-in Farmyard, a special area for demonstrating cows being milked, sheep being sheared, and horses being shoed, Mae turned the corner and bumped smack into the fence, misjudging her distance from it. Embarrassed, she kept on walking.

I did not see that wire fence, she thought, but Mae said, pushing her eyeglasses higher on her nose, "It's a little foggy this morning."

Harry looked perplexed, as if he did not have the faintest idea of what she was talking about. He simply nodded. A sudden gust of wind from the frigid north felt to Mae like it was blowing right through her parka as if the coat gave no more warmth than a crocheted Afghan.

"Ooh-wee, I hate the Hawk." Mae cringed, shivering. "I wish I were someplace warm."

Harry announced, "I'm going on vacation next week... to the Bahamas."

"Lucky you!"

"I guess I am," he agreed, shrugging his shoulders. "It's gorgeous there. The beaches are covered in white sand, like white sugar. The sunrises and sunsets must be seen to be believed. And the water is a beautiful turquoise blue." Harry reveled, "I'll be totally relaxing for a week.

"Have you ever been there, Mae?"

"I haven't," she shook her head no, feeling a tad envious since she had never had a vacation like that. "But it sounds marvelous. I wish I were there, right now."

Mae's first thought was that maybe she would go there someday. Then, on second thought, she doubted Barry would go there. Yet, she pondered about it. That spark ignited the dry tinder of desire in her heart for a similar vacation where it smoldered the rest of the morning.

Back at the Big Red Barn, the crew had about finished reloading. Harry thanked Mae, again, and clambered aboard the van, showing, for the first time, a hint of fatigue.

Mae realized, Harry's shift would be over soon, but she still had a full day ahead. She yawned and stretched, then morphed her stretch into a wave of goodbye to Harry and the crew in the departing van. She hoped the early morning TV appearance was worth her time and that the 10 o'clock event would draw some photojournalists.

*　　*　　*

Mae got in the yellow Rabbit and waited for the engine to warm up to the point where she was beginning to feel the heater thawing her near-frozen toes. Again, she felt that annoying itch. She ignored it, put her VW in gear and drove back the way she had come two hours earlier.

This time, Mae continued west across the visitor parking lot and onto where she could gain access to a different private driveway, which ran through a steel gate in the zoo's southwest outer wall and around to the back of the Administration Building, called Admin. In a tiny area of no more than a half-dozen parking spaces, Mae parked in her spot. She enjoyed the privilege of parking steps from a rear door that opened directly into her office. She could easily carry things to and from her car and meet the media in vehicles she authorized to be escorted into the park.

This morning, Mae entered through the main rear door and went straight up a long hallway, which led to the reception area where she checked for mail. Then she walked back half-way down the hall to the door with a stenciled PR/Marketing sign and entered it. She quickly passed the empty desk of her secretary, Callie, and went into her office where she would spend the next hour polishing up the groundhog fact sheet she had drafted at home the previous night.

Later, at the 10 a.m. scheduled event, Mae hosted not only a small gathering of people but a larger than expected group of news photographers, probably spurred by the TV coverage, including one from the daily *Southtown*

Economist. The temperature was 20 degrees warmer. Eddie performed adequately but, without Julio's help, was less frisky and entertaining.

After Eddie's weather forecast, Mae announced, "Everyone, let's move to Safari Lodge for cake and hot chocolate."

Moving to the indoor restaurant would allow the kids who attended — mostly from the nearby grade school — to warm up and enjoy a party. While celebrating with the children, Mae's boss, Grant Steward, the zoo's associate director of Development, dropped by.

He whispered in her ear, "Why didn't you notify the staff that the groundhog would be airing on Channel 2 this morning?"

"Grant, it was a spur-of-the-moment request. I barely had time to organize it."

"Well, next time notify me. It's important for everyone to be informed."

"Of course," she replied, feeling the itch.

Mae was in the middle of another busy day, hindered by that persistent itch.

* * *

Feb. 2, afternoon — Daydreaming about an exotic getaway

Back in her office that afternoon with a report for the Board of Trustees spread all over her desk and Callie holding her calls, Mae had a hard time staying focused. Usually, she did what was difficult first, and certainly she felt that way about completing the report for the Board. Her boss wanted to see her first draft as soon as possible. So, Mae felt a bit under pressure to create the crucial PR/marketing campaign to promote a new exhibit opening, titled Wolf Woods.

Mae chewed absent-mindedly at a pencil, daydreaming about getting away from it all. She wondered why everything had to be so hard, starting with the Chicago climate. It was either too hot or too cold. The summer damp made the heat feel hotter, and, paradoxically, the winter damp made the cold feel colder. Then there was her job. Mae admitted to herself that it was a circus, and she was sick of it: driving around in an endless circle to and from work, juggling her tasks at home and work, and performing a high wire act as the only person of African descent at the zoo. As much as she loved her work, she felt overworked, underappreciated, and stressed out by the daily grind to meet deadlines. She had vacation time coming in September, and she had "comp time" galore, but *never* a right time to take it. Mae felt like Alice being schooled by the Red Queen: it took all the running she could do to keep in the same place.

And, of course, there were the people: the people. The people she wished *would* show Julio's initiative never did. She wasted so much time showing Callie how to get things done that she might as well have done it herself in the first place. When 5 p.m. rolled around, Callie put on her coat and walked out the door, whether or not the work was done. It was Mae who stayed, sometimes well into the night, folding and stuffing press kits or whatever. Yet, Callie thought she deserved a raise. It was not only Callie but everybody, both higher and lower than Mae on the zoo's organizational chart. All had private agendas, and politics constantly reared its ugly head. It was hard to inspire the cooperative spirit needed to ensure the success of her efforts.

And, in the end, it was Mae herself. She knew she was feeling rundown, somewhat uninspired lately. She felt less energy and drive to do the creative work that she loved doing.

Living is like riding a seesaw, it has its ups and downs. This day, a weary Mae just wanted to hop off the ride and take a break.

Coming out of her fugue state, Mae decided to take a chocolate break. She dropped her pencil and opened the bottom right-hand drawer of her desk. Mae pulled out a secret indulgence: one single wrapped, giant myrtle from Long Grove Confectionery Co. She relished every morsel of the hulky milk chocolate, caramel, and pecan power bar. Munching away, her craving being quenched, Mae thought, "Chocolate is good, but what I need is *a vacation.*"

She imagined being in the Bahamas, although she had never been to a tropical island. In fact, she never had been on leisure travel, living in a hotel with room service. She could only imagine it based on what she had seen in the movies and on TV. In her ignorance, she thought it must be heavenly. Mae was so sick of the cold, snow, and ice. Her desire for a vacation in the tropics started to burn. It was as if the hot, tropical sun called out to her African blood. She ached to respond, here I come! Except an image of Barry wagging his finger and shaking his head, no, filled her mind's eye.

Barry, her kindhearted husband, possessed a generous spirit and never stinted on gifts or entertaining friends and family. But he had one desire: to own a home. They were saving for it. But try as they might, Barry and Mae, professional people with college degrees, never earned enough money to afford the American Dream. *Every* time they thought they had enough money to buy a house, the interest rates went up.

Mae heaved a long, slow sigh. Then, for the first time, she noticed the damage she had unconsciously inflicted on her pencil. She tossed it in the waste basket along with her power bar wrapper. She pushed back from her desk in a strategic withdrawal, if not quite in surrender, and slumped in her chair, pondering the twin problems: how to convince Barry of the necessity of an honest-to-God vacation, and how to secure the means to pay for it? Mae steadily convinced herself that she deserved to be pampered for one week in her lifetime. She thought if she could have a vacation, an exotic getaway, she would come back from it ready to tackle the world. If they started saving right now, they could have a real vacation by... Well, never!

She recognized the futility of that line of reasoning. There was never any money left over to save for anything, least of all an obvious luxury like travel. It occurred to her that they could charge the whole thing! The tempting solution sprang full-grown from her subconscious, where it obviously had not been buried very deeply. She blinked a few times and stood straight up, considering this possibility.

The Wrights were not unfamiliar with the concept of credit spending. They purchased their car on credit. They also used a credit card for emergencies like dental work and to provide for their son's needs. But Barry wielded the kind of brutal honesty that a zealous religious doctrine instills. He strongly opposed charging anything non-essential, and he considered travel downright frivolous. Mae's challenge would consist of convincing her husband: first, that they both not only wanted but needed a vacation for their well-being, and, secondly, that credit would be the best means of attaining it now.

She returned to her project feeling at least a little bit hopeful, having occasionally had some success where manipulating Barry was involved. She knew all his weaknesses and was not flattering herself at all in believing I am his #1 weakness. After all, he had asked her to become his wife, right? She resolved to bring it up to Barry that night.

Because of her extra-early departure that morning, Barry had taken the "L" to work. So, Mae made it a point to leave work at 5 p.m. sharp to pick him up. She did not want him to be in a bad mood because she ran late picking him up. She dialed in some smooth jazz on the car radio, hoping for something to mellow her mood as she suffered in rush-hour traffic with all the other drivers crawling on the Eisenhower Expressway toward the Loop. Traffic moved slowly yet steadily, until finally she pulled over, stopping in front of the Camelot nightclub on North Dearborn Street. There stood her tall, brown-haired, brown-eyed husband on the corner in his dark blue hooded parka, facing the Hawk like Nordic people as gusts of arctic wind whipped his legs and walrus mustache.

*   *   *

Barry gallantly waited as Mae got out of the car and walked briskly around to get in the passenger side door, which he held open for her. He leaned down to kiss her. She hesitantly met his lips, always a little bashful about kissing in public. He expected it, though, and she never disappointed him. Barry secured her door and got in on the driver's side while Mae fastened her seatbelt and locked her door. With confidence born of much repetition, he quickly adjusted the seat and mirrors, checked traffic for an opening, and smoothly pulled away from the curb. He flicked the radio to a hard rock station and turned up the volume. Barry caught Mae wince at the loud sound but said nothing. In fact, she smiled, and he smiled back.

"What's the joke?"

Mae said, "You're in relatively high spirits. You must have had a good day for a change."

He said, "Not bad, but my production crew still keeps calling me Scary Barry."

They laughed, knowing that moniker was ludicrous.

He could see that Mae was tired after her long day, so he adjusted the volume down to a "Mae-approved" level, then turned his full attention to driving. Mae glanced adoringly at him, no doubt grateful that he had read her mind and turned the sound down. She looked like she was going to say something more but instead relaxed back in her seat. Before long, the heated air inside the car and the gentle motion of traveling lulled the tired "PR lady" to sleep. While Mae slept, Barry watched her eyes moving beneath her eyelids, probably dreaming. She woke up just as he made the turn into their alley.

"What were you dreaming, Mae?"

"I dreamt about palm trees, white sand, warm breezes, and beverages served in pineapple goblets garnished with tropical fruit and little pastel paper umbrellas."

"Well, we're home," he dryly said, pulling into the garage.

It was twilight with the streetlights already on. The real world was a winter wonderland that consisted of leafless tree limbs swaying in the wind, snowdrifts, and a garage hung with such massive icicles that they had icicles of their own.

"Nothing so cold should look so beautiful," Mae remarked.

Barry came around to assist her with the car door as she bundled herself up and gathered her things from the backseat in preparation for the cold dash up the snow-drifted red brick walkway to the warmth of the gray frame bungalow that they called home. He closed the doors of the detached garage and quickly followed Mae inside the back door. Once up the rear stairs and through the kitchen door, he sat at the small kitchen table and tugged off his boots. Then he headed past the dining room for the front hall closet to put away his boots and hang up his parka.

Barry found his family in the living room. He was in heaven to see a blissful vignette of their simple life: Zac squirming in his mother's possessive hug, pulling away from her or at least pretending to resist her affection — something he had begun around the time he graduated to middle school. Mae held on tight until she planted an exaggerated kiss on his cheek. When Mae let Zac go, he moved quickly beyond her reach, taking her winter coat and knitted things to the hall closet where he hung them up. From the safe distance of the other side of the living room, Zac smiled a shy smile. Then he disappeared into the chaotic atmosphere of his room.

Barry could not help but see Mae whenever he looked at Zac. He had Mae's heart-shaped face. Their skin had the same warm brown tint, like coffee rich with cream and a dash of cinnamon. However, Zac was already taller than her and showed signs of developing the strong, lanky build of an endurance runner.

The couple went to their room to change clothes. Barry finished first, changing his work clothes for cut-off blue jeans and a sweatshirt, his usual at-home wear. As he left the bedroom to head for the kitchen, he noticed Mae scratching near her elbow. In the kitchen, he reached for the top of the refrigerator to turn off Zac's little black-and-white TV. Not so long ago, it would have been spewing cartoons or an adventure show, but it was currently tuned to something educational about the space shuttle. Barry decided to leave it on but lowered the volume. Next, he washed his hands and then began taking food out of the refrigerator to prepare dinner. Zac came into the kitchen and voluntarily hugged his dad. It may have been a ploy to get near the open refrigerator because he grabbed an apple from the crisper drawer and disappeared back into his room.

Zac lived primarily on apples; he ate as many as three or four a day. Barry was proud of his healthy, good-looking son and resolved to try and eat more apples himself. At the same time, his parental instincts made a mental note to be sure the apple core found its way out of his son's room and into the garbage pail.

Mae soon joined him in the kitchen, having changed from the Pendleton gray wool suit she had worn that day to her favorite well-worn Micky Mouse T-shirt, jersey sweatpants, and the fleece-lined slippers Zac had given her for Christmas. She washed her hands and then began to prepare a fresh green salad. Barry turned cooked ground beef into sloppy joes. Tomorrow or the next day, the leftover "joe" would not be wasted but blended into a pot of homemade chili.

When dinner was ready, they all ate together in the living room, in front of the TV. They talked, laughed, and did the things that families do, snug in the cozy, little house on Grey Street.

Barry thought how pretty Mae looked, as he always did whenever he saw her for as long as he had known her. He adored her heart-shaped face, and her voice was music to his ears. In his eyes, Mae was still his beautiful bride and always would be. He constantly marveled at his good luck in finding and winning *his* "Cinnamon Girl." And he tried hard not to let romance die at the hands of complacency. Then he noticed Mae scratching her arm again.

"What's wrong with your elbow?"

Mae, trying to brush him off, said, "Nothing, just dry skin I think."

He reached for her arm and insisted, "Let me see."

Pulling up her sleeve, Mae revealed a small dime-sized patch of skin, and jokingly said, "What do you think Dr. Wright?"

Barry carefully examined it, and said, "Looks like acne. Have the doctor look at it."

Taking her arm back and dismissing his advice, Mae smirked, "I'll put moisturizer on it."

"OK," Barry sighed, feeling like Cassandra in Greek mythology. "If only you and Zac would listen to me, you would save yourselves a lot of trouble."

Later they cleared their supper dishes to the kitchen. Zac retired to his room, where he probably would read for a while and then find numerous other ways to procrastinate before finally tackling his homework. While Mae cleaned up the kitchen, Barry took out the garbage, something Zac was supposed to do when he came home from school. But he did not mind that oversight. Zac really was very good at doing his chores. Besides, it gave him an excuse to get out of doing the dishes and enjoy a few minutes in the crisp night air with a warm house waiting whenever he had enough.

Outside, the wind howled as clouds raced past the moon. There was a clatter in the alley, coming from the direction of the garbage cans. Barry looked up in time to see the ringed tail of a big raccoon going over the fence. Once he reached the back gate, the interloper was gone, most likely high in one of the big cottonwood trees surrounding the garage. He disposed of the trash and made sure the lids were snugged tightly on the metal cans; the critters could chew through plastic cans in seconds. As much as Barry appreciated nature, these urbanized survivors lost their charm when they created a nuisance. But Barry never took it out on them. He believed that every living thing had a right to survive and held its important place in the ecology.

Although he had slipped on his boots and his parka, Barry stood enjoying the freezing dark in his cutoffs. He looked up at the clouds and stars. He watched his breath form into visible puffs and blow away. As a descendant of farmers, Barry was a city-dwelling man with a country-loving heart who was frustrated with renting instead of owning a home.

He bemoaned that their standard of living did not approach what he had enjoyed growing up in the 1950s and '60s, especially since neither of his parents had attended high school. His father came from farmers in Tennessee. His mother came from farmers in Wisconsin. They met and married in Chicago. His father, who had been the sole breadwinner in a blue-collar industrial job, at that, provided a comfortable lifestyle for them, including owning a home and paying for a college education for him and his two brothers.

The problem had to be the escalating cost of living in the United States in the mid-1980s. For example, his dad had to save up roughly 10 to 15 percent of his annual earnings to afford a decent new family car back when Eisenhower was President. Barry and Mae found themselves faced with car prices that amounted to *half* their combined annual salaries — and for a lesser car. Paying in cash for a car was out of the question, and the ensuing finance charges for an auto loan pushed the cost higher. Already he and Mae had had the humbling experience of explaining to their son Zac that they would not be able to afford the eventual cost of his higher education, which made it doubly important that he do his very best in school in the hope of qualifying for some serious scholarship money.

Somehow, the necessity of finding and keeping a paying job amidst the glut of jobseekers suddenly competing for a dwindling number of jobs in the America that emerged following the end of the Vietnam War had all but snuffed out his spiritual nature and left him more than a little bit cynical. Life is hard sometimes, Barry reflected, and our jobs are way too stressful. But when he stood there on the property where his family lived and considered that the three of them were warm, healthy, and well fed, it seemed worth it. He concluded, if we are lucky and careful with our money, someday we will own the house we live in, too. Barry stood a little longer, wondering why Mae was never quite *satisfied*, no matter what. He wished he could make her happy or make more money. Maybe the two goals were inseparable. But her positive, go-for-it attitude was the first thing he found attractive about her.

The cold, clear night was beautiful, but his ears were beginning to burn, as well as the tips of his fingers and the skin of his bare legs. So, he hustled, shivering, back inside the house, locking things up for the night as he went. Back inside, Barry realized Zac — still in his room — was not necessarily to bed, as the hour was not that late. But the door to his room would remain shut tight until morning, a young preteen jealously guarding his privacy or perhaps an unselfish son giving his parents some space. Mae had apparently gone to bed. But, no... The bed was turned down, but she was not in it or in the bedroom, for that matter. Then, he smelled the girlie scent of bubble bath as steam leaked out of the opened-just-a-crack bathroom door.

Barry took that as an invitation. About to softly knock on the door, he delayed a moment. He stood secretly watching Mae in the tub. Although married for years, it still gave him a thrill to see her naked, all steamy, wet, and vulnerable.

* * *

Feb. 2, evening — Taking the first step to achieve the goal

Mae, for her part, had gone to put her plan into action as soon as the dishes were all put away. She said goodnight to Zac and went to her room where she turned down the bed. She took Barry's huge, red, terrycloth robe to the bathroom, hung it on a hook behind the door and started hot water running into the big, old-fashioned, claw-footed tub. That grand bathtub was probably the single best feature of the aging bungalow. She measured in a couple of handfuls of bubble-bath crystals and was about to undress when she remembered she had intended to put on some music. She pitter-pattered barefoot down the hall to the living room and started a sexy Marvin Gaye record playing on the turntable. Then she boosted the thermostat a couple of degrees before returning to the bathroom where she made sure she did not quite close the door. Mae quickly disrobed and eased into the bubbly bath. She relaxed into the hot, fragrant water, thinking, oh, this is almost heaven. It would be so easy to fall asleep right here.

She waited for her husband to come in and find her. She teetered on the edge of consciousness for a few minutes until, without knowing it was happening, she floated off to sleep, again — right there in the tub — and slipped back into her vacation dream. This time she lay languid and naked on a beach of black diamond sand, eyes closed, feeling totally relaxed and sensual. Warm waves broke into foam all around her. The sun covered her with scorching kisses.

When she opened her eyes, it took her a moment to remember where she was and to realize that she had been dreaming. Barry stood watching her shyly from the cracked door. At first, she pretended not to have noticed but soon their eyes met. Both smiled at their little game.

Barry opened the door as quietly as possible, trying not to disturb Zac. He locked the bathroom door behind himself and slipped out of his clothes, joining her in the tub. He lowered himself into the still-hot water behind her, sliding her soap-slippery body onto his lap despite her teasing mock protests and the considerable amount of bath water that splashed over onto the tile floor. He wrapped her all up in his arms, cupping her breasts in his hands. They luxuriated together until the water began to cool, then dried themselves quickly. Giggling and shushing at each other, they moved from the bathroom to the privacy of their bedroom.

Mae, of course, wore the big, red robe. Barry managed to cover most of his nakedness with a standard-sized bath towel. In the bedroom, there was still more shushing and giggling under the cold bedcovers until they started to get warm, soon followed by hugging and kissing and lovemaking. Afterward, they lay together, comfortably basking in the afterglow.

Mae whispered, "Barry, are you asleep?" She shifted a little in the bed to get closer to him and put her arms around his neck.

"Almost," he murmured. "That was nice, Honey."

There was just enough light in the room for Mae to see his little smile. Here I go, she told herself, No guts, no glory!

"Honey..." she cooed, low and slow, in her most charming, baby-girl voice, "What you and I really need is... *a vacation.*"

There, she had said it: the dreaded "V" word.

Barry looked awake, then. Both his eyes were open, and the little smile faded to a non-committal expression. If anything, he looked a little puzzled. He tried to pull back to get a look at her face. But she held on to him tightly and her words tumbled out in a rush.

"I'm tired. I don't mean tonight. I mean in general. And I think we could both use some R&R. I mean, a relaxing retreat where they have room service. Not a four-day camping trip to Wisconsin or a week of puttering around the house. I want to go someplace exotic, far away, and, most of all, where it is warm and sunny. Like, maybe..." she swallowed, and then put all her cards on the table, "...the Caribbean or Hawaii. I've *got* to get away!"

With that said, expectant and hopeful, Mae relaxed her hug on her husband. She pulled back enough to see clearly into Barry's panicky brown eyes.

"Why not go to the moon? Impossible," judged Barry. "Look, I know you've been working like a Trojan, and so have I. You are woefully underpaid. It's a great job at the zoo, where you work for peanuts. And I work long hours for peanuts, too. But we don't have the money to do a vacation like that, not this year. Why can't you be satisfied with what we have?"

Which was exactly what Mae had expected him to say. She knew he did have a point. If the zoo ever saw fit to pay her what male professionals at her level of experience earned, the Wrights would be able to afford to buy a house closer to her work. Mae would be spared much of the time she wasted each day fighting traffic.

One battle at a time, mused Mae. That was a fight for some future day.

She studied his raccoon eyes and his splotchy face as well as she was able in the near darkness. Mae thought she found a small chink in his armor; a scintilla of hope sprang up. She told herself that it was going to take some work, but... She might stand a chance.

Mae whispered, pleading with her eyes, "Promise me you'll think about it?"

"I will, Honey. I promise. But, please, don't get your hopes up."

She kissed him good night, and before long he was sound asleep.

Mae was not. She knew Barry was very decisive. He had a philosophy about making decisions. Barry had two guiding principles. "Don't set mail aside for later; if you don't read it now, you're never going to read it." And "If someone asks you to do something and you have to think about it, the answer is no."

Mae set a goal: get Barry to say, "Yes."

While she scratched the inch, she pondered her next move before eventually nodding off.

CHAPTER THREE

Friday, Feb. 24 — Trusting primary care doctor

In a chilly examination room in Evanston, Illinois, Mae waited for the doctor to arrive. She desperately wanted to scratch the itchy sore on her forearm but resisted the urge, not wanting to inflame the lesion before the doctor had a chance to examine it.

Over time, the patch above her elbow had gotten worse. At first, Mae paid it little mind, scratching at it subconsciously whenever she could not bear the itch. None of the over-the-counter nostrums she tried did the slightest good. In the space of three weeks, the blemish turned from a small, thickening patch of abnormal skin into a raw, red lesion, a little larger than a quarter. After much concerned urging from Barry, she called the HMO and scheduled an appointment with her primary care physician.

At 4:05 p.m., 35 minutes after her appointment time, Mae still sat waiting for medical attention when, at last, she heard the rustle of her file being removed from the rack outside the door. Dr. Ian A. MacAreless walked in, softly drawing the door shut.

Dr. MacAreless was young, tall, and personable with blonde hair and blue eyes. He dressed in an Ivy League style and wore loafers that sported those little leather kilties. All his female patients found him absolutely charming. He always oozed comforting self-confidence, which made him incredibly popular as a general medicine practitioner and a frequent choice for primary care physician. There was *something* about his lanky, boy-next-door appearance that made people trust him. Mae certainly did.

On the other hand, Barry was unusual in that he was underwhelmed by Doc Mac, as he irreverently called him, and suspicious of his medical abilities. He accused him of practicing "MacMedicine," out of his depth practicing slipshod medicine. He told Mae that any confidence in him was undeserved.

Mae had a suspicion of her own regarding Barry's reaction. She knew him to be honest but maybe, in this case, a little jealous. At one time, Barry had hoped to go to medical school himself. He had seen that dream wither and die back in high school. Although he was adept at grasping anatomy, physiology, and pathology, he was unable to fathom enough mathematics and chemistry to do very well. So, he accepted that he would never be able to survive medical school, and he settled for a degree in graphic design. First, he held a position as an animation artist and then as a greeting card cartoonist before his career in slide production.

"How are you, Mae?" The doctor smiled, favoring her with a good look at his perfect pearly whites.

"I'm fine, thank you, doctor," she said, returning his smile with an impressive one herself. "Except for a little rash, I can't get rid of."

She pushed up her sleeve and raised her arm, exposing the affected area. Then she realized Dr. MacAreless was focusing his attention on her chart. So, she relaxed and waited.

"Well, congratulations! I see you've lost 10 whole pounds since your last visit."

"Yeah, I guess so," said Mae, who was pleasantly surprised earlier when the nurse pronounced her weight to be a svelte 115 pounds.

"What's this I hear? You have a little rash to show me?" He took a seat on a rolling stool and reached out for a spot lamp, wheeling it and himself over close to Mae.

"That would be putting it mildly." She flexed her left arm at the elbow, raising it up so he could get a good look at the blemish. "It itches like crazy, too."

Dr. MacAreless put on the eyeglasses he was too vain to wear except when absolutely necessary and, switching on the light, remarked, "That's the same elbow you broke in Colorado, isn't it?" That was all he could come up with to make conversation while he bought a little time to examine Mae's rash and think.

"Yes," she nodded, recalling her first and last attempt at street roller-skating.

Mae wondered what connection the earlier injury could possibly have to her present complaint. The strong glare from the bright light was utterly blinding to her. She turned her face away, as much as she was able.

Dr. MacAreless examined the sore spot, first with his eyeglasses on, and then, again, with his unaided vision. He maneuvered her arm this way and that. Mae wished he would hurry. The glare was beginning to inflict real pain in her sensitive eyes. Finally, he let go of her arm and switched off the irritatingly bright light.

He sat up straight, facing Mae, and smiled reassuringly. "I don't know exactly *what* it is that you've got there, Mae. But there is a thing or two in our medical arsenal that we can try that ought to knock it right out. If that doesn't work, we'll send you along to see the dermatologist."

The doctor was unable to make any specific diagnosis. Mae was not satisfied. She had never seen anything quite like it before in her whole life. She wanted to know what it *was*, and what it was doing on *her* arm. "What can it be?"

"Well, I can tell you that it's *not* eczema or psoriasis," he said. "It's probably a reaction to something in your environment. You're working at the zoo, now, aren't you?"

"Yes," Mae answered softly, as she watched him rummaging through the medicine cabinet.

"There must be a regular smorgasbord of exotic irritants around you, all day long. Here, use this regularly for a while," he said, finding and handing her a small sample-size tube of an unpronounceable ointment. "I don't know if it will help, but I guess it might be worth a try."

Mae, growing a little worried by his lack of any definitive statement regarding her problem, inquired, "Dr. MacAreless, it *is* going to get better, *isn't* it?"

He responded brightly, "Yes, of course it is." Then, added with his face growing serious, "I must be honest with you, though. There is always the chance that it might get worse." Finally, with his expression shifting to one of confident reassurance—the one that was paying back his medical-school loans—he contributed this final bit of wisdom, "Then, again, it might stay the same." He asked, by way of dismissal, "All right?"

"Well... I guess so." She rose to her feet and rearranged her sleeve.

While washing his hands, Dr. MacAreless said, "Give us a call if it gets worse."

Mae replied, being respectful and polite, "Thank you, doctor."

She collected her purse and followed him out the door, feeling more than a little disgusted. Back out on the street, heading towards her parked car, Mae could not believe that she had taken time from her busy work schedule to receive essentially no help at all.

Later, Barry said she had been handed a nice, professional snow job.

* * *

Saturday, March 3 — Ignoring fever on National Pig Day

Mae B. Wright held open one panel of the sheer voile curtains hanging over the double-hung bay windows in her dining room. She dropped it to scratch her elbow hard, unable to scratch deep enough to stop the itch. Unaware of what she was doing to herself, she gazed out the window in a fugue state, thinking about days gone by, that day and what the future could bring. The cold air slowly seeping through the double-paned window made her shiver.

Mae was supposed to be getting ready to leave the house for another Saturday at work but stalled to look at the latest weather threatening to sabotage another zoo event she had planned. The warm glow of diffused light did little to brighten her frown, glaring at the sight of the early morning arrival of snow. Big, white flakes floated down, gently landing, and collecting on the soggy, partially thawed ground.

Mae started, "If this winter doesn't end soon..." She dropped the drape, feeling too defenseless to finish her threat.

Since she began working at the zoo last September, Mae had developed a whole new respect for the weather. It was a critical component in the success of her outdoor events. The weather not only affected the turnout from the animals and the public but news coverage as well. The media might get too busy with weather-related incidents and have no time to cover a fun segment about the zoo.

She looked in on Zac, who was still in bed alternately snoozing and watching cartoons. She opened the door a little wider and greeted him softly.

"Good morning, Pancho," Mae said, calling him by the nickname she had given him as a toddler, based on reruns of a 1950s TV series they watched. "I'm heading out for the zoo."

She gave him a little goodbye wave from the door. At the same time, she spotted evidence that he had been eating cereal.

"'Bye, Cisco," Zac continued the comedy routine sleepily. Simultaneously, he attempted to casually slide the dirty bowl and spoon under the edge of his bed with one bare brown foot. "Are you sure you don't need me, Mom?"

"Not today," she said. "I'm going to be there a long time but thanks."

Zac jumped up from the bed, and they met to hug each other. Mae could not believe how tall he was getting and how much his face was changing, cheekbones gaining prominence over baby fat, jaw line growing stronger, a pronounced Adam's apple giving an angular new shape to his throat and a still-downy moustache on his upper lip. He was becoming a young man.

Mae almost teared up, thinking that her baby was almost ready to start shaving and wondering why time goes by fast when you look back. But she covered any show of emotion with a stern reprimand, "Oh, Pancho, you're not supposed to be eating messy stuff in your room. Make sure you take those dirty dishes to the kitchen."

He laughed, although a little bit shamefacedly at having been busted. "Oh, Cisco, all right," he conceded and hugged her once more.

They both laughed. Mae turned him loose and left the room, closing his door like she had found it. Wandering back to the dining room, she looked out the window, again, and fell into a fugue state.

When she first started working at the zoo, Zac frequently went along with her on the weekends. All the employees got a kick out of his enthusiasm and accorded him special favors and privileges. He rode the steam-engine train for both fun and as actual transportation, moving freely around the 315-acre park. He attended dolphin shows, often being allowed to toss the Frisbee to the intelligent, playful marine mammals during the finale. He got to know the zoo better than his Evanston neighborhood. Over time, he started to volunteer his help in her office or at her special events, wanted to impress her with the fact that he was not a little boy anymore or perhaps hoping that he would then be able to spend a little more time with his mother. But Mae was almost always too busy — talking with other people and answering telephone calls — to pay as much attention to her son as she would have liked. After a while, Zac lost interest and stopped coming along. She was surprised by how much she missed his company. Mae wondered if he resented the zoo for taking so much of her time and attention away from him. She knew pretty soon he would notice girls, and he would forget all about her. That time would come before she could possibly be ready.

Initially, she came home and excitedly shared the events of her day at the zoo with both Barry and Zac. They sat still, giving her their rapt attention. Her zoo stories would go on and on about what had happened to the animals and the people. Lately neither acted interested. Barry and Zac listened, if they had no polite way out. Then they hurried back to whatever it was they were doing —

watching TV, mostly. She wished she had time to spend a Saturday relaxing and watching some brainless, undemanding TV.

"Have you got time for this?" Barry's voice burst through her musing as he came out of the kitchen with a mug of coffee in his hand from a second pot of coffee he had made. The roasted aroma filled the house. "Don't you have an event today?"

"What's it to you? You a cop or something?" Mae grumbled under her breath; a bit irritated that he was minding her business.

There was a brief delay before he responded, "No, Ma'am. I'm not a cop. But I might decide to write a book someday." He chuckled, heading toward the bedroom door, "And then, wouldn't you be surprised?" He dribbled hot coffee from his full mug as he crossed the dining room carpet, catching the drips on his ratty sweatshirt where they disappeared into the camouflage of stains left by painting and various other weekend projects.

Mae rolled her eyes and quipped, "Yeah, right!"

She smoothed the curtain closed, followed her husband back into the bedroom, and resumed her search through the closet for an appropriate outfit.

"Barry, try being useful. Help me decide what to wear."

"Oh, no. You're not sucking me into your routine dilemma," he balked. "I'm sure I haven't got a clue as to what you should wear to make the proper Pig Day fashion statement."

Reclining on their bed, he sipped his coffee. Then, on second thought, he said, "Hey, wait a minute. How about your bibbed overalls?"

"As if I own such a thing!"

Mae threw a lint brush at him in mock irritation. Then she realized it really was time to stop *looking* and start *finding* something. She did not want to wear one of her corporate suits, which she had worn too often for her liking when she first started working at the zoo. What a joke that was, walking around 315 acres of zoological park in 3-inch-high heels! She walked at least 12 miles a day on the job. So, she had learned never to wear high-heeled shoes to the zoo — or any foot gear that could not withstand pee or poop.

Plus, lately her knees constantly ached. That past Thursday, Mae had hiked two miles over to Seven Seas Panorama, the marine mammals' complex, for the bi-annual physicals of the five Atlantic bottlenose dolphins: Angie, Nemo, Shauna, Stormy and Windy. The photo op for news media lasted four hours. In excruciating pain, she barely made it back to her office.

Mae searched in her closet for a casual but nice outfit for weekend management duty. She did not want to descend to the level of denim, especially not now after her husband's *Hee Haw* TV show jibe. But *it* was not in her closet, and she knew she did not have the money to buy *it* even if she went shopping and was lucky enough to find *it*, and then she would have to charge *it,* and Barry would hate *it*. She stared in the closet, lapsing into her obligatory fugue state.

"Hon-*ney*?" Barry called her back to reality. "You're daydreaming. Are you going to work this morning? Why do you wait until morning to figure out what clothes to wear, then make a futile attempt to get me to offer a suggestion? I refuse to play in this ritual."

Mae shot an annoyed look at him. "Well, I don't know why I bother asking the opinion of someone who takes his dress queue from the UPS guy."

She knew her daily ritual annoyed Barry because it made them run late some mornings. They depended on sharing the one car they could afford to get *both* to-and-from their jobs. Most workdays, they left home together with Barry behind the wheel headed south along the lakefront, first down Sheridan Road and then Lake Shore Drive, exiting at Grand Avenue and proceeding through Chicago's Gold Coast neighborhood. Barry would then get out at a particular three-story, renovated brownstone, where he spent his day doing a job he referred to as "slide butcher," overseeing the handmade 35-mm slide film production of images designed for multi-carousel projectors used by educators and businesses — predominantly charts and graphs.

Then Mae would take over the wheel, adjusting the seat and mirrors to her satisfaction. The good news was that she did not have to face the glare of the sun while she drove. Each morning the rising sun would be behind her as she traveled west to the Chicago Zoo, and the same was true in the evening, whenever her workday ended, and she made the return trip downtown to pick up Barry. One car to share for two jobs to be done. Sometimes he waited for her. Sometimes she waited for him. Either way, one or the other of them seemed to always be waiting somewhere, pissed off about it. They both realized that it was a sore spot in their relationship, and they talked about it often.

It always had been that way during the 13 years of their marriage. If Mae had things *her* way, they each would have their own car. She brought it up from time to time, but Barry would blow his stack, shouting sarcastically, "Okay, fine! Which of our luxuries shall we eliminate to pay for another car: heat, electricity, or gas? How about birthday presents?" Of course, she knew that if one took a strictly logical point of view, Barry was right. But Mae did not limit herself to logic. She revered the words of Goethe, "Whatever you can do or dream you can do, begin it."

She often thought to herself that one of these days she was going to surprise Mr. Spock and buy herself a car. And I'll find a way to pay for it. Not to mention, if he is too impatient to wait for me, Barry can always ride the 'L' downtown. Then Mae suddenly remembered he did not have to go to work. Free to ignore him, she took her sweet time.

She fussed, "Nothing I own looks good on me."

"Uh-hum." Barry was not listening but reading the *Chicago Tribune*.

Mae looked in the mirror and said, "Hey, I look like I'm wearing someone else's clothes."

Barry glanced up, "Are you complaining?"

"Not exactly," she replied, thinking she had lost another five pounds since she last saw her doctor. "If I lose five more pounds, I'll weigh what I did in high school, 105 pounds."

"It's probably because of all the walking you do around the zoo."

Mae had not been that slim since before she gave birth to Zac, thinking she should go out and buy a whole new wardrobe like some women she knew. She congratulated herself on her truly unspoiled nature, thinking Barry does not know how lucky he was. What if she started going to the beauty shop every two weeks? Still, they did not have a lot of extra money, and that way of thinking was getting her nowhere.

Mae decided she needed to make do and settled for a pair of blue jeans after all, but new ones and lined, decidedly not bibbed overalls. She pulled a white cotton turtleneck over her head and covered it with an old, but still nice, red-and-navy mohair sweater. Mae looked in the mirror, wondering if she looked like she was going to pick cotton. She affirmed to herself, no way! Then she pushed her feet into a pair of Frye leather boots. She grabbed the matching saddlebag purse from her closet and proceeded to fill it up with her stuff. Next, she aptly applied the minimal amount of make-up: lower eye liner, rouge, and sheer color lip gloss.

"Hey, Honey. Here's an article about the zoo's polar bear death." Barry read aloud, "'the zookeeper never noticed any unusual behavior, but Penny, the popular six-year-old polar bear, died from acute hepatitis.'"

"Yeah, I know. I attended the necropsy."

"You did! What was it like?"

Barry sounded interested in something happening at the zoo again.

"Well, the chief veterinarian wielded a scalpel, making precise, definitive strokes, but the first cut immediately revealed jaundiced tissues. There was yellowish fluid all over the drain. Poor Penny had disguised the pain, as you know animals do naturally in the wild to avoid becoming prey. I needed to know the cause ASAP so I could send out a news release over the PR Newswire, which I did to cut down on any speculation about the cause of death. I told you, we're inundated with inquiries, trying to respond to federal and state agencies as well as the media, members and the general public."

She added, "You know, what else was amazing to me? Since it was my first time in the interior chambers of the animal hospital, I got to see all the amazing stuff there."

"Like what?"

"There were elephant aspirins. The tablets were the size of Oreo cookies. I mean huge!"

Mae used her hands to indicate the size.

"And there was bird-sized birth control pills, assorted antivenins, and various sorts of tranquilizer darts. The equipment and supplies are huge but kept sterile. I never realized that the hospital not only performs veterinary services but also studies to prevent animal diseases. I've got to get some media coverage on the work they do."

Now, officially running late, Mae suddenly realized that she was not feeling entirely well. She felt very chilly, despite the heavy sweater she had on. She raised her hand to her forehead, futilely attempting to check herself for a fever.

"I think I'm feverish, again," she said, trying not to sound worried.

"That won't work," said Barry, pooh-poohing her actions. "Here, let me check."

He put down his empty mug and got up from the bed to lay his hand on her forehead. Barry was always eager to practice medicine without a license.

"Yep, you do feel a little warm," he confirmed, looking worried. "You've had unexplained fevers on several occasions lately."

Barry went into the bathroom. She heard him sorting through the ancient, dark-oak medicine cabinet. Soon he returned, vigorously shaking down a glass mercury thermometer.

"Lay down and rest for a minute, Mae,"

She bristled, a little. "I thought you were so anxious for me to get going,"

"Come on, Honey," he insisted.

With those words, she melted into submission, "Oh, all right."

Mae laid down, boots hanging over the edge of the bed and hands clasped across her tummy. Barry placed the thermometer tip under her tongue, then sat beside her and held her hand, trying not to be obvious as he consulted his watch. When 3 minutes had passed, he took the thermometer from her mouth and held it up where he could read it.

"You're 100 degrees, again," he said. "Honey, this isn't normal. Maybe you should stay home, call the doctor. You may have a virus or maybe a low-grade infection."

"Stay home? Are you kidding?!" She was already back on her feet and grabbing her purse. "Waste another day with the doctor? No way!"

Barry did not argue with her, having little faith in Doc Mac. "You're most likely tired."

She shifted gears and stopped rushing long enough to put her arms around him. He looked considerably surprised.

She cooed, "Honey, have you forgotten your promise?"

Barry hugged her tight, nuzzling her neck, "What do you mean?"

"Well, what do you think? Are we going?"

She turned her face to look him in the eyes and instantly knew by the blush creeping up his neck that he had no idea what she was talking about. She broke the embrace. Apparently, he had forgotten the promise he made. Her hands flew to her hips as she crossly confronted him.

"Barry Moore Wright, you don't remember, do you?"

"I…guess not, Mae. I'm sorry."

Mae jabbed a finger into the middle of his chest and reminded him, "You promised me you would think about our taking a nice vacation!"

"Oh, you mean *that* promise. Mae, I know you want a vacation. I guess I don't see how we can afford it, right now…"

"Well, let me tell you something, Mister. We've got to think of some way." She cut him off cold. She strode purposefully from the bedroom, heading for the hall closet, still talking. "I'm working 60-hour weeks, and I bring home every single penny I make!"

Barry followed behind.

"Other women go shopping for jewelry and clothes and…fancy red shoes!"

She pulled out her coat and resisted his efforts to chivalrously help her into it, shrugging it on by herself. "I didn't ask for a diamond ring or a big wedding.

I don't spend money at the beauty parlor every two weeks or beg to eat out in fancy restaurants, at least, not very often!"

Mae pulled her car keys out, ready in hand, and tried to leave, having had the last word.

"Dammit, Mae! Get off your high horse," Barry exploded, catching her by the sleeve and spinning her around to face him. He was quick to acknowledge when he was at fault and slow to anger. But he was not about to stand there any longer without coming to his own defense. "I work as many hours as you, if not more than you do. I work for brain-damaged jerks who break their promises and enjoy making my job a living hell. I bring home every penny I make, too. I don't sit in bars and drink. I don't gamble or run around. I even gave up my motorcycle for you!"

When Barry lost his temper, which was not often, his size made him very intimidating, a useful gift for a kind, sensitive man to possess. He used it sparingly, avoiding confrontations and Hulk-ing out only when he had no other choice.

For a moment, Mae wondered if he might hit her — something he had never done and one thing she would neither tolerate nor forgive. Barry must have seen the fear flit through her eyes because he dropped his grip on her sleeve along with his anger.

"Why are we fighting? *Honey*, I don't want to fight with you."

He read her mind, and it touched her heart. Her anger melted, too.

"Me either!"

Barry may not have been perfect, but she knew deep in her heart that she need never fear this good, gentle man who had married her. She let him take her into his strong, loving embrace and listened quietly while he went on, this time in his usual soft, even tone.

"Mae, I love you. I don't ever want to live without you. We've both had to make sacrifices. I don't know why life has to be so hard or why everything has to cost so much. And I really, really wish I could give you the sun, moon, and stars…"

He could not go on. Barry needed to wipe his nose.

"I know, Honey. I know. I'm sorry, I lost my temper…"

She found tissues in her coat pocket and offered one to Barry. He shook his head and dabbed at his nose with the back of his hand. She blew her nose and lifted her eyeglasses to wipe the tears out of her blurry eyes.

"I hope I can see to drive." She hugged her husband lovingly. "It's just that, if I don't get a vacation, and I mean this year, I think I might lose my mind. *Then* how will I earn money?"

Barry pulled back to look at her. They stood blinking and staring at each other until they both started to giggle. He hugged her joyously and kissed her sensuously. Mae started to return his kiss and then pulled away suddenly, remembering her slight fever.

"Honey, aren't you afraid you'll catch my bug?"

Barry's eyes twinkled and he spouted a bit of schoolyard poetry stuck in his head since the 1950s: "Kissing spreads germs, and germs are hated, so kiss me, baby, I'm vaccinated!" He made another grab for Mae, leaning his mouth down toward hers.

She surprised him with a quick peck on his forehead. "Better not risk it. I might be contagious," she cautioned, laughing. "'Bye, Honey!"

"'Bye, Mae," Barry served himself another helping of laughter. "Be careful!"

As customary, Mae responded, "I will. I was born careful."

She bounced down the back steps and out the backdoor to follow the red brick paved walkway, down the middle of the sodden back yard to the side door of the detached garage. Inside the garage, Mae raised the heavy, old-fashioned wooden door by hand, avoiding the liquid drips that fell from the bottom edge. She walked around to the driver's side and unlocked the car. As she opened the door, the dome light gave her the expected wink.

"Looks like it's you and me today," she told the trusty yellow Rabbit, sliding behind the wheel with ease. She started the engine, then put on her seatbelt and black leather gloves. Next, she popped a Paul Simon tape into the cassette player, a solo effort dating from the year of her marriage. She thought one of the songs had a reggae beat and wanted to give it a closer listen.

All set, she put the "Cwazy Wabbit" in gear and backed out. Thinking she was as cool as Mario Andretti behind the wheel, Mae sped off for another eventful day at the zoo, hoping that Barry would give in to taking a real vacation.

* * *

Sunday, April 22 — Falling down at Easter Parade

Long about the weekend of the Chicago Zoo's annual Easter Parade and Bonnet Contest, the Wrights got a solid clue as to what was ailing Mae.

As usual, Mae had to work directing the special event and catering to the demands of the public and news media on Saturday and, this weekend, also Sunday. The event went fine on Saturday, except Mae ran up and down the stairs to the outdoor stage set-up on Grand Square, a broad, piazza-like mall, so often that her already sore knees began to ache worse than ever. That night, both her knees hurt her so much they kept her awake. In the middle of the night, Barry got up to get her two aspirins and a glass of seltzer water, which did help a little. Mae listened to him snore for a while before she drifted off to sleep herself.

Morning arrived before Mae could believe it. She woke up at sunrise with her right knee crowing from pain. She took three aspirins and went in to supervise Sunday's activities. Around 1 p.m., during the judging of the bonnet contest, Mae hurried down the makeshift steps of the stage and her right knee flared up with a jolt of intense pain. The joint betrayed her, giving way and spilling her down the last four steps. She landed in an undignified heap, feeling embarrassed as she tried to get up.

Grant Steward, her boss, rushed to her assistance and helped Mae back to her feet. It took a minute of protesting that she was fine to realize that she was not. Her left ankle throbbed with pain. When, with a slight hold on Grant's arm, she tried to stand alone, that ankle screamed its refusal to bear any weight. Grant then asked Forest Bittern, the Human Resources manager, to take Mae to the Emergency Room at the nearby Maywood Hospital.

"I would be delighted," Forest said, offering his arm for support.

Mae took his arm and hobbled along beside him, relieved to be spared the indignity of a stretcher. They made it to Forest's Saab and proceeded to the hospital. Mae continued to feel sublimely embarrassed to be the cause of so much trouble. At the same time, she was grateful for the gentlemanly way the men had come to her aid when she needed help.

At the ER, Forest helped her out of the car and into a handy wheelchair. He pushed her across the emergency parking area and up the ramp to the door where they entered. Soon Mae sat in front of the admitting desk. Forest served as her knight-errant, helping to get her admitted. No doubt, as human resources manager, he could see that the zoo remained safe from a liability suit.

While waiting to see a doctor, Mae fretted, "Will Callie be able to handle things?"

Forest assured her that Grant was there and, of course, her trustworthy volunteer, Carolina Wren, whom they called Carol. "I'm sure they will all manage things."

Mae hated that they were now operating on ER Time, you know, emergency room time. An hour passed, followed by an x-ray. After the passage of another hour, her left ankle was pronounced "not broken but badly sprained." A nurse wrapped it tightly in a couple of yards of elastic bandage. With her ankle supported, Mae felt better and would be able to drive herself home if she took it easy. She told Forest to take her back to her office because she still had work to finish. Instead, Forest drove her back to her car.

He insisted, "Go home, Mae, and rest that ankle. We will have to get along without you for a day or two."

Mae arrived home to find a worried Barry waiting for her at the garage. She realized that, in all the excitement, she had not telephoned to tell him what she was going through, or to warn him that she would be running late. Barry was angry with her for not thinking of calling her family. Then he set eyes on her injury.

"I'm so sorry, Honey," he said regretfully in his soft, even tone. "I was feeling selfish."

Barry immediately gathered her up in his arms and carried her into the house. Zac held the storm door open. Barry huffed up the stairs to the kitchen and headed for the bedroom, planning to put Mae to bed.

She protested, "Not the bed, Honey, take me to the couch."

Mae wanted to watch some TV. About 10 minutes later, when Mae could not hold open her eyes any longer, Barry tucked her into her side of their massive, solid-oak, four-poster bed.

The next morning, Monday, Mae stayed home, alone. Barry went to work, and Zac went to school. She slept late, abandoning herself completely to this rare luxury. She loved it.

When at last she could lie in bed no longer, she took three aspirins with a tall glass of orange juice, and then indulged in a long, hot, bubble bath. She soaked her bruised and swollen left ankle and painful knees. After she toweled herself dry, Mae wrapped herself up in Barry's red Turkish robe, her favorite garment for home loungewear. In fact, it seemed she wore his robe more than he did.

Mae reapplied the elastic bandages as best she could. Flushed and still moist from her bath, she made herself a big bowl of popcorn in the kitchen; then proceeded to the living room. There, she collapsed on the couch and willed all thoughts of work and responsibility, "Begone!" She stretched like a cat and turned on the TV. A tiny electronic dot appeared on the screen, then blossomed into *Gilligan's Island.*

Mae spent the day watching mindless TV shows that flitted across her consciousness with no more impact than a migration of butterflies. the perfect therapy for an injured "PR lady." When Barry came home, she supervised him in the proper re-wrapping of her sprained ankle, then rewarded him with a kiss. Her knees and sore ankle felt better. She had not cooked, and he did not want to, so they called for a pizza delivery. Mae was still full of popcorn and not overly fond of pizza, so she contented herself with a single slice. She sat back and watched her big husband and growing son compete to see who could engulf most of the remaining pie. They matched each other, slice for slice.

Bedtime came, followed all too soon by Tuesday morning. Mae felt better rested with a slightly sore ankle but now further behind in her responsibilities. Back she went to work. She had a high threshold for pain and did not want to miss the morning senior staff meeting nor cancel an afternoon TV interview. The rush of adrenaline when a special event or media interview went well gave Mae such a good feeling. She had turned into an adrenaline junkie, craving that excitement without fear of the detriment to her health. Upon completion of the interview with WLS-Channel 7's Frank Mathie, spotlighting the giant Brazilian cockroach — the largest of all cockroaches, Mae barely made it back to her office from the Reptile House and collapsed in pain at her desk. She treated herself to her favorite power bar, a giant myrtle. Eventually, she made it to the car and made it to the pick-up spot for Gary.

Later that evening, when they watched the news coverage, Zac said he thought the giant Brazilian cockroach looked icky. Though still in pain, Mae joked, "That's why they call the study of insects, ichthyology."

Barry immediately corrected her, "The study of insects is called entomology, Zac. The study of fishes is called ichthyology."

They all laughed.

As each day went by that week — writing articles for the next members' quarterly newsletter, reviewing and revising Wolf Woods media campaign plans with her boss, pitching news about dolphin sonar research and completing other managerial projects, Mae's left ankle became more and more painful instead of getting better. Before long, both ankles and her knees pained her constantly. By Friday, she was forced to admit that she was in so much pain she could barely walk. Mae left the zoo early and drove straight home. Once home, she went to bed.

Barry had to take the 'L' home.

*   *   *

Saturday morning, Barry insisted on taking Mae to the Emergency Room at Evanston General Hospital because both her ankles and knees were visibly swollen. Once there, a nurse triaged her situation and left them to sit for a good long time. After all, Mae was not spurting blood nor suffocating from asthma nor suffering from a compound fracture. So, operating on ER Time, eventually Mae got her turn.

The pair of interns staffing the ER that morning performed an exam. Not exactly brimming with confidence, Barry wished he could see the medical school grades earned by this pair of geniuses. After they left the examination room, he went to the pay phone to call home and check on Zac. When he returned, with no regard for being overheard, he loudly inquired.

"Where are the Mayo brothers?"

"Stop that!" Mae scolded him for his sarcastic assessment. "They'll be back. They went to finish filling out my paperwork."

They killed ER Time until the two Mayos eventually returned. They announced that Mae was suffering from nothing less than acute rheumatoid arthritis. Barry, who always took a lively interest in matters relating to medicine, challenged them.

"What makes you so sure she has arthritis?"

"Well, we cannot be positive until we run the lab tests," said the taller Mayo.

"You should be able to discuss those results with your primary by tomorrow," said his accomplice, unpocketing a ball point pen and extending it toward Mae, along with a release form on a clipboard. "In the meantime, follow the recommendations you see here," he concluded, indicating a section on Mae's copy.

Mae signed herself out. Barry took the release form and saw that the recommendations consisted of instructions to "take 2 to 3 aspirins every four hours, as needed, for pain and to reduce inflammation."

Once again, Mae had consulted the mighty oracle of modern medicine only to be told what they already knew. As Mae limped out of the ER, hanging on to his arm for support, she resisted accepting the Mayo brothers' diagnosis.

"Aren't I still a young woman? What am I doing with arthritis? Isn't that something grandmothers suffer from? No one in my family has ever suffered from arthritis, not even my mother, who lived to be 87 years old!"

Though he had his doubts, Barry said, "But Honey, we cannot deny your considerable swelling and debilitating pain."

They rode the short distance home, giving each other comforting looks but in frustrated silence. Mae's tests did not confirm the diagnosis of acute rheumatoid arthritis, and, after a visit, her physician, Dr. MacAreless, could not improve on the ER prescribed aspirin therapy. Unfortunately, aspirin provided scant relief. Barry saw that Mae was growing more tired and drained with each passing day. To top things off, her arm sore was getting worse. It had become an ugly open lesion, the size of a stick of gum.

"My stomach aches from taking too much aspirin," Mae complained.

"You may need to take a stronger, narcotic painkiller," he advised.

"I don't want to take narcotics. They make me feel loopy."

He empathized, "But, Honey, you might have to resort to narcotics if they can't find a better solution."

Barry knew that what they needed was a *solution* not simply relief. With the skyrocketing cost of health care, however, they could not afford a second opinion.

While the Wrights were fortunate in that their respective employers paid for a portion of their health insurance, those employers used that benefit as an excuse to avoid paying either one of them according to their true worth. Plus, the contributions Barry and Mae were required to make to maintain their coverage went up annually. Like their standard of living, the quality of the health care they received was in decline, particularly with the advent of the HMO system. That is when the health care system changed hands from being provided primarily by non-profit organizations to for-profit corporations.

Barry would have liked five minutes alone with the genius who thought up that particular scam. As far as he could tell, only two segments of the population benefited: the giant insurance companies, already swollen beyond belief with boundless greed, and the lawmakers they lobbied in Washington, who were secure in their taxpayer-funded health care plans and had no reason to legislate any meaningful change.

*   *   *

Saturday, April 28 — Insisting on a "honeymoon"

One Saturday morning late in April, when neither of them had to go to work, Mae and Barry went out to run errands and do the grocery shopping. Mae joyfully identified the "mud-luscious" smell in the air and the "puddle wonderful" sound from her Frye boots as they headed to the back door from the garage. Spring had come to Chicago at last and not a moment too soon! Juggling a bag full of groceries, Mae cheerfully checked out the tender, green tips of perennials peeking above the garden soil along the damp red brick walkway — although it would be weeks before summer arrived with enough sunshine and hot weather to satisfy her. Thinking about hot weather reminded Mae that she had to keep working on Barry regarding what she now pointedly thought of as their honeymoon.

They never had a honeymoon. This would be her new pitch to get a real, restful vacation.

Mae struggled to unlock the back door, but she made it in and up the stairs to the kitchen just as Barry came upstairs behind her, his arms loaded. He set down his bags on the table and shrugged out of his coat. They both began putting cold things into the refrigerator.

She started, "Remember our last vacation three years ago?"

"You mean the time we drove to Virginia to visit my old friend Rick? Yeah, we went to see Colonial Williamsburg and went fishing on the James River. It was fun!"

"Parts of that trip were fun, but all the driving was stressful even with the two of us taking turns." This time, Mae plotted, "Well, I want to fly on a jet to some exotic place where I can enjoy beautiful scenery and new faces. Where do people go this time of year? Washington, for the cherry blossoms? No, Japan for the cherry blossoms!"

"Can you guess how expensive a trip like that would be?!"

"But it might solve all my problems," Mae snapped back, thinking about how best to continue to reel him in.

Barry quietly finished loading potatoes and onions into the storage bins in the pantry. He had been working a lot of 75-hour weeks during the winter with little expectation that his workload would slow down anytime soon.

"I know," he said, in a measured tone. "A vacation would be wonderful. Maybe we could start to plan a trip like when we drove to Virginia ..."

"No, nothing like that! A *real* vacation, Barry Moore Wright, with plane tickets, hotel reservations and room service. Barry, we deserve a chance to relax, at least once in our lives. You know, we never had a honeymoon."

"Well, I don't know, Mae," he started backpedaling. "I know it's what you want, but I don't see how we can afford anything like that."

He frowned and shook his head rapidly from side to side, as if trying to dispel the entire idea before it had a chance to start sounding good to him. While Mae had flown all the way to the island country of Japan, Barry preferred to travel by car. Even so, Mae had seen to it that they took an airplane to visit friends in Colorado. But Barry's good times happened in Wisconsin at The Dells, Hayward Lake Resort, or way up near Phillips for the excellent fishing.

Mae decided to propose her idea out loud and bravely let the words come out, "Why can't we do like everybody else and charge it?"

"Use the *charge* card for travel!" Appalled at the thought, Barry slumped into a kitchen chair. Mae worried that he had momentarily suffered a synaptic gap from that line of thinking, a way he deemed inconceivable, irresponsible, and downright dangerous. "No!" He adamantly wanted to close the subject, "We need to live within our means."

Refusing to let it go, Mae said, "Honey, why can't we ever have a *real* vacation like other people? They can't afford it either! They don't think about it. They wake up one morning and say, 'Boy, do I ever need a vacation, right now! I hear Aruba is lovely this time of year!' Then, off they go waving their charge cards and having a ball! And do you know what? Now and then, you just do it, whether it makes any sense or not!"

"Mae, you might be right, I don't know. You have every right to achieve your dreams, but I am a long way from ready to use a charge card for traveling. You need to give me a little more time to think about it! I'm not ready to shoulder credit debt for anything frivolous. Besides, I couldn't take off from work right now, even if I wanted to! So, let's think about it for a while."

Mae thought, all right for you, Mister! But resentfully she uttered, "Fine."

So, Mae did what any woman would do under the circumstances. She got up on her high horse and refused to speak to Barry at all, unless it was necessary. Barry, acting as if two could play that game, went back out to get a car wash and some gasoline.

*   *   *

The stalemate lasted about two weeks. During all that time there were no open hostilities, but each nursed their hurt feelings. Outwardly they presented an attitude of indifference.

Finally, one Thursday morning in May, when they were getting ready for work, Barry, tired of the silent treatment, stepped out of the shower close after Mae, who skirted him when he reached for his towel. He lost it.

Raising his voice and conceding defeat, Barry shouted, "Okay, Mae! I give up! How soon are we leaving and *where* do you want to go?"

Barry grasped two reliable guidelines about married life. One, the best way to have a happy life is to find out exactly what your wife wants and then give it to her, as quickly as possible. And two, if she could tell you what she wanted you were a lucky man.

"Honey, part of your problem, beyond the financial considerations, is your anxiety over new experiences."

With peaceful relations restored, Barry had to admit that Mae had hit the nail on the head. It was true. Mae had pinpointed his big dysfunctional behavior. He hated to go anywhere he had never been before. Barry needed at least a week to get used to the idea of going someplace new, like a new restaurant or a new theater. Suddenly, she was asking him to travel a long distance to a totally strange place, possibly to a foreign country, without so much as the security of his car. She could not just spring this kind of abrupt change on him.

"Well..." she said, seeming to be buying time as she wrapped her wet Afro with a towel, Bogart-ing the sink and mirror. "I'm thinking." She started brushing her teeth, obviously trying to come up with some place that they would both be able to enjoy.

"I don't want to go anywhere hot," he emphatically blurted out.

She rinsed her mouth and spat, then queried, "How about Europe? A co-worker recently returned from touring the vineyards of France and Italy, bragging about a wonderful time."

Barry, who had pushed in front of the mirror beside her and was applying a ribbon of toothpaste to his brush, jerked his head up and met her gaze in the mirror.

He bellowed, "Europe! It's not that interesting...and besides, Europe needs paint!" Sarcastically, he added, "If you want to look at a bunch of run-down buildings and ruins, why don't we visit your old neighborhood?"

Mae froze for a short time, lapsing into one of her fugue states, nostalgically thinking about Woodlawn, her old neighborhood.

"When I was a child in the '50s," she said wistfully. "Woodlawn was a beautiful, green Chicago neighborhood, an ethnically diverse community where sometimes, at the annual block club party, a Negro family earned 'The Best

Garden Award." Mae momentarily drifted into another fugue state, recalling that was before blockbusting, which isolated Negroes — as they were politely referred to during those years, and the advent of low-income housing projects, which succeeded in vertically warehousing families of African descent, ultimately conditioning gifted Black children to an unsanitary, overcrowded, and belligerent groupthink setting. In time, block-after-block of vacant lots and rotting or abandoned buildings made up too many neighborhoods like once-pleasant Woodlawn. The projects stood like monuments to despair, surrounded by the savage streets of the ghetto. These days her old neighborhood looked much like photographs of war-torn Berlin shortly after World War II — the legacy of urban renewal Chicago-style.

Mae finally came back with a salvo, "I'm sure that all continental Europe isn't poor and run-down. But, fine. If that's the way you feel. There's still a big, wide world to choose from. What if we went to a bed-and-breakfast in England?"

"England!" he exploded, a gout of foamy toothpaste splattering into the sink. He had to pause to rinse his mouth and wipe his chin. Turning directly to Mae, he insisted, "If we could still find a couple of corners of unspoiled English countryside, it wouldn't be worth putting up with the snotty British in order to see it."

Worried that she might be losing ground, Mae said, "We don't need to go out of the country. How about Springfield? We could see the state house, visit Lincoln's house in Salem, the state fair and..."

Barry interrupted, "Yeah... well, I hate to burst your romanticizing bubble, but you can see better artifacts and learn more about Lincoln at the Chicago Historical Society."

"There's no way I'm going to hang around here on another vacation," Mae vowed. "I'm heading someplace that requires airline tickets, hotel reservations and room service. Are you coming with me or not?"

Mae left the bathroom — in his red robe, as usual. Her feelings were crushed.

Barry suddenly came up with what he thought of as a good idea. "Hey, let's go to the Pacific Northwest." He rushed into the bedroom, "I've always wanted to go to Alaska."

"Uh-*las*-ka! It's too cold there," countered Mae. Sounding irritated, she said, "You want to go farther into the frigid North!"

"It's beautiful country up there, on a grand scale. Mountains... and waterfalls... and ..." He seemed to be thinking of something else to mention, probably wild grizzly bears, then thought better of it. "It's God's Country, Mae. We could fish and do some camping and hiking." He asked in disbelief, "Why do you look so shocked?"

"Hon-*ey*," she pleaded. "I don't feel like freezing my butt off on this vacation. Remember our long weekend camping trips to Wisconsin where it rained most of the time? We could barely get a campfire going to heat up canned beans, let alone stay dry long enough to eat them. I vividly recall holding a tin plate at an angle to let the rainwater drain off while I forked up sauceless, rinsed beans into my mouth as fast as I could without stabbing myself. And the nights, although romantic, were too darn cold for me to consider getting undressed."

Mae casually let the robe fall from her shoulders. She stood naked as she unwound the towel from her head.

"Think South, where it's warm," she said innocently. "How about the West Indies? Imagine turquoise waters, stretching out on white sandy beaches, looking at palm trees ... "

"And hot!" Barry managed to fire back, trying hard to focus on his objection to anything. "I hate anything that makes me sweat, except hot showers and sex."

She crossed the room, brushing ever so lightly against him in her passing. "Come on, it's not *that* hot," assured Mae, who had never been there. "I want to be pampered." She revolved to face him, but slowly, so he could not fail to notice all her feminine charms, hoping he wanted to be sweating pleasantly in the next few minutes; he already had his hot shower. Mae gave him a warm smile and continued, "The ocean breeze makes it feel cooler. Besides, it's not a jungle. I'm sure they have air conditioning. They must have all the modern conveniences. It's 1984!"

"I don't know, Mae. It's an awful lot of money to spend for one week."

He was *this/close* to unconditional surrender. She positively burned to walk around a small, tropical island in the sun, regardless of the cost.

"I'm sick of the city and sick of the cold," she fussed.

Ironically, at that moment, Mae had no idea how *sick* she really was, or for *what* she was really asking.

"I can see that this means a great deal to you," Barry said. "You know, I try to budget every penny, but I realize that there is more than money to account for here. In the final analysis, you deserve some special reward. You have suffered through a lot this year with very little complaint. And I'm pretty sure the Caribbean is cheaper than Europe, probably a lot cheaper than Hawaii." He looked at Mae lovingly and she could see the last bastion of his resistance fall before her long-standing siege. "All right, Mae, you win."

*   *   *

Barry knew Mae would never let this go until she ultimately achieved her goal. That goal-oriented drive was an integral part of the "wonder woman" he admired.

He smiled to see her instant delight. It would have been childlike if she had not looked so darned sexy. She clasped her hands in front of her chin and bounced on her toes, coincidentally rewarding him with a most wonderful jiggle.

Then she tipped back her head and hissed an exuberant "Yes-s-s-s-s!"

Playfully, he added, "I guess your old, arthritic bones could use a vacation."

"Oh, yeah...?"

Recognizing a vulnerable target, Mae whip-cracked him crisply on the buttocks with her soggy towel, another skill he had taught her. His reaction was immediate and satisfying.

Barry wailed, "Ow!" Snapping instantly upright, he turned around to face his assailant.

Positively hooting her laughter, Mae jumped into bed and pulled the covers over her head. Barry got under the covers so fast his wail still echoed off the bedroom walls.

CHAPTER FOUR

May 1984 — Choosing a tropical destination

The mornings were growing sunnier, though they still felt chilly to Mae, who arrived in her office about 8 a.m. on Friday, May 18. She found it hard to get started on any of the projects covering her desk and threatening to spill over onto the floor. Frowning at her work, she wondered where to start. Her eyes strayed to the bottom right-hand drawer of her desk. Mae distinctly heard it calling her name. There, inside the drawer, covering her giant myrtle stash, was a thickly stuffed manila envelope. Giving in to her temptation, Mae thought since she was not supposed to start work until 9 a.m. officially, she was on her own time right then.

So, she cleared a couple of projects off her desktop, pulled out the envelope and spilled out the contents. Out tumbled the glossy colorful travel brochures she had been collecting for the past couple of months. Mae decided it was a good time to get started. Since Barry had agreed that she could plan a "honeymoon," she applied her characteristic goal-oriented enthusiasm to studying the possibilities and making the arrangements at a location of her dreams.

Mae thumbed through dozens of travel brochures. She soon realized that they could never afford an ocean cruise. Too stuffy, anyway, she rationalized. Next, the expensive brochure from Lewis & Kent Expeditions, Ltd., an operator of upscale tours, particularly intrigued her. She drooled over every slick page. They offered safaris in Africa, walkabouts in Australia, balloon trips over the Alps, barges down the Nile and treks to the Great Wall of China. The glossy, full-color pictures promised the lifestyle of the very rich. That is what Mae and Barry would need to be to afford the accommodation that characterized L&K's 5-star luxury itineraries.

Mae regretfully decided, a little too rich for their blood. She considered the possibility of one of the wilderness adventures offered to zoo members. It would be physically challenging and absolutely no room service. She had a bit more pampered travel experience in mind.

Mae reasoned, there must be something in between. She lapsed into one of her patented fugue states, reflecting on her previous travel experiences. As a child, she took occasional long weekend trips with her family. Those were always trips driving down to Memphis where they would stay with relatives. The trips usually involved more than one car, but everybody stayed close together, a caravan of cautious Negroes, inching south, looking out for each other the whole way. They never strayed from Route 57, one of the trails used by Negroes traveling to Chicago during the Great Migration.

Little Mae watched how her family got rather quiet as they passed through Cairo, Illinois, that town was notorious for lynching Negroes. Even as a kindergartner she understood they had crossed some boundary, from a safer place into hostile territory where Black folks had to be especially careful around White people, avoiding them all together whenever possible. Some grown-ups would unfailingly caution the northern-raised children, scarily shaking and pointing a finger, "Remember Emmet Till," invoking the spirit of the naïve northern Negro boy murdered supposedly for whistling at a White woman down south — and the specter of Jim Crow emerged to haunt another generation.

But, once they got to Memphis, those southern sojourns became happy times. They were safe in the confines of family. There were good things to eat, swinging music, and poking fun at each other. Mae sighed away the childhood memories and moved forward through time in her mind. She recalled a summer camp trip to Wisconsin when she was 9 years old, and there had been the YWCA trip to Washington, D.C., when she was in 7th grade. Those memories made her smile, thinking of all those trips as grand. Then she recalled the grandest trip of all, six weeks in Japan! It was during the summer of her junior year in college. She visited several cities in Japan as an exchange student, part of a six-week cultural studies program. Smiling to herself, Mae remembered how she had a human revolution! Except, she missed Barry, and he missed her. He proposed when she got home.

They married in 1971, the year they graduated. The nearest thing to a honeymoon was a trip to Colorado where they stayed with friends. Although nice, it was not a honeymoon. Zac was born in '72, and the honeymoon was indefinitely postponed.

Now is the time, she mused. Then she noticed the clock on the wall read almost 9 o'clock! Speaking of time, she had to get busy. Gigi Blue, *People* magazine's Chicago bureau chief, was arriving at 9:30 a.m. to observe cataract surgery being performed on an eagle in the animal hospital by a renowned Chicago-area ophthalmologist.

The brochures went back into the envelope and drawer. Mae went to work.

* * *

On Saturday, May 19, the Wrights again considered their options for a vacation spot, carefully and seriously. After accepting the inevitable, Barry acted as if he were looking forward to the trip and participated imaginatively in the discussions concerning proposed destinations.

At one point, the two discussed a fantasy of Mae's as a possibility, a journey to Africa, the ancient Motherland of her ancestors.

"It would be wonderful to visit not only a *country* but an entire *continent* where I would number among the majority and be treated like a long, lost sister." She said dreamily, "I bet you would be recognized as a friend, if not a brother, since you married me, an African sister."

"Don't be idealistic, Mae. Having dallied with the hippie counterculture in my youth, I'm familiar with the concepts of peace, love, harmony, and brotherhood and not so sure that a trip to Africa would be all 'Mai Tais and

Yahtzee'. I've never seen those concepts conscientiously put into practice for any length of time," he said. "Sooner or later the pursuit of the almighty dollar gets in the way. There certainly would be language problems. Besides, the news out of Africa is always full of political chaos and warfare."

Traveling in Africa sounded like an adventure, but not the leisurely honeymoon Mae sought. In the end, she grudgingly agreed with Barry that Africa was both too expensive and risky, although she suspected Barry's fear of the new and untried was the true deciding factor.

So, after much thought, study, reflection, and conversation, they finally agreed on a destination. They would go to the fabled, tropical island of Jamaica.

Jamaica was perfect — all the color of a trip to Africa but closer and immensely cheaper. Jamaica offered the tropical beauty and weather that Mae craved along with a culture exotic enough to be as exciting as Japan, but where the people spoke English. She was quite sure her race and her husband's obvious lack of prejudice would make them welcomed visitors, able to move freely and safely among the smiling and carefree Jamaicans, as advertised by television commercials: "Come back to Jah-may-kah."

Mae was more than thrilled. She was beside herself with anticipation. Very soon she would be on her way to the sunny Caribbean, as she had wanted to be on that freezing Groundhog Day months earlier when the idea first had been planted in her mind. And Barry would be with her. They would have a romantic honeymoon, a *real* vacation, at last!

* * *

It was during her lunch hour on Wednesday, May 30, when Mae, on the phone in her office, discussed a special vacation package with a travel agent.

"Caw Park Beach Resort... Two stories, Georgian-style villa..."

Mae attentively took copious notes as the travel agent described the resort hotel to her.

The agent talked like she had experience and first-hand knowledge, "...Surrounded by tropical flora ...half mile of private beach in a secluded cove... A restaurant with terrace and..."

"What? What?" Mae said, feeling excited about this resort complex. It sounded great.

"The room has a private, oceanfront balcony!"

Mae practically squealed, "Right on the beach?"

"Yes, indeed. It's outside of beautiful Ocho Rios," said the agent.

It sounded exactly like the right place for Barry and Mae to stay in Jamaica, with the right package, meaning priced in the range Barry could live with, as well as one that would meet *both* their pleasure requirements. Barry did not want to stay in an impersonal high-rise hotel or club complex, and Mae did not want to stay anywhere she had to cook and clean up.

The two-story resort had rooms with balconies that faced the ocean, a private swimming pool and a half-mile private beach, separated from the encroaching rainforest by the mouth of the White River. Jungle treetops framed a view of the distant Blue Mountains.

Something occurred to Mae, "Where *is* Ocho Rios?"

She was concerned about venturing too far from the mainstream public.

"On the north coast of Jamaica. It's about a two-hour drive from Montego Bay," explained the agent. "You take a bus to the hotel."

"A bus?" Mae was a little skeptical. "What kind of bus?"

She thought of the bus ride Kathleen Turner took in the movie *Romancing the Stone*. Barry never would forgive her if she set up something like that, giggling at the idea of her big, fussy husband scrunched in a wobbly old school bus with stinky livestock and sweaty foreigners.

"Oh, you needn't worry. They are very nice, air-conditioned, modern buses. And the scenery along the way is spectacular, Mrs. Wright," the experienced agent said reassuringly. "They provide top-tier service. I know because I inspected this resort. It's a great price because you'll be there in September, just before the peak season begins."

The travel agent failed to mention that "the peak season" began at the end of hurricane season, which was from June 1 to November 30 in the Atlantic basin.

Totally ignorant about tropical cyclones and when they occur, Mae cheerily replied "Well, it sounds perfect! But I need to talk it over with my husband and get back to you."

"Of course, Mrs. Wright. But let me warn you, if you want to guarantee your reservation for September 15, you should get your deposit to me as soon as possible."

She wondered, "Why the big rush? That's four months from now."

"Yes, but if you want the discount rate on this package, you need to make a reservation at least six weeks prior to departure. I know that September 15 may seem like a long time from now, but you must keep in mind that the longer you wait the greater the risk that the resort may become fully booked." She added, "You may cancel at any time up to two weeks prior to departure, should you wish to do so and still get your full payment refunded. There is a stiff penalty, though, if you leave in the middle of your vacation and return home early."

"Well, I doubt that would ever happen. Still, I must talk it over with my husband before I give you a deposit," Mae insisted.

"Very well, I look forward to hearing from you soon. I'm sure you'll never regret it."

"Thank you." Mae concluded smiling, "Good-bye."

She grabbed a giant myrtle to celebrate.

Back to work, Mae began with the plans for the next big event, Teddy Bear Picnic. She picked up the *Chicago Tribune* to scan the paper for any coverage. There, in the "Inc." column, was the gossip blurb she had placed with Michael Sneed. Mae read aloud for Callie's benefit. "It will be 'Bears and Woo at the Zoo' when WMAQ-Channel 5's news anchor Suzy Woo hosts the Chicago Zoo's 4th annual Teddy Bear Picnic on Saturday, June 2. Woo, who is expecting her first child, owns over 100 teddy bears."

Mae was thrilled to have this announcement appear nearly three weeks before the event. She congratulated herself, *"Excellent timing!"*

"That's great," said Callie, swishing her hips into Mae's office and handing over a rare lengthy three-page news release for proofreading. Mae readily accepted the pages that listed the zoo's 1984 fall quarterly special events schedule. She anxiously wanted to get it distributed to news media with long lead times, such as periodicals, weekly publications, and broadcast community affairs directors.

"All *right*," exclaimed Mae, who felt like giving someone a high five. Instead, she handed Callie the tear sheet from the newspaper.

"Callie, please have Carol clip it and make copies. Send a copy to Grant, of course, and see that Dr. Buffalo gets one."

"Sure thing," said Callie, swishing back to her desk.

Mae had organized a full day of activities for the Teddy Bear Picnic. In addition to the personal appearance by the popular Asian TV news anchor as Grand Marshal of the parade, there would be real, live "Bear hugs" from four players on Chicago's favorite football team, called "Da Bears." Mae had worked with an advertising agency to get a radio station to sponsor each participating player to represent one of the four species of bears at the zoo: Kodiak Island grizzlies, Asian sloth bears, South American spectacled bears, and Arctic polar bears. Visitors were being asked to donate a dollar to help feed the species of their choice in exchange for a "Bear hug" from the designated player.

Mae had numerous other activities lined up for the Picnic, including a Quick-well Clinic for teddy bears in need of repair, Paw Readers, teddy bear face painting, and Bear Talks from the bear keepers and the curator. Of course, there would be the parade, which would climax in the grandest event of all: the Teddy Bear Contest with prizes given in 5 categories: most snuggled, best dressed, owner/bear look-a-like, smallest, and largest.

It occurred to Mae to ask Callie, "What's happening with West Suburban Band?"

"I heard back from the band leader. They're looking forward to performing the marching music for the Teddy Bear Parade."

"Great! Now, all that's left is finding a big bear to lead the parade."

Affie, the calm African elephant, usually led the parades at the zoo for Halloween and Easter. But such a highly sensitive pachyderm would not be right to lead the raucous teddy bear enthusiasts. So, a delightful, adult-size Tender Heart teddy bear costume had been rented. Mae only needed someone to play the loveable character. That day, the weather was unusually hot so early in the summer, with temperatures already reaching the high-90s, in stark contrast to the extremely cold previous winter. Mae had been contentedly enjoying the heat, all the while knowing that when the weather began to turn chilly again, she and Barry would be taking off on their "honeymoon." Because of the heat, no one she asked was willing to don the heavily padded costume and exert themselves for an hour, not even to delight a few thousand children.

* * *

That evening, upon hearing about her predicament, Barry unselfishly volunteered to become Tender Heart teddy bear for the requisite hour. Pleasantly surprised, Mae hugged him gratefully. Zac ran to the car and brought in the costume for his dad to try on. Even in the cooler evening air, the padded costume felt stifling, and everything below Tender Heart's waist would remain unexplored territory to Barry. After a few minutes, he had to remove the head.

"His head is as big as a beer keg," Barry said, pulling it off. His wavy hair was plastered with sweat and ran down over his forehead into his smarting eyes. "I hope you realize I wouldn't sweat like this for anyone but you," he flirted, puffing.

"I guess you've been type-cast, Honey," she teased, poking teddy in his ample midriff, which was maybe an XXXXXXL. "But no matter how hot it gets," she warned him, "you mustn't take the head off in front of the kids!"

"Please, promise me you'll rescue me when my hour's up," he pleaded, "and, if the teddy bear falls out, throw ice-cold beer on him!"

They all laughed while he damply removed the rest of the bear suit. Later that night when Mae had his attention all to herself, she told him about the Caw Park Beach Resort and the special rate if they booked right away. He asked questions but ultimately gave his agreement to the cost and date. Mae would book their vacation package the very next day.

* * *

June 1984 — Disregarding pain at Teddy Bear Picnic

Saturday, June 2, the day of the big Teddy Bear Picnic dawned warm and sunny, with every indication of being a scorcher. On the drive in, the Wrights were excited. Mae had the highest expectations for a successful event. Soon after arriving, Zac scurried off to his own devices, and Barry waited for his curtain call.

Thousands of people were in the park by noon, most came through the woodsy bottleneck of the North Gate, in wave after wave of every conceivable human being all dressed for summer weather and planning on making the absolute most out of such a perfect day. Everywhere you looked, children dragged, hugged, sucked on, and beat each other with teddy bears of every size, style, and vintage. There were whole families: grandparents and grandchildren; fathers with little girls or boy, or both on their shoulders; mothers pushing strollers; parents "packing" a tiny baby fore or aft; bare-chested dudes; and bikers and bra-less chicks. Chicago Zoo visitors carried picnic baskets, coolers, cameras, binoculars, blankets and, most importantly, cash to spend.

All Mae's activities were jam-packed, especially the lines for "Bear hugs." People were not so much voting for a favorite bear species as fans paying a dollar to get an actual, physical hug from their favorite home-team football player: defensive linemen Bert Hecker, Ray Guildenstern or Chevron Pummelweed, or tight end Avery Lessfoot.

Mae, who was in her element, barely flinched as her knees and head started aching. She was everywhere at once "like God with a bullhorn," flanked by her volunteer Carolina Wren, called Carol, who held her clipboard, and her "staff" Callie, who monitored the walkie-talkie.

At 2 p.m., Mae darted this way and that in her "surrey with the fringe on top" — an electric golf cart belonging to the chair of the board. She designated here and disciplined there, while she formed up the Teddy Bear Parade. Callie flagged Mae down and handed her the radio. Security radioed, alerting Mae to the arrival of the parade's celebrity grand marshal Suzy Woo.

Mae left it to Callie and Carol to finish sorting out the parade lineup and zoomed off to the South Gate to meet Ms. Woo. It took Mae almost 10 minutes to cross the park from Fountain Court to South Gate, because of the crowds, but that was the sort of delay she did not mind. Mae was almost positive that the zoo would set a new attendance record for that event day. She arrived at the gate to find a knot of thoroughly charmed security guards surrounding the local TV celebrity. Suzy Woo was gorgeous, gracious, and unbelievably pregnant. She was dressed in a white-cotton, designer sundress with a wide-brimmed hat to protect her porcelain skin from the sun's rays and clutched her favorite teddy bear.

Mae stopped the cart and switched off the electric motor. Several nervous security guards, some of whom seemed to be trying to remember the protocol for emergency delivery, gingerly helped Ms. Woo into the cart beside Mae.

"Suzy, how nice to see you," Mae said, in greeting. "Thanks ever so much for coming out to help us with our event today."

"The pleasure is mine, Mae. It was an honor to be asked. I love teddy bears!"

Mae wished she knew Suzy Woo's secret for staying cool and dry on such a hot day — *pregnant and everything!* Mae had one more "celebrity" waiting in her air-conditioned office. She pulled her cart around to the rear door. It opened and Barry emerged, dressed as Tender Heart teddy bear. He approached the golf cart, moving somewhat blindly with no way to see the ground at his feet. Mae switched off the cart, again, and hurriedly dismounted, dashing to Barry's aid before he fell and broke his neck.

"Jeez, Mae. I can't see my feet!"

Barry's muffled voice came from the vicinity of Tender Heart's superior sternal notch. "My God, it's hot! I heard on the radio that the high today is going to be in the upper 90s!"

Holding him by the elbow, Mae guided him to the cart's rear-facing jump seat. He sat down clumsily, barely squeezing all of his massive "teddiness" on board. He had to slump uncomfortably low to clear the fringed canopy with Tender Heart's keg-sized head.

"Take it easy, Mae." Barry fussed, "I'm barely on this thing. What *is* the temperature?"

"Don't worry, Honey, I've got a pregnant TV star on board, and the park is so crowded I couldn't speed if I wanted to."

Mae started the cart, full to capacity, and likely well over its load limit.

"Suzy," she began. "Somewhere inside this grouchy teddy bear is my long-suffering husband, Barry. Barry quit complaining and get into character. Say hello to our lovely grand marshal, Ms. Suzy Woo."

Barry waved at Suzy and managed to stay aboard the cart while he wagged his enormous head from side to side. The maneuver caused the entire cart to lurch, first to the left and then to the right. Mae fought to maintain steering control. Suzy laughed musically at the huge, overstuffed, costumed character.

"I know how you feel!" she sympathized, patting her tummy.

"Everybody, sit still!" shouted Mae — meaning Barry, who had no idea how close they had come to crashing into a pushcart.

Mae navigated back through the crowds once more to Fountain Court and the waiting parade. People waved and shouted happily. Suzy beamed and waved back, totally given over to the excitement of the event. She wore her celebrity status like stylish yet comfortable clothes. Mae was proud to have such a gracious grand marshal for her so far singularly successful special event. She cruised up to the sawhorse barricade that held back the leading edge of the parade. She looked around frantically, unable to locate Callie. Soon Mae spotted Carol steadfastly pushing through the crowd in her direction, clearing her way with a clipboard and reminding Mae of a jungle scout swinging a machete against the underbrush.

"Are we ready?" Mae queried Carol as soon as the volunteer had gotten close enough for her voice to carry above the noise the children made, which was louder than the occasional baboon free-for-all that could be heard coming from Ape Island. Carol nodded. Mae was out of the cart and moving around to help Barry get his "Tender Heart" unwedged from the jump seat.

She led Barry by the hand to where Carol waited, just clear of the barricade, and said, "Take Bar—, I mean, Tender Heart..." she corrected herself, aware of the big eyes staring up in adoration, "...to his starting position in front of the children." She pressed Barry's paw into Carol's hand. Barry, doing his best to whirl toward the departing Mae, yelled, "Hey! Wait a minute, Mae. Are you leaving me already?" he tried to shout above the clamor. "For God's sake, don't forget, you promised to rescue me in *one hour*!"

"In character, please, B— Tender Heart!" she called over her shoulder, already back in the cart with Suzy. Mae was on a mission to run this special event on time.

* * *

As soon as Tender Heart was in position, the barricades were removed and the children immediately mobbed him. Most of the kids were so short, Barry could not see the ones who surged in close around his knees. He was terrified of stepping on somebody's precious child. Through the inadequate eyeholes behind Tender Heart's bow tie, Barry could see the marching band. Beyond them, Mae's cart led the parade with Suzy, waving and smiling.

Barry was going to try and keep his eye on Mae and do his best to follow the parade route. Inside the mask, sweat was already stinging his eyes and his breath sounded like Darth Vader's. He could hear the blare of brass instruments, as well as the high-pitched voices of overexcited children calling his name and screaming for personal attention. Tiny hands patted, poked, pinched, and pummeled him all over. To top it all off, it must have been more than 120 degrees inside the suit!

Barry felt both elated and terrified. He wondered if he could already be shocky from dehydration or hyperthermia. He did not know what else to do, so he waved like a madman with his free paw. Someone, presumably Carol, still held the other one.

Mae and Suzy took off, followed by the West Suburban Marching Band and, in turn, Tender Heart teddy bear, shuffling into motion, afloat on a living wave of screaming, sugar-fueled children.

This must be what it feels like to ride a surfboard, thought Barry, hoping he did not wipe out! In about 30 seconds, when he had not stepped on anybody, he felt like he had the hang of it. This would be pretty cool, he told himself, if only it were not so darn hot. And, like all fools who start thinking they are pretty cool, he began showing off. He skipped and gestured to the children, putting in a few fancy steps here and there. In the process, he lost his grasp on the hand he had been holding. His was an inspired performance for the next two hundred yards, until he started to run out of steam from the heat and exertion. He soon realized that he had better start pacing myself or he would not last to the finish line.

He settled down to try to keep up with the band. The parade went on and on. First, they marched west, down the long main parkway to Ibex Mountain, then back east, past Fountain Court on the opposite side, and up the incline that stretched toward Safari Lodge.

Barry wished the parade were over. He wondered how long it had been. It felt like more than an hour, already!

For a brief moment, he was hit by the cool, wind-carried spray from Roosevelt Fountain, which spouted majestically at the center of a pool. With his limited vision, he caught a glimpse of a wailing toddler in a stroller being aggressively pushed through the crowd to his right.

The little sweetie wailed, "Tender Heart, wait! Tender Heart wait! Tender Heart, wait!" She looked to be about three years old, her piercing tone cutting through the noise made by the other children.

Fat chance, kid, thought Barry, intent on getting through his part in the parade. The heat was making him sick. He stopped thinking about cold beer at the end of his hour of service and misery. He felt nauseous enough already. Now, all he wanted was to get out of the suit and into a nice, cool shower, followed by a tall, chilled glass of ice water.

Mae and Suzy had reached the restaurant and were beginning to round the corner and head back up the main parkway to the Grand Square where the parade would disband near the stage. Mae would then step up to the microphone and announce the start of Teddy Bear Contest.

If I can make it back to the fountain, I'll stand in the fountain spray until Mae can swoop down in her cart and rescue me, Barry hoped, having difficulty forming coherent thoughts.

The stroller girl persisted, "Tender Heart, wait! Tender Heart wait! Tender Heart, wait!"

Barry marveled at the decibel-level such a tiny set of lungs could produce. The finish line was within sight, though, and he focused all his energy on just making it.

"HE'LL WAIT! DON'T YOU WORRY, CAROL ANNE..." came a gravel-throated voice, each word spoken like an epithet, "OR DADDY WILL BREAK HIS FUCKING BACK!"

"This situation cannot be for real," thought Barry, who had not been instructed on how to deal with threats of physical violence. Who goes around assaulting parade characters, anyway? He slowed down, unsuccessfully trying to get a look at the man who went with such a voice. You never know these days — not when you are dealing with the public. Better not risk it, he decided and broke off his purposeful stride to waddle toward Stroller Girl. He patted her head. She beamed with pleasure, but not nearly as broadly as her dad, whom Barry could finally see.

He was an outlaw biker, smiling a fractured, gap-toothed smile through an uncombed beard. The guy wore greasy cutoffs over a scarred and tattooed body, lumbering along in heavy engineer's boots. He might have been all of five feet tall. He looked like 300 pounds of attitude poured into a 90-pound sack, Barry thought with amusement. Not that he wanted to tangle with this dude. Barry knew a little about outlaw bikers from his old hippie days. They tended to enjoy violence and carry concealed weapons.

Barry chucked the child under the chin and waved bye-bye, a wary eye on her daddy, who appeared satisfied. The backpressure created by the delay caused the stalled marchers to surge forward, and Barry "caught the wave" and surged with them, trying to put quite a few people between himself and the potentially dangerous, unquestionably proud papa. He recognized the adrenaline rush that always followed a confrontation — not his favorite feeling. He willed himself to forget about it and resumed his clowning dance, using his last ounce of energy to end the parade as exuberantly as he had started off.

Regardless of Barry's expectation, Mae was not there at the finish line to whisk him out of sight so he could remove the costume and cool down. He was tired and dehydrated. The children mobbed him, again, surrounding him to the point where he was unable to move in any direction. Some parent thrust a child into Tender Heart's arms. An electronic photoflash went off in his face. Barry began to laugh and cry at the same time. He wondered if he died, would they bury him in the bear suit.

The child in his arms was switched for another one, followed by more flashes. The noise of the crowd was incredible. Still, Barry thought he heard someone calling his name.

"Barry!"

There it was, again. He knew then it was Mae calling him. But where...?"

"Get in the cart!"

Barry avoided being handed the next toddler. Holding his hands high, he revolved until he could see Mae, inching her cart as close as she dared. He shook off the children who clung to his legs, with the strength of desperation, and slowly waded the 20-foot distance to where the cart idled. He collapsed backwards into the cart, bringing the ragtop down in the process.

Mae cut the wheels sharply and pulled away toward the edge of the crowd. Tender Heart wrestled to disentangle himself from the white fringed canvas, without bouncing out of the cart. Barry could tell by the diminishing noise that they must have been leaving the crowd behind. When he felt the cart brake to a halt, he could stand it no longer.

Barry tore at the tabs that secured Tender Heart's big head. Mae came around to where he wrestled with the costume, grabbing the huge head by the ears and pulling with all her strength, one foot braced against the bumper of the cart.

With an "Ow-w-w-w!" from him, off came the head.

"Your face is red and wetter than a muskrat. Are you laughing or crying, or both?"

He kept making vain attempts to grasp the costume's zipper with his padded paws. Mae could not help laughing despite his obvious discomfort, but she did get hold of the zipper and pull it down.

"Easy, Honey. You'll tear the costume," she warned.

He sputtered, "I'm glad you think it's funny, Mae. My whole life passed before my eyes! Help me out of this thing before I die!"

Barry was not sure where they were, but satisfied that they were "behind the scenes," he shucked himself out of the wringing-wet ruin of once-proud Tender Heart. Barry's T-shirt and shorts were soaked through.

Mae took his hand and pulled gently, helping him get moving. "C'mon, Honey, it's air-conditioned in my office."

Of course! He recognized the location, now. Mae had her back door unlocked and was holding it open for him. He hurried inside, into the cool darkened office. Mae opened his gear bag and passed him a bath towel. He dried himself off, feeling surprisingly chilly already, and began to change into some dry clothes. That was when he noticed the clock. It was after 4 p.m.!

Barry exploded in disbelief, "You left me in that sweat suit for more than *two* hours?"

"I'm sorry, Honey. There wasn't anything I could do. I'm so proud of you for doing this for me!" She kissed him, extending an ice-cold can of soda. "Can I buy you a drink?" she flirted.

Barry grabbed the can and popped it open, upending it over his open mouth. The carbonated beverage burned down his parched throat. He was so thirsty; he didn't taste it. He sat down on her office couch and burped, beginning to think he might just "make it."

"Any permanent brain damage I should know about?" she asked, teasingly.

"I guess not..." he started.

"...But then, who could tell?" she finished, her eyes sparkling. "Put your feet up, Honey, and stay in here where it's cool. I've got a few things to finish up, and then we'll head for home."

Mae leaned down to give him a kiss, planting it in the middle of his forehead. Then she straightened, gave him a smile, put on her sun helmet, and went back out the door into the heat, totally in her element.

Barry, already feeling better, worked on his second soda. He sipped this one more slowly. He thought, he had better start getting used to the heat. That was only a taste of what it will be like in Jamaica. He wondered why Mae's happiness was so often inversely proportional to his comfort level. Then Zac came through the back door to Mae's office.

He said, "Hey, Dad. You were great!"

* * *

On Sunday, June 10, the Wrights celebrated Barry's birthday at home. Mae and Zac surprised him with a Seiko diver's watch, which he had wanted for some time. It cost more than $200. Mae knew he would never spend that much money on himself.

"You shouldn't have!" He admonished them, but he was thrilled.

Barry immediately strapped it on his left wrist, crystal toward his body to protect it from scratches and chips, the way he always wore a watch. It was a big watch, but Barry was a big man. So, it suited him. From that day forward, he wore the watch proudly. Whenever he consulted it, Barry was reminded of his loving wife and son.

* * *

By mid-June, Barry and Mae were looking forward to a vacation with mounting excitement. Sharing their anticipation helped make them feel very close, more so than they had felt in some time. They started seeking out background knowledge about Jamaica. Their research made them aware of Jamaica's troubled political and economic situation, which curbed Barry's initial excitement. But Mae ruled that they were not going to worry about it. Lots of people went to Jamaica. The Wrights were going and *that* was *that*. Barry smarted at being overruled but was pacified when Mae agreed that they should bring up his concerns to people they knew who had made the trip, see what they had to say.

Mae's brother Chester and his wife Maureen, who had been to Jamaica a few years earlier, laughed at his worries. They had traveled with another African American couple and stayed in one of the large hotels, never venturing further afield than the pool or meeting any Jamaicans other than the hotel employees. They loved it.

Barry told Mae, "I hope we will see the countryside and meet some real Jamaican people.

One evening after work, they talked with Carl and Arlene, a married couple who worked with Barry. The couple got married in Ocho Rios and took their honeymoon on the spot.

They both said they loved Jamaica. They were thrilled for the Wrights, recommending a restaurant where they enjoyed a local pumpkin delicacy called sunshine soup. In a long story, somehow Arlene's wedding band was stolen, but they still had a great time. Carl also touted the quality, availability, and affordability of the ganja.

"You owe it to yourselves to try it," he told Barry. "You don't have to be afraid of the law so long as you aren't blatant about it."

Curious Barry wanted to know more, "How'd you happen to come across it?"

"Oh, it makes itself available," Carl assured him. "A waiter at the restaurant offered to fix us up with a bag. I'll tell you this," he went on, "It was a hell of a lot cheaper than drinking. It made everything sparkly and fun, and more beautiful than it already was, and..." Carl laughed heartily, "I never forgot where I parked the car or woke up with a hangover!"

Mae asserted, "I'm sure we'll have plenty of fun. I don't think we want to fool around with illegal drugs, particularly in a foreign country." She turned to him, "Do we, Barry?"

"I suppose not." he pensively replied.

Their good friend Ron, a gifted artist who led a bohemian, self-sufficient lifestyle, came over frequently, especially in the summer for Mae's excellent barbecued ribs. One Saturday on a beautiful sunny day, high in the 80s, Mae stood watch over the spareribs sizzling on the grill in the backyard while they listened as Ron happily recounted some of his adventures in Jamaica. The backyard, primarily in the shade of cottonwood and oak trees, felt comfortable and lush with flowers in big beds winding around the outer edges of the lawn. Around them on Grey Street, the air was filled with the sounds of people outside manicuring their lawns, maintaining their houses, and balling out their brats, as well as the songs of birds and the summer "snowfall" drifting down from 100-year-old cottonwoods.

Ron asked Barry, "I know Mae once traveled to Japan, but have you traveled much?"

"Sure, I'm well-traveled," Barry joked. "I've been to Wisconsin many times." With a straight face, he offered to show a non-existent tattoo on his arm, "Here's my tattoo of a water-skiing blonde over the legend, "I've been to Tommy Bartlett's Water Show." He admonished, "Never get drunk in the Dells!"

They all had a hearty laugh. Then Ron glowingly recalled his time camping for free on the beach in Negril, where he did pastel paintings of the scenery after eating a hallucinogenic mushroom omelet, a specialty for certain local entrepreneurs. Ron specialized in traveling the world on a shoestring budget. In the mid-1970s, he had traveled throughout Africa entirely on his own, finding friendly people everywhere. While his experiences were not entirely unmarked by problems, he lived to tell the story and wrote off his troubles to his ignorance or plain bad luck.

Regarding drugs, he went on to regale them with lore of the "ganja," the Jamaican term for quality marijuana, a major cash-crop of the island's economy. He told them about *sinsemilla*, meaning "without seeds" in Spanish, and another special treat called lamb's bread or, more crudely, "goat-shit ganja." The story went that raw marijuana was fed to young lambs or goats.

Their digestive systems concentrated the herb into heavy, sticky pellets cured for smoking.

Suspecting the story was apocryphal, Barry asked, "How would that work?"

Ron responded vaguely and Barry let it go because there was little use in arguing with his opinionated friend. Instead, he asked, "Isn't that stuff illegal in Jamaica?"

"Of course, but *everybody* smokes dope in Jamaica! It's part of the overall experience. You have to be cool, that's all." By cool, he meant discrete. "It's up to you to take it or leave it, but I'd say you would be missing something if you traveled that far and didn't try it. It'd be like going to Paris and ignoring the wine or to London without sampling fish and chips."

Working among liberal, creative people in Chicago's art and film community, Barry was surrounded by drugs and recreational-drug users — many people he respected among them, going back to professors in college. Of course, he knew people who had ruined their lives with drugs, usually from cocaine, but not a single instance where potiguaya had been the culprit.

"Yeah, Ron," Barry responded. "But if we wanted to smoke dope, there must be at least a half-dozen people I know right here in the city that could 'turn us on'."

After a long, thirst-quenching pull on his beer, Ron replied, "It's not the same thing. The dope people smoke around here comes from Mexico mostly, and, unless you're lucky enough to get something legendary like Acapulco Gold or Michoacan, Mexican pot is for shit. Ganja is a quality product, some of the finest smoke in the world. There's something about the sun and the soil. The growers in Jamaica know what they're doing. Hey, haven't you been paying attention to the lyrics of those reggae songs you've been listening to?"

Mae turned the tantalizing slabs of meat and smoke swirled in the air. Squinting against the sting of the smoke, she looked at him to see what effect Ron's conversation was having.

Barry thoughtfully sat in the shade, peeling the label off an empty beer bottle. In his heart, he felt that marijuana was the victim of a bum rap; probably the gentlest, least-harmful intoxicant known to man. He thought that if the Founding Fathers had made their fortunes in hemp, instead of rum and tobacco, the laws would be different today. Tobacco had been proven to kill people and drinking ended countless lives and ruined at least as many. Nevertheless, marijuana was illegal, although scientists had yet to connect heavy use of pot to anything worse than bronchitis. After all, the cancer wards were not full of Rastafarians or Coptic people.

"Well, Mae, it looks like you're conjuring up another gourmet delight, as usual." Ron picked up the platter and held it, admiring the ribs. "Ah-h-h, Mae, you're the queen of barbecue."

Mae transferred the smoking slabs of meat from the grill. Barry carefully dragged his end of the picnic table, already laden with coleslaw and toasted garlic bread, into the shade, then set out the silverware and plates. Looking up, he directed a question at Mae. "Where's Zac?"

A voice came from the alley, "I'm coming!"

The gate opened and Zac came in, out of breath and pushing his 10-speed bicycle. He came up the walkway, being careful, trying not to damage the delightfully fragrant lilies-of-the-valley that lined the red bricks. At this stage in his growth, he ate like a killer whale and had an uncanny knack of showing up precisely whenever the meals were ready.

"Hey, Poncho," Mae greeted her son, wiping her forehead with the back of the hand that held the tongs before her perspiration joined the smoke in stinging her eyes. "You're right on time. Run, wash your hands and then all you 'Rasta-guys' can sit down and eat!"

As always, both the food and the companionship were superb that splendid afternoon.

Barry still wondered about Jamaica, but everybody painted a rosy picture of paradise and encouraged them to make the trip. All of them made it sound like so much fun.

For the rest of the summer, the Wrights read books, watched movies, and enthusiastically listened to Jamaican musicians, including Bob Marley, Peter Tosh, Jimmy Cliff, Third World, Black Uhuru, and Burning Spear, as well as others. They learned the difference between reggae and ska, and what was meant by "dub" music. Although not heavy drinkers, they experimented with the dark rum and orange juice concoction called planter's punch and found it a pleasant potable. Mimicking a tourism commercial, they counted the days until "Jah-may-kah, mon."

* * *

As for the Wrights' travel preparations, Barry, expecting to suffer in the tropical heat and humidity, bought some wrinkle-free, wash-and-wear tropical attire: khaki shirts and shorts. The big guy, standing 6'3" tall, tended to be a little overweight but his height let him carry his weight comfortably. Nevertheless, he was sensitive about his size and chose to pack plain tans and olive greens for an outdoorsy look rather than the florid Hawaiian-style clothes often worn by tourists.

Shopping was usually a daunting experience for Mae, but she was thrilled to find herself as slim as she had been in high school. She bought a new swimsuit. Although not about to go swimming, she wanted to flaunt her girlish figure. Beyond that, she had no plans to buy a lot of new clothes. She already had replaced a few clothes because of her continued weight loss and held back on wardrobe expenses to save money. Mae also resolved that she was not going to be one of those people who lose their mind when they go on vacation, packing everything but the kitchen sink. She planned to pack her soft-sided suitcase with the swimsuit, cut-off jeans, six summer tops, two pairs of Bermuda shorts, black chinos and a chic sundress for only seven days.

Mae started singing a little made-up ditty, "I'm go-in' to Jah-may-kah, mon, where I-will-be in the ma-jor-ity."

Of course, just because she was going on vacation in a couple of months, the business of her job did not pause. Mae, in truth, did not even slow down.

There were many animals from all over the world and many interesting things to learn and promote. Most of her days at the zoo passed by so quickly it was as if she were living them in fast forward. In the land where peafowl roamed and the ancient Galapagos Island tortoise had the right-of-way on the road twice each year when it moseyed from its winter to its summer home, there was always a special event: Olga the walrus's Christmas party and birthday party, a tooth extraction for a tiger, cataracts removed from an eagle and more. The big apes, dangerous snakes, ferocious cats, testy bears, skittish fawns, and nervous rams who lived on the grounds had photo opportunities. The animals had births, attended by joy, and the ever-present mournful reality of death.

Something was always going on with the animals and the people. Mae could never predict what was going to happen next. She would go into her office each morning with her day mapped out, and by the end of the day, which was whenever she had finished dealing with the latest round of surprises and emergencies, whatever she had planned to do remained largely undone. Luckily, she always had a giant myrtle around for a pick-me-up.

*   *   *

July 1984 — Realizing the eye problem

The Wright's expectations ran high for the most wonderful vacation of their lives, coming soon in September. Nothing could ruin Mae's ecstasy about it, except…

… She kept having problems with her vision. Now things looked vague and blurry to her *all the time*. Mae's gradual loss of acuity reached the point where it interfered with her ability to read, write, and even drive. She felt as if she were being slowly enveloped in a fog, and a new impairment pushed her over the edge. Her entire field of vision had grown randomly peppered with small, fuzzy, black spots that were not quite like her normal floaters. Not only was her vision soft in focus but the new tiny spots hovered noticeably, unmistakably before her eyes.

One Monday morning in July, Mae was forced to face up to the facts and finally admitted to herself that something was seriously wrong. Feeling terribly frightened and too alone to bear it, she rushed to be with Barry and shared her worries with her husband.

Astounded, he wanted to know, "Why didn't you tell me sooner?"

"You know, never complain, never explain."

"Yeah, I know, 'old lady moldy, hairy, what's-her-name.'"

"Barry," she swatted at him. "You know it's Lady Mary Wortley Montagu. Stop quoting John Crowley."

"Seriously, what does it feel like?" he asked.

"I don't know, exactly." But she remembered being four or five years old and playing dress up with her cousins down south. "It reminds me of wearing one of my grandmother's old-fashioned black lace-veiled hats."

"I can't believe you have procrastinated for so long," he said, looking alarmed. "I don't want to fuel your anxiety, but don't waste any more time, Honey. Go see Dr. Greene."

Mae made an immediate fit-in appointment to see Dr. Greene, her long-time, patient optometrist whom they both respected. He performed a thorough exam for Mae that afternoon.

Dr. Greene concluded, "I can find nothing wrong with her eyes beyond the indication of a very small change in her eyeglass prescription. "I strongly doubt that change could account for the impairment you described."

"Dr. Greene, I'm not imagining this," Mae insisted, feeling insulted, as if the doctor had called her a liar. "Something is wrong."

The doctor said assuredly, "I'm not doubting you. I just can't find the problem."

Hoping for a simple explanation, Mae felt her worries tighten into a knot of fear in her stomach. Dr. Greene seemed to sense her anxiety.

"We're not through, yet. You've got to understand that there's only so much I can do. What you need to do is go see your primary care physician, tell him about the trouble you're having. He can refer you to an ophthalmologist who *can* diagnose the problem. I'll send him a letter detailing my findings right away."

Optometrist to ophthalmologist, Mae thought it sounded dreadful! She fought the urge to cry but a great, big tear got past her defenses and rolled straight down the middle of her cheek.

While passing a tissue from a box nearby, Dr. Greene gently asked, "Are you all right?"

Mae wiped her cheek and nodded yes, rising to leave she said, "Thank you, doctor. I'm okay. Sorry to act like a big baby, but it's so frustrating."

"I understand," Dr. Greene empathized, escorting her to the door. "Everything's going to be all right. You'll see."

As soon as Mae stepped into the reception area, Barry, who had been waiting, jumped out of his chair and impatiently wanted to know, "What did the doctor say?"

"I'll tell you in the car," she whispered, feeling vulnerable in front of the waiting patients.

Going home, she tearfully filled him in. Barry held her hand gently, eyes on the road.

"He's right, Mae. There's got to be an answer, and we're going to find it."

* * *

"I don't see anything wrong," said her primary care physician Dr. MacAreless, peering into Mae's right eye with his pocket ophthalmoscope. "But you say everything looks blurry even now?" He peered into the left eye. "I find nothing observably wrong in either eye."

"Um, hmm," she answered, indicating yes, not wanting to speak out in case her breath was unpleasant. She had skipped breakfast and missed lunch in an effort to get everything done at work before she left early in order to make her 5 p.m. appointment.

"And this has been going on since February?"

Mae nodded yes.

"Well, Mae, Dr. Greene's report states that you are losing vision, but neither of us know why. I think we'd better have someone take a closer look at those pretty brown eyes of yours," he said, a somewhat quizzical look on his face. Dr. MacAreless sat down at his desk and began to fill out a form. "I want you to take this over to the hospital emergency room ... "

She blurted out in surprise, "The Evanston Hospital! *Now*?"

He looked up at her, momentarily startled by her outburst, then replied softly but firmly, "Yes, *right now*." He nonchalantly returned to filling out the referral form. "I don't think we should delay this. It shouldn't take long," he assured her, as he handed her the finished papers.

"Is Barry with you?"

Scrambling to recover her composure, she confessed, "Well, yeah."

"Good. They'll be dilating your eyes, so you need a driver. You two hurry on over. I'll call the ER and tell them to expect you."

Mae wanted to postpone this course of treatment. She hated hospitals and the waste of time swallowed in the ER. But Mae appreciated the fact that she did not have to face this crisis alone. With Barry by her side, Mae found her eyes being dilated, examined, and re-examined by doctor after doctor after doctor on ER Time, from 5:30 p.m. until almost 11 p.m.

Completely baffled, the eye doctors on duty finally called in a senior ophthalmologist, who had returned to his home on Lake Shore Drive in Chicago. Clearly a dedicated physician, Dr. Sheffer made the return trip to Evanston Hospital while Mae and Barry spent another worry-filled hour awaiting his arrival. He arrived around midnight, read through Mae's file, and then began his examination, using a slit lamp to illuminate and magnify the interior structures of her eyes. At first, he looked disappointed, seeing nothing out of the ordinary. Suddenly, he shifted the slit lamp to an unusual, extreme angle and resumed his examination.

Mae bore considerable discomfort from the brightness of the light and all the various drops that had been squirted into her eyes. But she ached for a solution to her problem. Barry stood nearby fidgeting. Silence dominated the cubicle, broken only by small, metallic noises whenever the doctor readjusted the slit lamp.

Long minutes ticked by, every second a tiny agony for Mae, when a low murmur of surprise escaped the doctor's lips, "Huh!"

He made one more tiny adjustment then peered intently into her right eye. He refocused on her left, as if confirming an observation. He sat back from the lamp.

"You may relax now, Mrs. Wright. *I know* what's disturbing your vision."

Although Dr. Sheffer was within her arm's reach, Mae could barely make him out because of her dilated pupils and the persistent after-images that swam before her face. Her heart thumped into overdrive, and she held her breath as she awaited a long-sought-after explanation, only marginally aware that her husband had taken hold of her hand.

"You appear to be suffering from a highly unusual occurrence of sarcoidosis. It's unusual because it has manifested in your *eyes*, rather than your *lungs*, as is commonly the case."

"Sarcoidosis?" Dozens of questions whirled through Mae's mind. She and Barry looked at each other momentarily then back to Dr. Sheffer who resumed his explanation.

"We don't know a lot about the disease, but I will share what information I can."

He sighed and began, "Sarcoidosis is a disease capable of attacking any organ of the body, most often the lungs. It tends to attack more Black people than White and appears in more women than men. In your case, Mrs. Wright, it has caused an inflammation in your eyes that has already destroyed a good many of the epithelial cells that line the interior surface of the cornea." He paused to ask, "Do you know what the cornea is?"

Mae was not sure. It all sounded scary. She was squeezing Barry's hand hard as he sank onto a chair. "I do," he replied softly. "It's the transparent covering of the eye. You see right through it, like a clear plastic skin."

"That's correct. But in your case, Mrs. Wright..."

Mae found her voice. "Please call me Mae."

"...All right then, Mae. Your corneas have lost some of their transparency. The loss of these vital epithelial cells, which serve to wick the eyes' natural moisture out of the corneas, has allowed those normally transparent tissues to become water-logged. Hence the increasingly foggy nature of your vision. In addition, there has been a considerable amount of scaring. Those scars are the 'fuzzy black dots' that create the veil-like effect you've been experiencing."

Stunned, Mae searched for coherent thoughts and kept thinking *sarcoidosis*. She played the new word repeatedly in her mind, trying to come to terms with this frightening new reality.

Barry, who should have been a physician, quickly peppered the senior ophthalmologist with questions. "Will you be able to cure her?"

Dr. Sheffer sidestepped his question. "There certainly are treatment options."

"This didn't just flare up. Mae mentioned blurriness to me a year ago, and twice she's seen Dr. Greene since then. Why didn't he or Dr. MacAreless see this sarcoidosis?"

Dr. Sheffer shifted on his chair, crossing an ankle over his opposite knee before he spoke. "You mustn't find fault with your doctors. Recently, I was lucky enough to observe a similar inflammation in the eyes of a known sarcoid sufferer. This condition is rare and requires that the slit lamp be set at a very extreme, obtuse angle. When I was unable to find any reason for Mae's problem, I took a 'shot in the dark.' I reset the angle, and there it was.

"Incidentally, Mae, you might like to know that you have made medical history. You have the honor of being the first person ever known to be diagnosed with sarcoidosis through the eye, provided your blood test confirms my tentative diagnosis."

Mae's mouth felt dry. She licked her lips and managed to find her voice, again. "What ..." she gulped past a 'lump' in her throat, "... happens to me, now?"

"I will call Dr. MacAreless in the morning, and he will call you. If your test results confirm sarcoidosis, he will see that you get started on a course of chemotherapy."

"Chemotherapy!" Her heart dropped. "Have I got ...?"

Mae could not say the word. Despite her promise to herself, big tears welled up in her eyes. She desperately tried to blink them back before they could spill down her cheeks. She felt Barry's free hand rise as he put his arm around her in a loving gesture of solidarity.

"Cancer?" supplied Dr. Sheffer, quickly continuing, "No. Sarcoidosis is no walk in the park, but it isn't as bad as that. Chemotherapy is used to combat many diseases."

Her tears did spill over then in relief, so she could not truly be accused of crying.

Barry's skin grew patchy red spots, which meant he was growing angry. "Are you telling us that Mae is going blind, and maybe you can cure her or maybe you can't!"

Dr. Sheffer, speaking to her, said, "I have a favor to ask of you, Mae."

She was beginning to see a little better as the troublesome after-images gradually began to fade, and she was fighting to regain her composure. "What's that, doctor?"

Eyes tightening, Barry chipped in, "Yeah, what?"

Ignoring him, Dr. Sheffer directed his request to Mae, "It would be of inestimable value to future sarcoid sufferers if you would allow our ER doctors to examine your eyes once again, so they know what to look for. You've been through a lot of discomfort already this evening, but would you be willing?"

Mae, who thought the painful examination under the glaring light was over, knew cooperating would bring renewed pain. But she courageously assented with a couple of short nods, unwilling to deny future sufferers the relief of diagnosis, perhaps saving someone's sight.

Barry asked her, "Are you sure?"

When she nodded yes, he squeezed her hand and then took himself out into the hall. For the next 20 minutes, doctor after doctor examined her eyes. Mae remained stoic and did not cry.

* * *

Barry was aghast that his wife's torture must resume, but he realized it was Mae's call to make. He fumed in his mind, "If Mae says so, I must allow it, but I'll be damned if I watch it!

He hated it when Mae was unhappy or hurt, and there was nothing he could do about it. He asked God, over and over in his heart: why Mae, why couldn't it be me? As usual when he talked to God, there was no answer.

Out in the hall, Barry heard her gasp one time, "Oh!"

He could not stand it any longer. He went into the men's room and compulsively washed his hands. As he approached the paper towel dispenser, he realized it was empty. He blinked stupidly at his reflection in the highly polished chrome while water from his hands dripped onto his shoes. He tore the paper towel dispenser off the wall and bounced it into a far corner. Wiping his hands on his pants, he returned to the examination room.

"I think that's enough," he said in a soft, even tone. Barry took her hand, urging her gently out of the chair. "Whatever debt of gratitude we owe Dr. Sheffer has been paid in full."

The Wrights signed the paperwork, collected their belongings, and went home troubled. Troubled also adequately described any sleep they got that night.

* * *

Next morning, Mae called in sick with minimal explanation. Fiercely protective of her privacy, she was not going to let anyone at work know anything about such a personal problem. Barry had to go in to work on a big International Harvester Company job, which had to be delivered that morning. He promised Mae that he would be home by mid-morning.

Around 11 a.m., Mae burned up nervous energy by housecleaning, trying not to let her thoughts dwell on her problem. She barely heard the telephone ring over the whine of the vacuum cleaner. Switching off the noisy machine, she hurried to answer the call. As she picked up the handset, she heard a car door slam outside in front of the house.

"Hello," Mae answered.

Turning toward the window, she saw Barry coming up the walk to the front porch.

"Mrs. Wright?"

Mae recognized the pleasant voice of Dr. MacAreless's secretary and replied, "Yes."

As Barry was coming in through the screen door, she bounced on her toes to get his attention. With her index finger to her lips, she signaled for him to be quiet.

"The doctor wants to see you right away. Can you come in at one thirty?"

Barry mouthed, *Is that the doctor?*

"Yes," she answered, responding to both questions simultaneously.

"All right, he'll see you then. Goodbye."

"Thank you. 'Bye." Mae hung up the phone.

Barry immediately wanted to know, "What's going on?"

Feeling warm from rushing home, he gave her a slightly sweaty kiss. She was glad to see him, having half-expected him to be running late and unable to accompany her.

"The doctor wants to see me at one thirty," she said, giving her husband a hug. "I'm so glad you're coming with me. Did everything go all right at work?"

He explained that he got a lot of flak about leaving early from Diane, one of his bosses. But his priorities were very clear to him.

"Family comes first, Mae. You are *way* more important to me than any job."

While dressing to go see the doctor, Mae fretted. It felt like a date with destiny.

*　*　*

About an hour later, the Wrights listened nervously as Dr. MacAreless did his best to answer their questions and allay their fears.

"Your blood test confirms Dr. Sheffer's diagnosis," Dr. MacAreless said, putting the report down on his desk and looking at Mae. "The findings explain your persistent, low-grade fevers, weight loss and arthritis-like pain. All are symptoms of sarcoidosis."

Mae slipped her sleeve back from her troubled left arm and tugged loose a homemade gauze bandage, displaying the angry, weeping lesions. "What about this?"

"Yes, your lesions could be sarcoidosis, too," he replied calmly but unable to hide the look of shock. "I'm surprised by the rapid progress the disease is making against healthy tissue."

Rising and coming around the desk, he pulled up a stool beside her. He snapped his hands into a pair of fresh rubber gloves. Then, from a tray within his reach, he picked up a sterile, non-stick cover sponge, a roll of porous plastic tape and a small pair of surgical scissors. Working to apply the fresh bandage, he said, "From what I've learned about the disease, sarcoidosis has been recognized as a distinct disease for only the last couple of decades. Earlier, it was often misdiagnosed as arthritis or tuberculosis."

Mae tried to listen intently, but it was hard because she was still feeling shocky. She was reeling from her lack of knowing anything about this disease or how she got it, just too confused to ask questions that worried her for fear they might sound stupid. She felt like an outcast.

As if he had read her mind, Barry spoke up, "Is this sarcoidosis contagious?"

After cutting the last piece of tape, Dr. MacAreless sat back from his task and spoke the word with confident finality, "No." He pulled Mae's sleeve back down and deftly fastened the mother-of-pearl button.

"Thank you," she said, a little embarrassed — as usual, whenever she found herself to be the center of attention. Mae liked putting the spotlight on other people. The time it took for the doctor to apply the fresh bandage had given her time to sort out some of her confusing thoughts, so Mae asked a question for herself, "How did I catch it?"

Resuming his previous position of superiority in the big leather chair behind the desk, the doctor said, "I wish I could tell you. We just have no idea what causes it."

There was to be no satisfaction *there*. So, Mae was ready with another burning question, almost too frightening to ask. Better to face it, now, she thought, bracing herself for the answer.

She blurted out, "Can I be cured?"

The doctor tented his fingers and briefly reflected. Like Dr. Sheffer, he, too, avoided a direct answer. "There has been a good deal of success with steroids in recent years…" He began filling out a prescription form as he spoke, "…So, I'm going to start you on a very potent dose of corticosteroids immediately."

Mae realized with chilling certainty: he does not know!

"These 50-milligram tablets need to be taken every morning and evening, without fail."

He passed the prescription to Mae, who held it gingerly, as though it might be hot to her touch. Barry eased it from her fingers, folded it once and placed it in his shirt pocket. Under a lot of stress, Mae felt frozen in thought, her usual fugue state. Suddenly, she swam up out of herself and, noticing her now-empty hand floating stupidly in mid-air, returned it to the arm of her chair.

Something *too, too awful* occurred to her. She asked softly, the hesitation in her voice betraying her expectation of a negative answer, "Does this mean I shouldn't go on vacation?"

"Where are you planning on going?" he asked soberly.

"Ocho Rios, Jamaica. We aren't planning on leaving until September," she pleaded for permission with her eyes.

"So, sun, sand and surf, that sort of thing?" He dropped his poker face and smiled. "Cheer up, probably the best thing for you!" He chuckled at the obvious relief on her face. "Sarcoidosis is a stress-related disease. Anything you can do to relax is an excellent idea."

Barry thought of something else to ask, "This medication, are there any side effects?"

Dr. MacAreless paused before he replied, "Some, quite a few actually, but right now we have no other choice, if we're going to halt the damage the disease is doing to your eyes." Then he spoke directly to Mae, "We'll be watching you for any adverse reactions. We'll take a blood sample monthly to keep an eye on your blood chemistry." Having warmed up to a comfortable level of confidence, he promised, "We'll have you feeling like a new woman in no time!"

Seemingly annoyed by Barry's questions, Dr. MacAreless pointedly continued to direct his remarks to his patient. "Mae, I'll be overseeing your therapy. But you'll also need to see our cornea specialist, Dr. LeFraude, at the vision clinic." He passed Mae the clinic's business card. He emphasized, "Call his office and set up an appointment right away."

Barry relieved her of the card as he had the prescription, but not before she read that the clinic was located within Evanston Hospital. He tucked the card away. Barry nodded and began to stand up, but Mae tugged at him to sit back down, and he slowly sank and turned his face to hers with a questioning expression.

Mae had to say something about a new problem that was causing her difficulty. She looked back and forth between Barry and the doctor. "Um, doctor …" she began.

Dr. MacAreless wore his most solicitous, million-dollar expression. "What is it, Mae?" He put down his pen, folded his hands and made a show of giving his patient his fullest attention.

"I've got a new lesion... on the small of my back."

Barry blurted out, "I knew something was up!"

Mae had been hiding the lesion from him. She had avoided undressing in his presence, just lately, acting like she was mad at him.

"Well, I suppose I'd better have a look at it."

He rose and directed his next remark to Barry. "Why don't you wait for Mae in the outer office, Barry? We'll only be a few minutes." Turning back to Mae, he added, "I had planned to examine you anyway before I turned you lose. Put the gown on. I'll be back in a minute."

As Barry left the room right behind Dr. MacAreless, their eyes locked, and Mae read his expression perfectly. He wanted to know why she did not tell him. She could see his feelings were hurt. She hunched up her shoulders, saying I do not know, and beamed an "I am sorry" reply with her eyes. As he closed the door, Barry looked more perplexed than hurt.

A few minutes later in the inner room, Mae sat on the examining table while the doctor studied the new lesion on her lower back. Finally, he said, "It looks like the other lesion. I'm pretty sure it's not cancer, but I want to take a biopsy so we can be sure."

"Oh, great." Biting her lower lip, Mae asked, "What will that involve?"

"I'm going to take a small plug of tissue from the affected area, but don't worry. It won't hurt at all, and it won't leave the slightest scar."

"Well, okay." Mae gritted her teeth and tensed up, accepting her fate.

"Good!" Dr. MacAreless swabbed the area with alcohol and performed the procedure.

Mae also got another prescription from Dr. MacAreless for a corticosteroid ointment to apply to her lesions. She gathered the only weapon of attack against sarcoidosis was steroids, first by mouth and now rubbed into her skin. Mae wished she could have a giant myrtle instead.

The biopsy hurt like hell — and Mae would carry the resulting scar for the rest of her life. The results of the biopsy came back negative for cancer, positive for sarcoidosis.

* * *

The next Thursday afternoon, Barry accompanied Mae to her first appointment at the vision clinic with the cornea specialist, Dr. LeFraude. The soon-to-become usual mind-numbing wait in his reception area was followed by a flurry of activity as a young technician administered a battery of stinging drops into Mae's eyes, which looked debilitating.

Mae had to be warned, "Keep your eyes open, or we'll have to do this again."

About 20 minutes went by before Mae sat in the *Jetsons*-looking chair while the doctor fussed with his slit lamp. He examined her corneas first, then, lowering the chair, her retinas.

Sitting nearby, Barry unconsciously chewed at the callus on his thumb — his fingernails were long-since gone. He sized up this latest doctor to hold Mae's well-being in his expertly manicured hands while waiting. Dr. LeFraude, darkly handsome in a Continental way, seemed perhaps a few years past his prime. Despite a close shave in the morning, he had a blue-black beard that perpetually shadowed his square jaw. His expensive clothes and shoes looked a few years out of style. Barry thought, unkindly, "Going to seed a little, aren't you doctor?"

Ready to talk about Mae's prognosis, Dr. LeFraude broke the silence, "Yes, I see your problem, very interesting. Tell me, is your vision worst in the morning when you first wake up?"

"Well..." Mae thought about it briefly, then replied, "...Yes, I guess that's true."

"That's because as the day progresses your eyes are open, and your corneas have a chance to dry out. You can dry them out a little faster by using a hair dryer, not too hot, though. Or I can give you some saline eye drops to accelerate the drying process."

"Saline, isn't that salt? In my eyes?" Mae gave a painful look. "Won't that hurt?"

"They do tend to sting a little, yes. But it might be worth it to improve your vision." The doctor continued, "I know your treatment is very intense. It is important to your success that you realize how lucky you are," he said. "Dr. Sheffer's report says you were well on the way to losing your eyesight *permanently*." He let his words sink in, for effect, before continuing. "I wish I had better news for you, but the damage to your corneas has been quite extensive already. Mae, you are going to require corneal transplants to restore your vision."

"Transplants! Surgery?" Mae did not want to believe what she heard.

"How could anything so serious happen so fast?" Barry interjected, trying to project a calm that he did not feel. "Are you recommending surgery? How soon?"

Mae nodded her desire for the answer to his questions, too. Barry knew they had to perform a mental juggling act: try to stay calm, understand her problem, accept harsh realities, and ask all the important questions. He wanted to be there with her so he could help ask the right questions and later aid Mae in remembering what the doctor had said.

Dr. LeFraude smoothed a hand across his longish hair. "Surgery, yes, *someday* — certainly not soon. We cannot perform surgery on an inflamed organ. "Our first job is to clear up Mae's uveitis, the inflammation." Narrowing his focus to Mae, he chose his words carefully. "Once that has been accomplished, we will determine how well you are able to see, what other problems you may be having, and whether or not the surgery is... advisable."

His grave expression softened. "Let me give you some good news." He permitted himself a brief, small smile. "Your retinas appear to be undamaged, no need for vitreoretinal medicine. For that, you should be grateful. We can transplant a cornea, but we cannot transplant a retina. I am prescribing a corticosteroid medication in the form of drops, one drop in each eye four times a day. I will need to see you once a week to supervise your treatment and gauge your progress. We may need to adjust your dosage or change or supplement your medication."

Dr. LeFraude paused the conversation to write out Mae's prescriptions.

Barry thought, a lot of steroids in her blood, on her skin and now in her eyes, while Mae posed a ready question, "What about possible side effects?"

Dr. Sheffer took the time to finish writing and passed over the prescription before he responded. "We will be observing you closely for any signs of glaucoma or cataracts." He sighed, "There is always a danger of either condition with prolonged use of steroids. That is why it is imperative, Mae..." He made eye-contact with her to be sure he had her full attention, "...that you use the drops *exactly* as prescribed and keep your weekly appointment without fail."

They thanked Dr. Sheffer and left the clinic. Mae, half blind, clutched Barry's arm for safety. As they reached their parked car, she made a snappy wisecrack, "I'm not sure which is worse, the disease or the treatment?"

*   *   *

The week after her treatment began, Mae felt extremely agitated. This unpleasant feeling came on gradually. In the privacy of her office, she confided in Barry over the telephone.

"I feel like I'm going to jump right out of my skin, like I could outrun Secretariat!"

"I don't know what to say, since you apparently have no choice but to take the prescribed meds." He asked her gently, "Did you tell Doc Mac about this?"

"Well...sort of. I told him I was feeling nervous."

"And what did he say?"

"He said that I am taking very high doses of a powerful drug and should 'hang in there' until my body can adjust to the medicine."

"Then that's what you need to do. Try to relax, Honey. Give it a couple more days." Sounding cheery, he joked, "You know, some people in my industry pay a lot of money for illegal drugs, just to feel the way you're feeling."

Confused and filled with questions. she gave a bitter little chuckle. "Honey, it's not very funny. I'm jittery, a little on edge, and it's not a pleasurable feeling."

Mae too had been a college student in the 1960s. She had resisted the temptation to experiment with drugs or smoke pot. Not that she was categorically opposed to it, she simply wanted to reserve all her brain cells for getting the best possible education.

"It's supposed to be a mellow feeling... a sense of well-being," she said, thinking she had a good idea of what it felt like to be high. "This odd feeling isn't at all like that. I feel all jumpy."

"Mae, you're under a lot of stress with this thing." He meant sarcoidosis. "Don't make matters worse for yourself by worrying. You've got to keep in mind that your doctors are all positive that these steroids are the *best* chance we have for saving your eyesight. You may have to accept these... feelings, for the time being."

"Well, I'm sure you're right. But knowing that doesn't make it any easier to take." She confessed, "It's so hard to act normal and do my job when I feel like my brain might boil over at any moment. I've even lost my craving for giant myrtles."

"I'm sorry you have to deal with this illness." He sounded empathetic. She remained quiet for so long, he asked, "Mae, are you there?"

"I'm still here," she said. "I wish I weren't. I wish I were on my way home."

"I know it's hard but try not to worry. You see two highly trained professionals at the peak of their careers. They're not going to let anything bad happen to you. I'm sure that given time, your body *will* adjust to the medication and the side effects *will* go away."

Mae nervously jumped in her chair when Callie knocked on her door and stuck her head in, apparently with something pressing on her mind. Mae waved for her to come in, then signaled with an upraised forefinger that she would be a minute.

"Uh-huh," Mae said, her voice all businesslike, not caring to let Callie know she was on a personal call and hoping Barry would take the hint. He did.

"Gotta go? All right. Try to take it easy and remember, I love you."

"Me, too." She rattled the phone when she spastically put the handset into its cradle.

* * *

Finally relieved to know what was wrong with her, Mae wanted to feel lucky about her chances of accomplishing a complete recovery. Yet the perils of the disease and the rigors of the treatment for a cure kept her on the edge of tears. Although a good deal of the foggy aspect of her vision had improved, she still had low visibility in the mornings that cleared up over the course of the day. And the spots caused by the scarring of her corneas would never go away until she had corneal transplant surgery. She would have to get used to them.

Mae wanted to learn all she could about sarcoidosis. When a search at the public library proved fruitless, she took her research to the library at the University of Chicago in Hyde Park, not far from Woodlawn, the South Side neighborhood where she grew up. Mae knew the campus had one of the finest medical libraries in the country. There, she sat at a computer terminal, familiarized herself with the software program, and then typed in s-a-r-c-o-i-d-o-s-i-s to launch her search. Three hours later, she had found few references. For the most part, her hopes had faded to disappointment. Half the materials were in foreign languages, most of them in Italian. The English references were obscured by Latin words and unfathomable medical language.

In the end, she was left with two small finds. The first reference was in a review document, which stated:

"The most common eye lesion is granulomatous uveitis. Acute uveitis tends to clear spontaneously, but progressive uveal tract inflammation may cause adhesions between the iris and the lens, glaucoma, cataract, and blindness.

Periphlebitis retinae, retinal hemorrhage, retinitis proliferans, band keratopathy, proptosis and exophthalmos are some of the other uncommon manifestations of ocular sarcoidosis."

And the other one, a short reference to skin lesions in an article, cited:

"The most specific cutaneous sarcoidosis lesion is lupus pernio. It consists of a raised, violaceous, indurated plaque affecting the nose, the surrounding area of the face and the nasal mucosa. Ulceration is rare."

That was it, all she had been able to glean from one of the finest medical libraries in the nation. Her last avenue of hope had proven futile. Mae wanted to know more about sarcoid but just did not know where else to turn.

*   *   *

When Barry realized that he was not going to get details on possible side effects from Doc Mac, he planned to consult a *Physicians' Desk Reference* (PDR) for himself. He needed the big, red book that listed all the medications: their actions, indications, usual doses, contraindications, and side effects., which he could see right on Doc Mac's shelf. But he knew better than to expect to get a look at that one. His research went a little better than Mae's since the Evanston Public Library had a PDR, but it was several years out of date. So, he walked home by way of the bookstore and bought the most recent edition at Kroch's and Brentano's on Sherman Avenue. The way things were going with Mae needing so many medications, he thought they could use this reference book again and again. After supper, Barry consulted the PDR. It listed two-and-a-half pages of possible side effects to systemic corticosteroid, many couched in such incomprehensible medical jargon that he was left to struggle through a lot of translation, referring to the dictionary and a glossary of medical terms.

But what he learned left him with little doubt that Mae's medication was suppressing her natural immune system. He realized that was the reason for all the blood testing. Mae would be defenseless against infections from bacteria and viruses like colds and influenza, which was serious. He pictured Mae in a plastic bubble and prayed it would never come to that. As far as other side effects, the list was long and daunting. He could understand why the doctors had been reluctant to open *that* Pandora's box. Every symptom imaginable, marveled Barry, who now understood why they needed to "wait and see." He closed the book and put it away.

Deciding not to worry Mae with any more information than she really needed, Barry found Mae in the bedroom. She reclined pensively on the bed, wiping her cheeks with a tissue, having finished wrestling with the difficult task of administering her evening eye drops.

"Did you get your drops in your eyes?" he asked.

"I think so," she looked up at him, blinking and hastily added, "I *hope* so. Sometimes my face gets so wet, it's hard to tell." She wanted to know, "What did you learn from the PDR?"

"Quite a bit," he answered truthfully. "Steroids suppress your immune system."

"What does that mean?" she asked with a hint of alarm in her voice.

"It simply means you are more susceptible to germs. You must be very careful to avoid infections, limit close contact with other people who might have a cold or the flu. And, if you catch it, your body won't be able to fight it like it normally would."

"Barry, I work with the public every day!"

"Yes, well... Now work with the public at arm's length. Be sure to wash your hands a lot. Stay away from people who are obviously sick," he warned. As Mae absorbed these new facts, he added, "If you cut yourself, treat it with antiseptic immediately and put on a sterile bandage."

Soon after, the Wrights tucked into bed for the night. Barry slept fitfully, dreaming scary nonsense about germs and nasty diseases.

* * *

In a few weeks, Mae got a new prescription for eyeglass lenses, which further improved her vision. She passed the cursory eye-exam required by the State of Illinois wearing her new aviator-style eyeglasses with a thin copper-frame. Mae joked that because her driver's license was issued, the state was not too fussy — a scary thought. However, her license specified for the first time that she must wear eyeglasses while driving.

Also, Mae's unpleasant, speedy sensation troubled her less than it had in the first weeks of her treatment. Although learning to live with it, she had become increasingly suspicious of people and their motives, to the point where she did not want Dr. MacAreless to know all her business, thinking he could not be trusted. She told herself, "I can only trust Barry."

One of the biggest adjustments Mae found that she had to make as a sarcoid patient involved putting doses of eye drops in her eyes, which was never easy. She hated to have anything hovering close to her eye, and she had to squeeze the bottle and let the big, harsh drops plop right in. She never knew exactly when the drop might fall, and, if she blinked and splashed the medication all over her cheeks, she would have to start all over. When first diagnosed, Mae had to go through this torture four times a day. Mae's vision soon stabilized under treatment. Things looked less foggy. Dr. LeFraude said the inflammation was beginning to come under control. He reduced her steroid drops to twice a day in each eye. Still, getting drops in her eyes continued to be a tricky feat. Barry, with his usual readiness to practice medicine without a license, wanted to help. But she preferred doing it herself. That way, she maintained control.

Mae developed a routine in front of the mirror each morning before her drops added moisture and made her vision worse. She searched her eyes and face for signs of sarcoid, not knowing what she expected to see. She leaned across the sink to peer closely into her reflected eyes, which looked like two deep pools of brown with the smaller black pupils showing their miniscule reflections of her head and shoulders. Leaning closer, peering, still seeing the world as though through a veil, Mae couldn't see anything unusual. Except, there was a place in her left eye where a little bit of brown pigment spilled out of her iris into the surrounding white. She discovered that little imperfection at 13 years old, the summer when mirrors got interesting.

Mae wondered what sarcoidosis looked like in an eye because she could not see it.

With no answer to be found in the mirror, only her eyes looking the same as they always did, her attention shifted. Mae held her left forearm up to the mirror and studied the three big hot spots. The lesions looked like acid burns, continuing to eat up her once-smooth skin. She touched the area gingerly with her fingertips, blinking, trying to clear her vision, wishing she could see it better — the largest the size of a silver dollar at present, the others not quite as large but every bit as raw and painful. Mae treated these lesions daily with a topical steroid ointment, which seemed to have slowed their advance against her normal skin.

That day, instead of long sleeves, Mae wore a dress with three-quarter-length sleeves, just long enough to hide the blemished forearm though a concession to the summer heat. Mae put the ointment back in her cosmetics bag. The bag now contained more medicines than cosmetics, and the ugly sores made her feel unattractive and damaged her feminine pride.

"Oh, well," she sighed, straightening and thinking, "Keep your chin up!"

Still, the mirror reflected sadness in her eyes. She tossed her head back and tried to put in her drops. Her fingers shook nervously as she pulled out the lower lid, making a cup to catch the drop — a trick one of Dr. LeFraude's technicians had shown her. In her habitual fugue state, Mae drifted back through time to the day the young woman had waited in the hall to speak to her privately. Barry stood on the fringe of the meeting, pretending that he was not eavesdropping.

Her name was Amanda. She was pale and skinny, almost pretty, but she had an odd, full-looking, moon-shaped face and a swelling around her eyes.

"We have something in common," Amanda confided in Mae.

Unsure of what she meant, Mae nodded and smiled, waiting to hear more.

"I have sarcoidosis, too. In my eyes, like you."

"Really?" Stunned, touched, Mae felt an immediate kinship with a fellow sufferer. "What a coincidence!" Brimming with questions, she asked, "Were you diagnosed through the eyes?"

"No, I was diagnosed through my lungs. I was already in treatment when sarcoidosis attacked my corneas. But *my* eyes were the ones in which Dr. Sheffer first saw sarcoidosis."

Mae responded warmly, "I'm so happy to talk to you! How are you doing?"

"I guess I'm doing pretty good, right now. My lungs are clear, and my vision is better." Amanda gave a small laugh. "But it hasn't been easy. How about you?"

Mae was so happy to know she was not alone that she let this stranger in on a little of her personal business. "I'm better, too. But I hate the way the steroids make me feel."

"Like you could jump right out of your skin?"

"*Exactly*," Mae concurred. She knew it was no coincidence the way Amanda had put her finger right on it.

"Me, too. These steroids aren't for sissies."

After that, Mae remembered she had watched for opportunities to speak with Amanda. Occasionally, they had found a few minutes to compare notes, and Amanda shared her tips on putting in the eye drops since Mae was having so much trouble.

The eye drops! Mae snapped out of her reverie, back to the reality of the bottle of drops still waiting in her hand. This morning, she seemed destined for trouble getting them in her eyes. Here goes, she thought, tipping back her head, upending the bottle as close to her eye as she could stand and managing to catch hold of her lower lid. Before she had formed her cup, down fell the drop — Amanda's trick not working. Mae decided, one more try. She took a deep breath and started over. She lost her grasp on the still wet and slippery eyelid from her previous failure. The drop fell at that precise moment and splashed on her blinking lashes.

"Dang it, forget it!"

Mae tossed the bottle into the sink where it made several orbits of the basin before clattering to a stop against the drain. With a hand tightly gripping each front corner, she leaned on the sink to steady her nerves and calm herself. She thought about how she had always taken her eyesight for granted. Mae suddenly grasped that she was a likely candidate for corneal transplants. But no surgery could be performed while the infection persisted. She had to get the damn drops in her eyes. What if she could never get that stuff in her eyes? What would it be like to go blind? She closed her eyes and stood still, imagining what it might be like to live without her sight, to never again see Barry or Zac.

"Let me help you."

Barry's soft, even tone startled her. Mae abruptly opened her eyes and almost lost her balance. She started to reel and grabbed at the sink, again, to catch herself from falling. Barry caught her and held her for a moment until he was sure she had regained her balance.

"Are you okay? More side effects?"

"Thank you...I guess so," she said, still feeling a bit rocky and giving the bottle to Barry.

Mae felt like sobbing, but more moisture was the last thing the situation called for. So, waiting impatiently, blinking, she turned her frustration into anger and then bottled it up inside. Barry got the drops into her eyes on his second try.

"Thank you," said Mae, grateful that the burning, stinging drops were in but silently cursing that she would have to go through this miserable routine again at bedtime.

* * *

August 1984 — Working overtime on Wolf Woods

With all its health-related developments for Mae, July had been an extremely hectic month at the zoo. Of course, events had not slowed to make her job any easier. The wheel of life continued to turn with routine births, deaths, and new arrivals of animals at the zoo, accompanied by the never-ending demands of both the media and the public. In addition, the sensational event opening in mid-August and the one to command the lion's share of Mae's time and talent, happened to be a new, magnificent, multi-million-dollar permanent exhibit, titled Wolf Woods.

The first Saturday in August, Mae headed to the zoo to catch up on her overload of work. But, this special day, both Barry and Zac were coming along because Mae had promised them a private tour of the soon-to-be-opened mega-exhibit. The Wrights piled into the car as day was beginning to break. Barry drove as Zac gave directions to the house of a friend who he had invited to come along.

"Okay, Dad, this is it!" Zac directed, his voice trailing off to a barely audible mumble. "Pull over and *wait here* while I run in and get...her." He rushed out of the car before it had quit rolling and loped across the lawn, heading for the front door of a modest ranch-style house.

Simultaneously, Barry and Mae turned their heads to goggle at one another. They said the same word, "Her?" Apparently, there were major changes taking place in their son's life, and he had relegated them to a strictly "need to know" classification. He and Mae shared a laugh over this new development but had to get over it quickly as Zac soon returned with his friend. The young preteens paused at Mae's open window. Zac made hasty introductions.

"Mom, Dad, this is Jan."

"Hi," Jan just managed to say before Zac stuffed her into the back seat.

Barry, who had not gotten a good look at Jan, studied her surreptitiously in the rear-view mirror as she fastened her seatbelt. Jan had straight red hair, almost colorless blue eyes, no visible eyelashes, a mouthful of scary dental appliances, and the pale-under-freckles complexion of the natural redhead — a 12-year-old beauty still in the bud.

Zac caught him studying Jan in the mirror and sent daggers with his eyes.

Probably a plea, Barry interpreted, for me to keep quiet and act cool. He said nothing but gave Zac a big smile and then shut up and drove.

While they traveled, Mae tried to ease some of the tension with small talk, telling them all about Wolf Woods and the story behind how it had come to be built.

Here we go, thought Barry, "Why do women always have to begin their stories at the dawn of time? Oh well," he decided, "It's a long ride, anyway."

Mae began with the first major exhibit she recalled opening at the Chicago Zoo, Seven Seas Panorama in 1963. Back then, she told them, the marine mammal habitat had represented the state of the art in exhibiting cetaceans, going on record as the first inland home for dolphins. Wolf Woods not only reflected the current state of the art but also boldly anticipated the "zoo of the future," shaping the direction for the 21st Century. The watershed project had been quietly under development for the past decade and under actual construction for the past two years. It represented the dream of a lifetime come true for zoo director, Dr. George R.A.B. Buffalo.

Dr. Buffalo grew up to graduate from the University of Michigan, earning his doctorate in zoology in 1957. Soon after, he became a curator and coordinator of research at the Chicago Zoo, serving in those capacities with distinction and resulting in a promotion to deputy director in 1970. As deputy director, Dr. Buffalo participated in the reconstruction of some of the zoo's aging exhibits and the planning and design of new exhibit projects like Tropic World.

He was named director of the Chicago Zoo in 1976. Though his love for all species made that appointment especially appropriate, Dr. Buffalo held a special fascination for wolves. He had studied wolves in the wild and in captivity, authored important books and was recognized as the premier American authority on the vanishing species *Canis lupus*, the timber wolf. Once he became zoo director/CEO, Dr. Buffalo was determined to spearhead the development of a wolf exhibit unlike any other in existence. Out of his experience and ideas, the concept of Wolf Woods had been born. The exhibit, located in the northwest reaches of the zoo amid old-growth forest, was expansive and set off from the rest of the park by a high, wrought iron fence.

At this point, Mae's "zoo story" was interrupted. They were at the zoo, and Barry had parked the Rabbit. Zac practically broke his neck getting out of the car and coming around to open Jan's door — not because he was such a gentleman but for fear that, if he didn't, his dad *would*, and he wasn't taking any chances on giving him the opportunity to say anything clever.

They waited in Mae's office while she checked for mail and got a walkie-talkie. Then all headed for the new exhibit. Mae might have requisitioned a golf cart, but she suggested the walk. It was such a nice day.

Soon they were crossing the park at a brisk pace, and Mae resumed telling her story. She went on to explain that Wolf Woods was Dr. Buffalo's dream come true: a highly naturalistic environment designed to exhibit a pack or several packs of wolves.

"The exhibit is large enough to encourage natural behaviors but constructed in such a way as to facilitate scientific observation, behavioral studies and, of course, public viewing." Mae continued, "While curiosity and sensation-seeking will bring the public to see the wolves, the zoo's mission is to educate. By helping people to understand the important role wolves play in the balance of nature, we may increase support for the preservation of this unique species."

Their walk soon brought them to the entrance gate in the wrought iron fence. There, the public would pay a special fee to enter the hardwood and glass, 30-foot-wide passageway. They did not. Mae led the way through the passageway, which could accommodate traffic in both directions. It flowed through unspoiled woods to an orientation area.

Barry followed at Mae's heels, but the young people started to lag a little behind.

"The site itself," Mae went on, "is a meadow surrounded by 11 acres of natural forest preserve, including some century-old hardwood trees."

They walked along a trail made of densely grained cypress planking, flanked by a floor of black slate tile. Where the floor met the glass walls, a border of indigenous plants, including ferns, May apples, Jack-in-the-pulpit, trillium, wild strawberries, poppies, and the like, blurred the line between the enclosed passageway and the forest floor outside. Overhead, a redwood ceiling ported at intervals by skylights had been designed to permit maximum available daylight, as well as to conceal the artificial lighting necessary for nighttime and bad weather.

The trail was pleasantly air-conditioned, smelling faintly of green lumber, mosses, grasses, and wildflowers with spicier undertones of fungi, rotting wood and rich, black loam. These were the clean fragrances of the living woods, originating at the fresh air intakes. They all thought it was "pretty neat" that they could observe the natural beauty of the woods through the glass walls, but their isolation prevented them from impacting on the environment by so much as a footprint or a gum wrapper.

"Sometimes," explained Mae, "particularly in the early morning, you might see wildlife in these woods, real, free-living, indigenous creatures that are not part of the zoo's collection."

"Like what?" asked Jan. At the very moment of her asking, they startled a white-tailed deer browsing in the forest, camouflaged by a scrubby stand of sumac. The deer's head came up and it regarded the humans warily, eyes almost as big as Jan's and Zac's had suddenly become.

"Oh...like that!" answered Mae, feigning a casual air for the fun of it, as though she had known they would sight a deer that morning.

In truth, it likely had been a lucky coincidence and surprised Mae as much as anyone else. The deer reared on its hind legs and spun away, all in one graceful movement, bounding off through the forest and disappearing.

"Another time you might see wild turkeys," said Mae, "or coyotes, or a red fox chasing after a vole. Lots of squirrels, of course; and raccoons and opossums..."

"I can see those at home in the back yard," Zac interjected, acting underwhelmed.

The party resumed walking, but alert for other surprise encounters.

Barry pointed out, "It's like the zoo concept turned inside out. Isn't it? I mean, we're confined in here, and the wild things can come and stare at us, in safety."

"Exactly," agreed Mae. "And they come and go as they please, and you never know what you'll see, or whether you'll see anything at all. Dr. Buffalo believes that as time goes by and the inhabitants of the forest realize that they're safe, sightings should become a frequent occurrence. But no one really knows for sure."

Mae was wound up tight about Wolf Woods, practicing her knowledge in preparation for the media turnout expected at the exhibit preview being held that Friday, August 8. Although Wolf Woods was no longer considered a construction site, Mae wore her yellow hard hat out of habit. Barry believed she enjoyed the look of the helmet and the air of authority it conveyed.

The passageway led to the primary exhibit structure and opened into a spacious court under a high vaulted ceiling. Soft light came from exterior sunlight on the translucent ceiling material, augmented as needed by computer-controlled banks of artificial lights. Traffic flowed into the court to the right in a handicapped-accessible upward spiral, first past the security station and then into a spacious orientation area. The main feature, a three-dimensional, cutaway model of the Wolf Woods exhibit, had collateral materials explaining its mission, history, and design.

Besides the model, there was also a mock trapper's cabin open for inspection, symbolic of man's encroachment on the wolf's natural habitat. There, on display among many frontier artifacts, were cruel jaw-traps and snares, gut-hooks and skinning knives, and the pelts, furs, skins, horns, bones, feathers, and teeth of many species, including animals that had vanished.

"Gross!" said Jan, and Zac nodded his sage agreement.

"Here, come take a look at the model," suggested Mae.

Zac and Jan did not look all that excited. But they grew interested as Mae pointed out details while she spoke.

"Wolf Woods is essentially a gigantic cocoon woven from a high-tech synthetic fiber. The cocoon is attached by steel cables from many points along its exterior to corresponding points on an external geodesic framework, giving the entire structure maximum interior volume while providing strength and a high degree of flexibility, which is conducive to withstanding the extremes of Midwestern weather."

The model showed the exterior of Wolf Woods to be organically shaped, spiky at the points where the cables stretched the fabric. On the inside, these points of attachment formed the high ceiling vaults. Mae then led the way up the gentle spiral ascent, past a sign indicating the trailhead to Howling Heights Scenic Overlook. As they approached a level landing, the light grew dimmer with enough illumination to see to walk safely. The hallway leveled out, and Mae with her entourage proceeded under an arch, into another spacious court. Directly ahead, a curved, panoramic window — the size of a movie screen — permitted an overview of the actual habitat, looking out and down from the mountainous terrain of the "high end" of the exhibit.

Zac and Jan forgot to act unimpressed as they rushed forward to the railing that kept the public a respectful distance from the glass.

"Awesome, Mom!" said Zac — a high compliment, indeed.

Jan, turning up the corners of her mouth in a shy smile, bobbed her head in agreement.

The landscape stretching out below was that of a wooded upland in the foothills of some North American mountain range. Unlike the air-conditioned indoor corridors and courts, the habitat before them was open to the sky and the weather.

"This is the neat part," continued Mae. "The exhibit design called for incorporating some of the best real features of the actual landscape into the naturalistic environment. There are 29 living trees of various sizes and varieties left rooted in the earth, as well as a natural outcropping of stratified limestone." She pointed to these features at the heart of the exhibit. "Construction took place *around* them and *above* them. The open area of the habitat is equivalent to two-and-a-half football fields, all exposed to the sky, the weather and the changing seasons, year 'round."

Barry felt the delighted expression of a child come over his face as he stood beside the young people at the rail. He said, "It reminds me of a 'lost world' from some 1930s pulp novel. I feel fortunate to have grown up at a time when there were still farms to visit, and the wilderness and wild animals hadn't been quite so scarce or threatened as today. I certainly see the value for the future in such a superb effort as this at preservation."

Wolf Woods sloped out and down from where the viewers stood behind the glass. They looked out from the high end, with its rocky prominences, cliffs, and caves. A wolf lay stretched out in the shadowy cleft between two boulders, panting in the summer heat. A spring gurgled out of the rocks to become a waterfall, cascading 25 feet from the limestone outcropping over their heads to its splashdown in a shallow pool stocked with rainbow trout. The occasional "missing" trout augmented the wolves' diet with natural oils, vitamins, protein, and calcium.

Two magnificent wolves lapped up water from the shallows, frightening the fish, which darted to safety in the deeper recesses of the pool. Water overflowed the pool to form a brook that babbled across the floor of the upland meadow, winding around and through the trees and shrubs that made up the woods at the habitat's core. Because wolves are primarily nocturnal creatures, their feeding happened during the night, after public viewing hours. After dark, because wolves see in black and white and cannot see color, red light bathed the exhibit — dark night to the wolves but the scarlet twilight of illumination would allow scientific study and human observation.

Mae urged them to continue forward along the counterclockwise spiral, which descended to a mid-level viewing gallery stretching away in front of them for what looked to be at least a city block. From points along this gallery, viewers could gaze up at the heights, into the woods or down toward the lowest level where a grassy knoll was penetrated by the entrance holes to the wolves' dens.

Jan wanted to know, "Why aren't there more wolves?"

"There *are* more wolves. There are 15 of them currently living in the exhibit. Keep in mind, wolves are primarily nocturnal," Mae explained. "They hunt and feed at night. "Right now, many of the wolves are in their dens. Would you like to see?"

Everybody nodded yes, and, with much nudging and smiling, they soon crossed the gallery to resume their spiraling descent. Mae pointed out the animal tracks molded into the floor of the gallery here and there to remind visitors of other wildlife to be found in the woods.

While they walked, Zac figured it was his turn to ask a question. "When is Wolf Woods actually opening, you know, to the *regular* people?"

He was clearly enjoying his privileged status, as well as this opportunity to demonstrate it before a suitably impressed classmate. Mae laughed.

"We call those regular people *the public*, and opening day is not quite two weeks away, on Friday, the 15th of August. "As I mentioned earlier, exhibit previews are scheduled between now and then. This Friday, it's for the media.

By then, most of the wolves will have had enough time to acclimate to their new home and should be exhibiting natural, unstressed behaviors."

Mae whispered to Barry, "I hope!" He knew about the ton of work she worried about completing with almost no time left to finish it.

The spiraling trail leveled off and opened up at its lowest public-access level. Lined up on the curving outer wall were banks of elevators, telephones, restrooms, and a gift shop. On the inner wall were the doors to the offices and workplaces of the curator and staff. There were also hatches to various utility rooms and restricted areas, and Mae's destination, a darkened alcove with the luminous warning *NO FLASH PHOTOGRAPHY* over a large window, which revealed the interior of the communal den where six or seven sleeping wolves could be seen.

The tableau was illuminated by red light, invisible to the eyes of the wolves but sufficient for human observation. Mae grinned. Everyone else's mouth hung open.

"I've got one last surprise," teased Mae, leading the group out of the observation alcove. Going a few yards further down the passageway, they stood before a segmented steel partition. She raised the cover of a small, wall-mounted keypad then punched in a combination. Rewarded with a green light, she proceeded to press and hold a button.

There was a hiss of pneumatics — *P-t-t-t-ush-h-h-h!* It sounded like the air brakes of a bus, thought Barry. The segmented partition began to open with panel rolling back over panel to reveal another alcove. The nook was like the first but fitted with several smaller windows, revealing the interiors of smaller dens. Only one den was occupied, this time by a single, female wolf engaged in the grooming behavior of licking her paws.

"These are the birthing dens," Mae whispered, something approaching reverence in her tone and attitude.

"Far out!" This time the hushed exclamation came from Barry.

The she-wolf continued licking her paws, oblivious to the watching humans.

"This special feature will allow Dr. Buffalo and his colleagues to observe the wolf giving birth to her pups, as well as a means to study their early development. And, when the pups are a little older, this alcove may be opened for public viewing."

After a few minutes, Mae called an end to the tour and closed the alcove. They took an elevator up to the surface and discovered they were back at the admission area, still inside the gate to the Woods, with the option to return to the exhibit or exit back to the main zoo grounds.

"What now?" Barry asked. Zac and Jan waited expectantly, too.

Releasing the kids, Mae said, "You two be back at my office by 5 o'clock."

Zac poked Jan in the arm. The two of them took off running in the direction of the steam engine train. Mae wistfully observed that her son was already outgrowing this summer's clothes.

"And…me?" asked Barry.

Mae smiled. "Oh, you're coming with me. I've got plenty of work for *you*!"

"That's what I thought," he chuckled, taking her hand.

They struck out across the park for Mae's office. Once they arrived, Mae set Barry up with a place to work at one end of her desk. She moved a lamp from the credenza behind the desk so they could share its illumination, then handed him a red pen.

"Uh, oh...looks like proofreading," deduced Barry.

He pulled over and settled into a comfy guest chair. Proofreading was never his favorite task, but he knew how important it was, and he was pretty good at it.

"Honey, the best way you can help me is to take a good look at these press kit inserts," Mae said, speaking in a soft voice, a little bit worried that someone might be listening. As she spoke, she opened a thick manila folder and held it under the lamp. "I've already done my best, but... I can't see well enough to be sure that I've caught all the typos and punctuation problems. Will you give them a last look?"

"Sure, Mae, glad to."

As Barry reached up to take the stack of papers, he noticed Mae struggling to control a vibration of her hand. The papers rustled softly until she relinquished them. Their eyes met.

"Mae, you have a slight tremor in your hand." Barry said, in a purposeful, matter-of-fact manner as he was able. "How long has that been going on?"

"Shush!" she hissed and hastily withdrew the tattletale hand, seemingly annoyed. "I've been trying to convince myself that it was only a slight tremor. Do you think everyone at work has seen my hands trembling? I bet they've been talking about me behind my back!" Finally, she answered him faintly, "A couple of weeks, maybe."

"Is it the steroids? It's probably another side effect of your medication."

"I guess so." Wrinkling her brow, she added, "But could we *please* not worry about it now? If you will help me finish this work, I won't have to be here *all* weekend."

Barry wanted to say something further, but he understood that Mae would continue to insist that it was neither the time nor the place. He surrendered, letting go of a long breath he had been holding. He turned his attention to the stack of typed sheets.

"Okay... So, what have I got here?"

"You're looking at the news releases, photo captions and other background documents that I plan to hand out in the press kits at the media preview on Friday. I must be sure that they're right because they need to go to the printer first thing Monday morning, or they'll never be back in time for Callie to stuff the hundred kits I need."

An edge crept into her voice when she mentioned her secretary. Barry had not missed it.

"So, what are you angry with Callie about, now?"

"Oh-h-h, I don't know whether to be angry with her or not!" Mae tried to explain her feelings. "I don't know if you realize how much is involved in a major exhibit opening like this one. Cultural institutions in big cities don't open new permanent exhibits every day, or every *decade*. It's very important to me, not to mention my career, that everything is a smashing success, especially anything coming out of *my* department.

"I'm adamant about that because my capabilities reflect not only on me, but my entire race and even my gender. There are very few females with the title PR/marketing manager, and still fewer African Americans. Callie doesn't get any of that," Mae complained. "I hate to complain. But it's *just a job* to her. She puts in her eight hours as painlessly as possible, then hurries home to 'have a life.'"

Mae leaned back in her armchair with a sigh. "I wrote and re-wrote every word of those inserts, but I can't do everything. Callie is supposed to be handling the typing and duplicating. I'd like to think I don't have to look at them again. But I can't shake the feeling that if I don't double-check everything, it's always wrong."

Barry quickly scanned the top sheet of copy, comparing it to the rough original with its marks and corrections. In less than a minute he said, "It looks like you were right to worry. I can see where several mistakes haven't been corrected." Pointing to a word with transposed letters, Barry acknowledged, "This can't go to the printer."

"I knew it!" hissed Mae, with a stamp of her foot for emphasis. Almost at the same time, she wondered, "Is it an honest mistake or is Callie trying to set me up to fail?" As stressful as the question was, Mae said, "I don't have time to worry about this now. There's too much to do."

Barry wanted to know, "What all needs to be done?"

"First, I need to write Monday's media alert, which will be sent by newswire. Then, I need to draft speeches for Dr. Buffalo, the curator, and myself. After all that, I still need to proofread and edit the copy for the weekly employee newsletter. I need to give that copy to Callie first thing on Monday morning for typing and in-house duplication. "If, by some miracle, I can finish these projects today, then I won't have to work tomorrow. I'll be able to spend some time with you and Zac."

"Well, let's get crackin'."

While Barry concentrated on his task, Mae "pulled focus" and pitched in to her work. After about an hour-and-a-half, Barry started to flag.

"I need to take a break, move around a little to give my eyes a momentary rest."

For Barry's part, he often found it difficult to focus on exacting tasks for prolonged periods of time. Although some of the text was interesting, his eyes were feeling the strain from reading. He did an awful lot of proofreading at his own job.

"I'm going to get a can of pop. Do you want one?"

"Well, okay..." Mae said hesitatingly. "I rarely allow myself anything to drink at work. I'm afraid I might spill it all over my papers."

Barry left through the side door, heading across the parking lot to Nyani Hut. In five minutes, he returned with two jumbo plastic cups decorated with lively zoo animals.

He passed one to Mae and grumbled, "Why did you wait until the last minute to get this stuff done?"

Mae closed her eyes and drew in a deep breath before answering, "Barry, I still don't think you understand everything I do here. I spend most of my time on the telephone answering media calls about events at the zoo. Most of those calls are unnecessary, because I've already sent them the information — don't ask me why, but media unfailingly wait until they're on deadline then call me to be spoon-fed the info over the telephone! But you know what? I don't mind. Do you know why?"

Barry felt pretty sure he was about to find out.

"Because *that* is my job. If I don't get the information reported accurately and at an opportune time, I've failed." Mae was getting warmed up. "Plus, there are the annual events to be organized, publicized and run, like the County Fair Weekend coming up in two weeks, and special activities: films, tours, seminars and lectures. Plus, the fiscal year ends September 31, and I need my department's 1985 fiscal year budget submitted before we leave on vacation." Mae paused to let that one sink in. Then she continued, "I could go on and on, but let's forget about all my routine duties for the moment. Let me tell you *some* of what goes into launching a new exhibit." She took a sip of her drink to wet her whistle.

"I've been planning for the opening in a general way ever since I was hired, but there was only so much I could do to promote it without knowing the opening date and budget. For a myriad of reasons, the opening date wasn't confirmed until three months ago, and that's when I established my production deadlines and started scrambling to meet them. It takes *lead-time* to get the wheels of publicity rolling, and there is never enough.

"In addition to distributing calendar announcements of the event and pitching story angles to news assignment desks, I had to make all the arrangements for the exhibit preview. That means setting the agenda in coordination with my boss, the director and curator, selecting and contracting with outside vendors, coordinating with security and the zoo's food services people, and developing and producing the special promotional materials for the big event — you know, first coming up with a promotional theme then applying it in the creative design of the invitations, stationery, press kit folders, and the program signage, audio-visuals, and handouts..."

She had to stop to take a breath before she finished in a last rush of words, "...and that's not the half of it!"

Barry nodded his understanding and held up his open hands in a gesture of surrender. "Okay," he chuckled. "I guess I understand. Sorry I complained about a little proofreading." His face brightened. "Hey, speaking of the invitations, didn't you hire Ron to do the artwork?"

"I sure did," she nodded. "He did a fantastic job! Want to see it?" She walked over to the stacks of materials on her coffee table. After rifling through the pile, she located one of the finished pieces and returned to her desk, proffering the printed invitation to Barry.

He examined it. Duly impressed with their friend's gorgeous artwork, he said, "Wow!"

Embellished with a realistic rendering of the head and shoulders of a magnificent wolf, the cover had a three-dimensional effect. Ron, both talented and nature-loving, had outdone himself. He used a painstaking airbrush technique, doing such an outstanding job that the artwork came alive with cold green fire shining from the wolf's eyes and a wet, red tongue lolling between sharp teeth. Inside, the copy announced the event and requested an RSVP. Members of the press, it explained, could schedule interviews with Dr. Buffalo or the curator.

Mae then showed Barry the finished press kit folder designed to complement the invitation. That artwork had an entire wolf pack, emerging at sunset against the background of some lost, old-growth forest with the stylized words "Wolf Woods" spelled out in the tangle of branches overhead. The impressive art, also the airbrushed work of Ron, looked to be a sincere homage to Maxfield Parrish, filled with detail, color, and the interplay of light and shadow.

The sheets that Barry had to proofread were the inserts to be placed in the press kit, which would be printed on complementary stationery. The inserts consisted of three news releases along with six captioned photos on the right-hand side of the folder, and, on the left side, exhibit design and animal fact sheets, staff biographies, historical data sheet, an exhibit map, and a four-color translucent window decal of a wolf with its cubs. Mae had outdone herself.

The Wrights buckled down to their tasks and the afternoon flew by. At 5 o'clock, Zac and Jan returned, carrying a complete collection of injection-molded animals, souvenirs made by a zoo vending machine. Zac had threatened to do this for some time but had not had the pocket change to pull it off by himself.

Barry and Mae packed it in, and soon the party of four were in the Rabbit, heading home with the hot-plastic smell of freshly molded animals permeating the car.

*　*　*

During the morning of the day before the Wolf Woods exhibit preview, Mae started to feel a little panicky.

"Callie," she called out to her secretary. "How are the press kit inserts coming along? Didn't the printer promise to have them finished and delivered this morning?"

Callie came into her office and nonchalantly consulted her production schedule, running a pencil across notations. "Um-m-m...no," came Callie's reply. "You said, '*tomorrow* morning."

Mae was aghast and hard-pressed not to show it. "Callie when I said *tomorrow*, it was still *yesterday!*"

From somewhere in Mae's mind, almost as if whispered by a sinister voice, emerged the unpleasant thought, "Nobody's that dumb! She must be setting me up to fail!" But Mae said, "Callie, the preview is in the morning. When were you planning to stuff the press kits?"

Callie stood there blinking, her mouth hanging slightly open but saying nothing.

Mae felt exasperated, but she pulled herself together. "Okay... Look, we have a problem and the only thing that matters right now is solving it quickly. Go, call the printer. You've been working with him. Make sure he understands that tomorrow is too late. Tell him that we need the inserts now, *today*, as soon as possible!"

Callie nodded and sleepwalked back to her desk to place the call.

It was quarter past four by the time the press kit inserts arrived. Mae could see there was no way Callie was going to get the kits stuffed in 45 minutes, and, with a pretty good idea of what was about to happen, she dropped her responsibilities to pitch in and get the job done.

Fuming inwardly, Mae thought, "If I had known that Callie was going to set me up like this, I would have called in my volunteer, Carol, to help." She could not shake off the nasty feeling that Callie had consciously plotted against her.

As usual and without apology, Callie gathered her things precisely at 5 p.m. and, with a half-hearted smile, said, "Goodnight." She left the building.

Mae could not believe she was all by herself, stuck alone, again! It was a little past 1:30 a.m. in the morning when she finished stuffing the last kit.

* * *

By the time Mae got home, and her head hit the pillow, it was time to get up. She was back in her office before 9 a.m. Mae was tired and nervous but drew upon her experience to be congenial and stay calm and in control. The program, which started at 10 a.m., was followed by two staggered tours of the exhibit: one led by Dr. Buffalo and the other by the curator of large mammals, Dr. Javan Leopard. The RSVP's indicated a turnout of 60 members of the press.

The weather was warm and beautiful, so the news media turnout was excellent. Reporters, photographers, and a few editors came from the AP, UPI, four of six local TV stations, three daily newspapers, and six weeklies, as well as one national newsmagazine.

Everyone from the zoo, including Callie, conducted themselves extremely well, everyone except the stars of the show. Much to Mae's distress, the wolves were not completely acclimated to their new home, yet. Not to mention that the dog days of August were not the best season for observing wolves. They still spent most of the daytime hiding from the humans, and the heat. Mae was chagrined. No more than two wolves ever came out of their den at the same time during the entire preview! Some underbrush camouflaged the one that came closest to the glass where only a few of the waiting photographers and videographers managed to capture a good shot or some clear footage. Mae's heart had been set on so much more.

Members of the press kept asking, "Where are the wolves? How many are there? Can you get a few to come over on this side while we interview the curator by the enclosure?" Mae thought, "What do they expect me to do, go into their habitat and drag the wolves out by their ears?" By the time she got home, she was beyond exhaustion. That night, she slept restlessly, again, dreaming she was in Wolf Woods at the mercy of the media. She was wearing her yellow hard hat and carrying a bullwhip and chair, trying to make the wolves jump through flaming hoops. Members of the press corps were chanting, "Higher! We need higher ratings!"

CHAPTER FIVE

Early September 1984 — Disturbing dreams begin at home

Every day Mae took her oral medicine in the morning as directed and clumsily instilled the eye drops twice a day, frequently with help from Barry. Not long after the public opening of Wolf Woods, while cruising along the Outer Drive expressway on their way to work, Mae once again confided in Barry.

"Honey, I've been having this weird dream lately."

He glanced quickly at her, knitting his brows, "Really? " Then he returned his eyes to the road ahead and empathically asked, "Like what?"

"I don't remember most of it but something about bad people breaking into our house."

Mae quickly clarified herself, "Not the house on Grey Street but some other place that I don't know. The scary part is they're not just robbers. They're trying to kill us. I don't know how I know that, but I do." She worried, "I've never had a dream like it. It's frightening, and, as time passes, I can't quite remember it, which leaves me with a disturbed feeling for the entire day."

"This is a recurring dream?" Barry, who was very interested in dreams, had studied a lot about vivid and lucid dreaming.

"Yes," she said, putting her shaky hand to her temple and closing her eyes.

"You still have that tremor in your hand."

"Honey, my dream," she said, dismissing his tangent and wanting to return to the subject.

"I used to have a recurring dream," he said. "The first time I had the dream I was nine years old. It was about going swimming, only something horrible happened and I would wake up too terrified to go back to sleep.

"I had the dream with increasing frequency, and, by the time I entered high school, I might have had that dream 30 or 40 times. It was always the same, although it grew in detail and realism after awakening until I was 16. It went like this: I was out with a party of people aboard a yacht. The yacht was riding at anchor in deep tropical water, out of sight of land. I dove into the water and swam for the pure pleasure of it, putting myself at some distance from the boat. I turned around and looked back at the way I had swum, treading water to stay afloat. People were waving and calling to me from the deck of the yacht. I thought they were having fun, and, while I continued to tread the water, I waved back.

"The sun, glinting off the surface of the water, made the light so bright and the water such a transparent turquoise that I could clearly see the length of my submerged body, many yards beyond into the fathomless, Technicolor-blue depths — no way to see to the bottom. Then I realized that the people weren't only waving, they were shouting. Some people screamed at me, making frantic gestures, and pointing to the water.

"I became alarmed and rolled forward in the water, kicking to become horizontal and then began a crawl stroke back to the yacht. As I swam, I could see below me in the clear water a rapidly moving *something,* dark, distant, and torpedo shaped. It didn't look too big, but it's hard to judge size and distance in the clear water. It swam quickly out of my sight. I could hear my friends screaming now. I swam as fast as I could. But you know how it goes in dreams."

"Let me guess," interrupted Mae. "You couldn't move your arms and legs, or you swam and swam without getting anywhere. That has happened to me in my dreams, too."

"Of course!" Barry chuckled.

"The next time I see the fish, it's much closer. And it's enormous! Crossing beneath me, this time from left to right and maybe 20 feet down, is a great white shark. I try not to panic, but my heart starts pumping like a compressor."

"Oh, Honey, that's not a dream." She put her hand on his forearm where he had rested it on the center console. "That's a nightmare!"

"Right! Now, I'm scared out of my wits. I struggle, trying to pick up speed, but I'm exhausted, swallowing water and generally getting nowhere. Suddenly, something slams into me like a runaway bus, knocking me sideways maybe 25 or 30 feet. I don't feel any pain, but I'm having trouble swimming. There is a big red cloud billowing around me, staining the water."

"Barry, stop! You're making this up to horrify me, aren't you?"

"I'm telling you my dream exactly as I remember it. Do you want to hear the rest?"

"Umm... I guess so."

"To make a long story short, have you ever heard that bit of conventional wisdom, 'You never die in your dreams'? Well, it's not true. I died in that dream, from shock due to blood loss and drowning. I lost consciousness. Everything faded to black. That was it! I woke up feeling physically ill from the stress of thinking that I had died."

"You don't have that nightmare anymore, right?"

Barry chuckled, again, but shivered like a goose just walked over his grave. "When I was 16, I promised myself to stay out of salt water. If I don't go in the sea, I can't possibly suffer a shark attack. Since I made that promise, I haven't had that dream. It never bothered me again."

"Honey, aren't you planning to go swimming while we're in Jamaica?"

Thinking for a moment, Barry solemnly answered. "I don't honestly know, right now. I guess I'm saving that decision until the time comes. After all, it's only a dream." Barry added, "And dreams don't come true, or do they?"

* * *

As each day came to an end, Mae faced bedtime with increasing apprehension. Her dreams of home invasion and personal danger grew more and more intense, with intricate detail, vibrant color, sounds and smells. It was getting harder and harder to tell when she was dreaming and when she was awake.

Thursday night, September 6, about a week before they were set to leave on vacation, Mae had the most disturbing experience *ever*. It was incredible. Yet, she believed she was wide-awake when it happened. She heard a noise that awakened her. She swam up from the depths of sleep at a rapid rate and came conscious with a shock, wondering what she had heard. She strained to hear, but the house seemed utterly still except for Barry's snoring. Mae pulled the covers up to her eyes and lay still. Fears of home invasion came intruding into her mind. She quietly turned over in bed toward her soundly sleeping husband, debating whether to awaken him. Her common sense told her that she should wake him up in case there was danger. He would want me to, she thought. But before she could touch him or wake him up, a funny feeling came over her. The feeling advised: *Let him sleep. He already thinks you're imagining things. If you wake him up over a noise you think you heard, he'll get mad and tell you you're silly. Then, the next thing you know, he'll run tattle to Doc Mac!*

There was something unsettling about having doubts about her husband. Mae knew that she had never doubted Barry's love or good judgment. She pondered about what had come over her. The house remained silent. Mae felt halfway assured they were safe and decided to let her husband sleep. She turned back over in bed and closed her eyes, trying to convince herself that their home was secure, and gradually composed herself, hoping to get back to sleep. She lay like that for a little while, and she got right to the edge of sleep and was balanced there, leaning a little toward the Land of Nod when...

...She heard the noise, *again*.

This time, she recognized it as a jangling of metal coat hangers. Rudely awakened for the second time within an hour, Mae opened her eyes and stared at the dimly illumined outline of her half-open closet door. She wondered if the door was standing open when we went to bed. What she saw next nearly frightened her out of her wits as she watched in terrified fascination. With a slight creak from a protesting hinge, the closet door swung fully open like it had been pushed from within. It might have been Mae's eyes adjusting or a trick of the available moonlight, but the interior of the closet grew slowly brighter until she could make out a *presence* in the front of the closet, in front of her clothes, a looming shape that resolved itself right before her eyes into the unmistakable silhouette of a timber wolf, a full-grown wolf as big as life! Its eyes reflected a phosphorescent silver green as they stared directly into her eyes. Its hackles rose. It pulled back its lips from its teeth and rumbled a menacing snarl.

Mae froze like a jack-lighted deer. She wished Barry would wake up, but he was still out like a light. Mae kept trying to somehow master her confusion and questioned if she was really dreaming this. But she did not think so. Everything looked real. She recognized her bed, her room, her sleeping husband, and her clothes in the closet. And her closet still had a wolf in it!

The wolf was still snarling at her, too. She reasoned that somehow a wolf managed to escape the zoo and follow her home. But that seemed crazy, she tried to convince herself. Then she regretted her choice of words, anxious as she was to prop up her sagging sanity. Her heart pounded. She was too scared to scream or even move, almost more frightened she would discover that the wolf really *did not* exist than that it *did*. Barry, dreaming, mumbled something incomprehensible in his sleep. Mae continued to lie still, listening to the wolf's snarls and the rush of her pulse pounding in her ears. Hypnotized by the wolf's predatory glare, she felt more and more like Little Red Riding Hood in the original version where the Big Bad Wolf tears her into bloody chunks and eats her!

Mae could make out the wolf's muscles bunching beneath its hide and knew it was tensing to spring. Suddenly, all that power and tension was released into motion. When it finally happened, it happened *fast*. Instead of springing at Mae, however, the wolf pivoted gracefully despite its size and the crowded confines, pushing through her clothes, and causing the empty hangers to jangle. The beast disappeared into the pitch-black recesses at the back of the closet.

Mae's paralysis let go. She screamed an awful, little scream-moan and got power over her right hand to slap rapidly at Barry's ribcage.

Barry awoke in a panic as a distraught Mae said, "I saw a *wolf* in the closet!"

"Wake up," he said, shaking her a couple of times while trying to come out of his stupor.

"I'm awake," she told Barry. Then, she asked him, "Aren't I?"

Barry took Mae in his arms. Holding her he said in a voice still heavy with sleep, "You've been dreaming, again."

"No, Barry. I wasn't." She rejected the very suggestion. "I know what I saw was real!"

But Mae knew while she was still speaking that what she was saying was impossible. She must have been dreaming, she thought. But it seemed so real.

Barry roused himself and checked the closet for stray wolves, pushing aside the hanging clothes to find nothing. He then walked through the house. just to be sure that all was secure. When he returned to bed, Barry snuggled up to her. They made spoons for more than an hour. Then he relaxed back into sleep. Mae laid awake, convincing herself it had to be a dream.

* * *

In the morning, Friday, September 7, Mae told Barry, "You've got to be right; I must have been dreaming. But it was the *realest* dream I ever had."

Nevertheless, Barry added closing all closet doors to his evening security regimen. He knew that Mae had been through a great deal and presumed that she was simply suffering from exhaustion and stress. Like Mae, he wanted to believe that their soon-to-come vacation would relax her and dissipate her fears.

* * *

On Friday, September 14, it turned rainy, and the wind blew in a chilly reminder that winter would soon come. Mae congratulated herself on her perfect timing. She and Barry would be leaving for tropical Jamaica on the next morning. But that afternoon she had her last pre-vacation appointment with Dr. MacAreless.

On the way, Barry encouraged her, "Be sure to tell Doc Mac about your bad dreams."

Her common sense agreed, but a queasy feeling warned her: not so fast, you cannot trust the doctor. Convince him that you are well, and he will take you off the wretched medicine. Later, alone in the examination room with Dr. MacAreless, Mae was given the results of her most recent blood test. There was an optimistic tone to the doctor's voice, and he smiled as he said, "I have some good news for you. Your sarcoidosis appears to be in remission."

"That's great!" she declared. "I'm sick of taking these pills..."

The doctor looked briefly confused then grew serious as he continued, "Wait a minute, young lady. That's not what I meant. We don't want to cut back your dosage, not yet." He said firmly, "Continue taking your medication as I prescribed until you get back from your vacation."

"But, why?"

"Well, the steroids have had a significant effect on your body chemistry, and your system has adjusted to accommodate for the daily dose." He warned, "If we discontinue the dosage or cut back too abruptly, you could very well suffer some serious withdrawal symptoms."

Mae wanted to know, "Like what?"

"Such as severe headaches, dizziness or... other discomforts." Dr. MacAreless presented a confident image to Mae, inveigling, "Please *trust* me on this. Okay?"

A discontented Mae acquiesced, "All right."

When the door of the professional building closed behind her a few minutes later, Mae crossed the sidewalk to where Barry waited in the car. Simultaneously she crossed a mental threshold from a place where her life was dominated by responsibilities and illness to a new place where her attitude changed. Summoning a light-hearted mood, she exalted. "At last, tomorrow we are going to Jah-may-kah. That is all I am going to care about, starting now!"

Barry shoved her door wide open as the radio began blaring the start of a newly released R&B hit that they liked. Mae dropped into her seat and started singing to the music once the lyric began, *"She dashed by me in painted on jeans..."*

Her door slammed, and Barry whisked her away, taking off like the proverbial bat.

* * *

Saturday, Sept. 15 — Transitioning from the U.S.A. to Jamaica

At 3 a.m., Barry lay awake in bed beside Mae, too excited to sleep. It was the morning of the long-awaited, magical day. In a few hours they would be leaving for Jah-may-kah, mon! While he hoped to have a good time, he had to admit to himself that doing something new always scared the hell out of him, whether or not it was expensive.

Barry listened to the rhythmic sound of Mae breathing and could tell she was fast asleep. Surely, she was more excited than him. After all, this whole vacation was her idea from the start. He knew that if not for her desire and willingness to make it happen, he probably would be too timid to ever go on such a vacation in his entire life. During their marriage, he had followed Mae's lead many times past what had at first seemed to be insurmountable obstacles. Her spirited confidence had given him the courage to try new things. Once tried and proven successful, he would gain the self-confidence to do those things again, maybe even by himself. But, in the wee hours of that special morning, Barry wished they were not going because then he would not have to face up to the ordeal of the untried and unknown.

What especially bothered him was having to wait. If he had to face up to a challenge, he always wanted to hurry up and get it over with, right now! He wished he was getting some sleep. Not only could he use the rest, but also it would pass the time. Mae's ability to sleep so soundly on such a special morning showed how badly she needed the rest. She had worked hard to see Wolf Woods have a truly special, historic opening. Then, before she could leave on vacation, she had worked harder to satisfy all the media requests and fulfill all the administrative obligations of her job. And the whole time, stress had robbed her of the rest she needed and plagued what little sleep she had been able to find with bad dreams and night terrors.

Suddenly, the rhythm of Mae's breathing changed. Barry listened to her take a sharp breath. Then he heard her mutter a word that he thought might have been, "No." Enough watered-down moonlight illuminated the bedroom for Barry to see her eyes darting, this way and that, behind her closed lids. He realized, Mae is dreaming, again.

An odd question occurred to him. Mae had tried her best to describe to him the increasingly foggy nature of her eyesight as well as the disturbing blind spots that now peppered her field of vision due to the scarring of her corneas. He wondered, when Mae dreams, is her vision impaired or does she see clearly like before she got sick? As Barry watched, Mae's expression began to show hints of increasing alarm. Looks like she is having another nightmare, he thought, they have been some real corkers lately!

Mae's eyes moved faster, and a frightened whimper escaped her lips. Like the sound a scared puppy might make, thought Barry. He shook her gently to awaken her from her distress.

"Mae, it's all right," he said in a calming voice that was loud enough to penetrate her sleeping state.

As she began to wake, Mae reacted to his touch by pushing away his intruding hand and struggling as though she thought he meant to harm her. Then her eyes popped open, but it took several seconds for her to shift her dreaming concept of reality to a waking awareness of what her senses were now telling her. She gradually recognized his presence.

"Oh, Barry. It's you!" she panted, relaxing into the comfort and security of his embrace. "I was having a bad dream. My heart is still racing."

"I know, Honey… Everything's all right."

Mae pulled away to sit up, then reached her hand to the bedside lamp and switched on the light, as if she needed to see for herself that no interlopers, human or animal, had invaded the bedroom while she slept. Glancing around the room, Mae kept her left hand pressed against her heart, but every breath seemed fast and shallow.

Barry worried that she might have an asthma attack, thinking that if she calms down soon, she will be fine. He would rather be headed for the airport than the emergency room!

"My dream seemed so real. It's still vivid in my mind," she puffed, while Barry, slightly dazzled, still squinted against the sudden brightness. "Bad men were breaking in again. This time they were right *here* in our bedroom. They were going to kill us!"

Barry scooted up beside her, propping himself with a pillow against the headboard. Settling, he stretched out his arm and draped it around Mae. She reached across his chest, hugging him and snuggling closer to rest her head on his shoulder.

"Are you all right, now?" he asked, solicitously.

"I'm fine." Then she added in a voice that revealed some exasperation, "I wish I could sleep through the night once in a while without having bad dreams."

Mae breathed more slowly and deeply enough that Barry judged, if she were going to have an asthma attack, she would have had it by now. He guessed that she would be all right. It occurred to him that Mae's chronic asthma had not troubled her in a while. He speculated that it was because of the steroids, thinking it must be some powerful stuff.

Trying to reassure her, he said, "Don't worry, Honey. You've been working too hard. On top of that, you've been sick. You're tired and stressed."

Mae nodded and sighed. He kissed her forehead.

Barry released her and sat forward abruptly, turning so Mae could see the impish expression he wore. "But you know what? There's a cure for that!"

She immediately drew in her extremities and started to curl up like a hedgehog, suspecting that he was about to tickle her, which was not what she needed right then.

"No, silly. *Look!*" he cried.

When she risked giving him her uncurled attention, he went on, jollying her along. "See, it's something new called a *vacation*, and you and I are leaving on one today!"

He clowned to make her laugh, adding boisterously in an exaggerated Caribbean accent, "Jah-may-kah, mon!"

Mae brightened and giggled but shushed at him to be quiet, "You'll wake up Zac." Then she whispered excitedly, "I know! I can't believe it!"

Barry kept up his antics to amuse her, much happier to be in the process of getting up than moping in bed in the dark. He sustained his attempt at an accent, "Well, woman. Now dat you've waked us bot', we might as well get up and get ready."

Mae looked at the bedside Westclox, a hand-painted, psychedelic, and glow-in-the-dark, authentic hippie artifact Barry had brought to their marriage. "It's still a little early for me to see the clock clearly," she said, squinting quite a bit.

"It's almost 3:30 a.m.," he said.

Tossing back the covers, she swung her legs out of bed and bounced up, giggling, "I'm ready. But, if you don't quiet down, Jamaica Boy, you *will* wake up Zac!" Heading for the bathroom, she asked Barry, "Are we still leaving at seven thirty?"

"Yeah, I thought we'd leave for the airport by then, at the latest." He added, "That's when I asked Julie to get here." He grew thoughtful for a second, then added. "I hope she'll be on time. Julie's young, and I bet she went out last night. She's not exactly a morning person either."

Mae paused in the hall, her hand on the bathroom doorknob, and chided him in a whisper, "Barry, don't start looking for things to worry about. If we didn't think we could count on Julie, we wouldn't have asked her to help." She went inside, then poked her head back into the hall and added softly, "Julie will be here in plenty of time. Go get your heart started and meet me in the shower in 10 minutes." She batted her eyelashes innocently, a couple of times — *wink, wink!* She disappeared, closing the bathroom door.

Mae and Barry had long had the habit of sharing the shower, since the earliest days of their intimacy. It made them feel secure in the other's love and helped stretch the hot water. Barry grunted by way of response, already on his way to the kitchen to make the pot of coffee he drank every morning to start his heart, a legacy of caffeine dependence brought about by long years of too much overtime and not enough sleep. He was getting an early start today, which was good. He was worried about having to use the plane's tiny, cramped restroom, and now he was going to have plenty of time to use his bathroom before embarking on the four-hour flight. As he prepared his coffee, Barry's thoughts returned to Julie and the question of her reliability.

Julie, he recalled, had come along to the slide production company where he worked, lugging her portfolio like all the other fresh-faced hopefuls who had finished art school and finally been forced to face the "flash" that they were going to have to make a living, *somehow*. When it had been ascertained that she was willing to work long hours for chump change and without benefits, on a loose contractual arrangement of questionable legality called freelance, she had been hired as a "slide butcher" trainee.

Julie had learned fast, worked hard and only complained a little. Those characteristics would serve her well in the demanding, pound-of-flesh world of 35mm slide film production. It also caused Barry, as the director of Operations and her boss, to be predisposed towards liking her. After he had worked with Julie for a while, he took notice that she always did the best job she could and had shown a willingness to perform responsibly.

Barry seldom encountered such a positive attitude among the artists, musicians, potheads, cokeheads, learning-impaired and misfits that generally populated the lowest stratum of the audiovisual food chain. He also discovered that Julie was intelligent with a ready wit and decided that she was "good people" in his book. She had become a friend, their relationship somewhere between avuncular and platonic but always mutually respectful.

Barry had invited Julie to his home for dinner and introduced her to Mae and Zac. Mae agreed that Julie was smart and made good company, and Zac thought she was fun. Soon they adopted Julie as a member of their extended family. Since she was young, single, and working part-time, her schedule was quite flexible, so Julie had been pleased to accept their invitation to make extra money by staying with Zac while they went on vacation.

A dyspeptic-sounding series of chugs and burps from the programmable coffee maker penetrated Barry's reverie, shuttling him rapidly back to the here and now. Too impatient to wait any longer for his first cup of coffee, he stole one by adroitly switching the pot for his mug, filling the mug directly with the scalding stream from the drip basket. While slurping noisily at the hot beverage, he reckoned he would know for sure if Julie were dependable by 7:30 a.m."

* * *

Daybreak on Grey Street thrummed with the morning-song competition of myriad songbirds, as if all their expended energy could stave off the approach of colder weather and spare the seasonal nesters the trouble of migrating to warmer climes. Soon the rays of the ascending sun would suffuse the still-chill air with warmth. But at that early hour the new day was still engraved with the announcement of much colder things to come as the first few falling leaves swirled down from the stately elms and skittered across the lawns.

Barry was outside at the front curb where he had just parked the VW Rabbit. He was ostensibly rearranging the junk in the trunk to make room for the suitcases and ensure nothing of value would be left in the car while it sat at the airport for a week. Mostly he killed time and watched impatiently for Julie's arrival. Before long, he heard the distinctive exhaust note of Julie's Japanese beater, chewing like a ripsaw through the more harmonious sounds of the new day. He looked up to see the aging, appliance-bronze Toyota round the far corner of the block, blowing a discernible cloud of startlingly blue exhaust.

Julie brought it to a stop behind the Rabbit with a parking-by-Braille technique that explained her much-damaged hubcaps and formerly white sidewall tires, making Barry wonder if he should provide his curb with boat-dock bumpers. She glanced at Barry and gave him a quick wave, then attempted to switch off the ignition. The car continued to sputter and wheeze for half a minute, then coughed and finally quit. By that time, Barry had walked up to the driver's side door and attempted to pull it open. He got it on the second tug, and it swung wide with a recalcitrant squeal. Julie emerged amid a clatter of oil-can empties that bounced out around her orange All-Star "Cons" and immediately rolled beyond easy reach beneath her car. She watched them go with patient acceptance, as if adjusted to moving through life accompanied by a fair amount of confusion. Breaking into a fresh smile with her short, auburn hair still wet from the shower, a white paper sack in one hand and a tall paper go-cup of coffee in the other, she said, "I made it," as if some doubt might have existed in her mind.

"So, I see," Barry chuckled, pleased to see she had passed the punctuality test. He truly liked Julie. "Go on in. Mae's still fussing around. Zac's waiting to have breakfast with you."

"He's my escort to breakfast this morning, you know. I promised to bring doughnuts," she explained, raising the bakery bag. "Oh, what about those darned cans?"

"Don't worry. I'll get them," he offered. "I've got some litter to dispose of already. I'll be coming inside in a couple of minutes."

"All right, thanks." Julie headed up the front walk, took the stairs and crossed the porch to get in through the front door while he finished his tasks.

Barry collected the litter and walked it all the way back to the trash cans, bidding farewell to his familiar stomping grounds with a last look around the backyard and garage to see that all was secure. He consulted his wristwatch and sighed, wondering if Mae was ready, yet. Deciding it was probably a good time to say goodbye to Zac, Barry walked back around the way he had come, locking the yard gates as he went. As he approached the front door, he could already feel the sun on the back of his neck and the warmth reflecting from the painted planks of the porch.

*　*　*

After her shower, Mae managed to get her steroid drops in her eyes right away. She also took her morning steroid pill. Just before Julie arrived, as Barry was taking the car around to the front and Zac sounded busy in the kitchen, Mae had a few minutes alone in the bedroom. She lifted the scarf on her dresser where she kept some money hidden in case of an emergency. Her little stash amounted to a couple of twenty-dollar bills. She reached for the money with ticcing fingers, then hesitated, having the oddest feeling of being of two different minds about whether to take the money along. She seemed to be "of two minds" about a lot of things lately.

Mae was truly in a quandary, mixed feelings struggling for dominance over what should have been an easy decision. The dilemma she felt was all out of proportion to the matter of allocating a mere forty! Her common sense told her that forty dollars was no big deal, one way or the other, so leave it hidden right where it, considering that we are likely to come home broke! But a strange *new* feeling inside her (the same one that had her doubting people and suspecting their motives) told her: *You never know what might go wrong, so you better take that money along. But hide it, and don't say anything to anyone about it — if you know what's good for you!*

The new feeling scared Mae from time to time. It was so cynical and unlike any other way she had ever felt before. But it was her feeling, she was sure of that, and she should listen to her feelings. Right? She stood there and agonized about it, watching the money tremble in her hand until she heard Julie's bright voice ring out, "Good morning!"

Mae's head jerked up. She jumped involuntarily when the screen door banged shut.

"Julie, hi," came Zac's response from the kitchen in the rear of the house.

Mae froze. Other than the tremor in her fingers, no part of her body moved, except for her eyes. She heard Julie moving along the hall. She followed her progress through the house in her mind's eye, while her actual eyes traced Julie's path on the bedroom wall, as though it offered no more resistance to her sight than a plate glass window. What she "saw" was so vivid that Mae wondered if superpowers came with her new feeling. Her common sense rebutted: ridiculous!

A moment later, Mae jumped again, in response to a second bang from the screen door. She deduced that it must be Barry; he must be ready to leave. She felt his heavy tread as he crossed the house. When he paused near the bedroom door, she panicked, expecting him to walk in on her at any second. Right then, she decided what to do regarding the money and regained her ability to direct her muscles.

* * *

When Barry entered the house, he started to go toward the bedroom, intending to hurry Mae along. He had almost reached the closed door when he changed his mind, thinking that if he rushed her now, it probably would piss her off and spoil the start of their trip. So, he quickly decided she would be ready sooner if he left her alone. Married to Mae for 13 years, Barry was occasionally able to demonstrate that he did not have a learning disability. He picked up his soft-sided black suitcase from the hall outside the bedroom door and carried it by the shoulder strap into the dining room, putting it down beside the black garment bag that contained the few nicer clothes they were taking, there to await Mae's companion piece. He checked for the third or fourth time to make sure he had the airline tickets and traveler's checks, then went to the kitchen.

In the kitchen, Julie was sitting down at the table, after having topped off her coffee from the fresh pot currently warming on the hot plate. Zac was returning the plastic 2% milk jug to the refrigerator after having finished pouring himself a tall glass of it.

As he closed the refrigerator door, Zac saw his dad come in and piped up with, "Are you guys leaving now?"

"In a few minutes, I suppose," Barry answered, gratified to see that most of the milk had made it into the glass. "Whenever Mom is ready. I guess it's time to say good-bye."

Turning his back to Julie, he opened his arms to his son. Zac sprinted over and gave him a manly hug. Barry gazed down into his son's upturned face with proud amazement, thinking Zac's growing up fast, not that much of a gap between us anymore. Then, filled with a father's love and pride, he thought Zac's got his own look now but still looks so much like his mother.

"Love you," Barry said, quickly adding, "Take care of things. See that you mind Julie!"

Barry suddenly felt all warm and runny, which he had not expected — Zac getting to be so big and all. The depth of all the emotions he felt somewhat took him by surprise.

"Love you, too, Dad," Zac replied. "And don't worry, I will!"

Julie had taken her chair by then. But when she realized goodbyes were already in progress, she stood up again to be polite.

Barry turned back toward Julie, saying, "Goodbye and thanks, again." He intended to give her a little peck of a kiss on the forehead — to let her know he thought of her as family. But, because she was standing once more and nearer than he realized, his kiss landed *way closer* to her mouth than he had ever intended. It caught them both off balance and embarrassed them equally. They both knew what had happened was an accident, and they were nervously laughing about it, saying things like "Sorry, my fault," and "Goodbye!" and "Be careful!" and "Have fun." Then they realized, as if the situation were not already awkward enough, that at some point in time Mae had joined them in the kitchen.

* * *

Once Mae was spurred into motion, her feelings sorted themselves out and the dichotomy in her mind evaporated. It was not long until she swung open the bedroom door. She took her soft-sided suitcase off the bed with the handle and, leaning a little to compensate for its weight, headed out of the bedroom and across the short hall toward the dining room and the social commotion she heard coming from the adjoining kitchen. Mae put her suitcase down beside the other and walked into the kitchen to say her goodbyes, arriving at the doorway just in time to witness the awkward kiss.

The unexpected sight of her husband kissing another woman left Mae stunned, and jealous momentarily, uncertain of what exactly was going on but certain that she did not like the looks of it. Her new feeling — no longer quite so strange, growing increasingly familiar due to its more and more frequent return engagements — surged forth, waving a red flag. But Mae's common sense prevailed. She soon realized by the blush that was spreading up Barry's neck and crimsoning his face, he already felt dreadfully embarrassed before he ever knew she was watching. Within the space of three seconds, Mae managed to surmise what had taken place, although still feeling disoriented in the wake of her initial shock.

Mae quickly composed herself and restored a smile on her face. She walked into the kitchen, took Zac into her arms, and hugged him as hard as she dared, glad for the diversion.

"'Bye, Poncho," she said, "I'm going to miss you! I love you."

He squeezed her in return, so hard she saw stars. "Me, too. Love you, Mom!"

Zac, having properly said goodbye to both his parents, bounced into his chair and turned most of his attention to examining the tempting, fragrant gobs of deep-fried dough. "Yum-m-m!" he happily intoned. Julie's selection apparently met with his approval. Julie, perhaps sensing Mae's momentary jealousy, appeared anxious to defuse the situation, awaiting her turn to say goodbye. As soon as Zac was out of the way, she stepped up to Mae and hugged her.

"'Bye, Mae. I know you guys will have a wonderful time! And, um ...I hope you know I didn't mean to get fresh with your husband."

Mae laughed appreciatively, gave Julie a heart-felt, sisterly hug in return, and replied, "I know. Thank you, Julie, for looking after... *everything* while we're gone." She had almost said Zachery but caught herself in time to avoid any insult to his preteen ego.

"Shall we get going?" Barry, who had fled the scene of his recent discomfiture, now stood in the dining room loaded down with all three pieces of luggage: two suitcases strapped over one shoulder and the garment bag held high by the other hand. He nervously patted his foot, impatient to be on the move, "Let's go, let's go, let's go!"

Soon, while a few elderly neighbors watched, Julie and Zac waved and called happy nonsense noisily from the front porch. Barry beep-beeped the horn and Mae waved joyously to any and all. The Wrights were finally on their way to a *real* vacation.

Mae felt practically beside herself with excitement. Less than a mile from home, she already had an exhilarating sense of freedom. She wondered why Barry did not have some lively music playing on the radio. Looking at him, she realized that he was still smarting! In the midst of sharing confidences, her husband once told her that he still felt upset about silly things he had done or said as long ago as elementary school. She knew he would get over the incident in the kitchen eventually, but he would probably never forget it.

Mae wished she could say something that would end his misery. Once she would have felt a lot more than a twinge of jealousy. But any doubts Mae had harbored regarding the depth of Barry's feelings for her had evaporated in the attention he had paid to her during her recent, intense medical treatment. He resolutely insisted on dealing with the situation not as Mae's problem but as *their* problem. He was at her side for every single medical visit.

"Now, we're off on our first *real* vacation. Our honeymoon," she corrected herself, feeling more like a bride by the minute. She felt truly lucky to have this man beside her.

As they buzzed down the expressway on their approach to Chicago O'Hare Airport, Mae captured Barry's right hand from where it rested lightly atop the shift knob and held it in hers. She kissed it and then hugged it lovingly to her breast because he had made her dream come true.

Brimming with anticipatory delight, she sweetly said, "Do you have any idea how much I love you, Honey? For a whole week I'll have your attention without work, worry or intrusion, while we seek pleasure on the fabled, tropical island of Jamaica."

Barry came out of his funk. A boyish smile ripened on his lips and split into a grin. "Thanks, Hon," he said, without elaborating. He brought her left hand to his lips and returned the kiss, then pressed her hand to his big heart, for a moment, before letting it go.

* * *

The huge, green-and-reflective-white signs that spanned the expressway spelled out various airport destinations, and Barry needed both his hands as he downshifted, goosed the gas pedal, and cut the wheel to change lanes. He followed the off ramp that led to "Remote Parking for the International Terminal." In practically no time at all, both Wrights — happily enjoying the holiday groove —grabbed their bags, locked up the Rabbit and found the stop for the shuttle bus that would take them to the terminal.

Their timing was excellent. Barry could see the bus coming already and, very soon after, so could Mae. When the bus arrived, Barry and Mae waited, smiling, while people got off. The returning travelers in this weary-but-happy-looking group were of various ages, all still in tropical attire, most everybody wore sunglasses and some wore big, intricately woven straw hats. One man made Mae laugh out loud because he wore a whole stack of hats. The jubilant people kept *coming* and *coming*, off the bus.

Barry whispered, "A regular conga line."

They carried an odd mix of luggage, vacation souvenirs, personal property, and whatnot — even an elderly lady protectively cuddling a sad-looking, pop-eyed, miniature Chihuahua that probably weighed about two pounds.

"Take me home," said Barry. "I'm imagining the tiny dog sitting in a China teacup with a cartoon balloon floating over its head. What's next, a fishbowl full of sea monkeys?"

At last, with the shuttle bus almost empty, the Wrights clambered aboard. They sat right up front, behind and across from the driver. They happily held hands, feeling like schoolchildren let out of an arithmetic test to go on a field trip, while the bus gobbled up the couple-of-miles-or-so distance to the terminal. The departure area of the terminal bustled with a thousand travelers from all walks of life and many far corners of the globe, all united in the common goal to board a plane and be somewhere else.

Northlake, the suburb where Barry had grown up, lay not far from O'Hare Airport. O'Hare had done some growing up of its own.

"It looks different every time I come here," he said.

Mae replied, "That's because we don't come here very often."

As they walked toward the bank of arrival/departure monitors where the gate for their departure flight would be listed, Barry reminisced, "I remember when I was little and people from the surrounding suburbs would take Mannheim or Irving Park Road to the airport and pull over to the side, anywhere along the cyclone fence, to watch the planes take off and land."

Mae had heard this story before but indulged her husband by listening politely, anyway.

Barry continued, "Times were simpler then. Remember, back when Eisenhower was president? People were used to making their own fun, and it didn't always have to cost money." He went on, "My dad had a two-tone, black-and-yellow 1957 Plymouth with real cool tail fins. Anyway, there we were, Mom and Dad in the car, my younger brother and I standing in the weeds along the dusty roadside, eating 5-cent candy bars and hollering in delight with the planes roaring right over our heads."

Mae got their gate information and made sure their flight was on time. Then they moved on to join the line for the detectors. Since they had their tickets and had carry-on luggage, they would be able to proceed through the metal detectors and go directly to the gate.

While they waited for their turn, Barry picked up the thread of his reminiscence. "In those early days, all the commercial airplanes were propeller driven. But O'Hare Field had an air force base, too, and sometimes we were lucky enough to see a real jet fighter take off. It was a few more years before the commercial passenger jets came to O'Hare. The roar of those Boeing 707s was unbelievable! I still remember the noise waking me up in the middle of the night, scaring me out of my wits and shaking the entire house. As a Seventh-day Adventist, I'd think, 'It must be Jesus coming!' It kept me nervous 'til I was fifteen…"

Mae interrupted, "Barry, move up. It's our turn." She put her suitcase on the belt where it disappeared into the maw of the x-ray machine while she passed through the metal detector. Barry was right behind her. Mae's suitcase made it through without incident as did the garment bag. Barry's suitcase, however, touched off a reaction from the bored-looking woman who sat facing the screen where the x-ray machine revealed the contents of each item. She signaled the security guard standing on the flight-gate side of the detection equipment. The young, muscular Black man waved Barry over to a table set to one side.

Mae stood by while a mystified Barry complied. The young man brought Barry's suitcase to the table. Barry stretched to get a look at the x-ray image, still frozen on the screen. He looked startled. It took him less than a minute to open his suitcase and satisfy the security guard, who thanked Barry quickly and cleared him into the restricted area.

"What happened," Mae asked when he rejoined her.

"It appeared that I had a gun-shaped object, smack in the middle of my bag," Barry explained. "Almost immediately they realized that what they were looking at was a *pair* of leather-covered, steel framed, eyeglass cases, one for my prescription glasses, the other, my sunglasses. The cases had shifted among my things until one overlay the other at an angle, presenting the near appearance of a semi-automatic pistol." He smirked, "Just my luck, huh?"

Moving in the direction of the departure gates, they laughed a little about his typical luck. Mae spotted the sign first, and said, "C-4, this is it!" She grabbed Barry by a belt loop on his jeans before he moved too much farther in the wrong direction and tugged him across the aisle to the waiting area for their gate. His belt loop tore loose in the process, much to Barry's annoyance but Mae's unabashed amusement.

Her mirth proved infectious because soon Barry was chuckling about it, too.

The Wrights checked in at the boarding desk, exchanging vouchers for boarding passes. They found a place to sit and wait for over an hour until departure time. Contented, they did not mind the uncomfortable plastic furniture as they watched the passing parade of humanity, and the big jets taxiing out on the tarmac beyond the plate-glass windows. The airplane they would board stood in near readiness as food-service personnel completed the transfer of in-flight meals, and the baggage handlers torture-tested the checked baggage when stowing it in the cargo hold.

Before long, the flight crew arrived and boarded. Soon after that, one of the attendants took her station at the gate and the passenger boarding process began.

* * *

The Wrights had been assigned seats toward the middle of the plane. When their row was called, they grabbed up their things and excitedly joined the stream of travelers presenting their boarding passes. They funneled through the gate, then along the level, mechanized passageway to the waiting plane.

Mae went first, past the smiling flight attendants and down the cramped aisle, awkwardly managing her suitcase so as not to bump it into anybody. Barry was right behind her, lugging the other two pieces of carry-on luggage. He had to duck a little to pass through the hatch, trying hard not to jostle anyone with his burden or his bulk, which was not the easiest thing for someone of his brawny size to do on a crowded airplane. Barry smiled at the cheery, welcoming attendants and moved slowly but steadily, being careful not to put one of his size-12's down on anybody's toes. He got a glimpse of the captain and the copilot on the flight deck then rotated carefully to his right, following Mae to their designated seats. He hefted both suitcases up and into the overhead bins with no problem. A helpful flight attendant relieved him of the larger garment bag, stowing it in a small bulkhead closet.

Finally, Barry lowered himself into the teensy-weensy aisle seat. He noticed that a honey-blonde, middle-aged White lady sat by the window next to Mae, who sat in the middle, buckled up and beaming. It took him a while to stop fidgeting and settle into the closest approximation of comfort that a guy his size could ever hope to achieve in a regulation, coach airline seat.

In the air, they chatted to pass the time and after a while the attendants served the typical, unremarkable airline fare. Mae had a glass of white wine and Barry had an imported beer, which would undoubtedly make him drowsy enough to fall asleep.

"The pressure on my ears is making it hard to hear you," Barry said, pointing to his ear and indicating discomfort.

Mae, who had been using her soft voice, smiled. She sat back in her seat to let him rest.

Just as he was starting to doze off to sleep, Barry thought he heard someone say, "Hi-dee, hi-dee ho." But, with his ears stopped up, he could not be sure that the nonsense syllables came from some Cab Calloway of his subconscious.

* * *

With a smooth and uneventful takeoff and finally in the air, Mae's dream was nearly real at last. Since her careful preparations had included making sure they had a non-stop flight from Chicago O'Hare (code ORD) to Montego Bay (code MBJ), Mae was elated thinking, four hours from now, when my feet touch the ground, we will be in Jah-may-kah, mon!

Mae, who had long since finished her little glass of wine, started to be bored with the airline magazine. She realized the lady seated beside her was looking at her. Mae shyly smiled.

The lady returned her smile and said, "First trip to Jamaica?"

Mae usually had no trouble at all being sociable but, for some reason beyond her understanding, being spoken to by this stranger touched off a shiver of anxiety that tainted her mood of pleasant excitement.

Feeling dubious, she still replied, "Yes, it is."

"Wonderful!" replied the lady, who then twisted in her seat to offer Mae her right hand less awkwardly while she introduced herself.

"My name is Heidi, Heidi Hough." Her eyes twinkled when she pronounced her name.

Part of Mae wanted to laugh out loud at the amusing name, indeed the lady looked as if she expected it. Mae's strange new feeling rushed to mind with an ominous thought, *Watch out!* Suddenly, feeling of two minds for the second time in a single morning, Mae did her best to cover up her confusion and managed a polite response.

She briefly took Heidi's hand and smiled, "Hello, I'm Mae..."

Keep your last name to yourself, her new feeling cautioned. So, Mae left her introduction hanging on a high note, incomplete. She wished this woman had continued to mind her own business. Mae, adding a dollop of claustrophobia to her mixture of emotions, felt trapped in her seat. Worried that the woman might think she was alone, Mae decided to introduce her husband, conscious or otherwise. She added, "...and this is my husband, Barry."

"Please, let him rest. Plane travel can be *so* tedious," said Heidi. "Pleased to meet you."

Barry's eyes stayed closed.

Heidi went on, "You're going to love Jamaica. I do. It's one of my favorite places. Will you be staying in Montego Bay?"

Mae mentally debated, on the one hand feeling like she was being grilled and wondering if this was a conversation or an interrogation. Her other sense rebutted, thinking the lady was just bored, trying to be friendly. Still, that other feeling — not so new anymore but still strange — insisted, *Don't trust her; you don't know what she wants!*

A cringe of fear ran through Mae's entire being, a raw, primitive emotion that made no sense to her because she could not connect it to any tangible threat. Her inquisitor looked harmless enough, and Mae did not want to waste one minute of her precious vacation cowering and jumping at shadows for no reason. With difficulty, she recovered her self-possession and attempted to present as normal a demeanor as she could. She answered Heidi's question since it seemed the most normal thing to do.

"My husband and I are headed to the Caw Park Beach Resort near Ocho Rios."

However, as soon as she gave Heidi an exact destination — too much information, Mae got punished with the awful sensation of near-overwhelming fear. That negative feeling hissed inside her mind, *Now you've done it, stranger danger!*

The emergency pump connected to Mae's adrenaline supply kicked on. She felt like she was buzzing all over, and it was all she could do to remain in her seat. Stranger danger! Stranger danger! Like a skip-rope rhyme or a stuck record, the phrase repeated in her mind, making it almost impossible for her to think. Mae questioned herself, wondering what was wrong with her. Her mind was in agony, trying to figure out what was happening to her common sense.

"...Do a lot of traveling," Heidi was saying, "and I particularly love Jamaica. In fact, I own a condo in Ocho Rios." She looked at Mae, somewhat concerned, "Are you all right?"

"I'm fine," Mae lied. "It's just... I've got a little headache. It's the altitude, maybe."

Mae's strange feeling lauded, *Brilliant!*

Her brain was working for her again, and she decided to blame the cheap wine. Mae, unaccustomed to duplicity, awkwardly added, "Or maybe it is the wine. It wasn't very good."

Heidi bought Mae's answer. "Oh, I know. Let a seasoned traveler give you a tip. Stick to vodka-rocks on airplanes. You'll never regret it." Heidi hoisted her drink as a visual aid and, looking at Mae over the top of the clear plastic cup, she toasted, "Here's to your happiness and a wonderful time in Jamaica!" With that, she took her own advice, swallowing everything in her glass but the ice cubes.

Apparently having succeeded in diverting Heidi from her seemingly relentless, nosy questioning with the application of a little white lie, Mae felt her sense of anxiety begin to simmer down. Her heart, however, went on pumping in double time. It was going to be a little while before her body could download all that adrenaline. Mae cast about inside her mind for any funny feelings that might want to help with a constructive suggestion about what she ought to do next. At first, no *one* or no *thing* volunteered. Then Mae's common sense, back from being unaccountably AWOL, caused her to think *she* should ask questions for a while.

"So, Heidi, what's so special about Jamaica?"

Heidi rose to Mae's bait, as though it was exactly what she had wanted all along. She launched into such a lengthy paean to the island nation that first Mae wondered, does she work for the tourism council? And later Mae wondered if she were trying to sell that condo she owned. It took Heidi 40 minutes and one more vodka-rocks before she started to wind down.

Mae remained so intensely focused on her pretense of enthrallment that she later realized she retained almost no memory of what the woman had said. Her cleverness in turning the tables had given her the time she needed to collect her wits and calm down until she felt nearly herself.

The next time there was a break in Heidi's monologue, Barry, who had been listening for the last 10 minutes, interposed a question, pointing passed Heidi out the window.

"What's that big green mass down there?"

Mae, relieved to have Barry taking an active part in the conversation, could relax her dubious control over the situation. It took Heidi a moment to stop trying to focus on Barry's fingertip and revolve her head to the scene outside the plane, and another moment to sort out the glimpses of intense green jungle from the obscuring clouds.

"Oh, you mean *that*," she began. But before she could finish, she was interrupted by the voice of the captain coming over the public-address system.

"Ladies and gentlemen, for those of you who might be making your first flight to Jamaica, the island you see off to the side is our near neighbor, the communist nation of Cuba, approximately 90 miles from the southern tip of Florida. In fact, our flight time would be reduced greatly if we weren't required to circle around Cuba to avoid violating her air space." The captain went on with a few details before concluding his FYI.

Upon becoming aware that he was awake, Mae had almost immediately latched onto Barry's outstretched arm and brought it down from the level of his gesture to the armrest of the seat that separated them. She interlaced her fingers with those of her husband and held on to him as though he were her sea anchor, counting on the contact to prevent her from drifting back into stormy, uncharted emotional waters.

Heidi observed that she had lost her audience and resorted to entertaining herself with a paperback romance novel.

Barry fussed, "I feel rather stiff from being cramped in this seat."

Mae felt a lot better, still clinging tightly to Barry and believing he was her reality check. She surmised that if there is any real danger, Barry will know it. She sighed and recaptured her pleasant excitement. She savored the thought of, at last, a *real* vacation. Almost in the winner's circle, she was about to achieve her goal. She took the credit for making this vacation happen.

When the Wrights finally got their first glimpse of the wished-for island paradise, Mae basked in the marvelous glow of anticipatory delight that had sustained her through months of work and waiting. The recent episode of anxiety faded from her memory, no more to her now than a nervous manifestation of stress. Being out from under her everyday workload, putting hundreds of air miles between herself and her problems *did* seem to be working wonders. As the airplane floated down from the clouds, Mae's mood was so incredibly buoyant she felt as if she did not need the plane. Reaching to hold Barry's hand, she thought, "We are flying like Peter and Wendy into Never Land!"

Mae could tell Barry felt the same by the way he squeezed her hand and the shy, understated way he smiled when he was really enjoying himself — as if afraid of admitting he was taking pleasure in something for fear of it being capriciously snatched away.

* * *

What the Wrights viewed from the little window delighted both. Down below, floating on impossibly turquoise waters, cumulus clouds ruffling along her coastline, covered in lush green growth, and crowned with blue mountains, sat the legendary island of Jamaica!

Barry spoke reverently, "Like a picture in a storybook. Treasure Island!"

Jamaica was the most perfect-looking specimen of geography Barry had ever seen. That feeling connected him to countless travelers, adventurers and explorers, stretching backward in time past the modern-day pleasure seekers and dope smugglers; past the British builders of empire with their destiny so manifest; past buccaneers and freebooters, sugar planters, African slaves and free-living Maroons; past the gold-fevered Spanish and past Columbus to prehistory and the first Arawaks who made landfall in dug-out canoes. To all these, and now to him and Mae, Jamaica looked exotic, peaceful, perfect: resplendent with unspoiled beauty, gifts of fruits and flowers, and everywhere abundance.

As the plane rapidly closed the distance, his perspective changed and Jamaica began to emerge in detail something like HO scale, model-railroad in definition. Offshore, cruise ships looked like marvelous bathtub toys; modern hotels fronting white-sand beaches dotted the coastline; a coastal highway hummed busily with colorific compact cars; and everywhere, everything hemmed in felt-green fields and rampant jungle. The plane banked and wheeled. Jamaica sank from his view. The window filled up with dazzling blue sky. There was a mellow "bong" from the PA system, and the little "fasten seat belts" signals lit up throughout the passenger compartment. The captain made his announcement, noting local time to be two hours ahead of Chicago and the weather in Jamaica to be perfect.

Ears popping, Barry said, "Perfect for whom? I'm getting ready to do some sweating."

Mae said, "I hope it won't be so bad. I want you to enjoy himself." Then she reminded him, "Remember to reset your wristwatch."

When he glanced at her, their eyes met, and her dimpled grin could not spread any wider.

His next glimpse of Jamaica showed the ground whizzing by, rising rapidly to meet them. Mae flinched at the jolt of touchdown, clutched his hand a little tighter and waited for the few seconds of brutal deceleration to subside. As the powerful jet slowed to a comfortable taxi and his stomach caught up, Mae looked less apprehensive.

They arrived at Sir Donald Sangster International Airport, Montego Bay, Jamaica, at 13:04 hours local time. Both felt high in spirits and never more in love. Seat belt buckles clicked open all over the cabin. The plane filled with the usual confusion as the passengers sorted out their belongings and restlessly clogged the aisle.

"You can smell the vacation time burning," mused Barry as he let Mae out first. She squeezed sideways past him into the crowded aisle. Then he gestured to Heidi Hough, with an accompanying raise of his eyebrows. She waved one pudgy, be-ringed hand in dismissal, a seasoned traveler to the end — not so excited, she could wait rather than suffer the crush.

Barry shrugged, stepped out to join Mae in the aisle when the line began to move.

At the top of the open ramp — so unlike the high-tech, robotic passageway in Chicago, they paused to savor the moment. Something about this relatively low-tech method of descending from the plane triggered in him a feeling of déjà vu. He almost had it... Oh, right! Ingrid Bergman in *Casablanca* — his fantasy reference-point for Third World airports.

Barry looked at Mae quizzically, his shy smile playing in the corners of his mouth. "It makes me happy to see the joy on your face, but we've got to keep moving." He gently nudged her into motion. Mae practically skipped down the steps. When their feet touched the ground in Montego Bay, Mae and Barry still thought they had entered paradise, still believed they would live Mae's vacation dream come true. They had no idea of the devastating power of the forces already working against them, no reason to suspect the trap that lay in wait.

Mae said, "We are going to have fun!"

And while neither put it into words, exactly, both Barry and Mae knew they were there to relax and rediscover the reasons they first fell in love.

* * *

The natural setting was breathtaking. The equatorial sun embraced the Wrights while a steady breeze off the Caribbean Sea caressed and cooled, rewarding them with exotic fragrances. Beyond the runways and the cluster of buildings, the airport was surrounded by a tumult of living green. Everywhere they looked unfamiliar plants and trees, as well as many they recognized, loomed imposingly, including numerous species of palm trees, bananas, strangler figs, color-splattered crotons, vivid hibiscus, impatiens, poinsettias, and other colorful flowers in an abundance beyond counting. Bright, iridescent hummingbirds darted and hovered among the sensuous blossoms. Among the many vines that clung to the trees in their skyward climb, they identified the familiar golden pothos, a humble little houseplant back at home on Mae's kitchen windowsill, but here grown to gigantic proportions in the rich tropical soil, sun, and rain. Its variegated, green-and-yellow leaves were the size and shape of shields, many as much as six feet in length.

From what Mae had been able to see so far, Jamaica was everything she had hoped for, and, while the intense heat was proving rather unpleasant for Barry, who already sweated from the slight exertion of managing their baggage, Mae, with her roots in Africa and her cradle in the Mississippi Delta, felt like she was coming home, like she was really, truly warm for the first time in her life with Chicago's harsh winters now a million miles away.

The syncopated rhythm of Caribbean music pulsed on the breeze as the Wrights followed the crowd of arriving passengers toward one of the large hangars, the one that housed Jamaican Customs. Mae swayed her hips to the beat. Barry would have put his arm around her, but, being burdened with their luggage, he dropped his head instead and gave her a quick kiss. They smiled at each other. The sun warmed their skins and love warmed their hearts.

Right then, when it was not too late, when they could have turned around and gone straight back home on the next flight out, Barry and Mae happily rushed to meet their destiny. Barry had been thinking *Casablanca*, but *Gaslight* was closer to the truth for Mae. Unknowingly, she giddily immersed herself in the moment.

"Barry, I love it here!" she gushed. "Now, aren't you glad we came?"

"I think I could get used to this," he happily, if only a tad grudgingly, concurred.

His voice sounded unnecessarily loud to Mae, who was walking right beside him. She wondered if he thought she could not hear him over the music.

Entering the customs building, all the tourists were as thrilled as happy children. The Wrights joined the hubbub of activity and were charmed to discover a live trio performed the spirited music. There, too, were Jamaicans, seeming to the Wrights to be a generally handsome people. There were smiling faces, stern faces, busy faces, in every possible tint and shade but predominantly warm tones of brown. There were people with black hair, brown hair, straight hair, cornrows, and dreadlocks. People with braided hair bejeweled with bright beads and colored threads gave evidence of someone's strong fingers and steady patience. People wore straw hats, stingy-brims, Third-World attachés, boonie hats, baseball caps and bandanas, along with clothing of every conceivable cut and kind, everything in a seemingly impossible riot of color. There, in that place, they first heard the real Jamaican accent, so thick that to the Wrights' unaccustomed ears it sounded almost undecipherable. It gave English a whole new rhythm and a strange sound, as if each word were dipped in molasses. Mae and Barry discovered they had to work hard to understand.

"Cool Runnings," Barry said softly, pointing at the legend printed across the back of a Jamaican man's T-shirt.

"Shush-sh-sh!" admonished Mae. "Don't be so loud, Honey. I can hear you." She smiled to let him know she was not mad, exactly.

He shrugged, "I don't think I was being loud."

Mae could hardly believe they were finally there, out of the 'States and away from their worries, on this magical island in the sun, feeling like newlyweds and falling more in love (if such a thing were possible). It was just what the doctor ordered and so romantic.

They did not mind the 15-minute delay in having their passports stamped. When it was their turn, the Customs agent, a short, light-skinned, self-important man, acted all-business like, making a cursory search through their suitcases. Posted on the wall behind the agent, a large notice caught Mae's eye. The words expressly forbid anyone from bringing firearms into the country, warned that illegal drug use, as well as use of non-Jamaican currency, particularly U.S. dollars, would result in punishment. Finally, with a flurry of official activity, much banging of his rubber stamp and an imperious sweep of his arm, the agent indicated that they had been cleared for entry. Mae collected their passports and rushed for the doorway that opened onto paradise, back into the heat and sunshine. Ahead of Barry, she hurried toward a crowded area full of busy, purposeful people, their activity focused on a lineup of big, modern motor coaches.

*　*　*

There was a crowd at the airport that Saturday afternoon, including quite a few newly arrived fish-belly-white tourists. There were lots of Jamaicans, too, including airport personnel, bus drivers, tour guides, taxi drivers and policemen.

And folks busy doing who-knows-what, fussed Barry to himself, hoping Mae knew where she was going because he certainly did not. He demurred to Mae's innate sense of confidence and tried to follow her lead, thinking maybe he did not always agree with Mae, but he could always trust her. He already had admitted it was the truth, he thought gratefully, feeling a little abashed: if not for Mae, he would not be here now.

Barry had grabbed their bags off the counter and hustled to try and keep up with the enthusiastic, often to the point of being child-like, woman he loved with all his heart. The next thing he knew, he had lost sight of Mae. She could be the dickens to keep up with her. He knew that from experience at many special events. She had this well-developed talent for cutting through a crowd quickly, ducking this way and that, taking advantage of split-second openings too small for her economy-size husband.

Barry paused, facing a half-dozen idling buses with no idea which one was the right bus. Unamused and frustrated, he wished Mae would stop doing this to him. On the hot pavement, precisely at that moment when Barry faltered, a strong Black man's hands roughly seized their bags from him and hard face filled his view, inches from his nose, *way inside* his comfort zone.

"Remember me?" the man demanded, all surly confidence as Barry worked at recovering his poise. It took Barry a second to decipher the Jamaican accent. Once he got the meaning, he goggled at what was an absurd question!

He attempted to make some sense of it. After all, how could he remember this guy when he just entered Jamaica for the first time in his entire life? Still, he could not be sure, maybe he was on the plane. Barry did not want to be labeled as one of those White folks to whom all Black people look alike.

"Where ya goin', Whitey?" the man demanded.

The whites of his eyes were yellow with jaundice, but his body looked as lean and tough as a leather strap. There was another two-second lapse while Barry's brain struggled to translate. Whitey, was that an insult? Anxious to regain control but suddenly out of his depth and unsure of normal procedure for Jamaica, Barry guessed this person must be the equivalent of a redcap.

"I, uh, we need the bus going to Ocho Rios, to the Caw Park Beach Resort," he sputtered.

Without another word, the man wheeled and strode off in the direction of one of the big, modern buses that stood dazzling in the sunshine in its polished aluminum and spiffy white and blue paint. Barry rushed after the Jamaican man to keep his property in his sight. Alarmed, he caught up in time to watch his impetuous porter toss their bags into a bus's luggage locker.

Yellow-eyes quickly rounded Barry, holding out his hand and snapping his fingers in Barry's face. "Take care of me, mah-n!" He insisted, "Take care of me, *now*!"

With a shock, Barry realized the man had no official capacity. He was just some predatory opportunist who had homed in on him in his moment of confusion like a shark smelling blood in the water or a wolf sensing weakness in his prey. Having just arrived and having had no opportunity to exchange his U.S. dollars, Barry had no Jamaican currency at all.

Great, he thought, peeling off a couple of dollars while his eyes searched guiltily for the secret police. Not in the country for half an hour, no further along than the airport, and here he was breaking the law!

Flushed with embarrassment, Barry thought next time he would not be such a chump. Yellow-eyes hooted derisively then disappeared into the hustle-bustle with his dollars.

Barry did a slow burn while he searched for Mae. Much to his relief, here she came, having located the right bus through some means of her own. Blissfully unaware of his disconcerting experience, she looked pleasantly surprised to find Barry standing beside the right bus, their bags already on board. She cheerily sought his hand and led him onto the idling bus.

Barry, having survived his challenge — lighter by a couple of greenbacks but none the worse for wear and maybe a little wiser, decided not to risk dampening his wife's high spirits. He kept the incident to himself. Putting it behind him, he resolved to try not to be such a rube!

* * *

The front seats of the bus were already filled, but they found comfortable, Mae-approved seats about one-third of the way back — no way would she sit anywhere that might be deemed the back of the bus. Barry gave Mae the window seat. By the time the bus had filled up with excited passengers, he was able to put the troubling airport incident out of his mind. The on-board air conditioning no doubt helped him to relax.

A pretty, young woman, wearing make-up, boarded with the last couple of passengers. She was brown-eyed and black-haired with a light-brown complexion and dressed to match the driver in the white, green, and gold livery of their tour company. She said something inaudible to the driver that made him laugh. Then she freed a small microphone from its clip on the bulkhead. Smiling, she spoke into the microphone and the pleasing tones of English spoken with a cultured, West-Indian accent came over the PA system.

"Good afternoon, everybody! My name is Natalie, and this is Darryl, one of our very skillful drivers whose job it is to be getting us all safely to Ocho Rios."

She ribbed Darryl good-naturedly. A nice-looking, medium-brown-skinned young man, he had the collar of his crisply pressed white shirt buttoned and wore his official green and gold, clip-on, bow tie. Smiling broadly into the oversized rear-view mirror, he showed another flash of gold amid pearly white teeth and gave his cap a tip to the passengers, who responded with a few waves, hellos, and a general buzz of amusement.

Natalie continued, "We'll be stopping ever' so often along the way, for some of you going to Falmouth, yes?" She paused a moment, until she got a response from someone among the passengers. Natalie then did the same regarding stops in Discovery Bay, Runaway Bay, St. Ann's Bay, one or two other stops before Ocho Rios and, finally, Caw Park Beach.

Mae and Barry raised their hands for the last one, along with two other couples.

"Now," said Natalie, "Is there anyone on board who thinks they might be on the wrong bus?" She checked from a list on her clipboard and did a quick head count. No panicked passengers piped up. "No? Very good, then. Mr. Driver, you may proceed."

Natalie took her seat and adjusted the PA. The bus was filled with the sound of reggae music. Darryl closed the doors and gripped the steering wheel firmly in his strong hands as he wound up the diesel engine. The powerful, heavily laden bus pulled out of the parking lot, gaining momentum, heading for the A1, the main North Coast highway. Mae's window looked out on the inland side, but the windows were large and plentiful enough for them both to enjoy the sights on the coastal side, as well. They left the busy, "Mo-Bay" area behind in almost no time and joined the reckless dash of trucks and autos hurtling over the rough, pot-holed, and curving highway, mostly on the proper-for-Jamaica, left-hand side of the road. Darryl kept the engine RPMs at the red line. He seldom resorted to the brakes and considered the horn the bus's most valuable piece of safety equipment.

Barry was more than happy to leave the driving to Darryl, who was quite adept at eating up the miles while avoiding head-on collisions with drivers who passed each other recklessly, even in mid-curve with a 10-ton bus bearing down on them. His initial impression of Jamaican drivers was that they all drove like madmen.

Traffic diminished to next to nothing as they gained a few miles' distance from Montego Bay, following the A1 in a series of curves along the coastline, trending first north and then east, until they reached the small municipality of Ironshore. No stopping there. From what Barry could see, it was little more than a wide spot in the road: a few shacks and stores thickly painted in brilliant colors or weatherworn, never painted at all. Most structures adjoined a small plot of land with every available square inch under heavy cultivation with lots of banana plants, nothing else recognizable. Chickens and children scattered at Darryl's vigorous honking, and Ironshore disappeared behind them.

From time to time, Natalie interrupted the music to provide a commentary on the sights they passed along the way. As they traversed the Jamaican countryside, she pointed out the brown cattle in the fields, attended by stork-like white birds called cattle egrets. In fact, many of the cows stopped to pick up hitch-hikers — egrets rode piggyback, their sharp-beaked heads mounted on long necks, striking snake-like at the flies and other insects stirred up from the tall grass as the cattle grazed.

"Looks like a good deal for both," Barry observed aloud to Mae. "The birds feast while they cut down on the flies tormenting the cattle."

"I can see how that arrangement would teach the cattle tolerance for the piggybacking egrets," she said. Then, she whispered, "Barry tone it down a little. You're talking too loudly. If the whole bus needs to know, I'm sure Natalie will make a general announcement."

In contrast to the white egrets, big black birds soared over the fields and the highway. Barry thought he recognized them as turkey vultures. Natalie referred to them as John Crows. The highway continued to follow the coastline, all enjoyed glimpses of "sand and surf" beyond mangrove trees. The sky filled with gulls and frigate birds.

With much delight, Mae said, "I see pelicans!"

On the inland side, green slopes went by while Natalie explained that once those slopes were covered by the sugar-cane fields of the great plantations. She mentioned two restored houses in particular, Greenwood and Rose Hall.

Barry thought, Rose Hall, hmmm... He remembered coming across some allusions to Rose Hall having had a dark and murderous history, some tale that figured prominently in Jamaican folklore. He could not recall the details, and Natalie did not go into it.

In a little under a half-hour, they reached the town of Falmouth. "This is the capital of Trelawny Parish," said Natalie, adding that they would be stopping soon to discharge some passengers at a hotel a little further east. Barry watched from the window as Falmouth went by, looking a bit poorer and tawdrier than the Jamaica they had met at the airport.

Then the A1 veered inland. The Wrights held hands and occasionally some sight caught their eyes, but the scenery they passed remained typical of the sort they had seen so far. In fact, Mae and Barry paid less and less attention to the view and Natalie's commentary, and more and more to being together. They were still excited and happy but tired because they had been up since 3 a.m. They were anxious to reach their hotel and end their intense day of traveling.

* * *

On the bus, from time to time, Mae would have a feeling of uneasiness that remained manageable and not too troublesome, as long as Barry stopped speaking too loudly and pointing around "like a big, green pumpkin roller," attracting strangers' attention.

"Hey, look at that," he yelled, pointing to a tall wooden post set on the verge of the road, like a telephone pole without any wires or anything. "I wonder what that's for?"

Mae watched about six people turn to look where Barry was pointing. She sighed.

The bus made its first stop about 3 miles east of Falmouth, turning coastward on an access road that wound down the green slopes to a high-rise hotel facing the turquoise-blue bay. There, the Wrights got their first look at a real Jamaican beach. The sand was white, the surf was gentle, the sun was hot and the breeze off the water was cool.

"It's like the brochures!" Mae felt thrilled, remembering winter's frigid mornings at home and the warm glowing promise of the glossy, four-color pamphlets.

Rolling again, lighter by several couples, the bus roared over a very old, steeply sloping stone bridge, leaving Trelawny Parish behind and entering St. Ann's Bay. At the next stop, Discovery Bay, fishermen tended nets there. That was where Columbus was said to have made his landing in Jamaica on May 4, 1494. The place was so quaint and the seascape so picturesque it was easy to imagine three small caravels bobbing at anchor out on the blue water of the harbor. Sadly, an industrial wharf dominated the West Side of the bay and disfigured its tropical beauty.

The bus drove underneath and right between the legs of a rusty orange giant that straddled the A1. Natalie explained that the tall steel gantries and gray conveyor belts were used to bring the bauxite down from the mountains and load it into the holds of waiting ships — mostly Soviet freighters. But nothing was being loaded anymore. The aluminum companies were closing and leaving Jamaica.

In St. Ann's Bay, the A1 dived to the south. The bus continued to follow the coastline east on the A3. After a while, when they were near Ocho Rios, Natalie interrupted the music to tell the passengers they were passing by Dunn's River Falls, one of Jamaica's most famous attractions. People could climb the limestone face of the popular falls, up or down the gently terraced, water-worn steps while bathing in the refreshing rush of the cool, clear water.

Finally, in Ocho Rios, the Wrights got a quick impression of the still developing, premier North Coast resort destination. The roads were narrow and full of brightly dressed people. The bus went around a circular midway downtown. There were banks and offices, as well as pushcart vendors and market stands. Turtle Bay was surrounded by a white sandy beach and dominated by two modern high-rise hotels. The bus stopped at each hotel.

Carrying the Wrights and one other couple, the bus pushed on to its last stop and final destination, the Caw Park Beach Resort. Back on the A3, flanked by rolling green hills luxuriant with flowers and crotons, they traveled eastward about two miles from downtown Ocho Rios. About 2 p.m., the bus arrived at their hotel at last. Very tired, since they had been up since 3 a.m., the Wrights still ran strong on love and the excitement of being on their first *real* vacation.

* * *

As they entered the resort grounds, the bus turned off onto a curving access drive through a Colonial-era iron gate. The drive descended, winding down the slope through a magnificent private garden and leveled off in a broad cobblestone courtyard.

Darryl parked the bus in front of the Caw Park Beach Resort.

The British Colonial-style main building was tucked away in a private cove. A two-story, red brick and white stucco mansion with a red terra-cotta-tile roof, it stood like a crown jewel in its setting of private gardens. A row of beachfront suites stretched eastward from the main hotel, for guests requiring more room or more privacy, or both.

"Grand" was the word that came into Mae's mind, as she approached the main entrance, flanked by colonnades of tall palms. The huge mahogany doors were trimmed in bright, shiny brass and attended by a uniformed doorman, who graciously opened and held the door. She felt a sense of decadence while she waited for Barry to catch up. Together, they walked across the parquet floor into the spacious, shady foyer. Daylight from the glass doors and mullioned windows reflected from more brass and many mirrors. In the foyer, on the left, were the doors to the terrace and a set of stairs leading down to the restaurant and bar. Or one could climb the five broad open stairs to the hotel lobby, which they did. Mae happily and nervously ascended, admiring the craftsmanship in the beautiful woodwork. Barry came up right behind her. In the wood-paneled lobby, the walls glowed softly with the red-gold warmth of mahogany. The floors were waxed and buffed amber hardwood, overlaid with expensive-looking Oriental rugs.

Mae noticed that most of the hotel workers were Jamaicans of African descent. Barry put down their bags in front of the main desk. Several young Jamaican men and women in navy-blue blazers kept up a sociable racket behind the desk, speaking in a rapid-fire delivery of words that did not sound like English, accented or otherwise.

"Must be patois," whispered Mae. They had read about the unique Jamaica Talk in their books that explained Jamaica was a bilingual country.

One young male clerk separated from the good-natured horseplay to wait on them. In accented but intelligible English, he asked, "May I help you, sir?"

"We're Mr. and Mrs. Wright," Barry said, handing over his gold card.

"Oh, yes, sir, we've been expecting you. Welcome to the Caw Park Beach Resort." The clerk ran Barry's card, then gave him papers to sign.

"I have a message for you from Ms. Simpson." The clerk explained, "She is the representative for Hummingbird Tropical Tours. She says, would you be so kind as to meet her in the lobby at half past four o'clock for a brief orientation."

"Thank you, that's fine," said Barry. Mae nodded yes.

Then Barry remembered he needed to do something about his cash situation and added, "Oh, one more thing. I need to cash a traveler's check, right away, as I have no Jamaican currency. Can you help me?"

"Certainly, sir." The clerk showed Barry to the area of the long, lobby desk where currency exchange services were provided, and stood nearby while an attractive young woman behind a grill cashed his check.

"Mr. and Mrs. Wright, we hope you enjoy your stay," said the clerk.

Barry tipped him what he hoped was appropriate, 10 Jamaican dollars.

The clerk accepted the gratuity quietly and presented the key to their room to one of two erstwhile young bellhops designated to convey the couple and their belongings to their accommodations. They walked down the hall to the right and then up the first flight of stairs on the left, no elevator, and then down the length of the hallway, stopping at the second-to-the-last louvered door. Beyond their room was one last guestroom, and at the end of the hall was a back stairway. The young man with the key unlocked their door.

Barry caught Mae totally by surprise when he hoisted her up in his arms and swept her across the threshold into a clean, spacious room dominated by a king-sized bed. He whispered as he gently set her back on her feet, "Our honeymoon, remember?"

Thrilled with delight, she giggled, "I want to pinch myself!"

The room was everything the travel agent had promised, and more charming than anything Mae had imagined. The bellhops adroitly stayed out of the way, keeping quiet and trying to look busy and important. They put down the baggage and hustled around, opening the louvered shutters to brighten the room and turning on the indirect lighting in the bathroom. One young man flipped a wall switch, and an American hit-parade tune from the 1950s trickled like warm syrup from a ceiling speaker.

"Jamaica National Radio," said one. "American music," as if that explained all.

Barry accepted the key, giving each young man several Jamaican dollars. The bellhops withdrew, and they were alone in their hotel room at last. The polished hardwood floor gleamed. The Colonial-style, four-poster bed, with matching bedside tables, had dark red, almost-black, hardwood limbs veiled chastely in sheer white mosquito netting that was strictly a decorative touch in the newly air-conditioned hotel. Across from the bed, a mirrored armoire stood on one side of a small dressing table and upholstered chair and, to the other side, a chest of drawers.

Beyond the bedroom area was an open space with a rug, a couch, a couple of chairs and a table, and beyond that were a set of louvered wooden doors. These pulled back to let in the sunshine and revealed a sliding glass door, which opened onto a private balcony with a table and chairs in white-painted wrought iron.

Mae went outside on the balcony and beckoned, "Barry, come see how lucky we are!"

Barry hurried to join her. Making sure to close the sliding door, he said, "I want to keep the precious, lukewarm air conditioning inside."

"Now, isn't this view terrific!"

He nodded his agreement.

"We are fortunate to have such a wonderful, panoramic view of the ocean."

Waves washed the sparkling sand less than a hundred yards from where Mae and Barry stood. A cool breeze truly did come off the remarkable turquoise sea. Palm trees swayed in the breeze, dancing against a shimmering sky as blue as Easter-egg dye in a white China cup. Sea birds soared near a rainbow-colored parasail.

"Our room faces north," said Barry. "We will be able to watch the sun rise to the right and set to the left; two spectacular displays every day."

"In the afternoon, our balcony is in the shadow cast by the overhanging roof of the hotel, so it will be shady during the hottest part of the day," observed an excited Mae.

"Beneath our balcony is a private terrace, then a brick walk, a low wall, and a bit of garden, and then the beach," Barry observed.

"Over there, to the left, is the lobby and main hotel," Mae pointed out.

They could not see it from their balcony, but they could hear music coming from the terrace. Looking one way *up* the beach was one private resort or hotel beach adjoining another, the white sand stretching as far as they could see, all the way downtown. They could see the tops of the high-rise hotels, glittering in the late afternoon sun. To their right, or *down* the beach, the hotel compound stretched about 200 yards, accommodating the private beachfront suites before blending into jungle where the property adjoined the banks of the White River. On the beach across the river was a shantytown, a ramshackle assortment of low shelters. The river looked shallow where it entered the sea. There was a ford, wide enough to wade across, and an occasional patrol by a hotel security guard to encourage the guests to stay on the hotel's private property and the locals to stay off.

The Wrights congratulated themselves on Mae's excellent choice of the smaller, further out, more private resort.

"Well, I'm going to save any further gazing at the view for later," said Mae, heading back inside the room. "I'm going to go put away my things and try to settle in."

Barry followed. Mae began unpacking her things immediately, bouncing happily around the room like a beach ball, from the bedroom to the bathroom to the closet. While she unpacked, she warmed up to her surroundings and began to appreciate the romantic, 18th century ambience of the room. She staked out her territory, choosing a side of the bed to sleep on, furthest from the door. She put her lotions, cosmetics, combs, brushes, and other stuff on top of the dressing table. Then she carried her medicines into the bathroom and organized them on the sea-green marble counter. She ranked and arranged all her pills and drops and ointments, according to frequency of application or dose. It was her system to make sure she got all her medicines when she was supposed to have them.

Barry held back, watching her until she had claimed her territory. Then he unpacked his things and put them away. While they were busy, they talked, telling each other all the things they wanted to do and wondering what to do first.

"I can't wait to taste some real Caribbean cooking," said Barry.

"Are you hungry already?" asked Mae. "It's still early. We should take a walk, maybe meet some native Jamaicans. There's still enough daylight for sightseeing."

"Well, let's not forget, we have an orientation meeting to attend in a few minutes," Barry reminded her. They decided the clothes they had traveled in, shirts and shorts, would do for the unexpected meeting.

Mae suggested, "Let's call Zac now and let him and Julie know we made it."

They did. Everything was fine at home, and they learned that Julie was going to take Zac and his "friend" Jan to see a movie later.

* * *

At 4:25 p.m., the Wrights locked their room and went down to the hotel lobby to meet with Ms. Simpson. On the far side of the lobby, they spotted an easel card with the familiar green and gold hummingbird logo of their tour company. The card stood beside a comfortable parlor grouping, club chairs and a sofa gathered around a low table. A pretty Jamaican lady was waiting there, and she smiled as she watched them approaching her. The woman, might have been in her late 20s, had a very light brown complexion with straightened black hair put up neatly with pins. Dressed for business in a gray flannel jacket and skirt and high-heeled shoes, she had a little green and gold hummingbird cloisonné pinned to her lapel.

"Mr. and Mrs. Wright?" she inquired. "How nice to meet you! I'm Prudence Simpson, your Hummingbird Tropical Tours representative." She exchanged brief, warm handshakes, first with Barry and then with Mae. "Won't you please sit down," she offered, smiling pleasantly, and giving the Wrights a chance to make themselves comfortable.

Continuing to stand, the rep explained, "We're expecting another couple...Oh, I think they've arrived."

Approaching the orientation area was a White couple. They were around the same age as the Wrights, both husband and wife with light eyes, light hair and sun-freckled complexions that suggested the nickname, Sandy. They appeared to be Americans but already had established tans.

He was wearing a lightweight, white cotton shirt, untucked, and blue slacks, no socks, and deck shoes. She was dressed in a sleeveless yellow sundress and white leather sandals. Somehow, they managed to look both vacationesque and highly presentable.

Like you could take them anywhere, thought Mae, admiring the couple's style.

Both the Wrights recognized the pair. They came all the way from Montego Bay with them, on the bus from the airport. Ms. Simpson introduced herself and the Wrights.

"Bruce Bennett, from Cincinnati, Ohio," said the man. "This is my wife, Cindy."

Barry rose. There were how-do-you-dos and handshakes, a grip, and a grin, all around.

It turned out that the Bennetts traveled a lot and stayed at Caw Park Beach the previous year. So, they were interested in the part of Ms. Simpson's presentation to come later. For the sake of the Wrights, Ms. Simpson began with general information to help them have a safe and happy vacation. She talked a little about the history of Jamaica, stressing the diverse racial and cultural makeup of the people. She carefully made the point, "Jamaicans are not a color-conscious people. We treat everyone with equal respect. 'Out of Many, One People,' is our national motto." She made suggestions to help the Wrights get along, emphasizing, "You don't refer to Jamaicans as *natives*. We find the term insulting. We are not in a Tarzan movie."

She explained that most Jamaicans were poor and unemployment was a major problem, especially now that the aluminum companies were shutting down. She also hinted that the Jamaicans could be aggressive, and some few might be tricksters, trying to take advantage of the tourists. But most people were honest with goods or services to sell, trying to make a living the best way they could. She stated that most things had no fixed price. Buyers and sellers normally engaged in spirited bargaining, called "haggling" or "higgling." This could hold true for services, too, such as taxicabs. So, it was important to arrive at a clear understanding up front. She spoke briefly about options for dining in and around Ocho Rios. There were several fine restaurants. The fancier eating places and the hotels generally presented American or European cuisine, with an emphasis on seafood.

"Is there a place we can go where we can get some authentic Jamaican cooking?" Barry inquired, "Some place where we might meet some Jamaicans, not too touristy?"

"As a matter of fact, there is, indeed," said Ms. Simpson. "It's called the Jerk Center, and it's very colorful and very popular." She elaborated, "Jerk is a Jamaican favorite. It can be pork, chicken, or fish, but something like what you Americans call barbecue, and always very spicy."

Among the few rules she stressed, a couple pertained to dress.

"It usually doesn't matter what you wear as long as you remember that swimwear is never appropriate except at the pool and on the beach, and that the nice restaurants, including the one here in the hotel, draw the line at seating dinner guests wearing shorts. Gentlemen needn't wear a jacket or necktie, but you must wear long trousers or slacks not jeans. Ladies, you may wear a skirt if you wish, but slacks are also acceptable if you prefer." There were some other tips and pointers aimed at smoothing the tourists' entry into the swing of things in Ocho Rios.

Ms. Simpson summed up with, "Don't make the mistake of confusing Jamaica with a theme park. We have a history and a culture. We are proud people who work hard, raise our families, and live our whole lives here."

Then came the part the Wrights weren't expecting to hear, but the Bennetts were waiting to hear it. Ms. Simpson made a low-key pitch promoting Hummingbird's exclusive daily tours and events, a calendar of additional-expense sightseeing trips. They were encouraged to purchase these excursions. Ms. Simpson hinted strongly, "You can get around and meet people on your own, *if* you know what you're doing. But the safest way to have a good time is to take the tours."

The Bennetts had several events already in mind and signed up for those and two or three new ones. Because of the way Ms. Simpson kept hinting at possible problems regarding their personal safety without clearly stating what she meant, Mae thought the Hummingbird events were a good idea. Besides, most of the activities sounded like fun to her anyway, so she thought they should spend the extra money.

Aside to Mae, Barry said, "I hate to have this option spring up on us. We haven't budgeted for any extras." He queried honestly, "How much do you want to do those things and how much of it is about trying to be like the Bennetts?"

With thought towards their limited resources, the Wrights compromised and signed up for two Hummingbird excursions. Sunday evening, they would go to Night on the White River, consisting of small boats ferrying the guests upriver by torchlight to a clearing in the jungle for food, music, and live entertainment under the stars. On Tuesday morning, they would take the Bauxite Mines/Blue Mountain Tour and Luncheon, involving a ride inland, all the way up into the mountains for a change of scenery, for a tour of a recently closed mining facility followed by an authentic, Jamaican-style luncheon.

Ms. Simpson concluded the session by saying, "Thank you for your kind attention. Hummingbird wants you to have the vacation of your dreams, so if you have any questions or need any assistance, I will be happy to do anything I can to help. Simply leave me a message at the hotel desk or call the Hummingbird office in Ocho Rios."

She left soon after, but the Wrights and the Bennetts remained in the lobby area a few minutes longer, getting acquainted. Bruce immediately invited them to dinner, and Mae looked at Barry as if to ask, *Can we?*

Barry made an excuse, "Thanks, but we've already made plans. Next time."

"I'd like that very much," said Cindy.

"Me too," said Mae.

* * *

The two couples chatted together for a few minutes longer.

Bruce told them an anecdote about a Jamaican man trying to sell him some marijuana immediately upon their landing at the airport. He suspected the man of being an undercover cop. "Although," he concluded, "you never know, some of these hustlers are incredibly bold."

It reminded Barry of his airport adventure, and he almost talked about his encounter with the yellow-eyed "porter." But he thought better of it. If he brought it up now, he would have to explain to Mae why he kept it to myself in the first place. He knew that would defeat the purpose of his having done so.

Soon they went their separate ways. The Bennetts left the hotel, and the Wrights returned to their room. As Barry and Mae walked down the hallway toward their room, Mae asked him a simple question.

"Barry, do you like the Bennetts? To me, they seem very nice."

Barry decided they were "rich people," disliking them immediately on pure principle. He had to tell Mae the truth, but he considered his answer before he spoke.

"I'm sure they're nice folks. I just don't know how much we have in common."

"You mean because they may have lots of money, and we don't?"

He got to the door and sorted out their room key from the stuff in his pocket. He motioned for her to enter, answering, "Honestly? I suppose."

Mae could read him like a book. He closed the door and turned the deadbolt, then took Mae's hands, looked into her eyes, and did his best to explain his true feelings.

"We're here on a shoestring budget. We're going to have to work extra hard to pay for coming here. And that's fine, we decided to do that because it means a lot to us to be here together, if only for once in our lives. People like the Bennetts don't understand us. They've got plenty of money and run around places like this all the time, spending it like it doesn't mean anything. I'm afraid that if we hang around folks like that, we'll be doing it too, spending money right and left, buying drinks and dinners and other things we can't afford."

"I understand," said Mae, her pretty brow a little furrowed. "But we did come to have a good time, right? We'll have to be careful, that's all." Her expression softened again. "Besides, Honey," she cooed, "I didn't come here to run around with the Bennetts, you know…" She went up on her toes and kissed him. "… I came to be with you."

Barry returned her soft kiss. "Me, too," he said, and gave her his shy smile.

"All right then." Mae stepped back and directed, in a good-natured command, "Go find something relaxing to do while I put in my eye drops."

Off she went to the bathroom. Barry idled on the balcony where the light took on a golden quality as it neared the end of daylight. Out over the ocean, huge clouds formed into towering, mile-high columns, incredible formations he never had seen in real life but recognized from paintings and photographs of the sea. The heat and the long day conspired to make him feel drowsy. Soon he returned inside. He fiddled with the thermostat, which he already suspected did nothing. He flipped the switch for the radio and got the Everly Brothers singing, *All I Have to Do Is Dream*. He took off his running shoes and laid down on top of the bed, thinking he would stretch out for a little while, just until Mae comes out of the bathroom. Then they could decide about dinner and what to do rest of the evening. He yawned. His eyes closed. Barry stopped struggling and drifted into a sound sleep.

* * *

Mae finished with her drops, thinking that the bathroom was very nice. The walls and ceiling were tiled in ivory with a deep-green trim, and the bathroom floor was tiled in sea-green marble to match the countertop. There was no bathtub, but a tiled and glass-enclosed alcove formed a generously proportioned shower, with the showerhead placed high enough that Barry would be able to stand beneath the spray without ducking.

Mae wondered if Barry had seen that feature yet. She felt certain he would be pleased.

She opened the door to go find him. And find him she did, fast asleep on the bed.

Quietly, so as not to disturb him, she laid down beside him. She knew how tired he must be because they both got an awfully early start that morning. Was it that morning? It felt like it was days ago. She sighed, thinking about how everything there was so nice... While she lay awake in that reflective frame of mind, Mae heard the soft squeak of a floorboard and what sounded like someone in the hall, pausing outside their door. She expected a knock — the maid, perhaps. But seconds ticked by and no knock followed. It came to her with a sudden and frightful certainty that someone was spying on them through the louvers of the door. A brief, unpleasant shiver of alarm passed through her at the thought of it! But who?

She strained to hear any further evidence of this invasion of their privacy. She listened as hard as she could. At first, she heard nothing except the radio softly playing a peppy ska tune. But soon she became convinced that she heard someone breathing, besides Barry. With that, she became frightened enough to squeeze his hand until she had succeeded in awakening him.

* * *

Barry opened his eyes abruptly and started to say, "Wh—?"

Before he could speak, Mae clamped her hand over his mouth, silencing him. Rolling over and sitting up, she turned her back to the door, brought her finger to her lips, and signaled for silence.

Puzzled, Barry kept still and mouthed, "What the hell?"

Mae whispered softly, exaggerating the formation of each word, "There's someone lurking outside our door!" Both her hands trembled, worse than usual.

Barry nodded once. He understood. He forced himself to relax his muscles, concentrating on listening. He could not hear anyone and could not be sure Mae was right. He rose quietly from his side of the bed nearest the inside wall to check it out, moving stealthily over to a position beside the door, hoping he was not visible to a possible spy. He still could not see anyone through the slits between the closed louvers.

Barry reached carefully and unlocked the deadbolt, then gripped the polished brass doorknob. His hand felt sweat-slippery on the cold, smooth metal. He quietly wiped his hand on his shorts and took a better grip... swallowed slowly one time... took a deep breath... turned the knob... and flung the door wide open ... to an empty hallway! If someone had been standing there, for whatever reason, they were gone now. He closed and locked the door. Turning toward Mae, he shook his head and raised his hands in a questioning gesture then realized there was apparently no longer a need for silence. They both giggled nervously.

Mae, relieved, bounced to the edge of the bed and rising to her knees, mock-slapped Barry on the arm. She insisted, "There was too someone there!"

"Maybe, but they're gone now." He changed the subject, coming back around to one of his favorites. "Hey, what do you want to do about dinner?"

"I know." Mae brightened, remembering about the fancy restaurant that their friends had recommended, "Let's go into Ocho Rios and find The Lemon Tree."

"It's so hot. The thought of pumpkin soup doesn't hold much attraction for me. Not to mention, I feel like we've done enough traveling for one day. Let's have dinner downstairs?"

"All right," she said, willing to give in, "if we can walk down to the beach..."

"... And get to bed early," he finished her sentence. Mae sweetly added, "And then, tomorrow we'll go into Ocho Rios?"

"Yes, tomorrow we will check out the town. Now, let's eat."

* * *

In the waning phase of daylight, they headed for the hotel's restaurant, going downstairs to the Grand Foyer then down to the lower level through luxurious mahogany wood doors that opened onto the terrace or into the bar, and through similar doors opening into the restaurant.

As they approached a young man, serving as host and making table assignments, Barry said confidently, "A table for two please."

"Excuse me please, Bah-ss," said the dark-skinned Jamaican youth, who then disappeared into the dining room.

Bah-ss? Barry looked quizzically at Mae. He had no idea what the youth meant by that. They waited, observing that the service looked gracious, the ambience charming, and the food smelled delicious.

The waiter returned with the maître d', an older man with light-brown skin, graying hair, and downcast eyes. The elder man politely but firmly explained, "I should like very much to be able to seat you, sir and madam, but regrettably, I cannot. It is the matter of proper dress."

"Oh..." Barry felt chagrined. Although warned by Ms. Simpson only hours earlier that very afternoon, they had nonetheless "spaced out" by dinnertime, showing up in their shorts. Both had forgotten the day of the week and the dress code. It had been a long day. Recovering, Barry said, "Of course. Pardon us, please."

Despite his embarrassment, Barry gave the older man a confident smile as they left and went back to their room. He felt mortified enough to consider going somewhere else for dinner.

"That would be silly," Mae surmised. "We're here for a week, and what we need to do is put on the proper clothes and get right back down there."

He agreed. So, they put on slacks and returned to the restaurant. When they arrived, they immediately were escorted to a lovely table on the terrace. Nearby, a calypso band performed lively island music while happy couples danced. The Wrights drank a potent concoction of fresh fruit juices and sweet, dark rum out of coconut shells festooned with blossoms and chunks of tropical fruit. They enjoyed a divine meal centered around grilled red snapper. As they finished dinner, an indescribably beautiful sunset emblazoned the entire sky.

"It's like heaven," Mae marveled. "I've never seen anything more beautiful in my life."

"I have," said Barry, gazing at Mae and covering her hand with his own.

Mae dropped her eyes and glowed in the warm light of their love.

Barry called for the check. Although most guests of the hotel were content to sign for their meals and settle their bill when they checked out, Barry wanted to keep tight control over their budget. So, when presented with the check for his signature, he settled the bill in cash, leaving a cash gratuity. He intended to continue that practice for the duration of their stay. To him, it made good sense to stay paid up, just as earlier he paid cash for their extra excursions.

Mae did not approve of this practice. She told him, "It's silly, but if it makes you feel more comfortable, why not?"

By the end of their meal, the stars had arrived to light their way for their first, romantic walk on the beach. They strolled along the water's edge, alone on the beach, far from the lights of the hotel. The lovers walked hand in hand carrying their shoes, walking barefoot with waves lapping around their ankles. Nighttime had settled over the island full and complete, but it was not totally dark, not with so many stars sparkling like a brilliance of diamonds scattered across the black velvet sky. The moon, a slim crescent of palest silver, rose and the trees in nearby gardens and the not-too-distant jungle rang with a reptile chorus. They walked until their hearts overflowed with joy and love and desire. They hurried back to the hotel without spilling a single drop. In their room, they made love like it was the very first time — but not until Barry covered the louvers of the door with a beach towel so Mae could relax. It was glorious. When they were satisfied, they fell asleep in each other's arms for the last, perfect time.

CHAPTER SIX

Sunday, Sept. 16 — Discovering Stranger Danger in Ocho Rios

Mae awoke early the next morning. She opened her eyes to find herself alone in the big, romantic bed. From the dimly lit room, Mae could see the sky through the open door to the balcony. The darkness was lifting. There were fewer stars left to twinkle and before too long the sun would be coming up. Yawning, Mae sat up and looked around until she spied Barry out on the balcony, seemingly entranced by the view, exotic fragrances, and the dulcet tones of pre-dawn twilight in the tropics. Barry rarely had such peaceful moments, so Mae held stone still to watch him, not wanting to do anything to disturb his seldom-observed tranquility.

Seeing him like that made her feel so good. She congratulated herself for being able to make their well-deserved vacation happen. She had taken him from his stressful job and the rat race of their ordinary lives to a haven of beauty and serenity. Barry, who looked like he was enjoying the cool air and the easy birth of a new day, must have instinctively felt her loving eyes upon him because he turned to look, and, when his eyes met hers, they brightened.

He smiled and said, "You look like a tousled African earth goddess."

"Well, you did the tousling."

"I happily remember," he responded, reaching out for her to join him.

Mae arose in the T-shirt she had slept in. She slipped on her white, softsole Thunderbird moccasins and joined him on the balcony.

"Honey, good morning," he said softly. "I tried not to wake you."

Mae slipped her hands inside the light cotton robe Barry was wearing over a pair of shorts. Putting her arms around him and pressing her cheek to the center of his chest, she felt his big heart beating and smelled his manly scent, both made her heart melt.

"Good morning," she sighed contentedly, still a little sleepy and snuggling cozily in his arms to join him in savoring the nascent day.

Barry hugged her and kissed the top of her head, then hugged her again. "It's cooler out here than in our room right now," he explained. "I thought I'd let in some fresh air. I didn't mean to disturb you. But I'm glad you're awake. I've been up for about an hour, enjoying this window on paradise in solitude." He said softly, "Although you were in the next room, I missed your companionship. Whenever we are apart, I feel like half a person. If we were separated for very long, your absence would become such a palpable thing it would feel like an alien presence."

"Oh, Honey. That's so sweet."

Mae's vision was not very crisp so soon after waking. Consequently, she saw the world like an Impressionist painting, details softened by her handicap. To her, the white-sand beach where they had walked last evening looked like a piecrust dusted with sugar crystals, sparkling, here and there, where it threw back some starshine. At that pre-dawn hour, the air felt warm, not hot. It must have rained while they slept. A clean, sweet smell still lingered on the gentle breeze.

The frogs and lizards that had kept the night ringing were silent. All was quiet, except for the sound of the waves lapping on the shore in soothing, hypnotic sloshes, and the occasional, plaintive cry of a sea bird. Soon all the birds would fill with cheer then spill their morning songs in greetings to the rising sun.

The husband and wife kissed, feeling lucky in love and entirely at peace.

Mae looked again into the quiet depths of Barry's brown eyes and could hardly believe that moment was not a dream. Although he had not felt it was something he needed, Barry had traveled with her to this faraway land, this magical sea island.

She knew Barry made this trip to make her happy. He never tried to push her around. He never tried to put her down. When Mae looked at Barry, she did not see the color of his skin. The only color she perceived was in his heart, which shone like pure gold. In her eyes, he was the finest man she had ever known.

"I love you," she chimed.

He spoke softly, "I love you, too."

Their lips met, and they kissed with gentle passion. No anxious thoughts clouded their minds. They did not care what day of the week it was. Each was free from the worries of their workplaces and the nagging chores at home. They anticipated a perfect time, a little slice of their lives experienced together in love and in paradise.

Mae thought, this was all she wanted, and — in that moment in time — believed, they would always remember Jamaica with love for as long as we lived.

*   *   *

When Barry looked at Mae, he drank in her beauty like a thirsty man. Hers was a face he knew by heart. She grew more beautiful to him with each passing moment, each second, hour, day, and year they shared together. That morning, however, he noticed something different. Her pretty face had somehow grown fuller, more rounded, despite her recent weight loss. *Puffy* came to mind, but that was an ugly thought, unfit to describe any aspect of his beloved wife. Yet, it would not be dispelled. He remembered seeing that slightly moon-faced look before, only worse. Not that long ago, but who? Then he had it. It was Amanda, Dr. LeFraude's young assistant. Amanda, who was also under treatment for sarcoidosis and who had reached out to Mae, a sister in suffering and sympathy. He guessed that it was probably the medication.

With that realization, Barry felt sadness and a rising anger because he was powerless to protect Mae or to relieve her of her burden. He chose not to reveal his observation to Mae, who would no doubt see it for herself soon enough. He did not want to diminish her happiness or upset her needlessly during their "honeymoon" — what was likely to be a once-in-a-lifetime event. So, Barry hugged Mae in loving silence, secretly swallowing his anger like bitter medicine, for her sake, because it was the most he could do.

As Mae held onto him and peered most likely foggily but happily at a twilit Jamaica, Barry was reminded of a slide he had once produced while experimenting with new, special photographic effects. It had portrayed an improbable, imaginary island, vivid green palms and orange flowers electric against a blue and gold sunrise sky, the whole image reflected in the surrounding sea. It was truly one of the nicer pieces he had created, betwixt and between the endless flow of graphs, type slides and statistical tables. He liked it too much to turn it over as a background for mundane business use. He supposed it languished somewhere amid art in his portfolio. That special slide to Barry may have somehow presaged this Caribbean experience.

Mae spoke, uncannily giving voice to Barry's thought, "Remember that slide you made…" she began.

"The one of the tropical island?" he interrupted.

"How do you always know what I'm thinking? Yes, that one. You called it Fantasy Island, and I said…"

He joined her in chanting, in Munchkin-like falsetto, "Boss, da plane! Da plane!"

They chuckled, entertaining one another alone on the balcony, awake and alert before dawn. The day had yet to begin for most people, who probably still slept deeply, snugly wrapped in confidence of at least a few more hours of z's since it was Sunday. But Barry and Mae, who each descended from farming families, seemed to have an internal mechanism like the genetic memory of roosters that crowed them awake by daybreak. Even on vacation, they were early risers, quick to be up and about, beating the crowds.

"I wish I had some coffee."

"I know you do," she responded empathetically. "Sorry, the hotel starts service at seven."

"I'll be fine until we get some breakfast," he assured her, so appreciative of the fact that Mae, who had never developed a coffee habit, understood that he generally scorned breakfast but needed caffeine to get his heart started. "I'm glad you're awake early, though," he confessed. "I was wondering if you'd like to go for a walk, look around while it's still cool?"

"Why not? I'm itching for an adventure."

Although an hour before sunrise, they showered and prepared to greet the new day.

After she toweled herself dry, Mae treated her lesions then inserted the drops in her eyes without too much trouble (perseverance was improving her aim). She dressed in a bright, day-glow orange tank top. resigning to an unhappy fact, "I guess there is no way I can hide my sore arm in the tropics."

She slipped into a pair of tan shorts and laced up her Adidas cloud white tennis shoes and then covered her head with a white baseball cap. Finally rolling her morning pill carefully in a tissue and slipping it into her pocket, she said, "I'll take my morning pill later when we eat breakfast. We might find a morning meal in town or along the road somewhere."

Barry had put on his olive-drab khaki shorts, short-sleeved camp shirt, and a tan pair of socks. He put on his brown running shoes and finally set an olive drab, Vietnam war-era boonie hat on his head for protection from the sun. He admitted, "I must look something like a giant Boy Scout. But who cares? Ready?"

Mae sprang to her feet, her eyes sparkled, and her head nodded as she said, "You know me, Honey. I was *born* ready!"

It was their pat answer to the question, a code between them. They were ready to leave the hotel and go meet the real Jamaica, up close and personal. They left their room, and Barry carefully locked their door. The hardwood floor creaked noisily beneath their footsteps in the hushed, softly illuminated hallways as they tried to quietly make their way to the main entrance. They met no one else in the hotel at that hour nor heard a living soul, until they reached the front door where a Jamaican man stood on duty outside, watching the brightening horizon. He wore a short-sleeved white shirt with dark slacks, looking a little surprised to see anyone exiting the hotel at such an early hour.

"Security," Barry whispered to Mae while opening the heavy door for her.

"Good morning," said the man to Mae, catching and holding the door.

"Good morning," she replied, adding, "Thank you," and rewarding the doorman with a flash of her smile.

The man held the door for Barry and said, "Morning, Bah-ss."

Barry, made a face upon hearing that word again but replied, "Good morning."

"Too early for a taxi, Bah-ss," the man explained, allowing the door to close.

"Thanks, we don't need one. We're out for a little walk."

"No problem, Bah-ss. Sun coming up soon. Gonna be a hot one today, for sure."

Barry walked a dozen steps up the slope, along the curving driveway, then turned and looked back to see the man staring at them and running his hand over his close-shaven head, still watching the interracial couple.

"Jamaica being such an enlightened country in terms of racial equality and all, what's so interesting about us?" Barry shrugged, "Well, it's not like we've never been stared at before."

The uphill grade pleasantly stretched their muscles. Their path was illuminated by small lights placed every so often along the drive's edge, where asphalt met the garden. In the nearly dark day, the garden looked deep and intriguing. Mae wanted to explore the gardens further.

"Let's do it another time when the sun is up and shining. We'll be better able to see it."

By the time they reached the gate, Barry started to sweat. He felt glad they had started before sunup. When they turned out onto the A-3, the highway graded and more-or-less leveled between the steep coastal slope they had ascended, and the gentler rise of the inland slopes covered variously in sugar cane and wilder growth, sometimes jungle. They put the glowing eastern sky behind them and struck out at a vigorous pace in the only familiar direction, west toward downtown Ocho Rios.

"If we walk all the way into town, I bet we could get some breakfast there," said Mae, taking three strides to equal two of his. Already she puffed a little for breath.

"I suppose." Doubtful if Mae could make it, Barry worried, "Are you all right?"

"Yeah."

Considering how quickly the temperature could rise once the sun was up and not at all ready to commit himself, he said, "Well, it's a pretty long way to walk, so let's see how things go. We should be happy to look around a little, get our bearings. We dashed by everything so quickly when we came in on the bus."

A few birds began calling from the treetops in long, looping, unfamiliar notes as the Wrights paused to look back and watch the sunrise paint the sky. Above the horizon, a band of glowing orange blended into streaks of hot pink and gold like a cosmic watercolor wash. They put on their sunglasses and watched the heavens, transfixed, until the glowing orb itself peeked over the rim of the world, and the intensifying blue had absorbed almost all the other colors. Then the sun was up, and the birds were jammin'. Butterflies flitted over the landscape as the Wrights walked happily toward town. Once they had passed beyond the sprawling limits of their hotel's compound and the unmarked, covert-seeming entry to the very exclusive compound next door, they soon encountered the epitome of Jamaican hostelries, The Plantation.

"Wow, this graceful, colonnaded hotel continues to operate in the spirit of the British Empire during what the colonial planters called 'the good old days' on the island."

"Not so good for the African slaves," said Mae, who looked a little pained.

Ironically, they came upon a cluster of shacks around the very next bend in the road, less than a half mile from the grandest hotel. It was an all-too-visible pocket of sobering poverty. There, again, every spare square-inch of soil was crammed with heavy cultivation. Between the fruits of the earth and the bounty of the sea, at least the Jamaicans were not starving. But there was little evidence of material comforts. Beside a corrugated steel-roofed, ramshackle store at an intersection where a rural dirt road met the A-3, stood several Jamaicans dressed in their Sunday best, waiting for a ride. The people stopped talking and stared at them, shielding their eyes from the blaze of the rising sun. Their reaction to seeing Mae, a Black woman with a short, coily Afro, strolling hand-in-hand with Barry, a White man with long wavy hair in a field uniform, was to eye them curiously but respectfully. Not to mention, Mae had on shorts, which Jamaican women rarely if ever wore in public, especially on a Sunday.

"Good morning," Barry said, in an amiable tone.

"Good morning, Bah-ss," said an obsequious, white-haired elderly man, who dipped his head to Barry, then pushed his heavy spectacles back higher on his nose. He wore an ancient, shiny, once-blue suit and carried a much-thumbed Bible.

"Morning, Bah-ss," chorused the others, a middle-aged woman, a younger couple, and a girl of 11 or 12. A pair of small, barefoot boys said nothing but peeked out, curiously, from behind the full skirts of the women.

"Good morning," Mae said, looking strained.

Barry and Mae continued up the road, leaving the group standing at the three corners to stare after them. As they walked, Barry wiped his face and neck with his handkerchief, an army-surplus bandana printed in a camouflage pattern of variegated greens, browns and black.

Once they had passed the group, a somber mood seemed to come over Mae. She said, "I found it hard to smile at those poor people of my own race. Those Jamaicans didn't look like the happy, beautiful people I expected to see. They looked more like folks in old Depression-era photographs, especially the old man in the double-breasted suit."

Mae hiked alongside him, quiet and retrospective, occasionally glancing past the road, trying not to stare but studying the shabby living quarters of Black people. Close up and viewed so soon after the grandiosity of The Plantation, the dilapidated assortment of shacks and shanties underlined a disparity in lifestyles that was impossible to ignore. Although the institution of slavery had been abolished on this British Crown possession 25 years before Abraham Lincoln signed the Emancipation Proclamation, most Jamaicans still lived an obviously marginal existence in poverty. Barry thought about the tragedy of so many human beings being robbed of their freedom, chained, beaten, starved, stacked like cordwood, and crammed into the filthy holds of slave ships. Thousands survived the hell of the Atlantic crossing to reach the sugar plantations of Jamaica where their straining muscles, hot blood, and copious sweaty brows wrung from the earth the unimaginable wealth conveyed back across the Atlantic.

That wealth, with its attendant privilege, was enjoyed by the highbrows — the cold-blooded, self-proclaimed world champion White people, who lived in luxury and leisure in the English noble houses. Perhaps it has something to do with humping along the road sweating instead of speeding past in an air-conditioned bus, he thought.

Mae confessed, "I'm not feeling so good anymore."

"Is it because of the exercise?"

She answered, "I don't know."

Barry suspected that the *real* Jamaica looked mean, decrepit, poorly drained, and nowhere near as charming as it had looked in the glossy four-color tourism brochures.

* * *

Mae hated to admit it, but maybe Jamaica was a mistake.

Thoughts of all the misery in the past, present and future lives of her fellow African descendants bounced around in her head like a pinball, ringing against bumpers of confusion, racking up a high score of wild and crazy speculations. That funny feeling, which she sometimes had these days — the one she did not like because it frightened her but kept growing too strong to ignore, rushed to the top of her mind like a bonus game.

Let's make it personal, it suggested, loud enough inside her head to command Mae's attention. She thought about what if she were locked up, could not go home, could not be with her family when she wanted to. What if all her personal belongings were taken, and she was given strange clothes to wear, fed slop, and forced to do things against my will? Scenario after grotesque scenario tilted her mind — too many balls in play. She tightened her grip on Barry's hand and looked to see how he was reacting.

He was sweating profusely now but still pumping along, breathing easily. He smiled, oblivious to her inner turmoil. She tried to return his smile, but it felt phony, even garish, as though she wore dime-store wax lips. If Barry had had a bad reaction to the plight of these Jamaicans, he gave no outward sign.

So, it must be all right, Mae tried to convince herself, struggling to pull the plug on the runaway Bally in her brain... Stop! The Gottlieb of her gray matter... Stop! Stop! The Rockola of her reason. Stop! Stop it now, Mae Bea Wright! At last! Thank goodness, she thought, recognizing the voice of her common sense: you knew about the history of this place when you decided to come here, didn't you?

"Yes," she replied, unintentionally speaking the word aloud.

"Hmm?" said Barry, turning his head to look at Mae without breaking his stride.

But it was not the same as seeing it with her own eyes, she thought, returning to her unvoiced, inner dialogue.

Caught yourself standing on the side of wealth and privilege, didn't you?

I never thought so, Mae considered now. She dropped Barry's hand and stopped walking.

Mae had an epiphany on the road to Ocho Rios. She thought, I may be Black, but I am not Jamaican. She decided, I am a U.S. citizen and an alien on this island; it is not up to me to judge or protest these people's way of life. This thought saved her, restoring her equilibrium and self-presence and silencing the tempest in the teapot of her cranium. But after this episode, Mae could not see Jamaica with quite the same childish delight.

A few steps ahead, Barry stopped and turned back towards her. He took off his hat and mopped his entire head. Crescents of sweat stained his underarms.

""Honey? What's up?"

Mae was tired as much from her mental jag as from the hike. She was ready to turn around and go back to the hotel. Still, she did not relish the thought of passing the waiting Jamaicans, again. Nor did she feel she could adequately explain her confused emotions to her husband, thinking Barry's only here because of me, and I am not going to spoil his good time.

"Nothing," she lied, feeling light-headed and a little queasy. "I'm fine."

She bent forward, resting her hands on her knees.

She wondered if she had gotten too much sun. But how can that be? She had never been bothered by sunlight not even down South, probably because of her African blood and all that — but it did not occur to her that she had never been in the tropics on steroids before.

"Let's get out of the sun for a few minutes," she suggested, straightening. She lifted her cap and, with the back of her hand, blotted ineffectually at her damp forehead.

"Sounds good to me," said Barry.

Looking around, he pointed at a big patch of shade where a tree's limbs stretched beyond the mint-green pickets of a small, fenced yard. He waited with his open hand poised until Mae clasped it in her own again. Then together they walked the short distance to the oasis of shade at the edge of the road. The doctor breeze, the gentle wind blowing steadily inland from the Caribbean Sea, played lightly around them, so cooling and restorative in the deep shade. In the little yard, propped against the bole of the sheltering tree, a half-dozen life-sized human figures stood staring woodenly at Mae and Barry. The genuine Jamaican folk art, each figure hand carved from a single tree trunk or limb, was ostensibly for sale to tourists. The newly painted, bright-yellow shack adjacent to the fenced yard was a beauty parlor, identified by the hand-lettered, scrap-wood sign jutting out of a bed of crotons in the dooryard.

Barry wanted to know, "How much further shall we go?"

"How far do you suppose it is to downtown?"

Barry pointed to a modern high-rise clearly visible above the trees and roughly a mile away. "See that big white hotel? If I remember correctly, that's on the edge of downtown."

"You're right," agreed Mae. "And it *is* getting pretty hot. Let's head back."

Barry agreed, "Nothing's going to be happening this early on a Sunday, anyway,"

He got that twinkle in his eye, which meant he was getting ready to make a joke. "Hey, why don't we buy 'poor old Kaw-Liga,' here?" Barry hooked his thumb in the direction of one of the bigger sculptures, a stained and polished wooden Rasta man. "You and I can shoulder it back to the hotel."

Barry laughed playfully, his good humor (one of the first things that attracted Mae) was infectious. Feeling better and ready to laugh again, she giggled at the thought of the two of them staggering along the A-3 burdened with a 200-pound souvenir.

"No problem!" She added, "Easy to carry on the plane, too! But first, let me run in here and get my hair done."

Mae surprised Barry with that last bit, and it cracked him up. When he got his breath he said, "All right, then, ready to head back?"

"We'll go into town later?"

"Sure, Hon," he promised.

Mae pulled the bill of her cap low over her sunglasses to help shield her damaged eyes from the ascending sun. "Then I'm with you!"

Back they headed the way they had come. From 50 yards or so they watched as a stake truck picked up the folks they had passed earlier, the men assisting the ladies and children in climbing aboard. The Jamaicans rode in the back with crates for seats and a couple of nanny goats for companions. Mae silently watched them shrink in the distance. Soon they disappeared, merging into the blurred world of light and shadows that existed beyond the limit of her vision.

The temperature climbed steadily with the sun, which glimmered hotly on the coastal waters and baked the worn pavement under their feet. Occasionally one of the brightly colored compact cars came tearing over the highway. They would jump for their lives as the ever-present Jan Crows, scouting for roadkill, soared overhead like omens.

Barry was sweating buckets, which was no surprise and a condition that he had accepted would prevail during their entire stay in the tropics. But Mae was hot and perspiring too, which was unusual for her. She never minded the heat in the same way he did.

Walking back to their resort went faster, in that odd, inversely proportional way that a return journey always feels shorter than the initial venture. They passed The Plantation, now showing signs of life with employees reporting for work. Next, they passed the crypto portal to the mysterious hotel, right then being exited by an enormous Rolls Royce Silver Phantom, all gray metallic and bright chrome with mirrored windows sheltering the passenger compartment. The car turned ponderously onto the A-3, guzzling precious fossil fuel as it headed east.

They soon covered the remaining distance to the entrance gate of their hotel. Once back in their hotel's compound, Mae was feeling more secure, and both her energy level and her curiosity were restored to her. She expressed a renewed desire to explore the gardens.

"Now, before we get cleaned up for breakfast and the day gets hotter," was the way she put it. Barry was agreeable, seeming to appreciate her logic.

* * *

The Wrights began their exploration at the top, quickly locating a path paved with flagstones. They linked hands and disappeared into the shade beneath the big trees growing in the upper regions of the garden. The path ran more-or-less parallel to the coast, descending in gentle switchbacks that made the garden seem much larger than it was. As they advanced, it grew sunnier and various palms, tall and small, dominated. With the garden all to themselves that morning, private and enticing, they found both old flora friends and made new acquaintances, each species identified by a neat, small label. There was eucalyptus, oleander, Canary Island pine, massive rhododendron, juniper, cork oak, and yucca. They discovered a splendid collection of orchids, lush bougainvillea, ferns, bromeliads, and tropical fruit trees, including breadfruit from the South Pacific brought to the British West Indies by Captain William Bligh. The air was filled with delightful fragrances, ranging from earthy cacao and coffee to sweet florals and tangy, aromatic citruses. In a secluded corner near the bottom of the garden, they sat on a carved stone bench beneath a Victorian trellis overgrown with velvet-red roses.

They watched as a striking black-and-yellow spider built a perfect work-of-art web. It was no mere bug. It was a significant life form. Then it was the spider's turn to watch with its eight intelligent eyes while the humans brought their lips together in a soft, sweet kiss. Feeling peaceful and content again, Mae and Barry exited the garden. They followed the path to its conclusion at the edge of the courtyard, 20 or 25 yards from the main entrance.

They could not help but notice the Silver Phantom parked in the drive. A liveried chauffeur busily polished invisible dust from the already lustrous chrome.

As they crossed the main lobby, their tummy alarms ringing for breakfast to be next on their agenda, the Wrights passed a Black Jamaican in a suit and tie speaking deferentially to a White gentleman dressed in a tan field uniform. Obviously, by his dress and reserved demeanor, he was an Englishman.

Barry put the gentleman together with the Rolls waiting in the driveway and figured that the guy probably owned the hotel. A second later, as if a light bulb went on over his head, he could hardly contain himself until he and Mae had crossed the lobby and entered the dimly lit corridor leading to their room.

"Guess what?" he stage-whispered as they walked. "I figured out what 'Bah-ss' means."

Mae wanted to know, "What?"

"Boss!"

"Why on earth would these Jamaicans be calling *you,* boss?" Afraid she knew, she guessed the answer, "Because you're White?"

They turned into the stairwell and made the short climb to the second floor.

"It's more than that, Mae. They think I'm *English.*

"Did you see that fellow back there in the lobby? These clothes I bought for the tropics are a parody of what he's wearing."

"So, you think they call the English 'boss'?"

They paused before their door. She waited while Barry produced the key from a flapped-and-buttoned cargo pocket. He pushed open the door, and they went inside.

"I'm sure of it! Why, I bet the English own *everything* worth owning in Jamaica."

*   *   *

In the hotel dining room, Mae appreciated the elegance of it all. The open French doors on the seaside let in a lovely breeze. A waiter led them to a beautifully set table with fancy silverware, China, and crystal glasses on fine white linen and a lovely centerpiece, a vase of colorful fresh-cut flowers. She opened her napkin and placed it on her lap, gazing around the dining room with satisfaction.

The dining room hummed with activity. There were almost as many servers as there were guests. The waiters were uniformly young, dark-skinned males, dressed alike in starched white shirts, black ties, red jackets, and pleated black slacks. One young man served them coffee; another supplied water, and yet a third arrived to take their order.

Barry wryly observed, "Must have punched these guys out with a cookie cutter." After tasting his first cup of Jamaican Blue Mountain coffee, he proclaimed, "Wow, this *is* good." He was capable of drinking anything if it had caffeine in it, but he readily loved that cup of Joe.

Never much of a coffee drinker, Mae enjoyed her sips of coffee, too, as she curiously watched the other guests arriving, being seated, and being served. Gradually, she became conscious of a peculiar thing.

Mae whispered, "Barry, see how the dining room is divided into two sections?" Her brows knitted. "Is it my imagination or is this dining room *segregated*?" Mae's indignation was evident in her tense tone.

Barry nodded. "I was hoping you hadn't noticed."

In Mae's mind, a red Mars light started to twirl and the siren blared on her racial prejudice detector: Warning! Warning! Indubitably the dining room *was* segregated. The alcove in which Barry and Mae sat contained one other interracial couple along with several Black families. They could clearly see that only White guests sat in the other section. As they watched, more White couples arrived and led to tables in the White people's section.

"Jim Crow, alive and well in Jamaica," she erupted indignantly, under her breath. "They don't mention *that* in the tourism ads."

She felt angry, betrayed, and hurt. Hating to admit it to herself, she knew this vacation's causing way too much stress.

"Now, Mae, this is a foreign country." Barry rationalized, firmly but gently, "We don't know how they do things here. Maybe it's not what it looks like."

When they made their choice for love and entered into an interracial marriage, Mae and Barry both expected to run into a certain amount of ignorance and prejudice. The truth was, they never ran into the prejudice they anticipated. When they did run into prejudice, it was in ways they never expected. Renting their first Evanston apartment had proved interesting, with real estate agents all innocently steering them towards certain buildings in certain neighborhoods. On their own, Barry and Mae found a suitable courtyard building on a quiet street in a nice neighborhood. The management firm had been reluctant to offer the Wrights a lease, stating the reason being that there were no children currently living there. Barry pointed out that it was illegal to deny them a lease on the grounds that they had a child. He contacted a lawyer from the ACLU, and apparently the problem went away. They got their lease after all.

Once Barry took Mae and Zac fishing on a lake in central Wisconsin. They overheard some other anglers talking. "Hey, lookit that White man with that *coon lady*," said one man, ignorant or insensitive to the way voices carry great distances over bodies of water. Mae knew the disparaging slur followed by a polite reference was oxymoronic, but it still irked her.

Mae wondered what she could do about it, at home or right now in Ocho Rios. She resigned herself to go on, never mind, for Barry's sake, no need to spoil the trip.

Next, as the couple ate their breakfast, Mae felt pestered by the many servile waiters. They irritated her like outdoor picnic pests. It seemed to her that an inordinate number of these strangers hovered around their table, fluttering back and forth bearing water pitchers, buckets of ice cubes, pats of butter, baskets of scones, pots of coffee and other assorted condiments and food courses. Mae knew she should be enjoying all the attention, thinking goodness knows we are paying enough for it. After all, she wanted to feel pampered. Then something finally started to become clear to Mae. She understood why the cadre of servants bothered her so much.

Mae thought, "I am the problem! I'm a hypocrite! On the one hand I say, 'Let my people go' and, on the other hand, I am relishing the royal treatment!"

Her heartbeat accelerated. The room began to spin. She did not know what to do with her hands and sweaty palms. Mae thought she must be sick, which reminded her to take her pill. She searched her pockets until she found and unrolled the tissue. She put the pill in her mouth. That pill felt huge, like she could never swallow such a thing. She reached for her water.

Barry commented about something, which sounded like, "What big eyes you have," and she tried to answer, "The better to see you with." But she could not form the words until she swallowed the pill. She lifted her glass to her lips with a shaky grip. Crystal rang icily against her front teeth. She gulped at the liquid like she had forgotten the simple mechanics of drinking, spilling some water as she returned the stemmed glass goblet to the table. Barry tried to assist her with her glass and his napkin.

"Thanks, Honey."

Barry was always trying to be so sweet to her, she thought, appreciating his helpfulness, and that made her happy. Yet, she still felt like crying. She took a chance on her voice and spoke.

"I guess I'm a little jittery this morning."

Mae heard her words echoing as if her voice came from a great distance away. She knew the way she felt was unnatural. She admitted to herself that these thoughts were not the sort she should be having on her vacation. The last thing she wanted was to spoil everything for Barry.

She willed her worries, *Begone!* Mae focused on convincing herself to be calm, do not upset Barry with her feelings of…what? "Never mind!" She told herself, "Stop exaggerating everything out of proportion! Be calm!" She did what she was learning to do, which she was coming to think of as maintaining her cool, hiding her confusion, trying to act and appear perfectly natural. Her self-control took hold, and she managed to settle down.

"Yes," Barry said to the latest waiter to busy himself at their table, who had offered to refill his coffee cup.

Barry said to Mae, "This coffee is delicious. The flavor is hardy with a hint of natural sweetness and a clean finish." After another sip, he declared, "It's the best coffee I ever tasted."

Mae declined the waiter's motion to refill her cup, "No, thank you," placing her cup wrong side up on the saucer. She wittily thought Barry would drink his share and her share for sure. Mae did not understand what was so good about burnt seeds steeped in hot water. All she got from coffee was an upset stomach and jittery nerves, the last thing she needed right then!

Barry looked a little surprised. "Don't you like it? I do."

Still trying to regain her composure, Mae heard Barry say, "I do." That's right, she thought, refocusing on their honeymoon and shifting her thoughts to how lucky she was to have a good man she could trust. Her faith in Barry helped her find solid ground to stand on while she waited for her nerves to subside. Still, she needed to say something.

Mae began shakily but as she spoke her voice gained confidence, "Well, it's surely the best coffee I've ever tasted." She could genuinely attest to that — happy to consider anything other than the unpleasant confusion orbiting into the radio silence on the dark side of her mind.

"You haven't touched your fruit. Is everything all right?"

Mae looked at her breakfast, noticing it for the first time. She did not recall when it arrived. Examining it, she marveled at the beautifully presented plate of toast and colorful fruits. She could tell that somebody had gone to an awful lot of trouble. The dish looked so special with juicy looking pineapples, melons, and other exotic fruits. Pleasantly surprised, Mae discovered she had an appetite and started eating. It tasted delicious. She became herself again.

"Well, you can have your coffee," Mae said, selecting from the beautiful dish of juicy fruits. "I love this fruit! It's so fresh and ripe."

She discovered a dish of yogurt, and, from the basket of piping-hot breads and scones, she selected a nutty brown muffin.

Barry ate more traditional fare. He had eggs and bacon, a muffin, and more Blue Mountain coffee.

Normal was what Mae wanted; it was how she needed to feel. She withdrew into the normality that existed. She looked no further than their table of good food, good service, and the best company.

When the check came, Barry continued his practice of paying with cash. He commented, "I'm a little amazed at how quickly our cash is evaporating. I'd better go over our finances."

The sated couple left through the French doors to the terrace where they had had dinner the night before. They looked out over the beach, so different this morning in full daylight, but still quiet with very little activity in the bay since it was Sunday and only around 9 a.m.

"We could go beach combing," suggested Mae.

"Sounds like fun," Barry assented. "But we need to go get our hats and sunscreen."

Mae had an idea, "Honey, let's go this way."

She took his hand and headed across the terrace, toward the pool and cabana area. Barry followed along, confident of her sense of direction. She always caught on to a new layout faster than he did. Mae found what she was looking for in the courtyard by the pool. There was a door to the stairwell at the end of the wing that housed their room. They could get in and out without going through the lobby. They climbed the back stairway to the second floor and soon reached their room. They took care of their business and headed back out for the beach. They wanted to have a little fun and see what the rest of the day held in store.

* * *

The Wrights left the beach to walk along the hotel's dock, which was a substantial, concrete structure that jutted at least 100 feet into the Caribbean Sea. Although Midwesterners, Barry, an ardent amateur naturalist, and Mae, the semi-professional "zoo lady," had practical knowledge of the seacoast environment. The couple blissfully ventured along, fascinated by the shoreline and enjoying quality time together. Above all, it felt *non-threatening* to Mae. There, on the beach, she felt apart of nature, free of the social pressures that fueled her cyclic mood swings — episodes of confusion and jitters that accompanied her increasingly frequent emotional upsets.

Barry and Mae happily discovered a great variety and plenitude of tropical marine life in the relatively shallow, crystal-clear water, including beautiful tropical fishes, large and small. They spotted a lot of crabs, recognizing the bulky horseshoes and the hermits in their salvaged armor. Barry pointed out stingrays and starfish, as well as a beautiful but dangerous Portuguese man o' war (*Physalia physalis*), gaily trailing multi-hued streamers in the form of many feet of potentially deadly, stinging tentacles. Even landlubbers like Barry and Mae knew how to stay well clear of them.

They spied a sunken pile of conch shells in the clear water. Each had been crudely broken open and robbed of the delectable mussel by someone eager to feast on its meat. What little they saw of the coral reefs, damaged, colorless, and dead looking, had suffered from enormous environmental impact in modern times and clearly had not come out on top. Reportedly, a living reef some distance from shore ringed the entire island and presently concerned ecological forces were at work to pass laws to protect what remained, if it was not already too late.

One second the two were alone on the pier watching the colorful fishes. The next second, the fish scattered as a beat-up wooden skiff came sidling up to the dock. Aboard were several Jamaican men, presumably local fishermen, who each offered a deal, a proposition, and cried loudly for the tourists' attention. Turned out, these Jamaicans were typical if not particularly imaginative hustlers. They had various ideas designed to acquire the rich Americans' money.

"Bah-ss, let me take you fishin' out beyond the reef!"

"What you like? I fix you up! Mebbe a barbecue in the jungle?"

Barry, mindful of avoiding scams and hustles, politely but firmly refused all offers. "Thank you, no. I don't think so."

Mae got spooked by the sudden intrusion from the sea and peered out from behind her large husband, unhappy with this unsolicited attention from these no doubt dangerous ruffians. Barry kept a friendly, noncommittal smile while he firmly held his ground. Before very long the fishermen got the idea and shoved off. They aimed their skiff toward a promising-looking group further up the beach.

Mae came out from behind her husband, looking relieved that the boatload of scruffy, smelly strangers had gone, leaving them in peace.

"Don't worry 'bout dem fellas, dey jus' a lotta big talk."

The voice came from the water below the dock, startling Barry and sending Mae back behind him for cover. From there, she peered out at this latest marvel, half-prepared to discover a talking fish. But no, a human head protruded from the sea alongside the dock where a strong swimmer treaded water. As they watched, the swimmer grasped the dock and boosted himself up to rest on his elbows, half-in and half-out of the water.

"You are Americans, yes?" asked the young Jamaican man with confidence in his smile, framed by full lips and strong white teeth. Water drained from his short hair and ran down the rich, dark-brown skin of his face and neck to collect in a puddle on the concrete beneath his chin. Looking short in stature, his compact frame was knotted with hard swimmer's muscles.

"Yes," replied Barry, somewhat wary of this latest interloper but willing to be friendly.

"I t'ought so," replied the young man. "I'm going to America soon," he added in an offhand way, meanwhile casually examining the couple from head to toe while he caught his breath. He frequently glanced around to make sure that no one else approached the dock, apparently feeling capable of a quick departure and, thus, quite comfortable.

"My name is Robbie," he said, still smiling and extending his dripping hand to Barry. "Pleased to meet you."

Clasping Robbie's hand but hesitating to introduce himself, Barry said, "Likewise."

Mae remained standoffish, suspicious of Robbie's motives.

Barry inquired, "Aren't you afraid of sharks?"

"No sharks inside da reef," said Robbie, ignoring Mae and addressing Barry. "You a businessman?" Without waiting for the answer, he went on. "I'm a businessman, too."

Barry narrowed his eyes, "What kind of business?"

"Little a dis, little a dat," answered Robbie, flopping his hand over and back in an accompanying gesture. He turned his head and cleared his nose into the water. "Mostly, I help people find what dey need, for a lickle somethin'."

Barry, and no doubt Mae, got the picture.

Robbie fixed his eyes not quite on Barry's, but on a spot just to the right of Barry's head, about even with his ear and directly above his shoulder. As though speaking to an imp or angel perched there, he made his proposition. "I can get you anyt'ing you need, mah-n," he assured Barry. "You wan' some ganja, you jus' look for Robbie."

"Honey, let's go," prompted Mae, realizing that Robbie was talking about marijuana. She did not wait for him but started backing away from this latest hustler.

Robbie continued to favor Barry with his smile, nonchalantly adding, "I got de best 'oly 'erb you gonna find anywhere in Jamaica. Real *sinsemilla*, all da way from Negril!"

Seeing Mae back-stepping towards the hotel, he replied, "I'll give it some thought."

"No problem. I be 'roun', whenever you ready. I take care of all da Americans, mon. I take special care of you!" pitched Robbie.

Robbie smiled one last time and eased gracefully back into the sea. He disappeared rapidly beneath the surface. Barry hurried to catch up to Mae.

* * *

It was mid-morning when the Wrights and got back to their room.

"What do you plan to do?" Mae asked softly, with a hint of reproach, "Are you going to buy some marijuana from that horrible little pusher?"

"I don't know," he answered truthfully. "Honey, he's not what I'd call a pusher."

Barry could see that Mae was perturbed but felt like she was making a mountain out of a molehill. His heart was genuinely torn. On the one hand, he had a burgeoning desire to have an adventure, a little illicit fun where nobody got hurt. He thought that was the trouble with vice, it is so tempting. On the other hand, while she had not expressed her feelings on the matter when it came up for discussion back in the 'States, he could now see that Mae disapproved of the whole idea and would prefer that he stand well clear of anything illegal. He wondered if she was right or paranoid. In any event, he seldom ignored his wife's feelings and went around behaving with selfish indulgence. Yet it was Mae's idea to bring him here, and he did not want to prudishly miss out on the fun. However, he wanted to hear her say, "Let's do it!" But that was not going to happen. It was beginning to look like he was on his own with this escapade.

"Well," she said, offhandedly, "You have as much right to fulfill your desires as I do."

They both felt the matter was far from closed, but neither of them knew what else to say.

After a few minutes, Barry remarked, "Don't worry about it, Mae. I'm going to give it some more thought before I make any decision."

"Remember, it's illegal, Honey. I don't want any trouble."

"Me neither, Mae. That's the last thing I want." He took both her hands and kissed her on the forehead. "I think smoking ganja in Jamaica is like fireworks back home."

"What do you mean, like fireworks?"

"Oh, you know, everybody knows they're dangerous and illegal, but an awful lot of people think they're fun and buy it anyway. Nobody gets arrested, not for just using."

She kissed him briefly, the softest brush of her lips against his, then opened her eyes and announced, "I hope you're right, because I get the feeling your mind is made up." She clapped her hands against her knees, stood up and headed for the bathroom.

Barry sighed, knowing, Mae was probably right because "if you have to think about it, the answer is no." But, at the same time, he already could hear the guys back home laughing at him for missing out on a golden opportunity.

Thinking about the possibility of making an illicit purchase reminded him that he needed to take the time to examine the state of their finances.

He checked the door off-handedly to be sure it was locked, then carried his wallet to the bed and got comfortable. Barry spread their resources out in neat little piles: U.S. dollars in one, Jamaican currency in another, and traveler's checks in a third. He began counting the cash when he was surprised to hear a key in their door lock.

It must be the maid, Barry thought, bad timing and called out, "Wait!"

But to no avail. Mae came out of the bathroom just as a big, young Jamaican woman in a maid's uniform barged right in. Her eyes grew large and round for the Wright's money. Not that much actually, but it must have looked like a fortune to a working-class Jamaican.

"Irie!" the woman screeched in patois, meaning "no problem, everything is cool." And she backed out of the room, closing the door.

There was an aghast silence. Barry and Mae looked at each other, both disgusted by this callous invasion of their privacy.

"Accidental? Since when do maids barge in without knocking?" said Barry.

"I don't know, Barry." Mae sounded skeptical, as if she knew better as the facts were churning in her mind. "First, someone was outside our door, spying on us. Now, somebody used a passkey to enter our locked room. I don't believe these are mere coincidences."

Barry watched her return to the bathroom then hurriedly completed his accounting task, returned their checks and currency to his wallet and his wallet to his hip pocket. Then he went onto the balcony, feeling more than a little perturbed not only by the business with the big maid.

He looked at the terrific seascape, at the horizon where cumulus clouds piled high into the incredible azure sky. Lowering his gaze, he spied Robbie, lounging against the trunk of a palm just beyond the border of the hotel compound, off toward the mouth of the White River where the fishermen had their shacks. As Barry watched, a couple of tourists that he recognized on the bus from Montego Bay, presumably staying up the beach at one or another of the hotels, approached Robbie, who rose to meet them.

Barry couldn't hear what passed between them. But it appeared greetings were exchanged, after which the couple followed the young man along the riverbank until the three were gone from his sight. He waited with heart pounding for a good 10 minutes. After which, the couple reappeared, apparently none the worse for their experience. They walked up the beach, laughing, enjoying themselves, hands in each other's hip pockets.

Stoned, thought Barry, longing deep down to be feeling as good as he thought that couple was feeling right now. He kept watching. Soon, Robbie returned to his position at the base of the palm. He looked quite pleased with himself, wearing a newly acquired pair of aviator sunglasses. Barry had the momentary feeling that Robbie was staring right at him, smiling an electric smile. He pulled back into the room, knowing that Robbie might have pinpointed his location. But he dismissed the thought as needless paranoia.

After all, what difference can it make? He surmised, Mae has us both jumping at shadows now.

He made an impulsive decision and proceeded inside to discuss it with Mae. He found her still in the bathroom, unhappily detangling her short, coily hair with a wide-toothed pick. He told her what he had witnessed and how nobody looked none the worse for wear.

"I wish you'd forget about it," she told him, frowning.

But Mae's disapproval acted to firm his resolve, as if he had something to prove.

Barry had never had the opportunity to travel to an exotic place until now, and he wanted to have an adventure. He hadn't smoked marijuana in years. Not since college, not much back then, and never anything of any quality, he admitted to himself. But he had heard plenty about the high-quality "bud" available in Jamaica. His more bohemian and better-traveled friends had assured him, time and again, that if a tourist is discrete, there is unlikely to be any problem.

"It's all part of the local economy, Mae," he explained.

Then he tried to lighten things up, borrowing an argument expressed by their friend Ron. "And what *do* you think makes that reggae music such a happy sound. Haven't you been paying *any* attention to the lyrics?"

Meanwhile, having no real idea how much money he was going to need, other than that he expected the price to be reasonable, Barry slipped 40 dollars in Jamaican money into each of his two front shirt pockets. It probably would be a lot more than he needed, but "just in case."

Barry left his wallet with the rest of their funds and his credit card on top of the dresser.

Mae caught up to him at the door, though, and kissed him. "Please, be careful."

He grinned, feeling boyish and excited, and answered in accordance with their private, established, lover's formula. "I was *born* careful. Lock the door 'til I get back."

Then, he slipped out the door and down the back stairs.

* * *

Mae locked the room door. She had given up and let Barry go looking for Robbie, but without her blessing. She went and sat down, her heart racing and not pleasantly either. She imagined that Barry's heart was racing, too, but with another type of anxiety. Without Barry, Mae felt lonely and wished she had found it within herself to be more supportive of his whim.

Suddenly she felt so insecure that she jumped up and checked the deadbolt, then hung the big beach towel over the door's louvers for good measure. She became worried that the big wall mirror that gazed decadently down toward the bed might be a one-way glass. Feeling scared and silly at the same time, she covered the mirror, too, thinking, at this rate, pretty soon I will have to ring housekeeping to send up more towels.

Mae did not want to be all by herself in the room anymore. She decided to wait on the balcony where she could watch for Barry's return. Her mind whirled frantically with thoughts of arrest and incarceration, or worse, her husband murdered and tossed into the river to float out to sea and feed the sharks, the great whites and hammerheads way out there, circling the coral reef.

Stranger Danger! It reverberated in her mind, and she wished Barry would appear.

*   *   *

As he jogged down the back stairs, Barry glanced at his watch, checking the time, which he noted was not quite 11 a.m. He exited the hotel through the door by the pool and came around to the terrace, already sweating from making haste in the oppressive heat. He hoped Robbie was still sitting by the big palm where he had seen him last.

Robbie was still there.

Barry crossed the sand casually, trying not to appear too eager. If Robbie saw Barry or recognized him from their earlier encounter, he gave no sign. He was staring at something within the compound. Barry, treading the loose sand with a good deal of hamstring-stretching exertion, revolved his head toward whatever it was that captivated the little hustler's attention. He spotted a very tall, very tanned White woman, a topless sunbather, which startled him.

When he turned back, Robbie, eyes still hidden behind his new sunglasses, was now grinning in Barry's direction. "She a German lady. Dey do like dat sometimes. She keep dat up at dis 'otel, da manager fin' out, he gonna kick 'er out."

Robbie laughed a dirty laugh, removed his sunglasses, and hung them on one hinge from the gold chain around his neck. They dangled against his bare brown chest. His red-rimmed eyes fixed on Barry as he spoke again. "So, Mista' 'I gonna t'ink about it. You make up your mind?" Robbie laughed his dirty, little laugh again and rose to his feet, dusting the sand from his hands against his only clothing, a pair of dark blue shorts. He took a couple of steps to stand close to Barry, head tilted, fixing him with one eye like a feisty little fighting cock, listening, hands on his hips.

Barry spoke softly. "I...*would* like to buy a little ganja."

Dirty laugh again. "A lickle ganja! How lickle?"

Robbie's eyes, mere slits, watched Barry closely. Barry's mouth felt dry as he said, "Enough to get high a few times, I guess...a half ounce?"

"No problem. dat not much. I can give you dat much right now."

"How much for a half, then?"

No laughter then, dirty or otherwise, money was being discussed. "I give it you at a good price...sixty dollars."

"Sixty dollars Jamaican?"

Robbie gave one sharp nod of his head. "Sixty dollars, Jamaican." He whispered hoarsely. "Dis da very bes'. She already clean and ready to smoke. No seeds, no stems. An', 'cause you a first-time customer, I give you a lickle taste. But if we gon' do it today, we got to do it now." He jerked his head toward the hotel terrace.

Barry nonchalantly turned and looked over his shoulder. Some Jamaican guy in a necktie was dividing his attention between Robbie and Barry, the persistent hustlers in the skiff — back again, and the semi-nude guest. The man turned and hurried into the hotel lobby, ostensibly to take some action against somebody or maybe everybody.

Out came another dirty laugh from Robbie. "So, what you t'ink?"

Barry hesitated. Robbie seemed like he might be interesting to get to know when he first solicited Barry on the dock but, at the moment, the smaller man was coming across as a very seedy character. Beginning to feel as if he did not much like Robbie, Barry also simply had no money to waste. He could afford to spend a little on fun, but he thought sixty dollars, even Jamaican, was a little high for such a small amount of dope. He wondered if he was supposed to haggle for it like the Jamaicans do for everything. He hated to do that; it went against his non-confrontational grain. He would rather forget the whole thing than waste their little bit of money.

Meanwhile, Robbie had begun to walk up the riverbank without waiting for Barry to decide. Barry had to act quickly.

"Robbie, wait a second," Barry called softly, starting after him.

Robbie turned around to face the big American, continuing to walk slowly backwards.

Barry tried to lie convincingly. "I haven't got that much. How about twenty?"

That elicited the biggest, dirtiest laugh yet. "Sure, 'Mr. Rich American,' you don' got no money. No problem, mon. Come to my office an' we work something out."

Robbie turned back and continued up the riverbank, the sand beneath his naked feet beginning to give way to a tangle of jungle growth, making the going a bit rougher.

Here we go, thought Barry, scattering loose sand as he took big strides to close the gap between himself and Robbie. His adrenaline kicked in as he realized he was following Homeboy here, into the jungle, his jungle, and doing it alone. Indeed, they were walking beneath big trees now, lots of them, and the undergrowth was thick enough to start Barry worrying about snakes. Then he remembered, Robbie did not have shoes on, and he did not look too worried. Barry hoped it was not entirely due to Robbie's being seriously stoned. He could no longer see the hotel, nor the beachfront suites. He concluded that was the idea.

Robbie led Barry to a path through a stand of tall bamboo grass. The path led directly down the gently sloping bank to a ford in the river.

Barry wondered what was going on, but the answer was soon apparent as Robbie began unhesitatingly to wade across. He reluctantly took off his shoes and socks, doing it quickly before he fell very far behind. No guts, no glory, he thought, pretty much amazed with his own daring. He entered the warm and sluggish water, holding his shoes and socks high.

Robbie was about halfway across, immersed up to his waist. He waited for the slow, noisy American, to be sure he was still coming, now that he knew he was in for a soaking. He sniggered at Barry's fastidiousness in keeping his shoes high and dry.

The water reached Barry's groin, thoroughly wetting his field shorts. His heart beat wildly in his chest at the thought of the mad thing he was doing, but he figured if the little bastard was going to kill him, he would have done it by now. By the time the unlikely pair staggered out of the water on the east bank, Barry, naturally high on adrenaline, was sniggering along with Robbie, though neither knew what the other was laughing about.

It did not matter. Barry was having his adventure. He hastened to get his shoes back on, pocketing his socks, then hurried after his guide. Up the bank and back into the green half-light of the jungle they went. Robbie ducked low under a tangle of vines and thorn bushes, beckoning for Barry to follow. Barry was forced to his hands and knees to make it through without suffering serious damage from the wicked-looking thorns. No one can rush up on us in here, not through that circle of thorns, thought Barry, thumbing the sweat from his eyes. Anyone coming in would have to do it low and helpless, like he just did.

Inside the thicket Robbie waited, in a clearing that looked to Barry as if it had been bush-hogged with a machete or something similar, maybe a cane knife. There was a blackened circle in the middle where the cuttings had apparently been burned, a few empty Red Stripe bottles and bits of litter, a wooden crate turned upside down to form a low table and banana leaves scattered about to sit on.

"Nice office," complimented Barry, waving away a few no-see-ums intent on entering his mouth and nostrils.

Robbie used a forked stick to drag a dirty burlap sack out from under a thorny burl of exposed roots. He untied a twist of wire from around the neck of the sack and removed a dark brown glass bottle. He unscrewed the metal cap and poured a small libation on the ground, then helped himself to a big swig, winced momentarily, chuckled, and extended the bottle to Barry.

"Have a drink?"

"Sure."

Barry took the proffered bottle, which had no label. He did not want the drink but did not want to offend either. He sat his wet ass down upon the relatively clean banana leaves, sweating profusely and puffing a little for breath. He realized that Robbie found him entertaining. The hustler watched, sack in hand, while he brought the mouth of the bottle towards his lips, catching the unmistakable aroma of over-proof rum. He wanted to, at least, wipe the mouth of the bottle, but, again, did not wish to offend. He matched Robbie's swig with a long pull of his own, hoping the high test kills any germs that jumped ship from Robbie.

The rum in the bottle was strong and nasty. Barry never tasted anything quite like it in his life. He guessed it was some sort of local home brew. Barry managed to swallow the rocket fuel without choking. The effect of the alcohol was interesting and immediate. It scorched its way down his throat and started a fire in his belly. He tried hard not to grimace but could not help himself, much to Robbie's amusement.

"Smooth," Barry managed to say at last, a big tear streaming from one eye.

That made Robbie laugh. "You aw' right, White boy," he chuckled, shaking his head from side to side and screwing the cap tight on the bottle, then placing it back beneath the snarl of roots. Squatting comfortably, Robbie reached into the sack and removed a round biscuit tin. He spread the now-empty sack over the crate like a tablecloth, then put the tin down in the middle and popped the lid. As soon as the lid came away, Barry got a big whiff of a heady, weedy, skunk-like odor.

"Come see," Robbie said to Barry, holding the inverted lid in both hands as the light reflecting from its silver surface painted the shadows beneath his chin, nose, and cheekbones an eerie jungle green.

Barry moved closer, to see inside the open tin. He had seen people's stash boxes before, with their usual plastic bags of grass, little books of rolling papers and assorted paraphernalia such as pipes and roach clips and such, like artifacts from the Earth's core or lost Atlantis. Robbie's biscuit tin contained a couple of huge buds, each made up of densely packed marijuana flowers, delicate green fronds sticky with potent, aromatic resin and dusted with red-gold pollen, and shaped like bananas, just as long and as big around. The tin also held an empty cigarette pack, a box of matches, a pair of pointy barber's scissors, and three small, craft paper envelopes stuffed thickly.

Robbie looked pleased with himself. Barry finished goggling at the big buds of marijuana and watched, fascinated, as the Jamaican proceeded to pick up the cigarette pack and open it out flat. It was made of an outer wrapper of heavy paper and an inner wrapper of aluminum foil; the foil lined with a delicate white paper, like the wrapper from a stick of gum.

Robbie expertly separated the paper and foil with his fingernails without tearing the paper. He discarded the foil and placed the flattened paper on the inverted lid of the biscuit tin.

"Now that's what I call recycling," appreciated Barry.

Next, Robbie separated one envelope from its fellows, straightened the little bent metal prong of its clasp and opened the flap. He shook a generous amount of manicured ganja onto the paper and passed the envelope to Barry for his closer inspection.

"Dat about a half."

Barry looked inside the envelope, shaking the product to see that it all looked the same and contained no unwanted wildlife or foreign objects. This was the real deal, meticulously pruned from the same buds as those in the tin. He could see and smell the family resemblance. There was one small problem. He was very sure it was not a half ounce. No way — not even if he counted the taste Robbie was busily getting together! It looked like about a quarter, he thought, then wondered if this could be some metric thing. The discrepancy did not necessarily have to be a problem, though. There was enough in the envelope to make Barry happy, if he and Robbie could come to terms on the price. Barry closed the envelope and held on to it.

Meanwhile, Robbie had finished fashioning a peculiar, fat, conical joint. He struck a match with his thumbnail and set fire to the fat end — in what Barry considered an extravagant waste of dope — brought the pointy end to his lips, and sucked noisily, inhaling the acrid smoke deep into his lungs and holding it there. He passed it to Barry, who handled it gingerly, afraid it would come apart. He never had held or seen a joint quite like that one.

Robbie spoke, his voice coming out pinched and small as he continued to hold his breath. "We call dat a spliff."

"Okay, I've heard of it," said Barry, thrilling to what he was doing and where he was doing it and with whom. Barry excitedly brought the spliff to his lips and tried to imitate Robbie's deep inhalation, but the quantity of hot smoke this delivery method produced was too much for him. He choked, cutting the volume of his toke far short of the little Jamaican's.

Barry fought to hold his breath for about 15 seconds, but the burning smoke expanded in his lungs until he could hold it in no longer. He coughed it out explosively.

That made Robbie burst into laughter, and he lost the toke he had been holding. A huge cloud of exhaled smoke hung in the air between them.

Barry laughed, too, powerless to help himself. The drug that had first seemed to expand in his lungs began to expand in his mind. The ganja was definitely a breed apart from the relatively tame Mexican potaguaya with which he was familiar. He thought, no wonder the guys back home kept insisting we had to try it! Next, he noticed the cacophony of bird song coming from the jungle all around him. No doubt it had been going on all along, but he had not registered hearing so much as a note until then. He got quite a rush from his single inhalation and knew he had to settle his business with Robbie quickly, while he still had his wits about him. He passed the smoldering spliff back to Robbie. One startling effect of the ganja on Barry's perception was to make Robbie's facial features look tiny and out of place in a head that seemed to have grown suddenly huge.

"Wow! Thanks," said Barry. "That's real nice." He cleared his throat and tried to focus on the business at hand. "Robbie, I'm here on a budget. I'm a working man. I'm not trying to insult you, but twenty is all I can afford."

Robbie passed him back the spliff, exhaling leisurely but his face got serious, "No, not for twenty, mon. I got my expenses."

Robbie sat down on the ground and fully extended his legs, folding his arms across his chest. He stared fixedly through bloodshot eyes at his bare feet for several seconds, then sat forward suddenly, slapping his thighs with his hands. "Tell you what I gon' do," he said. "I give you dat ganja for…" he looked at the forest canopy high over their heads and scratched casually at his throat, then dropped his chin and leveled his reddened gaze at Barry.

"…Twenty dollars, *and* your shoes."

"My shoes?"

Barry wondered if perhaps he had heard incorrectly; he wore a size 12, extra wide. Robbie, not much bigger than his son Zac, looked like he might wear a size 8. So, Barry could not imagine what he would do with his shoes, unless, maybe, there is a black market for shoes. They were nondescript, brown leather running shoes from the Sears Big and Tall catalogue and had cost him around $40 U.S. He had packed only one other pair, his black dress shoes, and he could not imagine himself beach combing in those.

Besides, if I pay the full $60 Jamaican, it is a better deal than that, he figured — although he knew math was never his long suit, especially with a head full of tetrahydrocannabinol. He had a fierce buzz going, probably due to mixing the smoke with the small-batch, over-proof rum. Although he really had not had all that much of either. The spliff in his hand had gone out and Barry was grateful for that. He did not want any more until this business in the jungle was over. He got up on his knees and put it down carefully on the lid of the tin.

Again, he told Robbie, "Thanks."

He untied the bandana from around his neck, intending to wipe the sweat from his face and neck, then paused with it forgotten in his hand as he reached a decision.

"Robbie, I'm not gonna trade you my shoes."

Barry unbuttoned his right shirt pocket and fished out the J$40 with two fingers. He laid the currency on the lid beside the extinguished spliff.

"I can give you forty. Have we got a deal?"

Robbie weighed the possibilities of getting anything more out of Barry. He came to a decision of his own and rose to his feet. "Okay, forty...and *that*." He pointed emphatically to the camouflage bandana in Barry's left hand.

Barry raised the square of damp fabric, "This?" Thinking it was a no-brainer since the hankie only cost a couple of bucks, he said, "Sure, no problem." He stood up and handed the little hustler the piece of printed cotton cloth. Barry, who's high had peaked and was beginning to subside, buttoned his purchase into the pocket from which he had drawn the money.

Robbie immediately tied the bandana proudly around his neck, laughing his distinctive, dirty laugh at the hard bargain he had driven. He casually pocketed the money.

The big American and the little Jamaican stood in the middle of the jungle thicket. They shook hands, each inordinately pleased with himself.

Robbie then returned his contraband to the tin, snugged down the tight-fitting lid, dropped the tin back in the sack and wired the end shut again. Then he held on to the sack, taking it with him as he scrambled out of the thicket the same way they had come in, with Barry trailing right behind him. Back at the ford, Robbie showed no inclination to cross the river and hung back. Barry pulled off his shoes and made the crossing.

When Barry Wright reached the bank and turned to look, Robbie had disappeared. Maybe moving his stash to a new secret location, Barry figured, now that he had been to his 'office.' Barry doubted he could find the exact spot again, anyway, but respected the little businessman for taking precautions. He followed the river back to the edge of the hotel compound and reentered civilization, anxious to share his adventure and its fruit with his wife.

*   *   *

Mae saw Barry from the balcony as he crossed the beach, and she burst into tears of relief. She rushed to the bathroom to wash her face, not wanting him to know how worried she had been. When she heard a key being fumbled into the lock, she rushed to the door.

"Barry?"

"Yeah, Honey. It's me," he answered, opening the door.

She hugged his sweaty neck and kissed him as he stepped inside, smelling of smoke and raw alcohol. Surprised, she wanted to know, "Have you been drinking?"

"Huh... ah, yeah. I took a drink with Robbie."

"And did you get... what you wanted?"

"I sure did," he said, obviously pleased with the results of his field trip.

He pulled the envelope from his shirt pocket and handed it to her. She opened it gingerly and peered inside, then handed it back to him.

"I see." Looking at him quizzically, she wanted to know, "Are you high?"

"I was, but I only took a little taste." He paused, as if checking his perceptions, gauging where his head was. "I guess it's pretty much worn off now. Wouldn't it be a lot more fun if we did it together and shared the experience?" He asked hopefully, "Will you get high with me?"

Fidgeting Mae said, "I don't want to. The truth is I feel high enough already." She softly refused, "I...better not."

"Mae, it won't be as much fun if I have to do it all by myself."

"It's too scary, Honey. You go ahead. I don't feel like it."

"Maybe later?"

"We'll see."

"That, means no. I'm disappointed. I wanted it for both our enjoyment."

"Really, Honey, you go ahead. I don't mind. Have your fun... I don't want any."

Barry then noticed the towel that covered the mirror, "What's this?"

Mae felt intensely uncomfortable at having to explain. She thought she felt all right now. Those feelings were gone. She simply needed to relax, so she said, "It's nothing."

"Mae, you're acting strange. Are you still afraid?"

He went over and examined the mirror, first removing the towel. "It's completely ordinary, hung against a blank wall, suspended from a picture hook by a piece of wire secured to the mirror's wooden frame."

Mae said nothing, acting both guilt-ridden and defensive at the same time. She retired to her side of the bed.

Barry did not pursue it. He took the towel with him to the bathroom. He stripped off his sodden shirt and shorts and washed up at the sink. He soon returned to the bedroom in clean clothes, with his shirt unbuttoned.

"I'll be having fun soon when I turn on." But he stopped in his tracks. "I don't have rolling papers or a pipe. I've got authentic Jamaican ganja, but how am I going to smoke it?"

Mae quietly watched while he began scanning the room for possible materials he could use. He considered using the thin paper of a Bible page, but this resort room did not seem to be equipped with a bible. Eventually, he solved his problem with the cardboard tube from a clothes hanger and a little bit of aluminum foil from some seltzer tablets. He cut the tube on the bias and wrapped the sliced end with the foil, shaping it to hold about a quarter teaspoon of dope and puncturing it repeatedly with a needle to create a screen.

"Problem solved," he said, examining his makeshift pipe with a small degree of pride. "Thanks to a design school education."

* * *

Sept. 16, midday — Soaking up sun in Paradise

Barry took his ganja and pipe out on the breezy balcony, checking to make sure no bystanders were too nearby. Then he got comfortable in an outdoor chair before proceeding to fire up, inhaling deeply and holding his breath. After about 10 minutes, Mae joined him on the balcony. He brightened, hoping she had changed her mind and offered her a toke.

She shook her head no, and said, "I just want your company."

Pretty soon Barry felt very gratified and relaxed. "Wow!" He smiled to reassure her because that was all he could say. Anything more required too much organized effort on his part.

He noticed the blue sky, humming with an almost invisible electric crystalline grid of rainbow colors that vibrated too fast to be seen by the unaided human eye. After watching for a minute or two he closed his eyes. The hallucinatory display persisted, strobing in the darkness behind his lowered eyelids. He blinked and rose from the wrought-iron chair, returned to the room, and put his pipe out of sight in his armoire, suddenly feeling a whole lot higher than he had anticipated. Not necessarily stoned but beautiful, he thought, and all of a sudden, he wanted very much to be outside, closer to the natural beauty the island so bountifully offered.

He met Mae as she came in from the balcony.

She looked at him quizzically, trying to gauge his mood, "Now what do you want to do?"

Barry acclimated to his altered state of awareness, like he never felt better in his whole life. He wondered, what would it be like to feel this good all the time? Energized and restless, he thought, we should go out to lunch. He was about to run that by Mae when his thoughts concerning the currently empty condition of their stomachs reminded him of something his mom used to say. Suddenly he had a great idea and blurted out, "Let's go swimming!"

Mae thought she heard him incorrectly, "Go swimming, now? Are you sure? It is midday. The sun's rays will be fierce. What about your recurring nightmare?"

Barry, already done pulling on his Black Watch-plaid swimming trunks, stood holding out his sunscreen expectantly toward Mae. "Robbie said there were no sharks inside the reef. From what I gather, the reef is far out, farther than I can swim."

He had to wait while Mae changed into the pretty swimsuit she had purchased especially for this trip. It was lime-green and looked nice against her light-brown skin. She took her time about it, too, fussing with her Afro and applying glossy lipstick on her lips.

When she was ready at last, Mae rubbed his pale back with the sunscreen. Then Barry pulled a gray pocket tee over his upper torso, and soon they hurried excitedly down the back stairway to the pool area. He chuckled a little more than was called for. They skirted the pool. Quite private compared with the beach, the pool attracted mostly available singles; youth, narcissism and near-nudity were the order of the day as couples paired off, working out the sleeping arrangements for the coming night.

It was well past noon by then and nothing less than a fabulous day. Major changes had come over the beach since their earlier excursions. The oceanfront was crowded and bustling. Sunbathers were scattered across the cozy sands and thrill-seekers were parasailing and water-skiing, towed by fast, powerful boats.

"Wow, the joint is really jumpin' now!" Barry admitted a yearning, something he rarely did, "What I would like to do is go snorkeling, but I don't have any gear."

"What gear would you need?"

"You know, swim fins, a mask and a snorkel."

"Couldn't you rent those things from the diving concession?"

"I suppose I could. But I don't want to spend the money. I can only imagine what the robber barons at the diving concession must charge. We've got to try and economize a little. I'll go in swimming, for now." He held out a hand to Mae. "Coming in with me?"

"Honey, no," frowned Mae, who was not much of a swimmer and rarely entered the water. "You go ahead." Mae had brought along a current, best-selling thriller. "I am looking forward to the sheer decadence of doing some light reading."

Mae chose to stay high and dry, a few yards above the tide line, showing off her slim figure as she lolled on a hotel chaise lounge in the fleeting semi-shade of a palm tree. Until that minute, Barry had not thought about what he would do with his wallet when he went in the water. But the way things were working out, Mae could hold on to it for him.

"Well, if you're not going to get wet, will you hold on to my wallet?"

He gave her his wallet, containing all their finances: U.S. dollars, Jamaican currency, traveler's checks, and credit cards. Mae, who absolutely understood what she was being entrusted with, protectively tucked it safely between her breasts, secure in the bodice of her one-piece swimsuit, then tied her white fishnet cover-up around her shoulders, shawl fashion, knotted in the front to conceal and help secure his wallet.

Barry, still more than a little high, stripped off his T-shirt and tossed it down beside Mae. Then he ran, splashing, and dove delightedly into the turquoise-blue salt water, striking straight out to sea in a strong, steady-if-not-too-fast crawl. After 15 strokes, he was beyond his depth and panting. tasting the salt of seawater for the first time in his life and having a great time. He rolled over onto his back, enmeshed in a silver skein of tickling bubbles, and waved joyously at Mae. She was looking down at something she held. He disappointedly recalled that she was reading her book. Then Mae looked up and did a quick double take, squinting at Barry. After which, she at last ventured a tentative wave to his delight.

Barry felt like a million bucks. Despite the high temperature and inescapable ultra-violet rays, the water kept him comfortably cool as he stretched his muscles. The refreshing water and exercise caused his "high" to rapidly subside to the point where everything seemed normal again to his five senses, but his thoughts kept coming rapid-fire, imaginative, quirky, and funny. He plunged beneath the water, having a ball, kicking toward the bottom to a depth of 10 or 12 feet.

Underwater seemed like another world. Barry willingly opened his eyes to the seawater's sting, but without goggles or a mask only saw a blur of bubbles, dancing sunlight and shadow on the sand and seaweed, and colorful, rapidly darting fish. He surfaced, blew like a seal or a porpoise, then refilled his lungs and dove once more. The water was warm but rejuvenating.

Barry mused, "Here I am, swimming around in the sixth largest body of saltwater on the planet. Can the sea really be the same temperature as my blood?" Thinking about blood led to wondering about what exactly keeps the sharks from swimming inside the reef. Thinking about the possibility of sharks made him wish he had a face mask so he could see things underwater.

*　　*　　*

Back on the beach in the direct sunlight, Mae soon felt little beads of perspiration on her forehead. Although her swimsuit was basically nothing more than a leotard, Mae wondered if she should have gotten a white swimsuit instead of green since white would have reflected the heat better. Wiping her sweaty upper lip with a forefinger, she felt hot but did not want to move. Mae had fallen under the spell of her book, totally engrossed in the story she was reading:

> *Susan crept down the dark, echoing corridor, frightened but too intrigued to leave this mysterious chamber that she had found behind the heavy door at the back of the wine cellar in her new husband's family manor. The walls were hung with primitive masks that repeatedly startled her — she kept taking them for living faces, swimming out of the dark in the meager light of her candle, imbued momentarily with a horrible semblance of life by the warm, dancing light.*
>
> *Somewhere in the dark, a door or window must have opened. A sudden, chilly draft made her candle flame flicker and shrink. She held very, very still, praying silently for the diminishing spark to not go out, standing stock-still in the darkness that advanced on her in a smothering rush when it did.*

In the pitch-blackness she had the sudden and certain, heart-sickening realization that she was no longer alone. She held her breath, fighting not to panic, while every nerve ending in her body shrieked. A floorboard creaked behind her with the weight of someone... or, maybe something... and a warm, moist breath fell on the back of her neck...

A big drop of perspiration rolled slowly from the nape of Mae's neck, down her spine in between her shoulder blades. She had the eerie sense of a finger running down the middle of her back. She flinched, dropping the book from her hands onto the sand. She assured herself that it was only a drop of sweat. She retrieved and dusted off her paperback, then leaned back to continue reading, looking around to see if anyone had seen her start and drop her book.

Along about then, the sun drove Barry out of the water. He tromped onto the beach exhilarated and rejoined Mae, telling her excitedly about his swim and how he survived another challenge by conquering his superstitious fear of seawater and sharks.

* * *

The hot, happy couple returned to their room, climbing the back stairs and releasing lighthearted peals of laughter like children, again in unsuspecting high spirits. They entered their room gleefully, him tickling and her giggling.

Mae watched Barry lock the deadbolt then go straight into the bathroom to start the shower. She removed his slightly damp but otherwise intact wallet from her sweat-moistened bosom and laid it carefully on top of the dresser for safekeeping. She wiggled out of her swimsuit, then gathered it up from the floor and carried it with her into the bathroom. Closing the bathroom door, Mae joined her husband in the steamy shower where they washed away the salt and grains of sand and played together happily. Soon, all worries and tension dissolved and ran down the drain with the hot, soapy water.

Following their blissful shower, the Wrights raced to the big bed and made gentle, exhausting love. They acted like carefree honeymooners, again. After the warm winds, fresh sea air, and exercise took its toll, the contented couple fell sound asleep.

* * *

Sept. 16, afternoon — Dealing with Barry's missing wallet

Forty-five minutes later, when Barry quietly eased out of the king-size bed, cooler air rushed in beside Mae, replacing her husband's big, warm body and awakening her. She opened her eyes in time to see him lumbering sleepily into the bathroom. Mae shook off the clinging cobwebs of a vague, disturbing dream. The threads disintegrated over the shifting dunes of her mindscape as she rolled over, struggling to recall where she was and whether it was day or night.

She picked up her wristwatch from the nightstand. Eventually, 3:01 p.m. registered in her freshly awakened brain cells. She looked beyond the sliding glass doors and beyond the balcony at the still sunny and balmy afternoon.

Mae realized dreamily, "Oh, yeah. Jah-may-kah, mon!" She stretched like a cat and jumped up with a wide, beautiful smile spread across her lips, energized by the joy she felt from remembering they were still on vacation!

Mae opened her armoire and took out two tubes of soft, comfy white cotton. Unrolling these items on the bed, she first shook out one, shaped like a square sack, with a slit at the top for a head and a smaller slit on each side for her arms. The other tube unrolled like a square sack to reveal a pair of shorts with a gathered elastic waistband. She slipped them on quickly and easily, then stood before the window, admiring the view. The scene outside looked fabulous. Mae felt as if she had awakened to find herself in a television episode of *Lifestyles of the Rich and Famous*. The idyllic shore of the White River Bay was filled with beautiful people under the clear skies. They played in the water and in the air; the familiar rainbow-colored parasail floated by. The piped-in music of Jamaica National Radio, surprisingly playing a current hit, broke into Mae's consciousness. The hypnotic, driving bass line made her feel like dancing. She started bopping to the beat, then soon began to sing along.

"...Now our hearts will beat as one... No more love on the run..."

A relatively awake Barry, returning from the bathroom, stopped in his tracks, a little surprised by her display of renewed energy.

"How happy you look! This vacation is turning out to be a great idea."

It had been years since Mae had danced with someone and she had never danced with Barry. She cherished the hope that, maybe someday... "Come dance with me, Honey," she pleaded, holding out her arms and still swaying her hips to the beat. But she knew he would not. Barry had never danced in his entire life. Dancing was against his religion when he was growing up, and now that he was grown, he was much too awkward and self-conscious. Sometimes she dreamt of dancing with him. He would show a lot of grace and style, and there was nothing to it. He did it with ease. But in waking reality, it was no more possible for him to loosen up and dance than to fly through the air.

"Now, Mae. You know I can't dance a lick! What I can do is show you the Big Baby."

Although Mae had seen him do this antic a dozen times or more, she laughed hysterically at the sight. Barry, in his T-shirt and briefs, pantomimed an eight-month-old tot attempting his first steps on his own. It started with the Big Baby struggling to balance on his rubbery legs, then progressed to a few faltering steps, leading to the Big Baby beginning to topple forward, barely managing with each step to put forward a leg in time to prevent his crashing to the floor. He rushed toward her, eyes big, a frightened look on his face, arms outstretched in hope and desperation, anxiously projecting *catch me, catch me if you can* — as if she had the strength. Gaining speed and sustaining the illusion of runaway Big Baby totally out of control, thrilling her with the possibility of an actual collision, then, at the last possible second when he reached Mae, reestablishing control. Rather than crushing her, Barry swept her up in his arms and gave her a quick peck on the mouth.

"Smack!" He then said, "Did we miss lunch? I suddenly have a ravenous desire to eat."

He had the dreaded munchies. So, at not quite half past three in the afternoon, he was raring to know, "What are we doing for dinner?"

"Tonight's the 'Party Night on the White River.'" She poked him in the chest for his forgetfulness, "Remember?"

"Oh yeah, *real* Jamaican food and some type of live show," said Barry. "Ms. Simpson said to meet the boats at the dock at six-thirty."

"So did you mean you want to get something to eat, right now?" she asked.

"I guess not. And I suppose there isn't enough time for us to go downtown and look around before the White River excursion. Can't dance, and it's too wet to plow," he joked, "So let's get high."

In other words, no excuse needed, and any excuse would do. Mae watched him cross to the dresser and carefully uncover his stash. She watched him select some nice, sticky bits of bud and load them into his makeshift pipe.

Barry hopefully motioned to her, "Do you want some?"

She shook her head no, "Are you kidding? Not on top of my medicine. I told you, I already feel... high," she explained, although not sure that "high" was the right word for what she was feeling. She guessed that that word would have to do.

* * *

Barry slipped on his shirt and shorts, planning to head out on the balcony to take a smoke. His pockets felt light and that started him looking around the room for his wallet, first on top of the dresser; no luck. Then he looked around the nightstand; not there, either.

"Honey, do you still have my wallet? Remember? I gave it to you on the beach, before I went into the water."

"It's on top of the dresser," said Mae answered casually, heading out onto the balcony.

A few seconds later, Barry slid back the sash and peeped out. "Mae, it's not there. Would you come here and help me find it?"

"Men!"

Mae said it in an exasperated tone under her breath. She marched confidently over to the dresser, believing the wallet was probably right under his nose. But to her surprise, he was right. His wallet was not there.

"I'm sure I put it right here," she insisted. "Are you sure you didn't move it?"

He nodded his head no, then stood and thought, plucking at his lower lip with a thumb and forefinger. "Well," he announced, "I seriously doubt it walked off by itself. I'm positive I locked the deadbolt when we came in. In fact, it's still locked, now. I checked it. If you're sure you had it when we got back to the room, then it's *got* to be here somewhere."

Together they searched everywhere. They moved out both the armoire, dresser and the nightstands to look behind them, and searched the bedclothes. They failed to find his wallet.

Mae said adamantly, "I *know* I had it when we came back to the room. I distinctly remember placing it on the dresser moments before joining you in the shower. I can picture it perfectly in my mind."

Barry wanted to believe her. Yet, he could not help harboring some doubts.

"Could you have misplaced it outside? Lost it along the beach without realizing it?"

*   *   *

Without warning, fears of conspiracy and persecution flooded Mae.

"Barry, I'm *positive* that I had your wallet when we came back to this room."

Tears welled in her eyes while they searched the room, yet again, neither speaking. Still, they found nothing. Mae shivered in fury and, out of exasperation, cried, "I know I had it!"

"I'll go look on the beach," Barry said, leaving the room.

*   *   *

Barry returned to the beach, to be sure the wallet was not lying out there, somewhere on the sand. He combed the entire area where Mae had been relaxing, as well as their route to and from their room. His search proved fruitless. There was no mistake, no misunderstanding. The wallet containing all their resources was gone.

He returned to the room to find Mae in a condition of escalating distress. He spent some time comforting her and did his best to reassure her that he believed she did have the wallet all along. This reassurance, however, left Barry sucking on the bitter taste of an unpleasant fact he was finally forced to swallow.

He stated flatly, "I guess we've been robbed."

Mae sniffled and nodded her agreement.

"Right here in our locked room. While we were in the shower, I suppose." Or, worse yet, he realized, maybe while we were asleep. But he held this possibility back from Mae, although he could have saved himself the trouble.

"I can imagine someone creeping around our room while we slept."

Suddenly, Barry's mind flashed back to the earlier, uncalled-for intrusion by the big maid. For the second time that Sunday, a light bulb went on over his head: Mae is right. It is not simply paranoia. Something else is going on!

This realization electrified Barry into action. He placed a call to the bank back in the 'States. Credit cards and traveler's checks were canceled, and arrangements were made for their rapid replacement in downtown Ocho Rios. Thankfully, the amount of cash in the wallet had been the smallest portion of their resources. Any loss, however, was a lot for the Wrights to absorb. Barry, of course, self-critically regretted his morning's nonessential splurge. His taste for ganja turned to ashes in his mouth.

He phoned down to the hotel desk and said to the young woman who answered, "Please let me speak to the manager."

"Sorry, suh, but da manager don' come to work onna Sunday. Is there a problem?"

Barry was reluctant to take up the matter with an underling. "Could you call him at his home, please, and connect me to him?"

The operator explained that the man could not be reached at all, for any reason, because, like almost all Jamaicans, he did not have a personal telephone in his home, and he would not be returning to the hotel until his work week began on the next morning. Because Barry was having a hard time understanding her accented English and because he took the ready availability of telephones for granted, she had to explain a second time before he comprehended what she said.

Mae stood by, wringing her hands and trying not to weep audibly. Nevertheless, big tears rolled down her cheeks.

Barry was growing increasingly angry and frustrated. There was only one thing left to do (a thing he somehow had hoped to avoid). "Then, I guess you'd better connect me to the police." His conversation with the police was brief and to the point. The policeman who took the call told him to stay put and await the arrival of investigating officers.

Hanging up the phone, Barry told Mae, "The police are on their way. I don't think there's anything they can do, but I feel so *violated* I think we shouldn't just let it go."

Further alarmed, Mae said, "I don't want to deal with strange, foreign policemen coming to our hotel room."

Suddenly, another frightening detail popped out, "Barry, aren't you forgetting something? You've got to get rid of that marijuana before the police get here!"

With his mouth hanging open, Barry looked at Mae as though she must be nuts -- thinking dammit he had spent good money on that stuff!

He said, "Gosh, Mae, I hate to waste it. Help me find a good place to hide it."

"No-o!" Mae wailed, feeling pressure that was defeating the purpose of being on vacation. "You saw that big sign at the airport! Please, Barry, get rid of it, quick, before they come and it's too late!"

Barry hesitated, so positive that he could find a secure hiding place if he tried. No, he decided, remembering his priorities. It is not worth the risk, and, for 20 or 25 American dollars, it was not worth the upset it was causing Mae.

"Okay. You're right, Honey. I guess I can see that."

He took his little stash to the bathroom and flushed it down the toilet. Then he destroyed his simple pipe, reducing it to tiny, nondescript pieces, which he took out on the balcony and littered to the breeze.

He remained outside with his dark thoughts for a while, awaiting the arrival of the local authorities. Before long, he noticed Robbie swimming back and forth beyond the hotel beach. He watched as he treaded water from time to time, as if watching the hotel. Barry glanced at his watch. It was after 5 p.m.

He went back inside and found Mae on the phone, talking to Zac. This contact with home had calmed her, at least a little. But he could hear that her voice was still charged with emotion. Then Barry took his turn, talking with his son briefly and then speaking with Julie, first making sure that everything at home was all right and then confiding to her the nature of the problem they were having. Mae talked to Julie and then a second time to Zac. After "Good-bye" and "Love you" and "Love you, too," the brief, stabilizing connection with home was broken.

A few seconds later there was a heavy knock at their door. Barry glanced at the clock. It was 5:15 p.m. when he answered the door to two startlingly unofficial-looking officers. These officers were not the uniformed "Red Stripes" Barry had expected.

These men were dressed in plain clothes if you could call it that. They wore stingy-brim hats, dark sunglasses in heavy frames and cheap suits that did little to hide the bulge of guns in waistband holsters. Their skins were shades of dark brown, but these men projected a degree of darkness way beyond skin color, as alien and unfathomable as any Mau Mau or Leopard cultist to Barry. Mae did not look the least bit reassured either.

The officers did not waste time on amenities but pushed in past Barry the second the door was opened. One detective, wearing a green suit, taller than his partner, eyes spaced wide apart in a pock-marked face but clean-shaven except for a pencil-thin mustache, flashed Barry an official-looking badge. The other shorter, stockier man, dressed in a tan suit with little pig's eyes, a wiry, black tuft of beard growing beneath his full, lower lip, and a wicked-looking scar running across his jaw from the corner of his mouth all the way to his ear, did not bother showing any identification. Neither officer introduced himself by name.

"You Mistah Wright?" asked the first policeman in a low voice. He removed his dark glasses and scanned the room while he spoke, then fixing his remarkably wide-set eyes on the big American, but one eye at a time like a bird of prey.

"That's right," Barry replied, adding, in a tone slightly spiked with irritation, "Won't you please come in."

He started to close the door, then hesitated. He left the door standing open and moved to stand protectively beside Mae, who was shivering noticeably.

The policemen ignored Barry's sarcasm.

Green Suit withdrew a pen and notepad from his inner breast pocket and jotted something down. Tan Suit paced slowly around the room, saying nothing. He frankly inspected Mae for a minute. He randomly opened drawers and closets, peering inside.

Green Suit snorted softly, "What makes you so pos'tive your wallet was stolen?"

Barry quickly explained the situation. Questions were asked and answered, descriptions of the big maid, the wallet and its contents were taken. A more intensive, still uninvited search of the room was made, leaving Barry wondering exactly what sort of civil rights did they have in Jamaica. He was thankful that he had listened to Mae and flushed his ganja. In fact, he was beginning to regret involving these policemen.

Both Wrights could sense a distinct air of menace coming off these men like a bad smell, and husband and wife were anxious for them to be gone.

Clearly, they were scaring the hell out of Mae. Her lower lip trembled, and she kept continuously wringing her hands.

Then Tan Suit came out of the bathroom carrying Mae's vial of pills, which he handed to his partner. Green Suit popped the cap off the amber plastic vial and looked inside, then capped it up again and examined the label.

"You sick, Mrs. Wright?" he asked.

Something in his world-weary voice suggested he seriously doubted it. Under the man's direct questioning, Mae's already badly shaken composure deserted her completely, and she could not answer. She broke down and began to bawl.

The impact of Mae's collapse was immediate. Tan Suit said something in patois, his voice coming out in a hoarse ruined whisper. The officers looked to be developing a sudden interest in conducting their investigation elsewhere.

"Yes, my wife is sick," answered Barry, stepping forward and surprising himself by adding, "if it's any of your business," holding out his opened hand for the return of the pills.

Green Suit flipped the vial of pills into Barry's outstretched palm. "We'll be in touch as soon as there are any developments," he said, and something about the way he said it made it sound as much a threat as a promise.

With that, the police exited the room, leaving Barry to comfort the distraught Mae. With the policemen gone and the door locked behind them, Barry wrapped his arms around his wife and did his best to calm her.

Mae found enough voice amid her sobs and hiccups to tell her husband, "Barry, those awful men can't be police."

"Of course, they are, Mae. Why wouldn't they be?" he responded. But he was moved to wonder himself.

He held her until she quieted, then softly reminded her, "We're still going out tonight, right? 'Party Night on the White River,' remember?"

"Honey, we've been robbed!" She sniffed a couple of times. "I don't think we should go anywhere, not now."

"Please, Mae, try and cheer up," he attempted to console her.

"It's not the end of the world. What we need to do is to go ahead and enjoy our evening as we planned." He tried adding logic, "Besides, have you forgotten that this evening's meal is already paid for? We can't afford *not* to go."

Finally, she agreed, but clearly remained emotionally upset and nervous. It was more than the robbery or the scary police. "The happy trip that I had imagined for so many months is degenerating into hassles and frightening experiences. I feel like it's all my fault, because you wouldn't have come here if I hadn't insisted on it."

"Everything will be fine." He teased, "You dragged me all the way to Jamaica to have a good time, didn't you?"

She nodded and wiped her nose.

"Then, that's what we're going to do, even though someone stole our money."

Suddenly, at Barry's last remark, Mae's head shot up and she brightened, "I just remembered something."

With Barry watching and wondering what she was up to, she grabbed her cosmetics bag. Her hands trembled as she opened it to find a little travel-size tin of aspirin, then popped that open. Inside was a small wad of much-folded paper in the unmistakable color of banknote green.

"At home the previous morning, alone in my bedroom, I wrestled with the quite trivial dilemma of whether or not to bring my little 'mad money,' I finally came to the decision to bring it but hide it."

She had shucked the few aspirin tablets into the wastebasket and nervously folded the money until it fit snugly into the emptied tin, then closed the tin and tossed it back into her cosmetics bag where it disappeared among the general clutter of makeup and medicine. She snugged the bag shut and packed it carefully into her suitcase. So, after their misfortune, she was glad she had given in to her creeping paranoia and brought the money along. She nervously unfolded the bills and gave them to her surprised husband.

"Well, well," joked Barry, his returning good humor attesting to his appreciation, "Say 'hello' to the Jackson twins. Hello, Andy," he kissed the first bill with a loud smack. "And hello, Drew." He moved to return the money to Mae, understanding that it must have been some little bit she had put aside.

But Mae refused it. "You hold on to it, Honey."

* * *

The thought that something, anything, she had done turned out for the best raised Mae's flagging spirit. In a little while, Mae, in accord with her improved mood, felt better and looked forward to the party, for the moment at least. She dared to hope that the evening would be fun.

So far, her mood swings had not developed any regular pattern but occurred when triggered by external incitement.

From late afternoon to early evening, Mae and Barry watched from their balcony as down below preparations were made for the extra excursion, Party Night on the White River. As an event planner, Mae was very curious to see how this special event was being handled.

While they watched, a dozen small boats were readied in the shallows along the eastern side of the hotel dock. Each craft was fitted with torches, fore and aft. More boats rode the gentle swells further out to sea, waiting their turn to moor at the dock as soon as the first flotilla had loaded its passengers and embarked upstream against the slowly moving waters of the White River. Soon the partygoers began to arrive, more people than the couple had imagined. Thirty or more couples arrived in the space of a few minutes, gathering excitedly on the beach at the dock.

Between curious peeks, the Wrights got dressed. They realized they had better get going and prepared to head for the dock. When they were ready to leave, as they turned off Jamaica National Radio, Leslie Gore started singing, "It's my party, and I'll cry if I want to…"

Mae noted that program choice with appropriate irony, wondering coincidence, what are the odds? A momentary twinge of fear ran through her mind, fear that someone was broadcasting a message to her in the form of those particular lyrics. She quickly extinguished that thought, stamping it dead out before it could give spark to any more incendiary ideas. As they departed for their evening of fun, Mae double-checked the deadbolt although she had watched while Barry locked their door, thinking bitterly that the lock makes no difference.

Mae and Barry were right on time. They joined the excited couples being helped into the rocking boats. There were lots of grasping hands, something Mae did not like. When it was their turn, Barry went first. He stepped down into the boat. The helping hands of the boatmen prevented him from falling until he regained his balance. He twisted to assist Mae, who was squirming in the boatmen's grasp and feeling none-too-thrilled about all that tippy boat business.

Barry helped her get seated. Then, they held hands.

Mae wanted to be with Barry and tried to push away any thoughts about the motives of those shifty-eyed Jamaicans. But, as she looked around at the sweating oarsmen who smiled at her, she suspected that their expressions of merriment were only masks. She was pretty sure that these men were disguising their true feelings. Mae didn't *think* these men capable of doing unwary tourists violent harm, she was *positive* they wanted to kill them and steal their money because everybody in Jamaica seemed to have an angle.

Not yet aware of it herself, Mae's mood was beginning to swing. Her heart teetered on the brink of that awful plunge. As the Wrights waited, several more couples were assisted into their boat in a similar fashion. Excited squeaks and squeals escaped from some of the ladies. With the boat full of people, the crew shoved off.

The Jamaicans' work-hardened muscles bunched under their dark, sweat-glossed skins as they pushed with long poles against the river's banks and bottom, propelling the boats upriver against the sluggish current. It was still early and still bright. Butterflies crisscrossed the river. As the boats passed beneath the forest canopy, they entered a zone of greenish twilight. The treetops closed overhead. The torches were ignited. The effects were both exotic and very romantic.

With a wrinkled brow and half-baked smile, Mae looked up at Barry, watching him. He gazed around in a tranquil mood, his eyes scouting the forest as if looking for something. She wondered what. Birds and animals or other natural wonders, she imagined since Barry has a good eye and does not miss much. That belief in her husband's powers of observation settled her mind momentarily.

Barry pointed and whispered, "Here is the ford where I crossed, not that many hours ago, following adventurously my little friend Robbie into the unknown."

Or maybe foolishly is closer to the truth, she thought, or maybe there is no difference.

"Too bad about my ganja. It would be a lot of fun to be high right now. I wonder how many of our boat-mates are stoned?"

Some were giggling a lot. Some were drinking from Styrofoam "go" cups garnished with skewers of fruit, presumably from the hotel's beach bar.

"Oh, well. It'll be a lot of fun, anyway," she concluded.

Mae glanced back the way they had come and saw a long line of boats, torches ablaze, moving up the muddy brown river. Black Jamaicans worked each boat, carrying partygoers. There was no snarl of outboard motors, only the sounds of nature: water splashing, wild birds calling, and the laboring boatmen who conversed in patois occasionally punctuated with grunts of effort. From somewhere upriver came the primitive rhythm of talking drums. Mae could not help but make the connection with another, earlier century.

That is all it took. Mae's mood took the plunge. Simultaneously, her body stiffened, and her mind began to race. Once again, Mae suffered the intense feeling, like she could jump right out of my skin, and that is what she did. She felt herself lose contact with the present moment, floating outside herself. She pondered that she had not been drinking or doing drugs... Then she remembered this sensation and felt pretty sure that it must be her medicine! She hung on by her figurative fingernails.

"Honey, you look uneasiness" Barry noticed. "I wish you would relax."

She was so tense that her nails dug into his hand. He gently eased out of her too-tight grasp. Mae snapped back to reality with his touch.

"Oh, was I hurting you?" She realized she was squeezing Barry's hand as tightly as she clenched her stomach muscles. "Sorry."

"No, that's all right," he soothed, giving her a smile and taking her hand again, but in a gentler grip. "Isn't this cool?"

"Yeah," she agreed feebly, looking around and noticing where she really was for the first time in a while. She took in the tranquil beauty and smiled at her husband.

Barry said, "Hey, is there anybody in there?" It was as if he could tell that she had only momentarily surfaced from some hidden depth. But he quickly laughed at his joke.

Their boat soon joined others, waiting at the landing in the jungle clearing. Torches were ranked along the wood-and-bamboo dock and the steps leading upward to the venue. Quite a crowd stood on the dock and lined the steps, waiting for their turn to move up and join the party. The sound of drums came from somewhere over the crest of the riverbank, accompanied by amplified music and a smattering of cheers and whistles.

Barry, watching and listening, said, "Wow, this is a much bigger deal than I imagined. It's like a rock concert."

Mae nodded, barely aware of Barry's remark. She fretted over getting out of the boat. Mae watched as the most recent arrivals were assisted from their rocking vessels. The crew steadied the craft ahead. Strong hands reached down to meet the passengers' hands reaching up. The partygoers were hoisted to their feet amid laughter and shouts and much merrymaking. They half-climbed and were half-lifted from the boat to join the noisy, expectant, happily milling throng. The emptied boat moved off, and the Wright's boatmen came to life, maneuvering their craft up beside the dock.

First to board, Mae and Barry would be the last to disembark. They waited while the other passengers were assisted ashore by the many strong arms and hands. The process made Mae feel very tense. She regretted ever wanting to be on this excursion. She wondered why. what in the world was wrong with her.

There is nothing wrong with you, prompted the ever-more familiar "voice" inside her head, telling her it was the tricky Jamaicans.

The Wrights' time had come. Panicky, wanting to say no, Mae realized that it was too late to back out now. She felt her heart speed up.

Barry indicated for her to go first while he assisted her from below. From above, callused big hands grabbed her soft, little ones and pulled her to her reluctant feet while the crew and onlookers laughed.

"No-o-o-O!" she squealed, but her cry of distress was mistaken for delight, and lost amid the party-time din.

Mae felt that she was being handled roughly, pulled up in a vertiginous conveyance from the rocking boat to the crowded dock, although she did not want to go. Given a choice, she would have returned to the hotel (if not immediately to America) rather than join this loud, rough mob. She barely got her feet down on the dock when the interfering hands released her *before* she had quite got her legs under her and fully regained her balance. Terrified, Mae began to topple backward from the edge of the landing. She gasped aloud and grabbed the nearest hand in the crush. She seized the hand, feeling it inexplicably *tiny*. She wondered what the hell?

She held on for dear life while she fought not to fall. Mae felt the small hand convulse in her grip and deliver a sharp stab of pain to her palm. Simultaneously, she felt a steadying pressure against the curve of her back, she hoped from Barry. The second she was safe on her legs again, hemmed in by the riot of people, Mae realized that whatever she had grasped, it had pulled free.

It couldn't possibly be a human hand… Her mind was boggled. Besides being small, it felt scaly, stick-like, and dry. She forced herself to look and, with mounting fright, she recognized the dried lower leg and foot of a chicken! The severed end was adorned with an ebony feather bound to the bone by an elaborate macramé of black thread. One long claw was wet with a rich, red drop of Mae's blood, from a small puncture wound in the center of her palm. She dropped the horrid thing as fast as she could and squeezed at the tiny wound. She hoped to make it bleed out any germs or poisons, being cognizant of what Barry and her doctors had warned about her immune system being dangerously weakened by chemotherapy.

"Barry!" she shrieked and turned, smacking into him where he stood, directly behind her.

He was smiling and excitedly awaiting their next move. "Yeah, Hon. I'm right here. What gives?"

She did not speak. She could not find her voice. Instead, she held out her hand for Barry to see the wound.

Barry looked perplexed, unsure what she was trying to show him, "Your steroid tremor?"

All he noticed was the usual steroid tremor. Mae dropped her gaze, staring at her hand like an expectant stigmatic. She saw the light flesh of her palm was whole, her skin completely unmarked!

Barry nudged her forward, along with the revelers who moved up toward the steps. She resisted, casting about with her eyes for the nasty thing she had thrown down, anything to shore up her slipping sanity! But it was nowhere to be seen, lost under the trampling feet or fallen between the boards of the dock.

"Mae?" Barry still nudged her. As usual, he was anxious, not to be the cause of any delay that kept other people waiting.

She could not remain on the dock and grope around on her hands and knees looking for the vile mojo. Helplessly, she moved up the steps, feeling scared that it had never existed and holding tight to her husband's hand, then looking to double-check that it was indeed *his* hand.

Mae worried that someone must have planted that ugly thing on her. But...who?

Belatedly she looked about her for the likely source, or to see if she could spot some culprit bearing away the macabre bit of evidence. But the press of people was too great. The makeup of the crowd shifted too rapidly for her to draw any conclusions.

Mae struggled to make sense of what had happened. She knew she had experienced a lot of frightening, disturbing feelings and emotions during the past several months. She knew these feelings were abnormal. But she had expected this vacation to relax away her stress and make her feel like her old self again. Instead, Jamaica was turning out to be a threatening place, and her experiences were going from bad to worse. If only the press of the crowd had not made it impossible to stay and search for the fetish! She thought surely she could have found it and showed it to Barry. He would have known what it was, the way he always knows weird stuff. And we could have laughed it off and forgotten it by now.

Mae suddenly realized that Barry had never seen it at all. She only had the evidence of her senses. She used to be able to trust her own senses. A new thought insinuated itself, unbidden, from her mind's darker recesses. It slipped into her brain, slick as a rapier. *Well, now that you ask, there was that business with the wolf in the closet.*

She postulated to herself that it was just nerves! Barry said so, too. But she knew she had never accepted that all-too-rational explanation as much as capitulated to it for lack of a better one or any other, at all. It was too real! She saw that wolf. She knew she did. And she knew she saw... what she just saw! Mae's heart continued to pump her a stimulating cocktail of blood, fear, and steroids. As she climbed the steps, she felt a growing conviction she was being persecuted by someone, most likely someone Jamaican.

*   *   *

Barry could tell that something was upsetting Mae. He assumed she was still disturbed about being robbed in their room and the confusing, intimidating response they got when they called in the police. He thought but did not say to her, "Well, don't feel like the Lone Ranger." He was irked to find himself elected perky, peppy cruise director when this entire business, right down to this "Party Night on the White River," rated XXX for "extra-expensive extravaganza," was all Mae's bright idea. He reasoned that she has been sick... Yet, here we are, supposedly getting the cure for her blues, only things are getting worse instead of better. That brought to mind the saying, "Sometimes the cure can be worse than the disease." But he did not want to believe that, not when they would be working the rest of the year just to pay for this tropical-vacation aspect of Mae's cure.

He wondered, if Mae was not having any fun, maybe they should try and cut their losses by heading home. Candidly, he was not quite ready to accept that idea, thinking they were lucky their losses had been small, and no one got hurt. We should get over it and try and get our money's worth out of the rest of this vacation. Finally, the only thing he could think of to salvage the situation was to pretend to be having fun in the magical hope that Mae would see him, believe it, become infected by it and finally be able to relax and enjoy herself. Then he could *really* have fun, too.

By the time the pair had made their way to the top of the steps, each was pretending to have fun, for the other's sake, out of love. For Barry, it required only a small adjustment. Mae, though, was forced to summon all her courage. If only they had shared their honest feelings, then they might have boarded the next plane out of Jamaica and forestalled their unhappy fate.

Instead, the Wrights walked out from under the overhanging trees together, precisely as the drums stopped. They emerged into a clearing the size of a football field, ringed by jungle on all sides. Barry accurately judged the size of the crowd, "A couple of hundred people, tops." Not thousands, as it had seemed at the bottleneck of the landing.

The venue in the clearing featured a modern concert stage. In front of the stage, an area of hard-packed earth served as the dance floor. Row upon row of tables and chairs filled steadily with guests. A big open tent sheltered banks of smoking barbecue grills and heavily laden serving tables. The entire scene glowed in the diffused light of early, still-steamy evening. Summer ease and jubilation surrounded them. From the stage, recorded music began launching thick sprays of notes into the air, rising, wheeling, and diving, thick as flocks of blackbirds. The air also hung fragrantly heavy with the savory aroma of hardwood smoke and tantalizing snatches of the meats sizzling on the grills, everything adding up to one hell of a party.

"This is what I wanted," Mae said. "I knew it. This should be fun."

But she looked nervous and leery of everyone. Still, she smiled when she looked at Barry and her hold on him grew tighter, as if she were more afraid.

Barry noticed the lines of revelers advancing on the food tables. Food, a particularly good idea, thought the perpetually hungry man. He spun Mae in that direction and pointed, saying, "Look! Shouldn't we...?"

Mae hesitantly nodded her assent to his gesture. On their way to the food service tent, Mae spotted the couple they met earlier. "Look, Barry." Mae gave him a helpful poke and added, "There's Bruce and Cindy!"

"Who?" Barry said, focused on *FOOD!* He had no clue.

"You know, *the Bennetts*, from the orientation, yesterday," Mae whispered.

She waved at Cindy, who waved back then paused to poke her husband. Soon everybody had waved or been poked or both. But there was no way they were going to find four seats together. So, the Wrights went one way, and the Bennetts another.

"Oh, too bad we cannot sit with the Bennetts,"

"Yeah," Barry said, feeling relieved.

Mae seemed to have some sense of safety in the company of other Americans, but not him. Barry did not want to be mean or rude about it, but he had no interest in mingling with the Bennetts. He returned his attention to the buffet that lay in wait.

"I suppose we should eat something," Mae said hesitantly.

"Now you're talking!" Barry answered jovially, once his fear that running into the Bennetts might further delay his dinnertime had dissolved. "Eat plenty. Let's be sure to get our money's worth!"

The Wrights joined the hungry horde besieging the buffet tables. Everything, even the Jamaican specialties unrecognizable to them, looked and smelled scrumptious to Barry, anyway. There were the astonishing Caribbean dishes that they both had hoped to try like spicy jerk pork and grilled chicken, and some mystery meat in the form of deep-roasted, crispy-outside, tender-near-the-bone, richly aromatic morsels.

Barry took some of each, including a scrambled-looking dish that they were informed was "ackee and salt fish" and grilled fish described as "shark" and "re' snappah" when they asked. Hot casseroles steamed in their pans, some exotic and others recognizable like red beans and rice (called "rice and peas" in Jamaica). There were unknown fruits and vegetables, singly and combined in strange salads, and familiar fare, such as baked breads, rolls, and an array of mouth-watering desserts. Beer foamed in rivers from kegs, overflowing plastic cups. Tubs of ice held headache-cold soft drinks and bottled waters. Rum punch poured from sweating pitchers.

Barry was a little thirsty and took two cups of beer to save himself from the trouble of going back. Mae was relieved to find a familiar green bottle of imported seltzer water. The Wrights left the food area gingerly carrying their trays and found two empty seats. They sat down to the feast amid the riotous company, the lengthening shadows, and the golden last light of the Caribbean gloaming.

Mae tried to be hungry but felt too keyed up, jammed like an over-wound toy. Having produced events like this one, she knew the painstaking caution that went into food preparation. So, she worried, not trusting the Jamaicans and fearing the food might be drugged or tainted.

Mae took only a little of the food, and none of the mystery meat. In her frame of mind, it looked vaguely human to her (perhaps all that remained of the last group of tourists lured away from their hotels with the promise of jungle indulgences). She tore chicken off its bones, moved bits and pieces of food around on her plate and made yummy noises, hoping Barry would not notice that she ate nothing. She drank thirstily from the bottled water that she had uncapped for herself, trusting she knew its provenance at least.

Barry drained his first cup of beer at a swallow, replacing some of the vital fluids he had sweated away copiously and constantly since his arrival in Jamaica. Then, he fell to eating his food like a harvesting machine. About the mystery meat, he said, "It has an almost lamb-like consistency and flavor, but a bit more delicate." He guessed, "Must be goat. Did you get some?"

Mae shook her head no, fluttering her lashes and smiling. Inwardly, she shuddered watching him tear into that unknown, suspect flesh with his teeth.

Barry spoke again with his mouth full, "Try some? It's different but really good. I do believe it's goat."

"No, Honey, you go ahead," she answered, thinking goat, yuck! She was quite sure she did not want any if it was goat.

Looking around, Mae could see the tables were packed with people. On stage, the band struck a quavering accidental chord, held it to the effect, and then followed it with a hard-driving rhythm in the key signature of a springy, offbeat melody. With the party well underway, bodies started swaying as the sunset scorched the sky fiery red. Then the band started jammin', rocking the clearing with powerful home-brewed reggae. Fireflies, locally called "blinkies," came out all over the clearing, and their little magic sparks flashed to the tempo of the music. Torches flared at various points around the venue. By the time the band finished their first number, the crowd had warmed up and their applause spiked with shouts and whistles.

Mae caught the intense, earthy odor of burning ganja, which wafted from somewhere, carried by "the undertaker breeze," the night wind blowing down from the mountains. She crinkled her nose at the distinct smell.

Something besides the band was happening on stage. The lights went down, except for a single spotlight. A man broke into the hot silver circle, the emcee for the evening's program of entertainment. The Jamaican man, colorfully dressed in a red suit over a yellow shirt accented with a bright blue necktie, made a jaunty impression like a pirate or a parrot.

"GOOD EVENING, EV'R'BODY!"

The emcee waved and smiled while the crowd roared its greeting.

"WELCOME TO PARTY NIGHT ON THE WHITE... RI-VAH!"

His amplified voice boomed across the venue, buoyed by the background music and the ecstatic noise from the audience.

It all sounded too terribly loud to Mae, who had put aside any pretense of eating. Barry sat beside her on his standard, church-basement-type folding chair, happily feasting and sipping his second beer, genuinely having a good time in the exotic arena. Mae imagined this party must be like Old Home Week to an ex-hippie like himself.

"My name is Michael Blackamon..." continued the emcee in a conversational tone.

The name elicited a strong response from some of the crowd. It meant nothing to Mae, but Barry whispered in her ear, "Must be a local celebrity, maybe a deejay from a local club."

"…And I'm your emcee for an evening of terrific entertainment." The emcee continued, "You and I are very lucky people. Lucky to be here enjoyin' all this good food… good company… Lucky to be in Jamaica, beautiful queen of all the islands, on this very special night."

Some wag in the crowd called, "What's so special?" Laughter smattered from various points around the clearing.

Mae thought that was what she would like to know! She wondered why did she think it was going to be so great to come here?

"What's so special?" the emcee chuckled, playing off the heckler. "What is special 'bout tonight is what's special about Jamaica."

He paused for effect, then spoke one word, "Diversity!" He said it again, a couple of times, emphasizing each syllable. "Let me hear you say it!" he cajoled the crowd.

The happy audience hurled back, "DIVERSITY!"

"Here in Jamaica, it is our motto: 'Out of many, one people.' If you doubt it, look around you." He laughed and swept the crowd with a pointing finger.

As he gestured, a second spotlight came on, sweeping back and forth across the rows of packed tables. "What do you see?"

"DIVERSITY!" called the crowd.

But, when Mae looked around, she mostly saw White people with money to burn. The light spun over the exultant faces one more time, then winked out.

"Yes, that's right…" the emcee went on, "…And I don't mean here, tonight. I mean wherever you go on this island. Jamaica has a rich history, and many fine traditions handed down from all her many peoples, European, African, Tainos, Middle Eastern and Asian… 'Out of many, must come one.'"

While the show went on, Mae sat on the edge of her chair nervously watching and listening as it grew darker. The night was ripe with alarming possibilities. She could feel it closing in around her like a black-velvet fog, making it hard for her to see anyone in the audience farther away than Barry. The spasms of torchlight did little to dispel the blackness and set the gloomy shadows free to be the first to dance.

Barry finished his final bites at last, and, feeling needy, Mae sought his hand and held it tight. He smiled at her. In the dancing firelight, he probably mistook the look on her face for that of a person having fun.

In the near dark, Mae noticed that several couples at their table openly shared a big "bomber." In fact, butane blinkies flashed all over the venue. There was enough ganja smoke in the air by then that the nonsmokers on the leeward side were getting a righteous contact high.

Mae felt ill, not so good, scared and nauseous. But she returned her fragile attention to the stage. The emcee looked different to her now, wicked and sinister — devilish was the word that breached the roiling surface of her mind. She averted her eyes, trying not to look directly at the dark figure dominating the audience. Abruptly she noticed the stage lights touching off points of reflected color from the shiny parts of the musical instruments.

To her astonishment, she saw the brilliant points of light scattering across the stage like burning phosphorus or showers of white-hot sparks. She tried blinking away the effect. Even when she closed her eyes, the shower of sparks continued behind her shuttered eyelids.

It was too freaky, she quailed. Her instincts told her to get up and run!

Mae reluctantly opened her eyes as the stage went completely dark. Fathom sparks still ignited in her field of vision, then went out one by one. The unseen emcee remarked about the evolution of music and dance in Jamaica.

"Tonight," the voice filled the darkness. "We pay a special tribute to our African ancestors, delivered in chains to these shores over 400 years ago. We invoke the spirits of our great-great-great grandfathers and grandmothers to join us in celebration..."

From near-total darkness, the backdrop lit up a livid red, the color of lava or a midnight mescaline trip lit by railroad flares. The emcee reappeared as a demonic silhouette, edge-lit in red and firelight, while the audience became awash with ruddy reflection. Spotlights flared on three drummers. The strong Black men energetically persuaded their instruments to speak together in the rapid-fire glossolalia of rhythms handed down from the dawn of mankind.

"The sonic booming of the drums is making my whole body vibrate right down to my bones like a long ride on a big, v-twin road bike," Barry whispered. "It feels good!"

Mae felt the same sensation as if her vital organs were being microwaved. She wanted out from under that punishing barrage of noise. Except, when she looked at Barry, Mae realized in utter amazement, he was having fun! She covered her ears against the assault and squeezed her eyes shut against the troubling unreality of it all.

* * *

Cowering behind her shuttered eyes, Mae missed some of what took place on stage next. But Barry did not miss a thing.

Two lines of lithe, naked female forms, visible only as voluptuous silhouettes, moved out from the opposing wings, bare feet and hips moving to the tempo, bodies swaying, hands and arms rising and falling, graceful as black swallows. They converged on center stage, forming two concentric circles, each dancer stamping, leaping, and twirling in place.

Barry, quite startled at first, quickly warmed to the current entertainment. He appreciated it to himself: now this is what he called culture, enough bouncing bosoms for everybody! He realized this tribute to Africa was an excuse for nudity, always a crowd-pleaser. Not that he minded, he admitted, enjoying the performance. The glaring red made it difficult to see much anyway. Which, he supposed, must be the whole idea.

As Barry's eyes adjusted, the flicker of the firelight added enough illumination to make it possible to see that the maidens were not as naked as they first appeared. Each wore a sheer, black body stocking that must have been sufficient to satisfy some local blue law or preserve the young ladies' modesty. And, at least as effective, thought Barry, as a light coat of spray paint.

*   *   *

While the lissome young ladies on stage charmed her husband, Mae drew on the last of her willpower not to jump up and run away. She wondered what hope she might hold for discreetly urging the entranced Barry out of there! She was too wired to sit still any longer and jolted out of her seat. She leaned her face close to her husband's, in hope that her eyes would speak for her, reflecting the desperation she felt.

"Barry, we've got to go," she hissed vehemently into his ear.

Barry looked at Mae in disbelief. Losing his patience, Barry started to say something, probably, "Are you nuts?" But he controlled any rude impulse. He could probably see that she was distressed.

He spoke curtly, "When the show's over. We are going to get our money's worth out of something on this vacation, if it's the last thing we do!" Barry's eyes searched Mae's for several seconds, then he pleaded with her. "Please, Mae, try and relax."

She got his message, but somehow in the darkness or under the unusual circumstances, he missed her urgent, unspoken S O S. Barry held her hand and returned his attention to the show.

Mae realized with a sinking heart, he's not ready to leave. She swallowed hard, throat and mouth completely dry. When she looked around, she caught frowning Jamaicans staring at her, here and there, signaling their disapproval of the way she called attention to herself. Of course, as soon as she spotted them, they broke off staring and feigned dumb, happy absorption in their jobs or the show. Expending the last reserves of courage, Mae sat her shaking body back down, thinking she had to stay and watch over Barry! She believed in her heart that she would take a bullet for him, and he would do the same for her because they loved each other.

A disparaging sarcastic remark ricocheted like a buckshot through her mind, *Some guardian angel!* And Mae was ceasing to find the familiar, second-person voice odd and beginning to think of it as Stranger Danger, who then said: *What do you think you can do?*

Trying to ignore her feelings, Mae focused on the show but what she saw looked shockingly obscene. Naked Black orgiasts engaged in cult worship, presided over by some piratical devil, some obeah man dressed like a Caribbean buccaneer. She thought she heard wolves or wild dogs snarling in the jungle or along the fringes of the venue, but it was impossible to be sure over the noise. Her nerves began to hum like guy wires in a gale-force wind and, despite the sultry weather, goose bumps rose on her skin.

Mae survived by doing what recent experience had taught her to do. Once again, she maintained her cool, trying to subdue her suspicions and panic anxiety while she still could. For Mae, it was getting harder and harder and scarier to do. This time while she dizzily hung on, chimerical colors and patterns like the rainbow-gossamer of spider webs throbbing on her neural net fizzed in the air wherever she looked, eyes open or closed.

Meanwhile, Barry looked like he was enjoying this act a lot. Perhaps because it had come as a surprise and because it was playfully sexy but not embarrassingly dirty. The audience around him enjoyed it, too. It struck the right note of innocent decadence.

With a musical crescendo, the dancers fled the stage. The lights came down to darkness again, to the last plaintive notes of the flute and appreciative noise from the audience. Mae abruptly became aware of a solitary figure, passing into her peripheral vision. The mysterious figure faded quickly into the darkness when she turned her head to try and see better. It loomed beyond the limits of any good, usable light. She pretended to watch the show while counting her rapid heartbeats. She hung on, hoping her panic would subside or some hero of her hidden mind would rush onto the flight deck of her forebrain, seize her controls, and bring her down safely.

There were lots more acts, featuring less and less continuity. Mae was beyond caring. But she could appreciate the value of "diversity" as a theme because you can present anything you have a mind to or costumes for. She was pretty sure there would be ancient Romans in it, if they had togas lying around.

*   *   *

Barry whispered, "All in all, it's a surprisingly good show."

Nagging at Barry was the fact that he felt sorry for having been so abrupt with Mae. It had been an unusual occurrence for which he blamed his stress and planned to apologize later. He winced, realizing that Mae had not said another word to him. She sat hugging herself, rocking a little in her seat and looking off into the darkness from time to time. He felt bad about ignoring her request to leave and hoped she was enjoying the show. Even if she would not admit it to him now, which is likely, he thought, women being the contrary creatures they are, he decided he was going to make it up to her.

For the next 45 minutes, music dominated the show, supported now and again with dancing performed primarily by the young ladies who had already generously shared their ample talents. There was some giddying calypso music from a steel-drum band and some fun acoustic music in a style called mento, a Jamaican roots of reggae music very popular in the 1940s and 1950s. Then the band returned with a couple of ska numbers followed by some Rocksteady. Finally, they settled back into a solid reggae groove, good and loud. Faces and diverse images flashed on the rear screen in a great light show with lasers and chasers and everything. The total performance had gone on for over an hour by that time. The number reached its climax, and the light show peaked and shut down.

The audience rose to its feet, clapping and calling, "More! More!"

For the next several minutes, only the flickering torchlight lit the venue, plus the moon and stars, and the occasional meteor. The heavens were awesome.

Barry said, "Mae, this is so cool. You know, the night, the sky, the party, and Jamaica."

* * *

Suddenly another of the obscure, bipedal shapes walked through Mae's peripheral vision. By that time, she knew better than to turn her head if she wanted to continue to see it. The shape stopped even with Mae, and only a few yards past the zone where the unsteady torchlight failed. She held her breath and tried to hold her visual field still. Only the near-total darkness made that possible; if the stage lights had been up, her eyes would have had to move her focus about to keep the afterimages of the brightness from temporarily blinding her.

Through the corner of her trembling eye, she saw the first figure joined by a second, and moments later, a third. They had circled the venue all night, seemingly being drawn to the show or the drums but afraid of the light, Mae supposed. She wondered who they were, party-crashers?

Mae thought maybe Barry could make them out. His eyes were way better than hers.

"Barry," she called to him softly, laying her unsteady hand on his forearm.

"Yeah, Mae?" He inclined his head and his nearer ear toward her lips.

"See those people over there in the darkness?" She punctuated her question with a very brief extended forefinger.

He squinted hard in the direction she indicated, then answered, "Umm, no... I guess not."

They were still there. She could tell from the corner of her eye. Barry was always spying details but with his unhindered, full-frontal vision. Mae had learned to use the entire seeing capacity of her damaged eyes, but she could not think how to describe to him the mechanics involved in being able to make them out using only peripheral vision.

"Okay, never mind," she told him, her hand quavering as she withdrew her touch.

Barry looked at her quizzically for a couple of seconds, then reclaimed her hand in his own. "It's a pretty good show, huh?"

"Yeah," she replied, without much enthusiasm, still worried about the light-shy lurkers in the darkness.

"Now, aren't you glad we stayed?"

No, she thought but for Barry's sake answered, "Yes."

Truth and lies were losing their sharper distinctions for Mae. Telling the truth had become a matter of telling Barry what she thought he most wanted to hear, to make him happy, and telling everyone else, particularly the Jamaicans, as little as possible, preferably nothing.

The show resumed. The principal lighting returned to brilliant red.

At center stage there stood two uprights supporting a horizontal bar, the necessary apparatus for dancing the limbo. Male dancers set the horizontal bar ablaze.

Mae, too nervous to stop scanning from the corner of her eye, saw a curious thing happen in the dark where she had last glimpsed the shadowy figures. Once again, the indistinct forms had moved, awkward and shambling. They came to the edge of the audience where they craned their necks toward the performance as though anxious to watch and no longer shy. Mae wondered, again, what on earth was happening? Then she noticed the creepy way they moved, and thought, there is something wrong with their legs. She spun around to look at Barry, who must have noticed them by now! But all he looked at, right then, was the flaming finale.

With her acute new perception, Mae looked at what was happening on stage. The daring performers risked a scorching as they duck-danced the limbo, lower and lower, beneath the blazing bar. She saw through the semblance of a pleasantly exciting entertainment to the hellish spectacle it concealed. Reality after reality peeled back like the layered skins of an onion until she saw not Jamaican performers but lost American tourists, threatened with a red-hot, roasting spit. All that flickering, fiery, red light was too intense for her to stare into for very long.

She returned to skittishly monitoring the movements of the unknown shamblers in the dark. She watched them push up to the edge of the crowd, almost but not quite in among the growing number of people now standing, applauding, starting to gravitate toward the dance floor. Oddly, Mae alone watched their mysterious presence; no other partygoer showed any awareness of their existence. And then it came to her. She theorized that it was the red light! If red light is invisible to them, they must think they are still concealed by the darkness, just like the wolves in Wolf Woods!

Nerves wired, neurons overloading and shorting out like a bad string of Christmas lights, Mae tried once more to get a direct look, and, that time under the red glow, she succeeded. What she saw would haunt her dreams for the rest of her life. Mae watched some very odd-looking people, Black people judging by their hair texture and facial features, although their skins were ashen and gray. Both men and women, dressed in tatters and patches — old-fashioned oddments of an earlier century, seemed drawn to the celebration going on in the clearing.

Mae rapidly blinked several times, but they did not go away. Puzzled, she thought they must be part of the show.

Then she saw the reason for their difficulty in walking, something seriously wrong with their legs. Her mind clattering like a bad clutch, reality slipping and failing to engage, she never stopped trying to make sense of what she was seeing. No way, she thought, their knees bend the wrong way! Mae felt her courage dissolving away when she realized more. Her mind affirmed, it is impossible, but their heads are on backwards!

Mae's terrified gaze leapt from one to another walking impossibility. Her mind flashed back to the chicken-claw fetish, could there have been a drug on that claw? Her mind then flashed on another factor, goat meat! A sacrifice? But she ate none of it! Reeling, Mae squeezed her eyes shut for a slow count to ten.

Then she tried blinking, but the poor souls with the alignment problem refused to be blinked away.

That did it! The lid was completely off the toy box now!

After what she saw, on top of the bizarre and frightening things she had witnessed all evening long, Mae had more than she could stand. No more *maintaining,* too many of her circuits were blown. Mae was reduced to her instincts, pure fight-or-flight panic possessed her.

"Barry!" she screamed, startling her husband, so much that he half-choked on a mouthful of beer and slopped the remainder down his shirtfront. Before he could turn in the direction of her place at the table, Mae was *gone.*

Looking back at him, Mae could see that he spun around on his chair, coughing suds, until he located her. He turned his chair over backwards in his haste to go after her.

She kept moving fast in the direction of the landing, staying close to the protective circles of torchlight.

"Mae, what's wrong?" he shouted. "Mae! Wait up!"

But Mae showed no indication of ever slowing down. She moved with a purpose, a big tear rolling down each cheek, and her chin quivering. Clearly, she was determined to leave the venue, *with* her spellbound husband or *without* him.

Barry, forced to get up on his toes and run to catch up, reached her at the top of the landing. Catching her by the wrist, he demanded, "What the hell is wrong with you?"

Upon first being grabbed, Mae bucked and whimpered. Then, recognizing Barry, she stopped struggling and tried to collect enough breath to answer him.

"I don't know! I don't know! I saw..."

Mae wanted to tell him about it. But it was too frightening to acknowledge, let alone attempt to explain. She formed descriptive words in her mind. But she stopped short of saying them aloud. She knew that what she was about to say would sound, could only sound, insane!

Mae improvised, panting, "Barry... I was dizzy. I... thought I was going to faint."

She jerked against his grasp, pulling in the direction of the stairs to the dock and the waiting boats below.

"What? I had no idea you were feeling sick. Now I can see *something* is wrong, you're hyperventilating."

"Yeah, I'm still feeling queasy. I'm... I'm nauseous."

"Is it something you ate?" Barry's eyes were still adjusting after the intense colors and bright lights. "It's hard to see what you look like by the moon and stars, and the unreliable torchlight. Do you feel like you're going to faint?"

"No, no. I don't think so." She did not admit that she had had nothing to eat since breakfast. "I don't feel good. Can we go back to our room?"

She pulled toward the steps again. Down below, they saw a waiting boat. The boat floated in torchlight, a fiery halo reflecting on the river's invisible gurgling surface.

Mae was terrified of the Jamaican boatmen. The dancing flames and capering shadows made the men look like minions of hell.

Stranger Danger, the voice in her mind spoke again, *The devil you know is better than the devil you don't.*

Mae did not like that advice, but it made sad sense to her. A boat had been their way in, and a boat would have to be their way out. From the top of the stairs, she stole a nervous glance back towards the clearing, afraid of the twisted shamblers' pursuit.

Barry, noticing how badly her legs shook, gave up all resistance. He let her lead him down the stairs.

When they reached the dock, a boatman beckoned Mae to come on. She flatly refused the suggestion that she go first,

"Uh-uh, no way! Barry, you go."

"But Mae…"

"No buts, just go!"

Barry and the boatman looked at each other, puzzled. He shrugged and, with the help of the boatman, stepped unsteadily into the boat.

Mae refused all help but her husband's, shrinking away from the Jamaican's helpful hands. Barry strained to help Mae safely aboard as the crew steadied the boat.

Mae huddled against her husband, as far from the boatmen as she could get.

"Irie," said the boatman, gesturing to Mae, no problem.

"Mae, you're shivering," Barry noticed with surprise. He thumbed the sweat out of his eyes. "Why are you chilled in the sultry night air.? I hope you're not feverish."

The boatmen plied their craft. They steered to the middle of the open river. Once there, surrounded by open water and with no pursuers in sight, Mae felt a slight relief. She stopped staring back at the top of the landing and concentrated her worries on the ominous boatmen. She saw that, intimidating as they looked, the Jamaican workers meant them no harm. The two men did their jobs and paid the Wrights no mind. Her worried husband slid his arm around her and pulled her close. Mae regretted that mysterious circumstances had robbed them of a sublimely romantic moment.

She sighed. Unhappy, but more in control, Mae looked at Barry and apologized, "I'm sorry to spoil your fun."

Barry accepted the situation and showed his consideration. "I don't care. You're not spoiling anything. I love you. And, if you're not feeling well, you belong in our room, in bed. So, that's where we're headed."

Mae's consciousness still fizzed and sparked occasionally, but the neural pyrotechnics were primarily over. Left frightened and exhausted from fighting phantoms, Mae's mood grew as black as the river and the burning kerosene smelled stinky. She clung to Barry and avoided looking at the boatmen all the way back to the hotel dock. The romance drained out of the night.

*   *   *

Sept. 16, evening — Feeling powerless and confused

The Wrights returned to their room around 10:30 p.m.

Mae's eyes darted around the room, marveling that the place looked like it had when they left it. Sinking down on the bed, she felt lost and empty with her emotions in a hopeless tangle. She looked up at her husband, a trembling hand pressed to her mouth, worrying about what he would think if she told him what happened and how could she describe it.

Barry seemed determined to find out if she was really sick. He stooped and felt her forehead. "You feel feverish. Could be sarcoidosis," he unhappily supposed. "Mae, did you take your pill this evening?"

Lost in her thoughts, it was several seconds before his words registered. Once they made sense to her, she started, "No... I guess I didn't."

"Here, I'll get some water," he offered. "You'd better take it right away while there's still food in your stomach."

Mae did not have the heart to tell him that she never ate a bite. "Thanks, Honey, I can get it." So, she walked to the bathroom on legs that still felt unsteady, got her pill, and swallowed it on an empty stomach. She remembered that she had not put in her eye drops either. While she worked at instilling the drops, she considered how best to tell Barry about her bizarre experience at the party.

Suddenly, she heard a loud banging at their door. Mae jumped.

She heard Barry say, "Just a minute." As he moved to answer the door, she heard him mumble, "Who in the world...?"

She stuck her head out of the bathroom, thinking on a positive note that maybe it was Bruce and Cindy Bennett. They might want us to come out for a nightcap.

Barry opened the door... to the two alleged policemen, who rudely elbowed their way past him into the room. Shocked, Mae inched her way into the room, keeping her back close to the wall and watching the whole scene as if it were surreal theatre.

* * *

Without the slightest small talk, Green Suit held up Barry's familiar billfold and asked, "Is this your wallet?"

"It sure is." Barry reached out and took the wallet. He immediately saw the cash was gone. But the wallet still contained the checks and credit card. He wondered how the thief knew they were unusable. Unless... Something smelled fishy. Barry asked, "Where did you get it?"

Tan Suit answered. His voice came out ruined, hoarse and whispery.

"An honest fisherman, he fin' your wallet, floating on the water. *I'm* t'inkin' you lose it there in the first place."

Barry felt the wallet curiously dry for having been found floating on the bay. He recognized the lie.

The first officer shot an impatient look at his partner then took control of the conversation. "This honest fisherman is waitin' downstairs. A gentleman would reward him, so why don't you put on your shoes, Mistah Wright, and come downstairs *now*."

One thing Barry knew, he would rather not go anywhere with these two jokers. But he put on his shoes, uncertain about these developments, thinking just fucking great!

Mae cowered where she stood, looking unsure. Barry did not want to leave her alone. Recognizing her concern, he gave her a reassuring kiss, a smile, and a chuck under her chin.

"Lock the door, Hon," he said casually. "I'll be back in a few minutes."

She warned, "Barry, be careful!" He mouthed, "I was born careful."

Mae followed the men, keeping her distance from the police. As they marched Barry out the door, she promised, "I'll be waiting for you!"

* * *

In an instant, her husband was gone. She shot home the deadbolt, which still did not make her feel safe. Alone in the hotel room, Mae worried frantically, tears filling her eyes.

How can this be happening? Why did they have to get robbed? How did the Jamaican police find Barry's wallet so fast? Why did the policemen come back to their room so late that night? Why did Barry need to go see the Jamaican who found his wallet?

The whole business put her mind in a tailspin. Their perfect vacation ruined by someone who had robbed them in their room, their only private sanctuary in Jamaica. The police had found the wallet but not the culprit.

The policemen had to be crooked. She did not believe for one second that those Jamaican men were cops. Mae did not *think* those men capable of doing unwary tourists violent harm, she was *positive* they wanted to kill them and steal their money. She felt powerless and confused.

Mae could not sit still. She paced back and forth around the bed wondering what she should do. She did not know anyone at the hotel, except the Bennetts. But she truly did not *know* them. She had no idea what room the Bennetts were in. She consoled herself by believing that they were in the hotel and no harm would come to Barry with other people around.

Would it? Oh, my!

All at once, she heard noises coming from the hallway or another room. Fear gnawed at the pit of her stomach, and she still felt like they were being watched. She got scared and quickly went and put towels in their proper place over the door and mirror. Then a startling memory started to haunt her mind.

What about the disappearing mojo and poorly glimpsed spirit ancestors with their heads on backwards? What was that all about? She shuddered to *think* about the White River party and the impossibilities she had witnessed there, happening along the ragged edges of her reality. Mae tried to put it out of her mind, but that only made it harder and harder to do. Could it be real? She wasn't superstitious. Her common sense revolted at that suggestion. She convinced herself it had to be nerves. If only she could relax.

But Mae remembered the fetish. She remembered things happening like a bad dream. She remembered how frightened she was at a lot of disturbing sensory perceptions. Mae also remembered feeling better when she relaxed in Barry's arm on the river, and it seemed like none of it was real when they got back to the hotel.

The spirits at the party looked as real as the wolf in the closet but 10 times scarier, she thought. Then her logic clicked. That's it! The Night on the White River was simply my imagination. I have been wound up too tight. My imagination is working overtime. I have got to relax. Mae reminded herself that they had worked hard, and would be working harder, to pay for this trip. But they owed this vacation, this time off, to themselves. And she planned to get things back on track.

Suddenly in a panic, she realized, those Jamaicans took away my husband! What if Barry does not come back?

She calmed herself, again, thinking you are going off the deep end when there is nothing to worry about! She told herself: Barry's gone to thank someone for returning his wallet; his wallet has been returned; we had a minor setback; and it is not the end of our vacation. Mae reassured herself, everything is going to be fine. She decided that she simply needed to relax and enjoy herself, and stop having these crazy nightmares.

* * *

As Barry's nightmare on the White River Bay got under way, he reluctantly accompanied the policemen down the back stairs. Flanked by two strangers who were armed and no-doubt dangerous, he tried to appear unconcerned, but his "spider sense" was definitely tingling.

Once on the ground floor, he started to head toward the lobby where he expected the fisherman to be waiting. But strong hands from either side seized his arms. Cruel fingers thrust deeply, seeking the shocked nerve bundles beneath his quivering muscles. Somebody gripped his right thumb, bending it backwards while his hand was jammed up between his shoulder blades. Resistance on his part would result in a dislocation or a broken bone. With exquisite pain enhancing his confusion, he was spun about and muscled out the poolside door.

Barry shouted, "Hey!"

Water witches lit the scene with their eerie, dancing light. The pool deck was deserted. No one heard his stifled cry.

He was instantly punished with more pressure on his pinioned arm. He saw stars and shut his mouth, gritting his teeth. His elbow was at the snapping point. Barry hurt too much to resist. He was muscled 30 or 40 yards into the deep shadows at the bottom of the garden. There, he was released with a vicious forward shove that propelled him, stumbling into the center of a small clearing. Shocked and shaken, he tried to make sense of the sudden crude treatment but couldn't.

All he could think was: What the hell is going on?

His arm throbbed and his pressure points still hurt. He was out of breath, and his startled heart hammered. Barry could not see the men until he separated their shapes in the darkness from the shadows. There they were a couple of yards away and closing.

Barry tried to collect his wits and slow his breathing. He hoped to salvage some control or come to an understanding, realizing that there was no sidestepping *this* confrontation.

The moon stood mute witness to the encounter. By its wan, silver light, Barry recognized the location, the secluded English garden. He faced the rose arbor and the stone bench where he and Mae had kissed. As never before in his life, he was full of adrenaline and jacked up like a clown. He grasped how much it meant to him to survive the assault and get back to his wife and their quiet, ordinary life.

In the web among the roses, another silent witness opened eight intelligent eyes.

Barry stood up straight in the darkness, willing his legs not to shake, and turned to face his assailants. With sobering clarity, he heard the faint music from the distant venue and the vibrato of the lizard chorus, underscored by the policemen's loud breathing. A shadow detached itself from the surrounding gloom and a small figure entered the clearing. The figure stepped up between the two policemen and spoke to Barry.

"So, here comes de White boy to show jus' how much he 'preciate my honesty." The voice broke into a familiar, dirty laugh. "You high, now, bruddah?"

The policemen joined in the laugh at that.

Something finally clicked in Barry's brain. Jackpot! He recognized Robbie. Things started to make sense. He felt certain, this is a hustle! Knowing that gave him hope they would not hurt him any worse.

Done with joking around, the small hustler pushed his face as close to Barry's as their difference in height allowed and hissed, "Take care of me, now!"

Barry was less afraid yet still pumped full of adrenaline. He felt humiliated and angry because he was set up and tricked into a shakedown. But there was no way out. He had to go through with it. Barry figured the smartest thing he could do was to get it over with. Give them what they wanted. He put his hand in his pocket...

"Slowly!" Green Suit warned.

Barry eased his hand out of his pocket. He held all the cash he had, a total of 40 bucks, American. As he handed it over, he realized, thank goodness I have this money because of Mae. He prayed it was enough to satisfy these predators.

Robbie greedily snatched the money from Barry. The little criminal's moment of happiness lasted about one second. In turn, Green Suit snatched the money from Robbie. He glanced at it quickly and then tucked the money in his pocket.

Robbie looked surprised, then angry for a second. He began to whine, "But, you said..."

Before Robbie could get out another word, Tan Suit grabbed him by his pencil neck. Moonlight glinted dully on the snub-nosed revolver Tan Suit held pressed against the startled hustler's skull. He cocked the hammer.

"Irie!" choked Robbie. He was not laughing anymore. "Everyt'ing's cool, bruddah!" He tried to pull away, certain all he could expect was a bullet in the brainpan.

Uh-oh, dreaded Barry, if this is how they treat their partners...

Green Suit said something urgent in patois, disrupting Tan Suit's concentration. Tan Suit turned to argue. Robbie, sizing up the situation with a hustler's resiliency, pulled free and slunk back into the shadows. The sound of progressive rustling, stumbling, and cursing from the dark garden marked his rapid departure.

Tan Suit cursed and started after Robbie but was called off by a hiss from Green Suit. That one waved Mae's two twenties in Barry's face. When their gazes locked, Barry did not like the meanness he saw playing behind the man's cold stare. He was not so sure anymore. Murder or no murder, was it all the same to him?

The Jamaican spoke in a clearly threatening tone. "You are a stingy man, you know? Sometimes, bad t'ings happen to stingy people. I know you *want* to do the right t'ing, now, don't you? Before somet'ing bad happen to you or maybe to your pretty wife..."

When he heard the threat against Mae, Barry felt like his heart choked on a big gulp of blood. He wished they were safe at home and had never heard of Jamaica. But he was "in" too deep to give in to fear, and he knew it, hoping his best chance now was to brazen this thing out. So, he refused to drop his eyes. He felt Tan Suit's hands as they pulled and tore his pockets inside out. He heard the man curse, again, at finding nothing.

Barry figured if they were going to hurt him, they would do it now.

Green Suit's cruel, wide-set eyes narrowed to slits... and then shifted to Barry's left wrist. He grabbed it roughly and, when Barry offered no physical resistance, went on more gently, unbuckling the birthday watch.

Holding it up in the moonlight, Green Suit appraised the heavy diver's watch briefly. He pocketed the watch and returned to staring directly into his victim's urgent eyes.

Barry summoned his courage and centered himself, awaiting the pleasure of the dangerous man with the equally dangerous partner who moved around in the darkness somewhere behind him. His heart thudded out the passing seconds until...

...The cruelty in the man's eyes suddenly shifted to amusement. He laughed and made a dismissive gesture to his unseen partner.

Still sniggering at his private joke, he told Barry, "Enjoy your stay!"

With that, Green Suit shouldered past Barry and disappeared. Behind Barry, Tan Suit sniggered, too. Then a heavy foot made rough contact with the base of Barry's spine and drove him forcefully, staggering and off-balance, across the remainder of the clearing. His shins collided painfully with the low stone bench. He tripped forward, falling into the rose bushes and scratching himself deeply on the thorns. His face went through the spider's web. Barry got up quickly, absurdly concerned that he might have accidentally injured or killed the pretty spider.

As his intimidators vanished into the night with his cash and his watch, Barry stood in the dark, scraped and bleeding, his whole body shaking. He felt very lucky to be alive and relatively unhurt. He tried to calm down. He heard the men's laughter somewhere up near the road. There was a brisk exchange in patois followed by the sound of car doors slamming and an engine starting. Tires chirped, and the car sped away.

Barry suddenly shivered and realized he had been sweating profusely. He picked up his bandana from where it lay since it was turned out of his pocket. He slowly walked the distance out of the darkness and back to the zone of muted light surrounding the abandoned pool. He started to wipe his stinging face. There was a scrabble of busy legs against his cheek, and Barry realized he was wearing the spider along with a good deal of its web. He freaked, fearful of being bitten. He swiped frantically at his face with his bandana, not wanting to squash the thing on himself. He managed to dislodge the huge but harmless spider, which fell to the ground and promptly disappeared into the hibiscus.

Alone on the pool deck, Barry felt a rush of nausea and his legs got rubbery. He sank onto a lounge chair, feeling like he had just walked away from a motorcycle crash, pumped full of adrenaline one minute, exhilarated, knowing how lucky he was to be alive; next minute shaky, exhausted, and self-pitying.

Everything is all right, he told himself. Mae is all right. He focused on remembering that he had managed to act like a man when it counted. The foolish impulse to cry passed with nausea, leaving him curiously drained of emotion. He urged himself up, remembering that Mae was waiting. Barry crossed the pool deck and entered through the back door.

As he climbed the stairs to their room, he worried about how much he should tell Mae.

* * *

Before he finished unlocking the door, Mae's voice quivered, "Barry? Is it you?"

"Yes," he replied, entering the room and closing the door.

She rushed into his arms, pressing her wet face into his neck, and whimpered, "Are you all right?"

"I'm okay," he said, glancing around the room and realizing that Mae had been busy. A towel hung over the door, another one covered the wall mirror.

"Honey, you're bleeding!" She examined the deep red scratches on the soft insides of his forearms and touched the stingy ones on his throat, which made him jerk away. Fresh tears welled up in her eyes. "What happened?"

Mae pulled him into the bathroom with only slight resistance. She began cleaning up his wounds, first with hot water then with peroxide and cotton balls from her cosmetics bag. Barry's need galvanized her out of her distress. She stopped crying, although she almost lost it again when she saw his badly scraped shins. While she cleaned his wounds, he told her what happened, trying to be truthful while minimizing the menace.

He told her that the "cops" (if they *were* cops) were definitely "in on it."

He left out the part about Robbie, feeling guilty for having dealt with the hustler against her better judgment and because he was unsure of the part the hustler played in the actual robbery. Perhaps Robbie was simply enlisted to round out the cast of characters then jettisoned as excess baggage when their elaborate scam deteriorated into an old-fashioned roughing off.

Sad and dazed, the Wrights had a lot of questions on their minds about what had happened and what caused their situation. Mae looked miserable but did not cry any more. She hugged her husband as if she were grateful to have him back alive. On a gut level, Barry felt more and more like a bullied schoolboy, angry and vengeful and anxious to report the matter to someone and get some action. But who? The American Embassy crossed his mind. On an intellectual level, however, he figured any agency powerful enough to do anything would triage their problem as too trivial to be worthy of its attention. In the final analysis, he concluded, ah, the school of hard knocks. He guessed they would be forced to chalk this one up to the high cost of tuition! But Barry could not let go of his injured macho anger. Initially he stored it out of his way, to be dealt with some other time, putting on an attitude of bemused resignation. To soothe Mae and calm her fears, and to cover his embarrassment, he joked about his injuries.

"It's no big deal. It looks worse than it is." He bragged, "Hell, when I was a kid, I got hurt worse than this lots of times, falling off my bike."

They laughed. But it was nervous laughter edged with apprehension. Of course, what Barry *was not* telling Mae was how close he probably came to being murdered. And Mae *was not* telling him about the unexplained sensory phenomena that reached a peak during the White River party. They both chose to spare each other the details of their fear and disappointment. Mostly, they wanted to know: why us?

The Wrights went to bed without answers, clinging to each other, restless and silent but unable to call off the parade of conflicting emotions. It was hours later, almost morning, before the sheer weight of exhaustion knocked them out. Mae first, then Barry.

CHAPTER SEVEN

Monday, Sept. 17 — Being encouraged to stay

Mae was the first to wake up the next morning. She looked over to see Barry lying beside her, still sound asleep. The first thought in her head was how much she loved him and how secure she felt to have him nearby. As she gazed at his face, she glimpsed the scratches on his throat and the memory of what had happened the previous night came flooding into her mind, filling her with anxiety.

She sat up instantly, feeling threatened. Her eyes darted this way and that, determining whether she and Barry were alone and safe. She rocked the bed too much.

Barry awoke with a start. "Mae, what's up?"

"Nothing," she answered quietly, sorry about waking him up. "Uh, when I woke up, I remembered what happened last night and I got scared for a minute."

"Oh, Honey. Are you all right?"

"I guess so," she sighed. "Are you awake?"

Rubbing the sleep out of his eyes, Barry said, "Yeah, now I am." He sat up in bed and started examining his forearms.

Mae leaned closer and peered over his shoulder to see, too. Her heart ached whenever she saw his scratches and scrapes and the colorful bruises on his shins. She caught his chin and turned his head to see his throat, as well. She noticed the scrapes were red and the skin irritated.

"How are you feeling?"

"Not too bad," he said with a wry smile, hunching his shoulders. "At least the scratches don't look infected. Thank you for cleaning them up last night."

Mae hugged him. Disappointed in their treatment at the hands of the Jamaicans, Mae contemplated about whether things would have been better if they had picked another destination. They had spent so much of their hard-earned money to get to Jamaica only to be treated so poorly. She blamed herself for bringing this bad luck down on their necks and started to apologize.

"Honey, I'm so sorry…"

"Don't be," he interrupted. "It's not your fault."

"But it is," she said, feeling overwhelmingly guilty. Mae slouched back against the headboard, feeling crushed. "I'm the one who insisted on taking this vacation."

He came around to her side of the bed and sat down beside her. Barry took her hand and generously said, "Yeah, but we talked about it. We both decided. Don't blame yourself."

Crumpling her face, she asked timorously, "Why did this have to happen to us?"

"I guess it was simply bad luck!"

Mae wondered if luck was all it was. In the clear light of morning, she thought it was more like a dream than a real happening. They were robbed and that was real, she reasoned. The crooks came back, took Barry away, and hurt him. That was real, too! Her periodic distortions were causing her to question her judgment regarding what was real and unreal around her.

Barry asked her, "How are you feeling?"

Mae despairingly answered, "Terrible!" Then, sobbing again, she added the unthinkable. "Maybe we ought to go home." She saw him wince at those words.

"Bail out in the middle of such an expensive trip!"

Of course, he still had no idea of the extent of the bitter disappointment and frustration that had come periodically to haunt Mae, since she continued to put on a brave face, for his sake.

"Believe me, I know how you feel," Barry settled down, gingerly touching the red edge of a scratch where it chafed against his collar. He blotted at the thread of fresh blood with his clean bandana before it could leave a stain on his T-shirt. "But we have to consider: if we leave early, we'll forfeit all the money for our lodging."

"I know," Mae said solemnly. She remembered what the travel agent had told her months ago. "And there's a hefty penalty for changing our airline reservations. *And*, on top of that, we already paid cash for the bauxite-mining tour and luncheon, tomorrow."

"Right," answered Barry. "Plus, we came all this way and haven't seen much."

"You know, Honey, if we do decide to leave early, can't we take it easy today?" Mae visualized, "I want to have a calm, relaxing breakfast, have fun mingling with some real Jamaicans at the open market, and enjoy an exotic Caribbean lunch. You know, *be* on vacation. Then we can decide what to do. How does that sound?"

"What has happened to our "honeymoon" isn't fair. You work so hard, and so do I. We deserve one easy day out of this trip. So, yeah. That sounds fine. We're supposed to pick up our traveler's checks downtown, anyway. Might as well go to the market then." His eyes brightened, "But, right now, let's get dressed and go have a leisurely breakfast. I could use some Blue Mountain coffee."

* * *

The subdued Wrights walked into the dining room where the wide-open French doors showed the rising sun had ushered in another beautiful day and loosed the doctor breeze to play, lifting curtains and tablecloths and peeking under ladies' skirts. Other guests breakfasted happily, but the milieu of gaiety was lost on Barry and Mae.

Lagging behind the maître d' and moving like a wooden puppet, Mae found herself lost in a world of thoughts when a whisper reached her ear.

"What's this hoity-toity, coolie royal Jamaican got to strut about, He's only some Englishman's house nigger!"

Mae started and turned her head. Shocked to hear someone say such a thing, she looked but saw no one nearby who gave any sign of having been the whisperer. Then someone laughed loudly. It was a Jamaican man at a not-too-distant table.

Mae took it personally, thinking I bet his joke was aimed at me! She stiffened and sulked. Her spirits dropped even lower when the maître d' led them, as usual, to a table in the colored section of the segregated dining room.

"I'm about this/close to being ready to go home," Barry admitted in a whisper, obviously bummed out about the seating, too. "The game may not be fair there, either, but at least we know how the game is played!"

Mae was not helping him feel better. She knew he worried about her and usually took comfort in her pleasure. But she had nothing upbeat to say.

They both spread their crisp linen napkins on their laps and desultorily gave their order to the prim, obsequious waiter. They sat listlessly, eyeing each other with comforting smiles and waiting for their order, when Bruce and Cindy Bennett, who were about to be seated in the all-White dining section, noticed them.

Cindy broadcast, "Yoo-hoo, Mae!"

Despite her mood, Mae cheerfully smiled and waved at the friendly White couple. Regardless of Barry's reservations regarding the Bennetts, she liked them. She thought, how pretentious can they be when she goes around hollering "yoo-hoo"?

Barry looked annoyed that those rich people wanted to join them, but he quickly reconciled to the situation, especially when he noticed how happy it made her.

Cindy bounced on her toes and said something in Bruce's ear. Bruce, in turn, said something to their waiter. The waiter nodded and stepped quickly aside to make room for the Bennetts to cross out of the "Whites Only" section and join Mae and Barry at their table.

Up close and in the clear morning light, Mae determined that Cindy and Bruce were a bit older than them. As Cindy merrily took a seat across from her, she admired her cool cotton sundress with its tasteful seashore-and-dunes print in peach, sand and green. Mae thought Cindy looked so cute! And Bruce looked dashing in a loud, tropical-print shirt, displaying brilliantly colored macaws and toucans against a black background.

Barry looked at Bruce's shirt and whispered to her, "I wouldn't be caught dead wearing that shirt. But it looks good on Bruce."

Mae started feeling self-conscious about what she had on. Her plain old, white sleeveless blouse and beige cargo shorts seemed "dressed down." Without thinking about it, she had automatically responded to her low spirits that morning. Her sense of discomfort increased as the waiter took the Bennetts' breakfast order.

The four Americans chatted about their activities during the last two days while they waited for breakfast. Bruce and Cindy went out a lot and hit all the hot spots. They also enjoyed nature, hiking, and such, the things of more interest to the Wrights.

"I've been doing a lot of snorkeling," said Bruce. "Nothing fancy, this time, no charters or anything." He swept his hand in a gesture meant to encompass the bay. "I've been having a ball right out here."

"It *is* beautiful," remarked Barry. Mae nodded in agreement.

"As beautiful as anything you'll find anywhere on the island, except, maybe, the Falls," commented Bruce. "Would you like to go snorkeling together?"

"We *might* take you up on that another time," Barry said. "But this morning Mae and I have some business we have to attend to."

Unable to contain her curiosity about Barry's scratches any longer, Cindy clucked her concern. "Look at you, you poor thing. Did Mae do that? Honestly, you two!"

Mae's head shot up, "What do you mean?" She looked slightly suspicious but risked a half-smile, suspecting her leg was being pulled.

"That's what Bruce said when he saw Barry scratched up. Well, what he said was..."

Bruce tried to interrupt. "Shush, Cindy!"

"...'Row-w-w-r-r-r! I bet Mae's a regular tigress in bed,'" Cindy finished her quote, batting her eyelashes innocently at Bruce.

Bruce blushed a little. "All right, you've had your fun."

Everybody laughed. The couples felt comfortable in each other's company. Mae did not mind the good-natured kidding. The lightness of the conversation with these Americans struck the warm note she needed.

Barry also seemed to find the Bennetts were not the snobs he imagined. The couple showed three traits he found most admirable. They were candid, down-to-earth and appreciated his brand of humor. Finding them pleasant, he forgave them their money and adjusted his attitude, accepting their offer of friendship.

When the laugh was over, things got quiet for a minute. Barry, with a sober look on his face, then said, "Bruce, let me ask you something. Do the locals ever... bother you?"

Mae's smile faded. She cut her eyes to Barry and wondered if he was going to tell them. She flicked her gaze to Bruce as he responded.

"Sometimes," he said. "I guess you get used to it. When they learn they can't get a rise out of you, they leave you alone."

Bruce had not missed the way Mae's eyes hardened, following the conversation. He inquired softly, "Why? Have you had some trouble from the locals?"

The four Americans sat blinking at each other in the awkward silence for several seconds until Barry spoke again. "A little."

That was enough to pop Mae's cork. She gushed, but in a stage whisper meant to carry no farther than the table and the ears of her husband and the other two Americans, "We were robbed in our hotel room!"

"Oh, no!" commiserated Cindy, her China-blue eyes getting big as saucers.

Cindy reached across the table and squeezed Mae's hand. There was no longer the slightest trace of ditziness to her voice when she asked, "Do you want to tell us what happened?"

Bruce nodded, then sat back, all attention.

Mae and Barry exchanged looks. Then Barry cleared his throat and began the explanation. They took turns telling the Bennetts their story. The tale unfolded across the breakfast table, ever so slightly sanitized, leaving out Barry's previous dealing with Robbie and, of course, Mae's disclosure of her personal illness and problems.

The Bennetts were properly shocked and sympathetic. Nevertheless, though they sympathized, as seasoned visitors to Jamaica they knew "these things happen."

Cindy told Mae, "I know you're angry, right now, but don't let it make you feel hateful. Try to remember, the average Jamaican is as honest and law-abiding as you or I." She crossed her heart.

Keeping his voice low, Bruce said, "The truth is, with the aluminum companies pulling out, unemployment is way up. The government is admitting to 30 percent, so the real figure is probably higher." A waiter passed within earshot, so Bruce waited until he was gone. Then he continued, "You were the unlucky recipients of a spontaneous economic adjustment."

That's an understatement, to say the least, thought Mae, bitterly. She said, "When the police arrived, they weren't even wearing uniforms." She went on, complaining incredulously, "It seemed like they had one badge between them and neither showed us any ID! How can you know who to trust?"

Bruce considered, "Well, there are plain-clothes detectives working vice and narcotics, things like that. Still, you can't be sure you ever really spoke to the police since someone from within the hotel made the connection for you. I don't know, but the whole thing sounds to me like it might have been an 'inside' job."

Barry and Mae nodded. It had to be a strong possibility.

"Or they might have been crooked officers, capitalizing on our bad luck to bolster their retirement plan," theorized Barry. "And the hell of it is..." he concluded, "...We'll never know."

Mae announced flatly, "We should go home."

"Oh, no!" chorused Bruce and Cindy. They looked at each other and laughed, tickled by their uniformity of thought.

Then Bruce sobered and explained, "That's exactly the wrong thing to do."

"Sure," Cindy chipped in, "You'd go home bitter and probably never travel again. Now *that* would be a real misfortune, and you don't need to let that happen."

Bruce said, "Guys, I wouldn't be saying this to you if I didn't believe it's true. That was a nasty trick someone played on you, especially for such a cute couple on their first time out. But think about it. How much money did you lose?"

Barry blinked a couple of times while he processed the math. "Well... around a hundred dollars in cash, American and Jamaican. There was our credit card and our traveler's checks, too. But I canceled those by phone, right away."

"Okay, then," Bruce nodded. "So, your cash loss was small."

"And my watch!" Barry interjected.

It was Mae's turn to pipe up. "Two-hundred and twenty-nine dollars," she whispered. "But that's not even it. It was special, from me and Zac, for his birthday!"

"All right then, three-hundred thirty dollars. The point I'm trying to make is, if you had to spend that much on a *car* repair, would you throw away your car?"

Mae and Barry thought about it for a minute.

Before either could speak, Bruce added, "Think of it as a *vacation* repair, then, if that makes it any easier. Don't throw away the rest of your vacation! But, while you're at it, think about this, too..."

Before Bruce could finish making his point, Cindy pressed his arm to signal him to let her make it for him. She leaned across the table and spoke softly, in a serious but upbeat tone. "You're practically guaranteed disaster proof, now, 'kiddies.' The chances of anything *else* happening to you guys are astronomical! So, remember," She resumed her more usual, comfortably ditzy persona, shrugged her shoulders, and smiled, "As the Jamaicans keep telling us, no problem!"

Mae liked Cindy's attitude and wished it were only true.

Cindy has no idea of my problems, she bemoaned. A lot of scary things had happened to her, which she had not shared with Barry. Day by day, incident by incident, Mae grew more suspicious of her medication, more reluctant to take it and more likely to forget. But the price she already paid with a portion of her eyesight served as a constant, depressing reminder of what she was in for, if she chose to forego the steroids that held her blindness at bay and kept her sarcoidosis from killing her.

Come to think of it, Mae realized, I have not had my pill yet this morning!

She needed to take it soon, but she felt nervous and reluctant to do so in front of Bruce and Cindy, and the hovering Jamaicans for fear of revealing any weakness that might increase their image of vulnerability. Two Black servers who began setting the food on the table annoyed her. Mae thought they were obsessed with the table arrangement, adjusting and rearranging the place settings to accommodate the addition of the Bennetts. Soon a third waiter who came to refill the coffee cups bumped into her.

Mae's new voice was conjectured up, *All this fuss is a smokescreen to allow these sly Jamaicans to hover over our table, lending their sharp little ears to our conversation.*

She tried to inconspicuously take her pill. During a long sip of water, trying to make the damn pill go down, she tried to convince herself that Cindy was right: there is no problem. The coffee steward, about to refill Mae's cup, distracted her. About to put down her glass and tell him, "No, thank you," Mae made momentary eye contact through the transparent glass, a kind of fisheye, magnifying effect.

She set the glass down with a thud and a splash, doing a double take because Mae thought she saw green, neon dollar signs glowing from deep inside his pitch-black pupils! She knew, no way! Another glance affirmed his eyes were quite normal. But Mae's anxiety made her feel as if a cold finger probed her innards.

She shifted her gaze from the waiter to Barry. They made eye contact, and he winked at her, which startled her into wondering what that was supposed to mean. Mae's questioning brown eyes roved to Cindy, then kept moving until they locked with Bruce's confident half-squint, and she felt fidgety. She thought he was waiting for me to say something, anything.

So nervously Mae asked, "Do you think we can...*relax?*"

The coffee steward beat feet back to the kitchen.

"Of course, you can relax," Bruce assured her. "Vacation repairs, remember? Come on," he said, smiling his best salesman-of-the-year smile. "Lighten up. It's not such a big deal. You came a long way to have some fun, so don't let a little mishap stop you now." He added specifically to Barry, "I'm sure you'll be fine. But if you're still a little uncomfortable and you want to play it absolutely safe, stay in the hotel compound or stay with your tour company's organized trips."

Barry replied, "Well, perhaps you're right." But Mae suspected that he was thinking, "Sure, more field trips would be a great idea if we had your income."

Finished with breakfast, the Bennetts said they planned to spend much of the day beach combing, sunbathing, and snorkeling. The Wrights admitted that they were not sure what their plans would be, yet. So, they exchanged well wishes before parting and promised to get together again, if the Wrights decided to stay.

Barry and Mae traversed the hotel's corridors and climbed the stairs back to their room. Mae felt jitterier than she did before breakfast. Still, she regretted leaving the company of the Bennetts. They appeared to be a loving couple, like herself and her husband, trying to relax and get away from their ordinary routine. They seemed normal and agreeable to Mae.

Upon reaching their room, the Wrights locked themselves in. They gravitated to the pleasantly breezy balcony and sat down.

Mae sat passively watching the waves, the breeze teasing at her short strands of hair. She realized she was seeing better. Speaking of seeing things, she worried, then tried to put the troubling thought out of her mind, unable to deal with the question of the reliability of her own senses. She thought about telling Barry about her sensory perceptions in the dining room and at the White River. Yet, thinking about it was enough to bring on a certain creepy feeling, an automatic stab of high anxiety.

"Maybe now we can decide whether to stay or go," Barry began. "What do you think?"

Unsure of what she wanted to do, Mae said, "Well, I don't know if I feel better or worse after talking to the Bennetts." Then she added, "One thing I do know is that I don't want to talk to anyone else about the robbery. It's too eerie. Whether we stay or go, I just want to get on with our lives. Yesterday's gone."

Barry sighed, then shrugged. Then he brightened, as if he had a bright idea. "Since we don't *know*, we're going to have to trust our feelings. So, how do you feel?"

Mae thought, this whole thing keeps going round in circles. She did not answer his question. Instead, she asked one of her own. "Barry, do you think we're safe here?"

"I'd like to," he replied. "I mean, as safe as anybody else. I guess I don't know why all our friends came to Jamaica and had such a great time. Yet, you and me..." his voice trailed off.

"Almost like there's a curse on our vacation," Mae let slip, very casually.

Barry looked serious. "Well, let's not go *that* far." He reflected for a moment, then said, "You know, Bruce and Cindy made a good point, about the odds being pretty slim of anything else happening to us."

"Do you really think so?" Mae wanted to believe it. "It sounds logical."

"Also, something else. We will lose a lot of money if we go home ahead of schedule."

Mae spoke slowly, thinking about her words. "Well, maybe we should stay... and keep to the hotel compound for the remainder of the week."

"Except we were *in* the hotel when we were robbed," Barry reminded her. "And, *on the hotel grounds* when the police assaulted me and robbed us some more. I can rationalize the loss of the money, but the theft of my birthday present!"

Taking the watch made it personal. Barry would never stop smarting over it. He gazed across the beach, scanning the fringes of the hotel grounds, the waters of the bay.

"Are you looking for your little friend Robbie?"

Failing to discover his whereabouts, he said, "For the first time, the little bastard is nowhere to be seen. I'd like to pound the diminutive hustler into sand like a tent peg."

Mae remembered another flaw in the plan to stay close to the hotel. "I wanted to go to the open market downtown," she said, imagining the market like a cross between the Saturday-morning farmers' market in Evanston and a reggae Renaissance Faire. Working up her enthusiasm for staying, she stressed, "So did you!"

"True," Barry nodded his agreement. "That still sounds like it ought to be fun, Honey. Although we can't afford to spend much, I *would* like to see more of the local arts and crafts."

"Well, let's go downtown, pick up our traveler's checks and maybe mingle a little with the people, at least." Mae concluded, "Then we can decide whether to go home after that."

Before they settled on it, the telephone rang. Barry went inside to take the call.

Mae, although curious about who might be calling, fell into one of her fugue states, considering for the hundredth time if she was being silly. Could she be imagining a threat that did not exist? If she was right, she thought, the Jamaicans were plotting to hurt them, and she wanted to go home! Then, she thought, again. But what if she is wrong? If they leave, and she is wrong, they will be throwing away everything! They were supposed to eat, drink and be merry. The money is spent. So, they might as well enjoy it! Right? Cindy was right about one thing, if they went home now and wasted money, Barry would never travel again — not ever!

Barry started talking, before he finished opening and closing the balcony door, "That was a Mr. Dunbar, the assistant manager of the hotel. He's coming to talk to us about the robbery."

"Now?" Mae felt iffy about another strange Jamaican coming into their private quarters. "Oh, no! Didn't you tell him we didn't want to talk with anyone else?"

"Yes, but he was persistent. He seemed like a nice enough person, so I gave in."

* * *

Sept. 17, mid-morning — Meeting with a real cop

Barry opened the door for Mr. Dunbar about quarter past nine in the morning. Mae stood nearby anxiously, hoping they would get this business over in five minutes.

While Barry scrutinized the man's identification, which did have a black-and-white photo and job title on it, she appraised his appearance. He wore a bright yellow short-sleeved shirt and nicely pressed, dark brown slacks. She also glanced at the man's shoes, which were black, shiny, and extra thick-soled, but wondering if they the good, supportive footgear of a big man or could this guy really be a cop. After the dubious presence and frightening impact of the other "police," Mae thought him questionable. This guy looked more like a real cop, or at least some security professional, than the ones who identified themselves as the police. Still, she felt far from ready to trust another Jamaican stranger.

In a stand-offish manner, Mae conducted the man similar in build to Barry out onto their balcony. Barry, a little taller than Mr. Dunbar, brought up the rear. Once they got comfortably seated around the small outdoor table, Barry did all the talking. This clear, brown-skinned man with an open face and a beautiful set of ivories listened to their story with evident concern. He simultaneously seemed to be taking their measure. After Barry had his say, Mr. Dunbar asked for more-detailed descriptions of the "big maid" and the nameless policemen. His face lit up in recognition of something. He shook his frowning head and muttered, "I see." He did not explain. He pondered. When Mr. Dunbar swam up out of his thoughts, he returned his attention to them.

"I'm getting an idea of what happened here." He paused and then went on, "I regret this thing happened to you and in our hotel. I assure you, we will do everything we can to make sure such a thing never happens again! Please accept my sincere apology."

"Well, thank you," said Barry. "We appreciate your concern. But let's get something straight, right off the bat." A ragged flush crept up Barry's neck as he confronted the Jamaican. "We're only here for a few more days if that. We sure don't want any further involvement with the police."

"No, I should think not," agreed Mr. Dunbar, taking Barry very seriously. "But trust me when I tell you, there are... *certain* people in Jamaica who concern themselves with putting a stop to this sort of thing. I'm thinking of an important man in Kingston who would be very interested to hear your story. I need to call him."

Barry tried to object, "Please don't trouble yourself..."

"I must," insisted the assistant manager. "It's my job."

"Well understand that we don't want to meet with any more police, in our room or at a police station," Barry informed him.

"Well... In the meantime, please don't let this unfortunate incident spoil your fun." He said very plainly. "Nothing else like it will occur during the rest of your stay."

Mae wondered sourly and increasingly suspiciously if that was a guarantee and how much was it worth?

Mr. Dunbar broached a new subject, smiling and his brown eyes twinkling. "There is one thing you can do for me. You mentioned that you have business at the travel office. I would consider it an honor if you let me drive you downtown."

Although pleasantly surprised by his offer, Mae's distrust of Mr. Dunbar and his true motives deepened. She worried about what sort of ride he planned to take them on.

She promptly replied, "Oh, no. But thanks."

"I think we *should* go with Mr. Dunbar," Barry quickly overruled her.

Mae trusted Barry, but she thought Barry does not see things the same way I do.

"Well... If you say so," she yielded, worrying that Barry was awful quick to trust this Jamaican bozo.

"Good," said Mr. Dunbar.

They agreed to meet him in the courtyard in 10 minutes. He left the room.

Barry seemed shocked by Mae's rapid dismissal of Mr. Dunbar's kind offer.

"Mae, I certainly trust Mr. Dunbar much more than any local, certainly more than some strange cab driver."

"I don't know, Barry. Do you really think that guy is an assistant hotel manager?"

"What I think is that he's a strong, self-assured fellow, whatever his exact profession. And I, personally, very much want someone like Mr. Dunbar on our side."

Mae applied to her trust fund and found it bankrupt. She decided she would follow Barry's lead but remained distrustful of Mr. Dunbar and his motives.

Maybe I'm being overly suspicious, she admitted. But, in her heart, she could not ignore a dreadful feeling, like a timer ticking down toward doomsday.

* * *

In the courtyard, they found Mr. Dunbar in an even brighter yellow car than the shirt he wore. He pulled up in his tiny, two-door import, which was in nice condition. Barry folded the seat forward to gain access to the back, but before he could make his move, Mae ducked in, inserting herself into the back so her longer-legged husband could take the roomier front seat. She did this automatically, in the same spirit that caused her husband to open doors for her and make sure she got served first before he would eat.

With the three of them arranged as comfortably as the compact car design would allow, Mr. Dunbar showed every confidence in his little four-cylinder engine's ability to pull their combined weight. Revving the engine, a lot, and feathering the clutch a little, he got them climbing up the drive to the highway.

Barry complimented Mr. Dunbar on his nice, clean car. "Is it almost new?"

Mr. Dunbar smiled. "This car is 10 years old. Would it surprise you if I told you that it has over 300,000 miles on it?"

"Really!" Barry looked impressed. "You obviously take excellent care of it."

Mr. Dunbar laughed. "I do. I had the engine rebuilt once, and I just had it painted last year. In Jamaica, a person counts himself lucky to have a car at all. We can't afford new cars, so we take the best care we can afford of the one we have."

Mae knew he had to be talking about the mixed-blood middle class since she was pretty sure the majority of Jamaicans counted themselves lucky if they owned so much as a bicycle. But she kept her comment to herself and listened while the men talked.

Mr. Dunbar was a good driver, capable of holding his own in the erratic, aggressive Jamaican style when necessary. Most often, however, he exhibited a more reasonable, defensive-driving technique.

Suddenly Mae noticed a rare road sign and began worrying about their fate, wondering where he was taking them. Experiencing a renewed flutter of anguish, she asked suspiciously, "Are we on DaCosta Drive? I thought this highway was called the A3."

"That's true. But it is called DaCosta Drive in 'Ochi'."

"Ochi?"

It was the first time Mae or Barry had heard the nickname for Ocho Rios. So, Mr. Dunbar gave them a little background.

"Ocho Rios means 'eight rivers' in Spanish," he explained. "But it is a corruption by the English of the Spanish name 'chorreras,' meaning waterfalls. Ochi was a quiet little fishing village when I was a small boy. It was quite a different world, back then. But bauxite mining began, and the aluminum company opened a deep-water pier to handle the big freighters. Before long, that meant cruise ships, too. We were discovered. In the 1960s, the resort development began. The serious tourist industry started. Today, Ochi is the second busiest tourist destination in Jamaica." He became quiet for a moment, his thoughts turning inward. Then he added, in a voice grown almost wistful, "It's a good thing, too. The aluminum companies are all gone now."

It became obvious to Mae that Mr. Dunbar wanted the Wrights to stay on in Jamaica. In his low-pressure way, he seemed determined to do whatever he could to convince them. He went on talking, pleasantly telling them quite a bit about the variety of attractions in and around town: the beautiful beaches, the spectacular golf courses, the dancing and parties of one kind or another, the many botanical gardens, the colorful birds and fishes...

...*The dangerous, dishonest people,* Mae, in her covert voice, finished for him. Well sure, suspected Mae, if we go home, it is money right out of his pocket. She suspected none of this was a coincidence; things were becoming clearer, details still emerging to support her suspicions.

They had reached the center of town. Mr. Dunbar showed them the civic clock tower as a landmark reference, spun them through the traffic roundabout and pulled them up in front of a gray stone building. He waited in his car while the couple went inside and got their travelers' checks restored. However, they were unable to secure a replacement for their credit card. It would take a week to 10 days, so they might as well be directed straight to their home address, which is where they would be by then. They were going to have to get along without it.

The building that housed the travel office was primarily a bank, so Mae and Barry seized the opportunity to exchange some checks for Jamaican currency at a better rate than they had received at the hotel. Once again, they had cash in their pockets.

While clambering back inside Mr. Dunbar's tiny vehicle, Barry asked, "Is it very far to the open market?"

"No, not so far but too early. It's only 10 o'clock. The market opens at noon."

So close, and yet. For the time being, the smartest thing to do was to return to the relative safety of their hotel. Disappointed, the Wrights rode back with Mr. Dunbar to Caw Park Beach Resort. Primarily Barry conversed with him.

Mae remained withdrawn, outwardly quiet and passive, inwardly far less trusting of this Jamaican than her husband. She kept wondering, "What is this guy's angle."

Mae Bea Wright had arrived at the distinct conclusion that in the eyes of every Jamaican they met, their presence represented "a few more dollars." To the Jamaicans, they were not people, Black or White. They were *tourists*: fools to be bested in trade or witless sheep with money in their pockets, waiting to be fleeced.

Mae's new voice sarcastically surmised: *Going into town and spreading some cash around might be a good idea. Maybe that's the solution. If we spend more money, all the scary bullshit might stop, and the Jamaicans will leave us alone. Then we could have a good time!*

Pulling up in front of the hotel around 10:30 a.m., Mr. Dunbar asked, "So, what will you do for the rest of the day?"

Barry told him, "We want to visit the open market. So, no doubt, we'll be returning to the downtown area later by taxi."

With her skeptical voice persisting, Mae thought, *Honestly, what a big mouth Barry's got! We should keep our own counsel!* She considered, somewhat in jest, *Don't tell that phony Jamaican our plans. He is likely to send more thieves after us!*

Mr. Dunbar courteously wished them a pleasant day and left.

Mae and Barry walked back to their room, passing several Jamaican employees of the resort in the hallway. They could not help checking out the gossiping women, but there was no sign of a particular "big maid."

Sheltered in their room, Barry admitted, "I think we *should* stay."

"What makes you think so?" whispered Mae, as if someone might be listening.

"Well, Mr. Dunbar is looking out for us now. The hotel management certainly has taken an interest in restoring our good opinion."

"It seems like it, doesn't it?" she replied, not so certain. But there was no denying that Mr. Dunbar had been accommodating with his manner and time.

"I'm beginning to think no one would *dare* bother us again while we're here."

Mae looked pensive. She rattled her head, disgusted with her cynicism but unable to ignore all the unhappiness and distress they had endured. Even a good rattling failed to dislodge the negative feelings clinging to her like so many bats tangled in her hair. She knew how she felt. Then, again, she had not exactly been feeling normal throughout the trip, even before they had been victimized. She did not know what to think; how she could be sure. The only thing she felt sure of was Barry. She totally trusted his instincts and judgement.

"If you're sure," she replied. "Let's stay."

"Then it's settled. We're staying and, from here on out, nothing's going to stand in the way of us having a great time!" He hugged her tense body, and cajoled her softly, "The marketplace is coming to life about now. Let's get going if you still want to go."

"Yeah, I do," she said, kissing him, then slipping out of his embrace to get ready. She tried to adjust her attitude, reminding herself that they were returning to the downtown area for a day of shopping and exploring. Finally, they would get to see and interact with real Jamaicans.

They headed downstairs, trying to figure out how to go about rounding up a taxicab with a trustworthy driver. It turned out to be easier than expected. Downstairs, surprisingly they met their tour rep at the front desk. Apparently, someone (presumably Mr. Dunbar) had already appraised her of their misfortune.

Quickly hanging up the courtesy phone when she saw them, Prudence Simpson approached them and said, "Are you two all right? I am so, so sorry to hear what happened."

I'll just bet you are, thought Mae's cynical self, growing fascinated with the woman's very sharp-looking incisors, which bobbed and flashed, respectively, as she talked. *You're probably in on it, you Creole fraud!*

Mae seemed to be growing beyond trusting *any* Jamaican.

Barry sighed and said, "Well, we were pretty upset, but we're trying our best to forget about it. We're about to catch a taxi downtown."

Unable to avoid staring at Barry's scratches, Ms. Simpson asked softly, her pretty brow furrowing, "The police did this to you?"

"Yup," he answered, "If they *were* police. But it's really nothing."

Ms. Simpson made no further comment, momentarily lost in thought. Then the concern in her face evaporated, replaced by a sudden illumination. "I have an idea that should help smooth out the remainder of your vacation," she said. "Sometimes it's a good idea to find one particular cab driver you can trust, then use him exclusively for the duration of your stay. If you do, you can work with him to schedule your transportation needs. Usually, the prospect of your steady business will encourage him to offer you a better rate.

"Let me introduce you to a cab driver I know you can trust. His name is Henry. Henry has always been a very fair man in his dealings with me. I think I saw him outside at the cabstand a few minutes ago. If we hurry, I bet we can catch him."

"Sure," replied Barry, looking at Mae, who was not saying anything. He reached out his hand for hers. They followed in Ms. Simpson's wake, through the foyer, out the front door and across the courtyard to the line of three waiting cabs.

Ms. Simpson strode purposefully across the cobblestones in her pumps like she was born to walk over irregular surfaces in high-heeled shoes. She made for the first cab in line, an all-white, late-model minivan.

"Henry? Is that you?" she called as they approached.

Henry thrust his head outside the window, "Yes, Miss?" His eyebrows raised like twin question marks in a handsome, milk chocolate face.

"Oh good. It is you," she replied. Ms. Simpson stepped a little to one side and ushered up Barry and Mae to a position beside the window, so she could make introductions. "Mr. and Mrs. Wright, allow me to introduce Henry."

"Hi. Nice to meet you," said Barry.

He extended his hand, meaning to shake Henry's hand through the open window. Henry rapidly killed the engine and swung open the door, dismounting from the driver's seat to respectfully stand while he shook Barry's hand.

"How do you do."

Henry's grip was manly, firm but brief. His mouth twitched, intended as a smile. He had a bashful demeanor and sympathetic brown eyes. The clean, brown T-shirt that he wore had silk-screened across the chest in white the legend "Cool Runnings," the Jamaican equivalent of "have a nice day."

Mae said nothing, not much moved to trust yet another Jamaican. She fretted in her head, *How do we know he won't kill us... for our pocket change?*

"Henry," said Ms. Simpson, "Mr. and Mrs. Wright are my guests. This is their first time in Jamaica, and I need you to take care of these nice people. They need a regular driver they can trust to see they get safely to and from wherever they wish to go."

"No problem," Henry said quietly. Then he asked, "Are you going someplace now?"

"As a matter of fact, we'd like to go to the market," Barry answered.

"No problem," replied Henry. He opened the side door of his van for the Wrights.

Mae entered the vehicle first and situated herself on the roomy bench seat. Barry, pausing before climbing aboard, asked Henry, "How much is the fare?"

"To the marketplace, nine dollars."

Barry calculated the amount to be about $3 American, which seemed reasonable enough to him. "All right, then." He turned to Ms. Simpson and said, "Thanks, we appreciate your help."

Mrs. Simpson smiled and nodded. "You're welcome. You two have a good time!"

Once Barry was inside, the cabby shut the door then got himself back behind the wheel. The sun blazed 15 minutes from its zenith.

Henry did not smile or say any more than was absolutely necessary, answering most questions with his usual reply, "No problem." He proved to be a skillful driver in the high-speed, wrong-side-of-the-road, Jamaican fashion. He took only a short time to cover the same distance that seemed so far when Barry and Mae had taken the walk on the previous morning and less time to reach downtown than when they took the road earlier, riding at a more sedate pace with Mr. Dunbar. Around the corner from the clock tower, Henry pulled up at the corner on the south end of the marketplace, almost at the beginning of the stalls. Barry paid Henry, remembering to "take care of him."

Henry got the door for the Wrights and politely asked, "How long will you be?"

"How long do you think we'll need?" asked Barry.

"Oh, the market is not so big…" Henry raised his hand to stroke his throat while he was thinking. "Maybe, one hour," he said, continuing to hold the door until Mae had safely reached the pavement.

Barry said, "Then please pick us up in an hour."

"No problem," said Henry shutting the door. Then he tapped his forefinger against Barry's forearm to get his attention and stressed, "Don't leave the market, please…" He pointed, "I'll pick you up right there, under the clock, in one hour."

"No problem," said Mae, with an innocent smile and a hint of sarcasm.

"All right. Thanks," said Barry, shooting Mae a curious, mildly reproachful look.

Henry, having reinstated himself behind the wheel, aggressively pulled a very skillful U-turn directly into the manic flow of the downtown roundabout traffic and disappeared.

"Well, here we are, at last!" said Barry.

"And there goes our transportation," griped Mae, feeling defenseless in the busy downtown sidewalks full of people, some Jamaicans already appearing to take an interest in the new arrivals. "That's probably the last we'll ever see of good ol' Henry."

"What makes you say that?" asked Barry, seeming a little annoyed that she would take such an attitude since they had resolved to stay and *enjoy* the rest of their vacation.

"He's a Jamaican, isn't he?" she said under her breath, her voice a little too soft for Barry to catch her response.

Barry let it go. He glanced uselessly at his bare wrist, then craned his neck to see the clock overhead. "Shall we?" he asked, offering Mae his arm and conveying some encouragement with a loving smile.

Mae let out a breath she had been holding, "Sure." She took her husband's arm, managing a mirthless smile of her own. Entering the market lane, she kept remembering "no problem." She repeated the phrase in her mind like a personal mantra against the onrush of anxiety steadily overtaking her.

First the sidewalk and then the entire lane became crowded with noisy people, many tourists numbering among the Jamaicans. A riot of high-spirited activity, the market fulfilled their every exotic expectation of what the Third World must be like. Crowded colorful stalls, both permanent and portable, offered everything from necessities like fresh produce and basic clothing to luxuries such as art, fashions, and jewelry. Loud music competed from various quarters, and a great many dealers sold records and cassette tapes — some legitimate, but a lot of bootleg stuff was being offered, too.

Everywhere they looked, a hubbub of people browsed and shopped, many buying, selling, haggling over prices, calling out, complaining, laughing, shouting, trading quips and insults, eating, drinking, and smoking — you name it, folks were doing it. The crowd occasionally made way for pushcarts and motorized carts. Mopeds, motor scooters and small motorcycles seemed to be common means of transportation.

Almost immediately, in an action that would be repeated numerous times by various young men before they would leave downtown Ocho Rios, a Jamaican youth brushed into Barry and whispered, "Coke?" When Barry did not acknowledge him, "Rass," he cursed softly, giving Barry a last, contemptuous look from over his shoulder as he passed.

Mae, trying not to stare blatantly, kept nervously checking on the young man until she was certain he was gone. Then, in a quavering voice, she asked her husband, "What did he say?"

"He was hoping to sell us some cocaine."

Mae nodded her understanding and sighed. She got a better grip on her husband, lacing her fingers through his. But it was not only her insecurity, although it was certainly the biggest part. While they walked, she thought, a little pot is one thing, but cocaine is entirely another story. I must not let Barry get any more bright ideas.

The marketplace took some getting used to, shocking their systems like the unexpectedly cold water of Chicago's Lake Michigan on a hot July day. But they plunged headlong into the color, noise, and excitement, striking out quickly through the fresh food stalls, past the fruits and produce, the fresh meats and baskets of still-flopping fish. Soon grasping the layout, Mae and Barry quickly cut to the craft stalls. They held hands and strolled along, looking at the various exotic items being offered for sale. Coral and silver jewelry, stuffed dolls, bankra baskets, large earthenware yabba bowls, straw and leather crafts, paintings, silk-screen printed T-shirts, and other souvenirs, each had its space and its Jamaican higgler.

They also spotted a man rigged out as a one-man band, keeping up a rhythmic, occasionally melodious racket, doing his part to add to the market's overall tumult. Musical instruments and noisemakers hung from the old man's entire body. A child-size accordion spanned his thin chest, and a small drum stood out from between his shoulder blades. Stopping to watch and listen for a minute, they discovered the man had a little spotted dog. The dog sat up in front of Mae and begged happily, its tongue lolling with the heat. Mae soon realized the frisky critter was missing an entire front leg.

"Aw-w-w," Mae said, putting her hands to the sides of her face while the pathetic mutt nudged her excitedly with his remaining front paw. She implored, "Barry?"

"Sure," he said, pulling out his money. He peeled off a Jamaican dollar. The hat, he noticed, was on the ground several yards away, beside the erstwhile musician. On an impulse, he extended the bill toward the dog.

The dog went, "Rowlf!" It left off prodding Mae to hop-trot adroitly over to Barry and seize the bill in its teeth. It then covered the distance to the hat in a flash that belied its handicap, dropping the single amongst the collected coins and small bills.

Facetiously Barry said, "I'll bet that smart little doggie could make change, if needed."

The "band," a stick-thin older man with gray hair and beard, left off hooting the harmonica part of his rig briefly, and with an accompanying bob of his woolly head, said, "Thank 'ee, Cap'n." Then he switched his sonic frontal assault to a battered cornet, redoubling his efforts as a gaggle of White seniors, mostly ladies, arrived to see what was going on.

Mae began to move on with Barry. The little dog started rolling over in front of one elderly lady after another while a succession of pocketbooks could be heard snapping open. At first charmed, Mae then unhappily thought, could the old man have purposely maimed the dog? The more she pondered the question, the more she deemed, I wouldn't be surprised.

"Barry, let's go," she nudged.

Although Barry's hat shielded him from the sun, the heat was a bit much for him to endure. The little bit of shade that existed had a stall or a pushcart under it. Here and there, vendors pushed red-enameled wooden carts loaded with soft drinks and beer in buckets of ice. So, it was no surprise when he asked, "Would you like a cold drink?"

Mae was thirsty, but she feared that somebody might have tampered with the drinks. She too-vividly remembered her experience at the party in the jungle, and she was too scared to buy anything to eat or drink from a strange Jamaican on the street.

"Maybe I'll have a sip of yours," she replied.

The Coke Barry bought came in a familiar, curvy, green glass bottle. He offered it first to her, but Mae declined. So, he drank most of the pop in three or four swigs then offered it, again, to her. Although Barry had not cramped up with poison or started hallucinating or anything, Mae still distrusted it. She handed the bottle back to him and offhandedly said, "I think I'll wait."

Barry shrugged and killed it. He looked around for a trash can. A mob of half-dozen small boys suddenly surrounded him, each pleading noisily for the bottle, eager to return it for the penny deposit. Then a cute little boy of five or six snatched the bottle away from his unresisting fingers. The children ran off.

Barry said to Mae, "I had a momentary Tender Heart Teddy Bear déjà vu."

Mae, the first to take a backward glance, stopped in her tracks and alerted Barry when she saw what was happening. Shocked, they watched as the lucky little boy was pummeled to the ground and robbed of the empty bottle by an older, bigger youth. Several grown-ups shouted at the meanness. A woman rushed to rescue the smaller boy, but the bully got away with the prize.

"Dammit!" Barry said, "I wish I had carried the bottle back to the hotel."

As the shock of the bottle incident wore off, they again found themselves immersed in the exotic sights, sounds, textures, and smells. A great deal of aggressive marketing was going on all around them. They came to a stall where a heavy-set woman was selling shirts and blouses sewn together from washed and softened sacking, the recycled material utilized in ways that left the finished articles decorated with the labels and pictures originally printed on the sacks. Some of the artwork was quite nice, old-fashioned trademarks and such.

Barry slowed down to look, probably considering a purchase because the shirts appealed to both the designer and the ex-hippie in him.

"You think she's got anything in my size?"

Usually that was way too much for him to hope for, especially with anything different or trendy. As usual, Mae could see from where he stood all the garments appeared to run toward small sizes. But the big islander did not fail to notice his interest, though. She came out higgling and landed on Barry with both feet.

"You! Good lookin'!"

The big woman began with an intensity that startled Barry and frightened Mae into retreating behind her big husband, a fallback position that she never assumed back home but that was becoming SOP in Jamaica.

"Yeah, you! Big White mah-n wid de Black sistah! Mama's got shirts fe you!"

She quickly draped a rackful of garments over an arm as big as a linebacker's. Then Mama waddled out from behind her crate-and-plywood counter to start draping shirt after shirt over Barry's shoulder.

"Oh, per-feck! Per-feck fe you! Dis one you' cullah, too!" she insisted, holding one of her least attractive offerings, a burnt orange and bilious frog-green graphic, to his cheek. "Cheap, too. Only forty dollahs," she declared.

If Barry had not been warned about this particular aspect of the culture, he would have been horrified. But he expected this confrontation and handled it. "Hey! Hey!" He punctuated the arrival of the two latest shirts to land on his neck with the exclamations to get Mama's attention. Raising his hands in a dismissive gesture, he smiled and responded, "No."

"No? Why no? Okay, thirty-fi' dollahs, but only 'cuz you me fust customah, today."

The aggressive woman had a head like a bowling ball, crowned with a straw hat. Her dark brown skin had little beads of sweat, especially standing out all over her face.

"Why no?" sputtered Barry, emerging from under the pile of shirts by thrusting them back on Mama. "They're nice. But you have nothing to fit me. That's why no!"

"You t'ink no? Waddabowda ext'a large? Dat one on sale, too/ Thirty dollahs!"

She waddled in place, making one complete revolution. Like a large moon or a small planet, marveled Mae. When Mama came around to face Barry again, she had dropped her inventory on the counter except for the XL, which she now held spread by its short sleeves across her ample frontage. The shirt's antique-style graphic was that of a sugar company, showing the British lion striding regally from a cane thicket, the picture and lettering printed in red, yellow, black, and green on unbleached muslin. It was nice, but Barry could see it did not fit.

"No way, just too small!"

Mae was experiencing a queer, mixed tingle of both fear and amusement as she gradually risked emerging from behind Barry. These loud, pushy strangers flat-out frightened her. Yet, she was determined to buy *something*. She had not forgotten her resolve to spend money and thought that shirt looked like it would fit Zac. She contemplated buying it, wondering whether Zac would like it enough to wear it?

Mae decided she wanted that shirt. But she had not gotten quite used to the idea of higgling. While she was trying to decide what price she might offer, as well as to work up the courage to go toe-to-toe with the imposing Mama, Barry shut the transaction down cold.

"No, not today. Thank you, but no."

He found Mae's hand and began leading her briskly away.

"Irie!" Mama cried after Barry and Mae. Then, mumbling and fanning herself with her hat, she went about returning her merchandise to the hangers and racks.

Mae thought darn! She wanted to buy that shirt for Zac. But she had not decided soon enough. Now it was too late. The next moment, just as they left the crowd and crossed the market at the near-deserted end of the lane, she heard someone say, "The Americans are being tightwads, again." She knew it was true; she did not need to hear about it from strangers. But if the Jamaicans were complaining aloud, she figured she'd better buy something whether Barry likes it or not. And though she had only thought it and not spoken it aloud, a reply came back.

Good for you!

This time, there was not a soul nearby except Barry, who was within 10 or 15 yards. Though the sun was a blazing furnace overhead, radiating its heat unsparingly down on the marketplace, Mae felt a chill.

For a few seconds, her teeth chattered, "D-d-d-did you say something?"

"Uh-uh," Barry replied, leading her back in the direction of the teeming market, this time on the opposite side of the square. A rivulet of sweat snaked out from beneath his hat and ran down his temple. He stopped and let go Mae's hand while he lifted his hat and mopped his head and neck with his bandana.

She wondered, if not Barry then who? Mae's chill passed and she was warm again, just that quickly. While she tried to sort it out, they kept walking. Then her eye caught sight of a flashy display. She guessed that it looked like a fashion show.

"Barry... Honey, what's that?"

"I'm not sure," he replied. "Want to check it out?"

Mae looked again, carefully sizing up the colorful attraction. She could see a number of tourists already gathered and watching the presentation. She did not feel well. Mae felt frightened and nervous, but she knew what she had to do to placate the hateful, mercenary Jamaicans, *We've got to spend more money!*

Mae screwed up her courage and answered, "Sure."

Barry seemed glad she finally was getting into the spirit of the thing, and they crossed the lane for a closer look.

Some pretty, young, caramel-colored women dressed in bikinis smiled down from a small stage. Over their swimsuits, they were modeling various styles of dress achieved by folding, arranging and tying a rectangular piece of brightly colored cloth, somewhat like a West-Indian sarong wrap.

There was another pretty lady, slightly older, using a microphone to provide the crowd with a running commentary while the "girls" demonstrated the garment, wearing it as a cover-up for the beach, as a dress, a skirt, a top, and so forth. The actual merchandise was being sold by another pretty girl, out of the open doors of a van parked alongside the stage.

The Wrights started watching and before long Mae decided that the garment might be nice. Just as Barry started to move along, tugging gently at her hand, she spoke up.

"Honey, wait."

Relaxing his tug, Barry wanted to know, "What's up?"

"I want one of these wraps." Mae paused, put her hands over his shoulders, touching the back of his neck, batting her eyes, and pouring on the charm, then wheedled, "Buy one for me?"

Looking surprised, Barry said, "Of all the silly things to spend money on! You'll never wear it." Then after a second's thought, he acquiesced, "What can I say? Buy one for yourself. It'll be worth it if it cheers you up. It's basically a big bandana. How much could it cost?"

Mae thought for a minute because she was frightened enough of the Jamaicans to want to avoid the whole higgling experience. But she decided maybe it would not be so bad. A voice in her ear said, "No guts, no glory."

Startled, she realized it was Barry. He watched her to see if she would take up the challenge, his eyes twinkling and a smile teasing at the corners of his mouth.

"All right," she announced, although not with her usual confidence but at least with a reasonable facsimile. She released his neck and found his hand, not completely ready to let go. They approached the back of the van. A lady tourist, quite pleased with herself, concluded a transaction. Mae was next.

Not wanting to appear weak or dependent, Mae quickly released Barry's hand and stepped up to the folding card table. From the rainbow of colors on hand, she quickly selected a lovely turquoise print, the color of the Caribbean on a sun-splashed day. She picked up the folded cloth and approached the smiling vendor. The instant the vendor smiled Mae freaked out. She still held her ground, pretending that she did not notice the vendor's devilish grin, believing that it must be a test of her ability to keep their secret.

Standing nearby and watching her with a keen eye, Barry inquired, "Why are you acting like you're afraid? This isn't like you, Mae. You usually do so well with people." He wanted to know, "Is there something going on with you?" Barry did not mean her illness or her reaction to their bad luck. "Lately you've been acting... a little weird. Maybe I should buy it for you."

"No, I've got this."

He looked relieved that she had regained her old confidence and was having fun.

"Fin' one you like?" the smiling girl asked Mae. "Oh, very pretty, like you!"

Mae's new voice worried, *This one's got those pointy teeth, too — worse than that Simpson woman.* Mae stifled her inclination to back away and continued as the cloth fluttered with the tremor in her hands, "How m-much for this one?"

"Fifty dollars," replied the young woman whose smile faltered as she looked at Mae who kept staring at her teeth. She self-consciously shielded her mouth with a dainty brown hand.

See! She knows you know. Mae fretted, uncertain what she should do next. She still had to pass the test, though. *Better play their game. It will not look right unless you haggle.*

Mae wanted to run and hide, but she hung in and made her deal. Mae handed over some money and in another second the young woman pressed a paper-wrapped parcel into her hands. As Mae turned away, she caught sight of the girl getting out a compact mirror and, looking more than a little confused, checking her makeup and her mouth.

As soon as she was close enough to be heard, Mae, anxious to know Barry's reaction, proudly announced, "I got it for thirty-nine dollars."

Barry imploded, "My God! For an oversized hankie?" He must have seen the needy look in her eyes and how badly she wanted his approval because a second later he wrapped his arm around her shoulders and managed to say, "Good for you."

Mae disappointedly knew Barry thought she paid too much. But she also felt that Barry's tight rein on spending did not make sense. He does not know what I know.

Again, a voice whispered, *"Saving money won't save your lives, but spending it might."* With a jolt, Mae scanned the surrounding crowd of Jamaicans and had no clue who said it. She decided there and then that she needed to throw more money around, even if she had to do it behind Barry's back. She thought, why should he care? It's her money, too!

The Wrights had seen what there was to see at the market.

"It must be about time to rendezvous with Henry," said Barry. Suddenly, noticing a building across the square from the open market, he diverted Mae on an impulse, "Let's go check that place out. It'll only take a minute."

Mae looked and saw an uninviting, whitewashed storefront with no windows and a single door at the far end of a shadowy vestibule, beyond an opened burglarproof gate. A sign above the door had been painted over except for a single, fading, disembodied-looking word, which read *Spirits.* A chill came over her, again. Mae froze in her tracks.

"C'mon, Honey," encouraged Barry. "Must be a liquor store. I wouldn't mind getting a bottle of some good Jamaican rum. That way, if we want a drink, we won't have to pay high bar prices. Also, I'd like to try something the islanders prefer instead of the usual, extra-sweet stuff they push on us tourists."

"C'mon," he encouraged again, grasping her hand. "Mae your skin feels hot," he sounded worried. "It's probably time for both of us to get out of the sun for a while."

The double meaning of the word "spirits" hanging up nearby frightened Mae. It had first put her in mind of ghosts and manifestations of the restless dead. Now, she understood that it was a liquor store. However, that knowledge in no way diminished her feeling of dread. She willed her legs and feet to move, one step at a time, and followed Barry across the street slowly, feeling like she was pushing her way through Jell-O. She hoped Barry was right and it was merely a liquor store.

But the voice worried, *Why that particular word? What if it's up there as a warning?*

It seemed as surely as there were unknown conspirators arrayed against them, somebody was trying to help, leaving clues and warnings they knew she would not miss. Try as she might, she could not imagine who.

The word on the sign loomed over her head as Barry drew her into the shadowy portal. She gulped and closed her eyes. Inside the liquor store, which was relatively cool and dark to her sun-dazzled eyes, Mae risked a peek. They stood on a worn wooden floor, separated from the merchandise by a heavy wire mesh. Beyond the mesh, a skinny man dressed in black slacks and a white shirt counted bottles from the ranks, shelved floor to ceiling, along the back wall. He smoked an odd cigarette, taking his time, keeping them waiting for a couple of minutes before approaching the cashier's grill.

The store clerk appeared to be a Jamaican of East Indian extraction. "Out of many, must come one," buzzed Barry in Mae's ear, "I recognize the man's smoke as an Indian brand called Sher Bidi. I encountered it while exploring the smoke shops and boutiques along Wells Street in the Old Town neighborhood during my youthful sojourn among the hippies." He recalled, "Each cigarette is wrapped in a small, whole tobacco leaf instead of paper and tied closed with a piece of white thread. If you aren't used to them, they'll give you a brief 'headache' high."

Finally, the clerk spoke, "Something I can get you?"

Stunned by the high, nasal tone of his voice, Mae jumped. The store clerk sounded like a chipmunk breathing helium. Although his voice alarmed her, Mae felt glad to see he was in the flesh and had his head on straight. She continued to scan the darker corners nervously and stayed close to the wall so nothing could creep up behind her.

"Yeah," Barry responded. "We'd like a bottle of *good* rum. We'd like to try something Jamaicans appreciate. Is there something you might recommend?"

The man squinted against his cigarette smoke and gave it about two seconds thought. He seized a bottle of a golden distillate from an opened case on the floor.

"Fifteen dollars," he demanded, pushing it towards Barry but keeping it on his side of the grill.

Barry looked at the label. "It's an estate bottling of a brand I've never heard of, 90 proof and measuring one liter. I like the crudely drawn cutlass and compass rose, which brings to mind pirates and adventures on the high seas."

But as far as the liquor's quality, they had to trust the charming purveyor.

"I'll give you 10," proposed Barry.

"No higgling here," impatiently squeaked the man. "Government sets the price, and the price is fifteen." He crushed his cigarette into an ashtray and rested his hand on the bottle. "Well?"

"OK," said Barry, his face reddening. He peeled off the bills and slid them under the grill.

The clerk slipped the bottle into a brown paper bag then thrust it rudely at Barry. Immediately he went back to taking inventory.

The Wrights retraced their steps back out into the sun-drenched streets. Barry appeared satisfied with his purchase. Mae clutched her parcel, feeling jittery but relieved they were putting distance between themselves and the gloomy establishment. They returned to the rendezvous point at about five minutes 'til one. Henry had not yet arrived.

"What should we do for lunch?" Mae felt hungry, contemplating how long it had been since they had breakfast. It seemed like an awfully long time since then. "We've practically had a full day since breakfast. Are you ready to get something to eat?"

Barry, who never needed much encouragement when it came to getting something to eat, answered according to formula. "I was *born* ready." Then, on second thought, he asked, "But do you mean eat while we're still downtown?"

"Well…" Mae hesitated.

Knowing it was really her decision, she paused to think about it. She knew Barry, left to his own devices, would never venture out to try something new. He would continue to eat in the hotel because he is already accustomed to it. But she had several things on her mind. She was still remembering that morning's frightening interaction with the coffee steward. The alarming experience had spoiled her enthusiasm for patronizing the dining room at Caw Park Beach.

Originally, she had yearned to experience real Jamaican cuisine. So far, every time she had the chance, she wound up frightened that the food might be unsanitary, if not actually drugged or poisoned. She did not remember being so nervous while touring Japan, where she had been exposed constantly to unappetizing and truly bizarre viands such as baby octopus, rotisserie-broiled whole and served on a stick. Her Japanese hosts had eaten theirs with gusto, after bobbing the unfortunate mollusks in each other's faces for a while, for the fun of it. In the end, she had at least taken a taste. The critter cuisine turned out to be rubbery and flavorless.

As far as eating Jamaican style, she decided this was an opportunity to give it another shot. And, if they ate downtown, they would be spreading more money around, which ought to make the Jamaicans happy. Besides, it was probably a good idea not to be too predictable. That way, the Jamaicans would not be lying in wait for them, she hoped.

"I know," Mae said, having an inspiration. "Let's go to the Lemon Tree!"

"Aw, Mae, not right now. I'm too hot for a fancy restaurant, and I still don't feel like soup." Before he could come up with a compromise, Barry spotted their cab approaching. "Hey, here comes Henry now," he announced happily. "Why don't we ask him for a suggestion?"

Mae strained to make out the cab and soon enough espied Henry's minivan maneuvering fluidly through the traffic. "I guess it won't hurt to ask."

Next moment, Henry arrived, and the Wrights scrambled into the cab. Henry looked back over his shoulder and sat patiently awaiting instructions.

"Henry, we'd like to go someplace for lunch. We don't want to go to some tourist trap," Barry assured him. "Can you suggest a place where local people might go for some good food?"

When Barry used the word "trap" it had simply been a figure of speech, but the loaded word made Mae's taut nerves jangle unpleasantly. She watched Henry slyly for any telltale signs.

Making it sound like the only solution, Henry confidently replied, "Jerk Centre,"

If Barry's choice of words triggered any reaction, Mae decided that Henry hides his feelings like a pro!

"All right?" queried Barry of Mae.

"All right," she answered, wrinkling her forehead at the inauspicious name while remembering that Prudence Simpson had mentioned that place.

"No problem," said Henry, who flicked his eye at the side-mirror. He twisted the wheel over hard, gave a blast from his horn and accelerated back out into the madly dashing traffic.

Mae puzzled over whether it was good or bad that everybody wanted them to go to the Jerk Center. To her shock, she heard an answer come back to her from that unpleasantly familiar voice: the one that spoke from inside her skull; the scary voice that had not bothered her for a while; the mad one that she hoped had gone away; the malevolent mentality that put her in mind of things she had never dreamed of before.

Stranger Danger, the voice in her skull boomed hysterically like a cranked-up 1950s TV game show announcer, *It's time to play Hoodoo you trust!*

Mae squeezed her eyes tightly, fuming inwardly shut up, shut up! She did not want to hear it. Her common sense cried out inside her mind, "Oh, God! I feel paranoid enough!" She tensed and waited, but she heard nothing more from the voice of Stranger Danger.

* * *

Barry noticed Mae riding with her eyes closed and had no doubt that it was the traffic making her nervous. He watched as Henry swerved to avoid a head-on collision with a bus.

"Me, too," he admitted to himself.

They did not go far in the Jamaican taxi, about a five-minute ride. The Wrights easily could have walked the distance in 15 minutes if they had not minded the soaring, midday temperatures and if they had retained the confident, adventurous spirit that had sent them hiking up the highway on Sunday morning, innocent and unafraid.

The Jerk Centre, near the coast, across the highway on the inland side, stood beyond a small, tree-ringed parking lot, over a short rise where billows of smoke blew spicy, mouth-watering whiffs. Barry settled the fare with Henry. But, to Barry's surprise, Henry parked his cab in the small, gravel-strewn lot and joined the Wrights, unexpectedly taking the lead up the well-worn path in the direction of the fragrant emanations. Mae looked alarmed.

In his usual terse manner, the Jamaican cabby wasted no words on explanation but seemed intent on keeping his pledge to Ms. Simpson by providing them "safe conduct" all the way to the eatery. When the trio topped the rise, Barry saw what amounted to a rustic picnic grove: a smattering of rickety, brightly painted wooden tables and benches scattered about an area of hard-packed earth surrounded by a hedge of flowering shrubs and shaded by trees.

The big American and his nervous wife followed Henry across the grove in the direction of a yellow-painted, wooden shack. The tacky-looking shelter was open on the side facing the grove. Overall, to Barry, the place gave the impression of having been hastily thrown together (as if provided a pick-up truck, they could easily break camp and be gone in 10 minutes). This image of impermanence did nothing to inspire Mae with confidence.

Alongside the shack was the source of the smoke and the heavenly aroma: four huge iron grills suspended over shallow pits and filled with white-hot, hardwood coals. Each cooking surface was loaded with pounds and pounds of pork cutlets, at least a flock of split chickens and schools of fish fillets. It looked like a sweating pygmy manned the grills, but it was a youth wearing nothing but the briefest, cut-off shorts and absurdly a hair net. The joint's open side was spanned by a bar provided with eight or 10 stools, where several customers already sat eating and drinking.

"Henry!" cried the proprietor, a burly Jamaican, his full beard framing a toothy grin.

He put down the funnel he was using to refill several differently labeled bottles from the same mysterious demijohn and came out from behind the bar. Wearing a bright red T-shirt, plaid shorts and a pair of green rubber flip-flops, the bartender grasped Henry's outstretched hand and pummeled the cabby's shoulder in greeting. A much-stained apron covered his worn but clean clothes and his barrel of a body. And a shark's tooth hung from a thong tied around his bull neck.

The two men exchanged a few short words in patois. Then the bartender gazed past Henry, staring quizzically at the interracial couple. Henry made an introduction.

"Mistah 'n' Missus Wright, dis eh my good frien', Aaron."

"Hi," and "How do you do," said Barry and Mae, respectively.

"My pleasure," replied Aaron, beaming and kneading his hands together 'til his muscles flexed, as though he were cracking walnuts between his palms.

Henry continued, addressing his remarks to his friend, "Dese are *my* people." He hitched his thumb in the Americans' direction. "Take good care fe dem, Aaron."

"No problem," came the ready reply.

Next, Henry addressed Mae and Barry, saying, "I'll be back in one hour."

"Fine," replied Barry.

A cloud passed over Henry's face as though it hurt him to finish his thoughts out loud. "Don't go anywhere else, please. Wait for me *right here*, at da Jerk Centre."

"Sure," agreed Barry. He turned to Mae, "Where does he think we'd go?"

Henry twitched the corners of his mouth to show his rampant delight, then turned, and with a wave to Aaron, departed over the rise.

* * *

Mae heard Henry's last remark with escalating anxiety. In fact, she imagined that this place could be another set-up. She felt her stomach knot and her intuitive Distant Early Warning System come online. She had no good reason to trust Henry. And now, she marveled that Henry had handed them off to Bluto, here!

The Wrights were still standing in the sun.

Barry said, "My tongue must be hanging out!"

Instinctively, he moved toward the shade, and the bar. He took a stool toward the middle, placing their purchases at his feet. Excitedly he whispered, "I'm getting that 'pirate-vibe' again, makes me think of the buccaneers and their fabled propensity for wild pig, spit-roasted over an open fire."

Beyond that, Mae could tell he was thrilled to be experiencing another taste of Black Jamaican culture from as close to the inside as a White tourist was likely to get. And this time, it was legal.

Mae climbed warily onto the stool to his right. She glanced around apprehensively.

There were some rough customers seated at tables and even rougher looking, "colorful and quaint" characters at the bar, including one gap-toothed White man seated two stools away, to her right. A sweat-stained digger hat, a style worn mostly in Australia's outback, topped the fiercely sunburnt face. Mae tried not to stare for very long at anybody, but the more glimpses she risked toward the Aussie, the more she scrutinized the man until she realized that the ugly man was a woman! And she must be with that awful looking Black man seated to her right.

Next second, Mae got caught looking at them. The woman winked at her and raised her bottle. Mae forced a wan smile. Then as casually as she could, trying to act like she had been planning to do so all along, she moved to the vacant stool to her husband's left. The ugly woman laughed out loudly, and her drinking companion sniggered and choked. Mae resisted the urge but looked their way in time to see beer foaming out of the Black man's nose, which made the coarse pair laugh harder. With that, they rose to stagger off over the rise, arm in arm, supporting each other amiably, the White woman singing and her companion humming atonally along.

After watching the rough-and-tumble departure, giving the bar a swipe with a cloth and collecting a few soggy bills, Aaron inquired pleasantly of the Wrights, "So, what you want?" He hiked his thumb over his shoulder and the Wrights hunted down the menu. Their eyes adjusted, and they found it, swinging from the rafters in the form of a crudely hand-lettered sign. It read:

> # JERK PORK - JERK CHICKEN - JERK FISH
>
> ## MEDIUM, HOT or CRY YOU EYES OUT!
>
> ## SMALL, MEDIUM or LARGE

Below the sign, in the cramped recesses of the joint, a turtle-faced "chef" was preparing individual orders. From time to time, the young grill man passed him sizzling portions through a crude window knocked in the wall.

"Honey?" inquired Barry politely, inviting her to give her order first.

To Mae, his voice rang in her ears as if he were shouting.

"No, Barry, you go," she insisted, no longer feeling anywhere near as hungry as she had felt at the conclusion of their market excursion, less than 20 minutes earlier. She waited moodily, wondering why Barry had to talk so loudly.

Barry partly read her mind, "You want to know what I'm going to order? All right, then. Let's see... I'll have the large jerk pork. Hot, please. And give me a Red Stripe if the beer's good and cold."

Barry sighed, removing his hat and sunglasses. He ran his bandana over his wet forehead, face, and neck. His skin looked hot and irritated.

Aaron chuckled and called out the order to his backup in patois, then reached under the bar and produced a frosty amber bottle, popped it open with a church key and slid it down the bar top, where it stopped like it had brakes, precisely in front of Barry.

"You, Missus?" Aaron asked pleasantly, eyebrows raised, and full lips pursed.

Mae felt his voice thundering at her and winced. Then she shakily placed her order. "Give me... a small jerk chicken. Medium, and..." She remembered someone once telling her that brand-named bottled beer was usually safe where the water might be questionable. The brew was pasteurized, and the bottles were sterilized. "I'll have a Red Stripe, too."

Besides, she reasoned, if she could not drink it, Barry would.

Barry pressed his blessedly chilled bottle to his forehead and rolled it back and forth, as if relishing the decadent chill. Then he took a big swig, held the cold, foamy beverage in his mouth momentarily, as if savoring the hoppy bitterness on his tongue, and finally swallowed. With that, he lapsed into the guttural male language understood in every corner of the globe, "Ah-h-h-h-h."

He followed it with a politely stifled burp and almost immediately said, "I feel a hundred percent better." He pronounced the Jamaican brew superb in both taste and temperature.

Mae's beer had appeared magically in front of her while she was watching Barry. His obvious refreshment sparked her to try a sip, and, to her surprise, she found she approved, "It's so cold and so thirst-quenchingly wet!" She was enjoying it despite her former aversion to the taste of beer. For the first time in her life, Mae could appreciate the universal appeal of good, cold beer. Her face must have given away her approval because Aaron and her husband were both watching her, looking pleased. She noticed Barry's first beer was almost gone, and took another, larger, restorative slug of her own.

"Ps-s-s-t, Mae," she heard Barry whisper. When she looked, he had a fresh beer in one hand and was pointing at something with the other. Her first thought was that she wished he would stop pointing like that, followed by, but at least he has stopped shouting. When her eyes followed where her husband pointed, she had to admit he had spotted something interesting.

On one wall, hanging between some primitive wooden carvings of African-looking faces and a fading cricket poster, was an illuminated plastic beer sign of a kind once typically found in taverns all over the American Midwest. The sign presented a photographic image of cool, tall pines and sky-blue water. It glowed softly lit from within, engineered to give the waves the optical illusion of motion.

Mae found the incongruity of the North Woods artifact hanging in the tropical locale charming — and somehow, settling. A little reminder of home, she admired. A promise that if they can hang in, they will live to see home again. She suspected their mysterious guardian must have arranged for the sign to be there, a symbol of hope to be recognized at that time and in that place by the beleaguered Mae.

Meanwhile, the Jerk Centre had drawn a lively crowd of customer, mostly local Black Jamaicans. Music poured from a big, old, Art Deco-style wooden radio, and the air was abuzz with noisy conversations in both Jamaican English and patois. No one bothered the Americans; no one begged for money or offered any tempting proposals. The magic gloss of protection thrown over the couple by Henry, and somehow maintained without any visible effort by Aaron, held strong.

In almost no time the big Jamaican barkeep was placing their food orders in front of them, doled out generously onto clean banana leaves bolstered with newspapers to catch the grease. The spicy smell of the fresh, hot jerk, redolent with allspice and cayenne, sizzled in their nostrils. They salivated like Pavlov's dogs and Mae's appetite was instantly restored. The Wrights ate happily with their fingers, punctuating their delightful repast by cooling their taste buds periodically with Red Stripe. The jerk flavor was hot but pleasing. Mae and Barry debated over what had gone into its preparation, already conspiring to figure it out so they could recreate it at home on their backyard grill. When the piquant sauce threatened to run down their wrists and chins, Aaron brought them extra paper napkins.

Mae, surprised by how good she was feeling, fought to control her laughter between bites. But it was no use, Barry regaled her softly, but in sidesplitting terms, with quips and comments on the restaurant, the decor and the people until at last she was laughing out loud, more heartily than she could remember ever laughing before, and tears bred of hot spice mixed with pure childish joy ran down both her cheeks. She detected Aaron listening to Barry, too, whenever business brought him nearby. Fortunately, he had a good sense of humor and apparently felt amused rather than offended by what he overheard. His black eyes twinkled when he looked at Mae, and her opinion of him softened.

She thought, not Bluto, Aaron is more like a jolly Black Santa Clause!

By the time they judged the lunch hour to be about up, Barry had consumed three beers, and Mae had finished an entire bottle of Red Stripe, all by herself. Barry settled their bill with Aaron and discretely left a generous tip, enough for not only the bartender but the chef and the grill man as well. So, Mae knew Barry had to be feeling pretty good. The pleasant thought magnified her happiness.

Mae's internal voice came back with a fair amount of self-justification, *See what happens when we spread our money around!*

* * *

The Wrights gathered their belongings and prepared to venture back out into the sunlight. Their vacated stools were appropriated instantly by Jamaicans who had been standing by. As they crossed the grove, they could see that almost all the rickety tables were occupied by feasting customers, except for two tables situated completely in the direct glare of the merciless sun. Just before they reached the rise, a soft, halting voice came from somewhere near Barry's elbow.

"Scuse me, Bahss."

Barry turned and looked down into a pair of the saddest, most bloodshot eyes he had ever seen. The eyes belonged to a short Jamaican of indeterminate age. Cupped in his hands, the sad little man held a trio of stylized birds carved from a hard, reddish wood. The man forced a smile he clearly did not feel and extended his handiwork hopefully toward the big American, at the same time bracing for the expected rebuff, as though he feared Barry might deal him a blow.

Barry thought he recognized the symptoms of acute alcohol withdrawal. Rather than putting him off, the man's shaking hands reminded Barry of Mae's, and his heart was touched.

"Did you make these yourself?" he asked, taking up the little wooden birds and examining them.

"Yes, Bahss." The man risked showing a small degree of pride. "You like my lickle birds? They yours, fe three dolla'."

Barry knew he saw better craftsmanship back at the market. Still, at least this man had done some work; he was not just begging for a handout, which was worth encouraging.

He looked at Mae and showed her the carvings. She shrugged, then nodded.

Barry decided, "All right, we'll take them." He gave the man a five-dollar bill, then stowed the birds in one of his cargo pockets.

The man stared at the five. With a worried look coming over his face, he began, "I got to get some change..."

"No," interrupted Barry. "You can keep it."

The man looked bewildered. "Truly, Bahss?"

"Truly," Barry chuckled. "See, I'm an artist myself. I know you had to put a lot of time into creating those birds."

"True," replied the man. The money disappeared into his ragged pocket, and something almost like a smile crossed his unhappy, young-old face. "Thank you, Bahss." Then he surprised Barry with an odd request. "Show me your hands, Bahss?"

"My hands? Barry wondered why but passed the parcels to Mae. Then he held his hands out for the little artisan to examine.

The man touched Barry's hands lightly, first turning his palms up, then running his fingers over the smooth skin. "Scuse me, Bahss, but how you can be an artist?"

He held out his palms for Barry and Mae to examine. The Wrights beheld the heavy calluses, the scars from nicks and cuts. Barry ran his fingertip over the thick, work-toughened skin, then chuckled.

The small fellow smiled impishly — for the first time, a true smile — as though he had caught his customer exaggerating. He shook his finger at Barry. Then he said, "Cool runnings," departing in the direction of the bar.

Once the stranger was gone, Mae looked lovingly at him. "I'm doubly pleased. You showed compassion toward a troubled soul and performed the important act of parting with some more money." She muttered, "Another test?" Gazing around, as if expecting to see someone watching, she said, "I hope we passed!"

Barry took back both parcels as they topped the rise and looked out across the gravel. There were a couple of unattended cars parked in the lot, but Henry had not arrived yet.

"Well, I guess we must be early," said Barry. He spotted a small patch of shade, cast by a clump of palm trees at the edge of the lot. "Let's wait for Henry over there."

"Are you sure we shouldn't go back to the Centre?" asked Mae. "Henry said…"

"Henry said not to leave the *property*. If we go back to the bar now, we'll have to wait in the sun, and I can't take too much of the heat. Anyway, I'm sure we'll be fine in the parking lot," he rationalized his need. With Mae in tow, he bore anxiously down on the umbrella-sized circle of shade, worrying that if they did not make their move fast somebody else would likely pull in and park right there.

They waited quietly, huddled within the slim column of only slightly cooler air, watching for their ride. While they waited and watched, cars went by on the highway. A stand of mangrove trees hid the beach from view, but seagulls and frigate birds soared in the sultry blue air. A tall Jamaican youth, wearing a long-sleeved shirt despite the heat, walked across the parking lot, staring at the Wrights quizzically as he advanced. As an interracial couple, the Wrights had grown used to attracting stares, so they paid him little mind. The youth crossed the road, checking back in their direction once before disappearing down toward the beach.

From time to time, sounds of merry making from the Jerk Centre reached their ears. Barry yawned and wondered, what time was it. Absentmindedly, he checked his bare wrist. He fanned himself briefly with his hat. Mae was asking to borrow the hat for a moment when Barry noticed the tall youth returning from across the road. This time he acted like he paid no attention to them but managed to pass much closer than he had the first time, giving the Wrights a sidelong glance. He strode quickly to the top of the rise, stood plucking his lower lip and looking down on the Jerk Centre side for a few seconds, then seemed to arrive at a decision. He reversed his direction of travel and, this time, strode rapidly straight at Mae and Barry. Now flanked, it was too late to scoot back to the safety of the busy eatery.

Mae obviously didn't care for this development. "Barry," she began, her voice quavering slightly, when she realized he already had his eyes on the Jamaican's approach.

"Here, take this," Barry commanded softly, passing over the parcels, but retaining the paper bag-wrapped bottle of rum, which he cradled against his chest like a two-pound glass baby. He casually took a step forward, then sidestepped, angling to put the sun directly behind him and positioning himself between his wife and the advancing stranger. Maybe it is nothing, he hoped. Still…

"Hey!" called the young man.

He had a close-shaven head, a stud in one ear and a cold light in his eyes. He stopped two or three feet from the big American, stared for a second at the wrapped bottle Barry held, then spit on the ground between his worn tennis shoes.

"Hey, yourself," replied Barry, who did not stare but kept the Jamaican covered while mostly looking past him, hoping to spot Henry. "What's up?"

Barry tried to keep his voice casual, which could be hard for him during a serious confrontation. Stress tightened his vocal cords and, if he was mad or scared enough, made his delivery shaky. Exasperated, he thought, Mae does not need this bullshit! No way this punk's going to get through me!

"Come 'cross da road with me," said the punk. "I show you da waterfall."

He indicated the direction of the beach with a toss of his head. But he never took his eyes off Barry.

"No thanks," said Barry. "We're leaving."

"No, Bruddah. You gonna come wit' me," insisted the punk. He was getting cocky, as if he were warming up, beginning to enjoy himself.

The intimidator smiled wickedly. To Barry, the smile conveyed an implicit threat.

*   *   *

To Mae, this harasser awakened a primal fear like staring into the mouth of a hungry shark. Her happy mood turned upside down. Her heart pounded so hard she felt like it might burst. In her mounting fright, she backed up until she bumped into the trunk of a palm. The sudden, rough contact scattered what was left of her wits and shook loose a ripe coconut. The heavy nut hit the ground with a thud. Everybody jumped.

Mae almost fainted. She swayed but somehow held on to her consciousness, knowing Barry might need her! She cast about, seeking some weapon or somebody to scream to for help. There was nothing. No one on this side of the rise and no way anyone on the Jerk Centre side would hear her over the general din.

She wondered, "Is this 'the movement of Jah people'?" Why was this guy doing this to them? Mae agonized in thought, while at the same time she guessed she knew.

*   *   *

The punk menaced, "Come wit' me, 'cross the road. NOW!" He jolted an aggressive step forward, closing the gap between himself and Barry to inches, pushing *way* inside Barry's comfort zone.

Barry dreaded, "Here we go, again…"

Fear mixed with anger jolted between his temples like shock therapy. He kept thinking, last time I was alone and outnumbered… last time, I took it… not this time!

Something inside Barry snapped, and he spat out, "Back up!"

The younger, lighter man flinched then glowered. He reached his right hand behind him, into his waistband at the small of his back, under his shirt.

Barry held his ground, his heart thudding like a pile driver, wondering... What's he got? A gun? Knife? Nunchaku? He guessed it didn't matter. He had one chance. Barry gripped the heavy bottle by the neck with his right hand and swung it out to his right, determined that if that punk so much as moves again, he would break that bottle against his skull!

Nobody moved. For 10 long seconds, the air between the two men was so charged with tension it almost crackled.

Mae stifled an urge to whimper with her fist; bit her knuckle to keep from crying out.

Right then, Henry arrived like a SWAT team of guardian angels. He sized up the situation from the highway, jerked the wheel hard and tore into the lot without slowing, then panic-stopped the skidding minivan, sending dangerous chunks of loose gravel flying. Henry's door was open before the cab had stopped. He was out and moving up on Barry's assailant, unarmed, spitting words in patois, softly but with emotion and authority. The scowl on his face made him look like a savage jungle cat, the bitter smile like he was confident of an easy kill.

Barry did not budge. The bottle shook in his fist from the unrelieved tension in his muscles. He wished he understood what Henry had said.

Forced to divide his attention between Barry and Henry, the punk found himself outnumbered and on the defensive, and his meager stash of mean courage ran out. They watched the confidence drain from his face. He eased his right hand back around the front, raising both empty hands in a submissive gesture and edged away from the confrontation.

"Irie!" he said, with a forced laugh, then turned and sprinted quickly away.

Henry and Barry relaxed as they watched the young man disappear.

Barry's grip was numb on the bottle, the brown paper soaked through with perspiration. As soon as the troublemaker was out of sight, Mae rushed into his arms.

"Are you all right?" She sobbed.

Barry's blood percolated with adrenaline and anger. "I'm fine," he assured her, his voice cracking like a teenager's. He hugged her tight, pressing his scratchy cheek against the soft, flushed skin of her face. "He never touched me." But he knew it had been close, *too close!*

So much for disaster-proof guarantees.

"It's all right, Mae," he comforted. "Nobody got hurt, right?"

Mae gave him a look so full of shock and pain it broke his heart. Then her eyes hardened. She struggled visibly, pulling herself together. "Right," she murmured and straightened up, wiping her nose and cheeks. Barry handed over his bandana. He felt terrible, but he was pretty sure, Mae would be all right in a minute.

He suddenly remembered their savior and, raising his head he gratefully said, "Thank you, Henry."

"Yes," sniffed Mae, all done crying and hoping she did not look too awful. She disengaged from hugging her husband and turned to face Henry. "Thank you, so much."

"No problem," Henry quietly replied, his face composed and his emotions an enigma, again. He opened the minivan's door for the couple.

The threesome rode in silence all the way back to the hotel.

*   *   *

Sept. 17, afternoon — Meeting with the man from Kingston

It was a little after two o'clock in the afternoon when the Wrights returned to their hotel. Mae and Barry had more-or-less recovered from their encounter with the creepy punk but not their shocking breakthrough: Jamaica was no paradise. It was obvious to both of them that they needed to steer clear of the hostile locals.

Anxious to get back to their room and re-group, they rushed through the foyer. In the lobby, they ran into Mr. Dunbar at the front desk.

"Good afternoon, Mr. and Mrs. Wright. Are you having a pleasant day?"

"Swell," said Mae like the enchanted island of her dreams had lost its charm.

"Mae," warned Barry, fearing her post-traumatic mood verged way over the edge into outright rudeness.

"Swell?" Trying out the word as though he had not heard it before, Mr. Dunbar said again, "Swell... Does that mean good?"

"Yes, it does," replied Barry. "We had a good time at the market and a nice lunch at the Jerk Centre."

He refused to talk about their subsequent encounter, thinking what is the point?

"Very good, then," the assistant manager replied. "Are you on your way to your room?" Allow me to walk with you."

Barry wondered what now? But he said, "Sure, why not?" Mae looked puzzled.

Mr. Dunbar came around the desk and fell in step between them. Their footsteps echoed in the quiet, darkened hallway. At the stairwell, Mr. Dunbar touched them both lightly on their arms to communicate a halt. He faced the couple and spoke quietly. Mae and Barry listened.

"I was looking for you to let you know I telephoned the man I mentioned, the important man from Kingston. Remember? As I expected, he is most anxious to speak with you." He let that sink in for a heartbeat before going on. "As I told you, this man is one of my countrymen who is deeply concerned with seeing our tourist industry flourish. He was most unhappy when I told him of your experience and would like to hear the facts directly from you."

Barry did not want any more surprises or confrontations. Nor did he relish the idea of doing or saying anything that might incite repercussions from the "police" in this country.

He began, seeking to phrase a polite refusal, "Mr. Dunbar..."

Mae butted in with a sharp question, "Does this man have a name?"

Mr. Dunbar looked at Mae quizzically for a second before giving her an answer. "Yes, of course he has a name. You must understand, the work he does is of a *sensitive* nature. I prefer to let him introduce himself."

Mae looked puzzled — like what the hell does that mean?

Barry tried again. "Mr. Dunbar, I don't think there's much point..."

"Mr. Wright, I know the meeting will not change your experience," Mr. Dunbar pleaded. "But it might make a difference down the line, for somebody else's vacation."

Barry did not know what to think anymore. After today's episode of fun and games, he was secretly regretting their decision to stay. He wished they had decided differently and gone home. He could not think of a good enough excuse to refuse. So, he looked to his wife. "Is it all right with you, Mae?"

"Why not?" Mae agreed fatalistically.

Barry stared into his wife's eyes, wishing he could get inside her head for a few minutes to find out what she was really thinking and feeling. More and more he was sure that he was not getting the full picture. Meanwhile, Mr. Dunbar stood waiting for an answer.

"All right, then." Barry conceded. "But no more strangers in our room!"

"Very good!" said Mr. Dunbar. "Let me see... I'll reserve a table for you on the terrace, in my name, and you can meet with the man from Kingston there. Shall we say, three-thirty?"

Barry looked at Mae, who said, "Fine."

"Okay, then," said Barry, wishing he felt surer of the right thing to do.

He was out of his depth in this foreign country, though, and he knew it.

"Swell," said Mr. Dunbar, grinning. "I'll tell him. Three-thirty, then."

He excused himself, and the Wrights continued to their room.

* * *

Back in the room a few minutes later, Barry sat at the table dismally thumbing through his wallet, wondering where did the money go? He watched Mae nervously fidgeting about, putting away things and simultaneously checking for signs of intrusion.

"Mae, we need to talk."

"Yeah, I know," she said stoically resigned. "I realize Jamaica isn't Japan. Obviously, it's not safe to walk among the people. It's probably why they plan those side trips."

"True, I guess we've learned our lesson. But that's not what I want to talk about."

"Oh?" came out of her mouth, but she could guess what was next.

"Well... I'm worried that the money we have left won't last until we fly out on Saturday. I'm starting to think we may have been under-budgeted *before* we got robbed. All we have left are our travelers' checks, which, depending on the daily exchange rate, will amount to between $425 and $450, Jamaican. It means, if we don't spend another nickel today, we can only spend an average of $85 a day for the rest of our stay."

"What are you saying?" asked Mae, already tired of the subject.

"Look, Honey, please stay with me on this. Today, for example, we spent almost $40 for breakfast, $55 or so at the market, another $25 at the Jerk Centre, and around $30 on cab fare and gratuities. Which is what?" He paused to do the math in his head, "$150 and the day's not over!"

Mae stared at her husband as if she were having trouble understanding English. Then she replied, "But Barry, we're on vacation!"

She walked past him into the bathroom. She had not closed the door, though. So, he followed her in. Barry found her changing into her bathing suit. Ignoring her outburst, he said, "Mae, listen to me, please. All I'm saying is, we've *got* to economize. We have no choice. There are five days to go. We don't have a credit card for emergency backup, anymore. Remember?"

If she was still listening to Barry, she gave no sign.

"Mae?" Barry pressed, close to losing his patience, wondering if she did not see the reality of what he was saying then what?

"They've been in here again, Barry," said Mae, struggling with her trembling fingers to get the swimsuit straps to lay straight on her shoulders.

"What? Oh, sure, they changed the linen and made the bed." Instinctively, he felt for his wallet and found it safe in his pocket. "Don't worry, we're not going to leave anything valuable lying around."

Suddenly acquiescent, Mae volunteered, "We can skip dinner tonight if you want. Will that help?"

"Thanks, Mae." Barry was relieved to know he had gotten through to her. "I think it would be smart, that and anything else we can do to stretch our money from here on out."

"No problem," she replied "You're right. Maybe if we eat only one or two meals a day, we could set aside a little money for souvenirs. I want to find something nice for Zac, at least." Then she glanced at the travel clock, "Hey, isn't it time to meet the man from Kingston?"

"Almost. If you're through in here, I'd like to use the bathroom, and I'd better change into something more comfortable."

*   *   *

Three-thirty arrived to find Mae and Barry being escorted by the maître d' to a very nice, well-shaded table on the terrace, with an unobstructed view of the beach and the bay.

Mae wore her newly purchased wrap over her swimsuit. Barry had on his khaki shirt and shorts. They planned to spend the afternoon and evening on the beach, after their interview with the man from Kingston. And, to play it safe, they had secured their checks and travel papers in a lock box at the front desk.

The waiter came and asked Barry, "May I serve you something to drink, compliments of Mr. Dunbar?"

Barry forwarded the question to her, "Mae, would you care for something?"

The heat was relentless, even in the shade. Mae felt thirsty, but it was too hot for anything alcoholic or too sweet. "I'd like an iced tea, please...with lemon."

Barry asked for the same.

Soon, they sipped their cold drinks and sat waiting for the man, conserving their energy and observing the people up and down the beach. It looked like life as usual on the White River Bay, complete with a number of the local riffraff finding excuses to annoy the guests on the hotel's side of the river. On the opposite bank, on the beach between the river's mouth and the fishermen's shanties, several cooking fires were being tended. A few Jamaicans idled about, no one moving fast or far, except for the children who ran and played, seemingly oblivious to the heat. Otherwise, even the dogs had sought out spots of shade and hunkered down for siestas.

By 3:45 p.m., when the man from Kingston had not materialized, Mae began wondering why Mr. Dunbar set them up on the terrace like this. That line of thinking started to make her nervous again, her anxiety complemented by a continuous rattling sound beginning to intrude on the edges of her consciousness.

"Listen!" said Barry, interrupting her thoughts. "What the hell is that noise?"

"You mean, you hear it, too?"

"Of course! It sounds like…"

The sound grew steadily louder, becoming a roar as two flying metal monsters blasted over the hotel, emerging directly above their heads a scant 50 feet in the air. The olive-drab Huey Hogs split the sky with the roar of their powerful engines and the whirring clatter of their rotors.

"…Helicopters!" finished Barry, his jaw dropping.

Their paper cocktail napkins took off. Dust blew up from the terrace and surrounding gardens. They jumped up from their chairs in surprise, shielding their eyes and shutting their gaping mouths against the grit.

Barry's chair went over backwards, and their table rocked, upsetting their mostly empty glasses. On the beach, blankets and sun umbrellas flapped while startled people scrambled to their feet and gazed at the helicopters in astonishment.

The Hueys crossed the beach in a split second and headed straight out to sea. Then the military aircraft banked and circled above the bay, heading back toward the beach. People from the bar and the dining room crowded the terrace to gawk at the unusual activity. Both copters slowed, hovering over the beach on the extreme western edge of the Caw Park Beach Resort property, then settled noisily to the sand.

Nervous sunbathers gathered their belongings and began retreating toward the hotel. Mae and Barry had spectacular ringside seats and no idea what to expect. Suddenly, men in military fatigues began streaming from the doors of the idling aircraft. At least 10 soldiers with automatic weapons swept across the beach, ignoring the tourists and employees but driving the trespassing locals eastward, toward the river. The usual boatload of Jamaicans gave up harassing guests along the dock and headed straight out to sea.

The Wrights watched in troubled fascination as the soldiers continued their show of force until all the riffraff had been swept to the far side of the river.

The skirmishers splashed straight across behind them, machine guns held high and dry.

"What's this all about?" Mae worried aloud, latching onto her husband's arm. She did not see how it could, but she prayed the incident had nothing to do with them.

"I haven't got a clue," said an amazed Barry.

The startled Jamaicans of the fishing village abandoned their shelters and cook fires and ran for the cover of the jungle. Dogs barked as the soldiers pushed through the squatters' encampment, poking into the huts and shacks with their gun muzzles and issuing orders that must have amounted to "clear out!" Within minutes the shantytown had been reduced to a ghost town. Then the troops formed up and slogged back across the river.

They humped rapidly back to the landing zone and scrambled aboard the helicopters. Raising a storm of wind-blown sand, the Hueys revved up, lifted into the sky, and surged south with their staccato roar fading as they disappeared toward the interior.

There was a hubbub in several languages from employees and guests alike, as people moved off the terrace and returned to their work and play. Members of the hotel staff were quickly mobilized to straighten up and return things to their proper order.

Barry righted his chair, and the couple sank back into their seats, thunderstruck. Neither had ever seen anything like that before in their entire lives. Though no one had been hurt and not a single shot had been fired, the aggressive display had frightened and upset Mae to the point of plunging her once again into a condition of raw nerves and full-bore anxiety.

She turned to Barry, "W-what do you think?"

"You mean about what just happened, or waiting any longer for the man from Kingston?"

Before Mae could respond, a gruff voice growled, "Excuse me."

The Wrights jumped in their chairs, then turned to see a Jamaican man standing nearby on the terrace. He was average in size and solidly built, with graying hair and a dark complexion. His features were broad and unhandsome. His clothes were medium gray and crisply pressed, his black shoes polished to a high luster. He stood very straight, his posture contributing to a generally military aspect.

The stranger asked, "Are you Mr. and Mrs. Wright?"

"Yes," replied Barry, who started to get to his feet.

The man gestured for him to remain seated. "Please don't get up." Then he walked around the table to face the Wrights. Producing a leather card case, he placed it before the seated couple where they both could read it. "My name is Reaper," said the man from Kingston.

Mae took a direct hit on her dwindling peace of mind the instant the stranger pronounced his name. She squeezed Barry's hand and looked away, refusing to look at the man or his card.

*   *   *

"May I sit down?"

The man from Kingston did not wait for an answer but seated himself across from the Americans, his broad back to the beach.

"Of course," said Barry, who then concentrated on the I.D.

He saw the man's name shown there as Colonel John Reaper. The card *looked* official, and the attached photograph showed him in a military uniform. In the little picture, he reminded Barry very much of an African dictator. Still, Barry noted that nothing about the identification detailed Colonel Reaper's job title or explained his connection with the tourist industry. So, all Barry knew about the mysterious stranger was what Mr. Dunbar had told him. He closed the wallet and slid it across the table. The colonel tucked it back into his pocket.

The waiter arrived with fresh glasses of iced tea for the Wrights and a cup of Blue Mountain coffee for the colonel. When the waiter left, the man from Kingston spoke.

"Mr. Dunbar tells me that you two have had an unpleasant experience. I'd like to hear what happened, please, in your own words."

Mae looked terrified, no doubt tired of reliving their misadventure and anxious for the interview to be over. She shook nervously, avoiding eye contact with the strange man with the disturbing name. His arrival, mere minutes after the assault on the beach, was too much.

Barry regretted that Mae, already sick and nervous, had to be exposed to such a troubling military action — if you could call it that. He thought whenever they involved the authorities, their troubles went from bad to worse.

Still, he had agreed to the interview. So, Barry cleared his throat and told Colonel Reaper the story of their being robbed in their hotel room. He also detailed his subsequent encounter with the so-called police. When he had finished, he licked his dry lips. He took a sip of tea to wet his whistle, glancing at Mae. Then he looked deep into his glass, as though something unusual but highly interesting had appeared there like a tadpole, perhaps.

Mae sat stock still, gripping her drink and staring down into her lap. The corners of her mouth twitched slightly, betraying her tension.

Colonel Reaper flicked his gaze from husband to wife then back again. After reflecting for a second, he asked Barry, "Is there something else?"

Barry sipped a little more tea, delaying his reply. He could feel the red flush creeping up his neck. He was thinking that he still did not know who he was talking to, or why he wanted to know. Finally, he decided to keep on putting his trust in Mr. Dunbar, which meant extending it to the colonel all the way. With a sigh, he resumed.

"As a matter of fact," he began, then added the details of their confrontation with the punk outside the Jerk Centre.

Colonel Reaper listened closely while Barry unraveled the rest of their tale. As he was speaking, the colonel studied him openly, then Mae, too, although less obviously, observing her with little shifts of his eyes.

* * *

While Barry jabbered on, Mae could feel the man from Kingston staring at her. She felt his eyes crawling over her face and body like flies. She kept her eyes lowered. Her mind would not rest. Thoughts and images, worries and fears, roiled through her consciousness. Mae doubted that she could sit still in his presence for another second. She listened to Stranger Danger, who said, *Smoke and mirrors! Nothing is as it seems here! Nobody is what they pretend to be! Who is this guy? What does he really want? Whose side is he really on? How can we trust him when the truth is obvious. I don't know why it isn't clear to everyone: the Jamaicans are out to get you!*

Her absolute certainty drained away. She filled with grave doubts, wondering how she could be sure of anything. Her worst fears batted through her brain. Half the time she was hearing things and seeing things that could not be real. Or could they? She could not shake off her dreadful anxiety, did not want to face the fact that unless she could come up with a rational explanation, she must be losing her mind! She put *that* thought down like a rabid dog.

Deeply confused, lost in an agony of questions, she pleaded to the powers that be to know why this was happening to them. She wished she had never heard of Jamaica, longed to be home safe in her little house with her husband and son. A command came to her from inside, where the chilled winds blew through the vaults of her cranium and the haunted darkness expanded, threatening to possess her mind. It came in the form of an urging she was powerless to refute, this time from distances not so vast and depths not so unfathomable as a mere few days earlier.

Stranger Danger hissed to her, *Look at Reaper, NOW!*

And her gaze involuntarily lifted. Her focus zoomed and locked on the face of the man from Kingston. Mae watched his visage change. His flesh softened, then slid on his skull until another truer face emerged.

The change that she watched come over his face was subtle, at first an exaggeration of his features. But it did not stop. She watched his face morph and meld until it was beyond grotesque. Petrified, Mae could not move, rip her eyes loose or blink the nightmare away. What was so awful about the way he looked was not only that his eyes bulged like they would pop from their sockets. It was not simply the obscene rolls and folds of sweaty black hide puddling like melted licorice where his head met his neck or the way his veins crawled like living things under his skin. It was mostly his mouth, gaping open like crude surgery, a liver-colored gash exposing red tissue and splinters of bone. The man's mouth made Mae's poor heart sink like a murder victim wired to a manhole cover. She saw, in perfect detail, each tooth terminated in an unnatural point as though it had been sharpened with a file!

Horror sat at Mae's table on the terrace, staring her in the face and grinning with cannibal teeth. Mind spinning, sick to her stomach, her heart pounding in triple time, she finally tore free of his hungry glare and forced her eyes back down, struggling not to cry or whimper out loud in the extremity of her emotion.

All this time, Barry's voice droned on. Mae struggled to understand why he did not see the monster, wondering how he could sit there and chitchat with this horrid beast.

There are lots of things good ol' Barry doesn't see as clearly as you and me, teased Stranger Danger.

Her ice cubes clinked rapidly in her tumbler. Mae knew she could not think straight. Betrayed by her senses, she flat-out refused to look up or direct her gaze toward Colonel Reaper, equally afraid of what she might or might not see.

The lid blew off the toy box again. The wolf from her closet escaped along with all the other unspeakable things she had witnessed and thought she had safely locked away. For Mae, it was Party Night on the White River all over again, only worse!

* * *

When Barry saw Mae tense up, he knew that the interview was frightening her *big* time! But he could not see why. He saw her staring jumpily at her iced tea, her lips quivering and both hands gripping the sweating tumbler so tightly that it squeaked. Fearfully, he thought that Mae had better relax or she was going to break that glass!

"I guess that's about all," Barry hurriedly finished his story.

He could tell by Colonel Reaper's puzzled expression and occasional flick of his eyes that the man was aware of Mae's acute distress.

"Well...," said the colonel, who pushed his coffee cup away, wiped his hands and mouth with the linen napkin and rose to his feet. Then he paused as Mae recoiled as far from the table and him as her chair would allow. This time, he kept his eyes on Mae. "I'm sorry for all the unpleasantness you've both endured." He took his eyes off Mae and returned his gaze to Barry, "Everything you've told me will be included in my report." He extended his hand.

Barry rose and manfully gripped the outstretched hand, relieved that the stressful interview was over. "I hope we've been some help?" His voice was steady, but he felt the red blotches on his neck and face attested to his painful, nervous tension.

"Yes, of course, thank you," said Colonel Reaper. "Your experiences will help us prevent such destructive mischief in the future."

He looked at the troubled woman again, hesitated, then said, "Mrs. Wright, I can see you've been upset by all this. I hope you can forgive us. But let me assure you, thousands of visitors enjoy their visits to Jamaica each year, and there is no reason you and your husband shouldn't enjoy the remainder of your stay. I certainly hope you do." He tried his smile on Mae once more, hoping to put her at ease.

The man sounded gruff but so genuine in his concern that Mae risked raising her eyes for a second, then clenched her eyelids shut. She fought to take control of her disordered mind as two big tears welled, hung trembling on her lids, then tumbled wetly down her cinnamon cheeks.

The colonel's face fell in consternation. Frustrated, he brought the interview to a close, saying, "Goodbye, Mr. and Mrs. Wright, and good luck to you."

With a curt nod of his head, he departed, leaving the terrace through the French doors to the interior of the hotel.

Mae whispered, in a shaky, baby-girl voice, "Is he gone?"

"Yeah." Barry turned back from watching the man's departure. Worried for his wife's safety, he eased the glass away from her. Her hands were wet and chilly when he took them in his own.

"Mae, what's going on?" He begged to know, "What's the problem?"

With the frightening man gone at last, Mae risked opening her eyes, looked around, then gulped and words gushed out, "Didn't you see that man? Didn't you see the way he looked at me? Barry, his horrible face and his *teeth*!"

Barry's brow furrowed in puzzlement while he attempted to process what his wife was saying. "Well... I agree he was no Prince Charming, but..." He did not know what else to say. He sat still, worrying and waiting for her to say something he could understand, something he could respond to or deal with.

* * *

Thrown off kilter by Barry's mild assessment, Mae darted about with her eyes. She kept checking to see who might be listening. She thought, no Prince Charming? Is that all Barry can say? The man looked monstrous or subhuman, or, or...

Stranger Danger suggested, *Like your worst Halloween nightmare?*

This time, Mae spun her head rapidly to look. As she expected, there was no one there. But this time, Mae knew who had spoken: Stranger Danger. Not only inside her head either, but she had also heard the voice sounding clearly in her left ear, on the side opposite where Barry sat patiently waiting with loving concern etched all over his face. And oddly enough, Stranger Danger did not seem odd to her at all, not anymore.

Mae *almost* spilled the beans, right then and there; she *almost* blurted out what she had been thinking and feeling and fearing, and seeing and hearing, before Jamaica. Her desperate brown eyes searched Barry's for the answer to the question that seared her soul. Would he still love her if she told him all? She would rather die than lose his love.

Stranger Danger whispered in her ear, once more, *That can be arranged.*

The morbid suggestion echoed in her head then died away slowly. Mae let it go. She read the urgent questions in Barry's eyes but could not bring herself to risk forming the answers. She could not find the words to explain herself. She watched his hope of understanding fade from the expression in his eyes. Rising from her chair and leaning down, she let go his hands to embrace him, pressing his head to her breast, his ear to her wildly beating heart. Slowly, gently, first one and then the other, Barry's arms encircled Mae's waist.

"Honestly, are you two 'at it' *again*?"

It was Cindy Bennett, standing a few feet away at the top of the flagstone steps from the beach to the terrace, pretending to be shocked.

Startled by the interruption, Barry and Mae disengaged from their hug.

Bruce was right behind his wife, stomping sand off his sandal-shod feet. He carried a diver's mask, a snorkel and a pair of swim fins clamped under his arm.

When he noticed the Wrights, he chimed in, "Don't you people have a room?"

The Bennetts laughed pleasantly, enjoying their teasing. The happy sound of these other Americans' laughter was pure music to Mae's ears. Like that morning at breakfast, Barry was disconcerted by the timing of the Bennetts' arrival, but Mae was relieved to see Cindy with her easy-going confidence. She felt a stabilizing sense of camaraderie with the other Americans and secure in their company.

"Hi, guys," greeted Mae, getting the boost she badly needed to summon her strength and pull herself together. Though still scared and shaky, Mae did her best to hide it. She brushed at her tearstained cheeks, wondering why she always had to look so awful whenever they ran into the Bennetts. "Join us?"

"All right," Bruce replied and laid his gear on a chair beside the table. "But I could use a beer. Anybody else?"

"No, thanks," said Barry, "We're all set. We're drinking iced tea."

Cindy declined, too. Bruce nodded and went over to the bar, returning in a minute with a Red Stripe.

Surely Cindy could see that Mae had been crying, but she pretended not to notice. She pulled up her chair and said sweetly, "Ooh, Mae, what a cute cover-up! Did you find that here?"

Mae nodded, still feeling insecure. "I... bought it at the open market."

"Well, you did good! Now I'm *sure* I want to go shopping with you. It suits you, too, a perfect color against your pretty skin." Cindy held up a freckled forearm, pouted, and said, "I'm jealous!" Then, she lightened up and laughed.

The compliments worked like a magic charm. It was exactly what Mae needed, Cindy's self-assurance and her familiar, home-style conversation.

Mae desperately needed a big helping of the normality that swirled around Cindy. Nothing she had encountered in Jamaica equaled Cindy's confident personality in its power to relax her, help her feel safe, and make her believe that things were going to work out fine.

Wanting to have "girl talk" only with Cindy, Mae said, "Cindy, let's take a little walk." She inquired considerately, "Barry, do you mind?"

"Of course not," he answered, observant to the fact that she was acting more like herself.

"You two go right ahead. Bruce 'n' I'll sit here and swap some lies."

"All right!" said Cindy, leaning down and adjusting her sandals. Mae observed that Cindy had on a prettier wrap over her swimsuit, Asian in style with a mandarin collar, black but mostly sheer and worked with dragonflies in gold thread. When the fit of Cindy's sandals suited her, she bounced to her feet. "This is our chance to meet some good-looking *young* men, huh?"

Cindy winked at Barry and gave Bruce a peck on the cheek. She put on her floppy straw hat and the new-found friends left the terrace and started walking across the beach.

* * *

Barry and Bruce watched their wives walk off.

Bruce swigged his beer. Then he asked, "What was all the excitement a while ago?"

"Damned if I know," replied Barry, "but I'll tell you what we saw. We were sitting right here when the helicopters buzzed over our heads, scared the hell out of both of us! They landed right over there. Maybe a dozen soldiers got out carrying automatic weapons. They pushed all the locals off the beach, all the way across the river, too!"

"Huh!" said Bruce, in a small exclamation of amazement. "Shoot anybody?"

Barry drained the last of the ice-melt from his glass, then shook his head. "Never fired a shot. But they moved through the village over there, kinda like they might have been looking for somebody in particular. They ran all the locals into the jungle, and then they just came on back and took off. Pretty weird," Barry concluded, without mentioning the man from Kingston.

"I guess!" agreed Bruce. "We were up the beach when it happened. I was snorkeling when I heard the helicopters and I tried to tread water and see what was up, but it was hard to tell at that distance. And Cindy cannot see very far without her glasses," he explained, then added, "One thing about Jamaica, it's full of surprises."

Barry got quiet for a minute, thinking about all the excitement he and Mae had experienced over the last three days. Bruce interrupted his reverie.

"Have you guys made up your mind to stay?"

"Yeah, I guess so."

"Good!" said Bruce. He gave Barry a playful punch in the arm. "I'm glad to hear it. I know you won't be sorry. And I think the girls have hit it off, don't you?"

"Yeah." Barry pondered whether to trust Bruce with a little personal information. "It's that..." he spat it out quickly, before he could change his mind, "...Mae's been pretty sick. We took this trip as a treat for her. She's supposed to be relaxing. So far, we've had nothing but hassles. I'm afraid it might be doing her more harm than good."

He got quiet and watched their wives dodging waves in the surf at the water's edge.

"But we've made up our minds to stay, so I hope you're right," Barry concluded.

"Is Mae taking steroids?"

The question caught Barry by surprise. "Corticosteroids, yes. How'd you know?"

"I've seen that... uh, fullness in the face before," Bruce said. "Steroids can do that, I know." A cloud passed over his face. "Say, she hasn't got cancer, has she?"

Barry answered, "No, thank God! Sarcoidosis."

Bruce shrugged and shook his head.

Barry nodded, "I know, no one's ever heard of it." He explained, "Some sort of rare immune system deficiency. I thought she was doing pretty good until... Well, until just lately."

Barry, not expecting the conversation to take this turn, was beginning to feel disloyal for talking about Mae's problem behind her back. But it was a relief to talk about it with someone.

"Well, I'm sure she'll be fine," encouraged Bruce. "Things have a tendency to work out."

"True," Barry agreed, looking at Bruce's snorkeling gear lying nearby on the chair.

He really wanted to try snorkeling. Swimming in the Caribbean was fun, but he wished he could see clearly under the surface. He thought the use of a mask would help him accomplish that, and a snorkel would make it possible to keep his face underwater for longer periods of time.

Barry asked Bruce, "Did you rent that gear?"

"No, in fact it's mine," replied Bruce. "Say, would you like to borrow it?"

"Oh, no thanks," Barry did not want to put Bruce out, but he thought about the state of their finances, knowing that he had to economize. "I don't mind renting some from the diving concession. I was wondering what it would cost."

Bruce insisted, "Please, don't rent from those greedy bastards. They're way out of line! You're more than welcome to borrow these, anytime."

"All right, thanks," said Barry. Although he was planning to go in the water and would like to borrow the equipment then, he declined. "I appreciate the offer, but not today."

That was part of Barry's nature to resist favors and avoid feeling beholden. Still, he was pleased that Bruce had made the gesture, thinking he might take him up on it later. It was a way Barry could indulge in his wish without spending any money, so he reasoned that every little bit helps. Barry noticed Bruce had finished his beer.

"You know, I think I'm ready for a beer. May I buy you one?"

"I thought you'd never offer," Bruce joked. "You're on, big guy!"

Bruce relaxed in his chair, squinting against the glare to check out the girls, while Barry went to the bar and ordered a couple of Red Stripes.

*   *   *

Earlier Mae yearned to talk to Cindy Bennett — as a fellow American and as the only woman she knew at all in Jamaica — about their ongoing misfortunes. Mae had debated the pros and cons of confiding in Cindy about her excessive nervousness and unexplainable, frightening spells but then hoped Cindy, with her broader base of experience, could help her discern whether there was any substance to her suspicions of being targeted by the Jamaicans. With these things on her mind, Mae had asked Cindy to join her on a walk.

But once the two women started out across the sunbaked sand, they engaged in pleasant, lightweight conversation. Mae felt so comfortable talking with Cindy, so downright *normal,* she chose not to destroy the mood by exposing her troubled nature. Being with Cindy made Mae feel secure, like the next best thing to being safe at home. Feeling so close to this well-off White lady, like she had found herself a true sister, felt ironic in the wake of her perceived rejection by her Black Jamaican "brothers" and "sisters." Mae did not reason it all out clearly and logically. She could not. But she decided not to risk losing her new friend by sounding like a lunatic with tales of persecution, black magic, or madness. So, she talked about her son Zachery instead.

They carried their sandals and walked along barefooted. Mae did the talking while they waded in the ticklish mixture of warm sea foam and pleasantly churning sand where the waves broke on the beach. Mae finally finished bragging.

"He sounds like a special young man," Cindy said. "You must be very proud of him."

"We are!" Then she realized she had not given Cindy a chance to talk about her family. She asked, "Do you and Bruce have children?"

Cindy gave Mae a funny look, lip trembling a little. "Not yet," she said. Then she forced a little smile. "But we want to have a baby more than anything in the world."

Uh-uh, thought Mae in dismay! She did not mean to broach a painful subject.

"I'm sorry Cindy, if you'd rather not talk about it..."

"Oh, bless your heart, Mae! You didn't say anything wrong, sweetie!" There were big tears in Cindy's blue eyes, but she was smiling. "In fact, I'm glad you brought it up. I'm dying to tell *somebody*." She palmed her eyes dry, mumbling, "Oh, God, don't look at me! Sometimes, I'm such an old softie!"

She sniffed and laughed, then stopped with her hands on her hips, tossed her head and made solid eye contact. "Can you keep a secret?"

"Yes, I promise!" Mae nodded, confused and curious. Cindy made Mae feel very special by sharing her secret.

"Bruce and I have always wanted to have a family. But years have gone by, and although it seemed like all our friends were having children, somehow, we were never blessed with a baby. Then the doctors finally found out why. I had a medical problem. I was heartbroken, and I'm sure Bruce was, too. But he never let it show. He was an absolute angel. He treated me like a princess and told me he loved me more than anything in the world, and nothing else mattered. But, of course, it did. I wanted to be a mother, and I knew Bruce was hiding his disappointment. Meanwhile, my biological clock kept on ticking..."

"Oh, Cindy! I—"

"No, wait! I'm coming to the good part! Anyway, this year, I started a new treatment. And I don't want to say anything to Bruce until I'm absolutely certain, but I'm pretty sure. I'm pregnant!"

Cindy spread her fingers on her flat stomach, patted them there a time or two, and positively beamed. Mae was touched that Cindy shared something so personal. She grabbed Cindy's hands and gushed.

"Oh, how wonderful! Cindy, I'm so happy for you!"

They both squirted a few happy tears while they splashed up and down, giggling like schoolgirls. Eventually, they started back toward the terrace. Mae, delighted with Cindy's company, hoping to share some more time together later that evening.

"What are you and Bruce doing tonight?" she asked.

"We're going to the Lemon Tree for dinner. Have you been there?"

"Not yet," said Mae, "But we've heard it's very good."

"It's great! It's probably our favorite restaurant in Jamaica. Say, would you and Barry like to join us?"

Mae was about to answer, sure! Then she remembered she and Barry had made a pact to forgo dinner that evening to save a little money.

"Oh, sorry. We can't tonight. But we're staying now, for sure, so let's go out together another time, okay?"

"All right, Mae. That sounds fine."

They were almost back on the terrace when Mae had a thought. "Cindy, are you and Bruce going on the bauxite mining tour and luncheon, tomorrow?" Mae had not paid any attention to the other couple's choices when they all signed up for special excursions.

"No, we didn't sign up for that one. Are you and Barry going?"

"Mm-hmm," Mae said, wishing Cindy and Bruce were going, too. But the two couples had not known each other when they made their choices.

The boys were sitting where they had left them, like a couple of good dogs. Nothing much had changed, except Barry had joined Bruce in having a beer.

Mae hoped Bruce was a better influence on Barry than his art and film buddies back home. She felt Barry had had his "walk on the wild side," and she did not want it happening again. No use looking for trouble, it finds them easily enough! That thought, along with the prospect of parting company with Cindy, had drawn Mae's stomach into a tight, anxious knot.

The women stepped off the beach and climbed the short flight of flagstones. Their husbands watched their approach.

Cindy announced, "We're back, you lucky boys!"

Mae took her chair, but Cindy walked around behind Bruce and mussed his hair, saying, "C'mon, lover, we'd better get going."

He smoothed his hair and said, "Already? It's my turn to buy Barry another beer."

"Save it," ordered Cindy. "Barry will give you a raincheck. Let's go!" She stamped her feet and tried to tug out Bruce's chair.

"But it's only five-thirty! Our reservations are for eight!"

"I know," said Cindy, "Fortunately, as we can all see I was born naturally beautiful. But I need time to be *gorgeous,* starting with a nice long bubble bath! And you need a nap. I'm planning on keeping you up late. So, get up! Up! Up! Up!"

"Oh, all right," Bruce capitulated. "'Bye, guys. Sorry, Barry."

Bruce pushed with his feet while Cindy pulled, and his iron chair scooted back with a squeal. He got to his feet and hitched up his swim trunks; they had dried while he sat, except for the seat, where the still-wet trunks clung clammily to his behind. With an appropriate face and as much dignity as any human being could muster, given the circumstances, he pulled the offending shorts loose so he could walk without looking like a jerk. Everybody laughed, including Bruce. He gathered his gear, still chuckling and shaking his head as Cindy took his arm and looked back once, waving goodbye.

Mae returned the wave, feeling the carefree moment flit away, leaving her feeling anxious and wistful and thinking that the confident Bruce and Cindy seemed to enjoy some magical protected status. Nothing bad ever happens to them, Mae determined. Even the angry coffee steward had restrained himself from doing more than glowering his displeasure at her in the Bennetts' presence. Stranger Danger added, *Or maybe the Jamaicans are too clever to make any moves in front of witnesses.*

*   *   *

For the next hour, the Wrights walked up to the beach and back again, enjoying the late afternoon serenity. The beach was almost deserted. Most folks were inside already or headed that way, giving thought to dinner. No familiar parasail glided by, but Barry spotted an ocean liner cruising on the horizon. He tried to show it to Mae, but there was little contrast between the ship and the pale-blue edge of the sky. So, she was never quite able to say she saw it. But then, she first spotted the school of flying fish, flashing silver in the sunlight, their splashes creating brief, fragile rainbows.

Barry pronounced that sighting, "Pretty cool!"

When Barry got too hot, he peeled off his shirt and dove into the surf. He tried to get Mae to follow him in, but she contented herself with shortening her wrap and wading up to her knees. They splashed each other in good fun, then held hands while they walked along the water's edge, back to the Caw Park Beach Resort proper. When they reached the pier, they walked out to the end, observing the stingrays and the pretty fish darting here and there in the clear water.

They were met at the deep end of the pier by strong swimmers, two of them this time. A pair of young Jamaican boys hung on the edge, calling to Mae and Barry with the usual propositions that amounted to anything and everything.

One youngster offered, "We gedda boat fe me uncle an' take you to da nude beach!"

"No," Barry said, laughing at the outrageous offer from someone about nine years old.

"Okay," said the other boy, "Wha'choo like? We got da bes' coconuts, mon. Wanna buy some?"

Mae fussed, "No, thank you!" Surprising Barry, she said a Jamaican word, "Irie!"

"Mae, wait!" said Barry. "Maybe there *is* something…"

"Like what?" she asked.

"Like, some fresh fruit," he answered. "We could bring fruit up to our room for when we want to save money on meals. Not a lot, only what we can eat over the next couple of days."

Mae thought about it and had to admit, "It makes sense. I would like some fruit."

"Well?"

"I guess so," agreed Mae. "Sure!"

Barry put it to the boys, "How about it, can you sell us some fresh fruit?"

"No problem!" chorused the boys. "Whacha wan' us to bring? Coconut?"

"Maybe one coconut," said Barry. "And a bunch of bananas, about six…"

"And some mangoes," added Mae, who had discovered the juicy fruit in Jamaica.

"Pineapple?" suggested one of the boys.

"No, no pineapple. It is too messy. A coconut, a few bananas, and two mangoes," outlined Barry. "Can you get that?"

The boys answered, "Sure! No problem!"

"How much?" asked Barry, tickled but hiding his mirth behind a businesslike front.

"You give us five dollas?"

"Okay," agreed Barry, perhaps a little bit too fast.

"Each!" demanded the bolder of the little opportunists.

Barry calculated the exchange rate in his head and figured that at that rate he would be losing money. "No! Three dollars each," he offered.

"No problem!" The boys kicked off, swimming like turtles. "Soon come!"

The Wrights had been idling along the pier for about 15 minutes when they finally saw a beat-up boat approaching. The weathered dory was being rowed by one of the boys while the other kept a sharp eye open for trouble. Seeing no one around except Barry and Mae, they pulled into the pier and handed up the fresh fruit.

It looked good. The coconut had been stripped of its outer husk, and there were seven bananas and two large rose, orange, yellow and green-hued mangoes. Barry handed down the money and the boys each took an oar and rowed swiftly away.

"Not bad," pronounced Barry, well satisfied with their purchase.

"Not bad at all," agreed Mae. "It was really a great idea!"

The sun was low in the western sky as the Wrights headed back toward the hotel, carrying their prize of fresh fruit. They spied Mr. Dunbar watching them from the terrace.

"Hello," greeted Barry.

Mae worked up a half-hearted smile for the assistant manager, who had been responsible for springing the horrible man from Kingston on them.

"Hello," said Mr. Dunbar, pleasantly. "What was that about?"

"Oh, nothing," answered Barry. "They weren't bothering anybody. We just bought some nice, fresh fruit from a couple of young fellows."

"You did. I see," said Mr. Dunbar. He showed no emotion, only posed the question, "And where do you think those boys got the fruit they sold you?"

Barry had not thought about it. He glanced at Mae and saw that she was looking worried. Turning back to Mr. Dunbar, he answered truthfully.

"I thought… That is, I guess I assumed they went and bought it somewhere and marked it up a little to sell it to us."

Mr. Dunbar was sadly shaking his head.

Barry shook his own. "No, huh?"

"No," said Mr. Dunbar, "I'm afraid that's very unlikely. The little rascals no doubt stole that fruit from the garden of some poor, hard-working person."

Mae looked completely crestfallen.

Barry thought of many cuss words and hoped Mr. Dunbar was not going to insist on reporting the theft to the police. "Mr. Dunbar, we didn't know..."

"No, of course you didn't," he replied. "It's not your fault. There's nothing to be done now, except to enjoy the fruit. He stressed, "Just avoid any dealings with tricksters in the future!"

Chastised, Barry and Mae entered the hotel from the pool deck and mounted the stairs to their room, clutching their most-likely-stolen goods and feeling miserable, as if they could not do anything right.

* * *

Sept. 17, evening — Drinking and avoiding thinking

As they reached the second-floor landing, Barry and Mae passed a pair of young Jamaican maids who were on their way down the stairwell. They glanced at Mae, then carried on a few words of conversation in whispers. Although the exchange was spoken in patois, Mae believed that she understood every word perfectly.

Startled by what she overheard, she managed to control herself until the maids had disappeared. Before they reached their room and Barry unlocked the door, she asked him in an urgent whisper. "Did you hear what those maids were saying?"

Opening the door and letting her in first, Barry responded hesitantly, "No, why? What did they say?"

Mae quickly circled their room looking for signs of intruders while Barry locked the door. She placed the colorful mangoes on the table beside Barry's bottle of rum as she assuredly stated, "The first one said, 'Those ugly Americans don't spend enough money!"

Barry looked bummed as he brought over the rest of their fruit and completed the impromptu still-life composition. He looked more depressed when he looked up at her expression. His brows knit. "Mae..." he started to interrupt.

Mae shushed him for being too loud. Then she softly continued, "Just listen, Barry. Let me finish! The other one said, 'Too bad! Somebody might get killed.'"

"Mae, please. I don't..."

She grabbed his shirt, feeling scared to death. "...Honey, what are we going to do?"

Barry gave her a shocked look. Then he pressed her down gently in the chair, easing his shirt out of her grasp. He sat down wearily in the other chair, holding her hand.

"Mae, I don't know exactly what you heard. But whatever it was, it was in patois, and *not* what you said."

She stared at him in disbelief, wondering how he could be so thickskulled and plain wrong. She felt certain she understood the maids, which meant their lives might be in danger. Mae wanted to share her fears for their safety, but she struggled to come up with the right words to convince him. Soon she resigned to the fact that Barry had no reason to believe her. She had to find proof.

"We don't have time for this," said the voice inside her head. *"How on earth do you put up with him? Never mind, just tell Mr. Bluster he's right and get it over with, so we can all get on with our predictably short lives!"*

Suddenly calm, Mae adamantly proclaimed, "Well, you're probably right. I guess I don't know what I heard."

*   *   *

Although Mae's tone of voice warned him that there was no point in arguing with her, Barry still could not believe she had heard any such thing. He found himself confused, wondering if he could be wrong. He suddenly became the one full of doubts. Dead tired of trying to figure everything out, Barry glanced at the bottle of rum on the table and distinctly heard it calling his name. He deemed it time to put the world and its worries on hold, at least for a while.

Barry sighed deeply. He got up and went into the bathroom

He quickly returned with two little glasses and said, "I don't know about you, but I'm going to have a drink."

Barry seized the bottle and cracked open its metal screw top with a quick twist. He poured himself a couple of fingers of the amber fluid, then hesitated with the mouth of the bottle poised over Mae's glass.

"Join me?"

For once in her life, Mae decided a drink was not a bad idea. "All right, I will."

He poured her an equal amount, a couple of fingers. She picked up her glass, looked in it, and then passed it back and forth under her crinkled nose.

"Am I supposed to drink this straight?"

"Why not? We haven't got a mixer. Try it," and he demonstrated, draining his glass, letting the rum dwell briefly on his tastebuds and then swallowing it. He grimaced and shuddered, which told Mae all she needed to know.

Mae set her glass down giggling and teased, "Smooth, huh?"

"No," he answered truthfully, adding, "I wish we had some Coke."

He tried to smack the not entirely unpleasant but too-strong taste out of his mouth.

"Well, why don't we get some?"

"Aww, Mae," he griped. "I don't want to go out anymore tonight. It's been a hell of a day. I'm hot. I'm tired. Now, I smell like I've been drinking…"

"No problem," chirped Mae. "I'll get it. Let me put in my eyedrops. Then, I'll run down to the bar."

In a few minutes Mae returned from the bathroom and held out her hand. "Give me a couple of bucks."

Barry had no objections. He was a little surprised but appreciated her willingness to go solo. He passed over his wallet. She extracted a few bills. He walked with her to the door and turned the deadbolt.

"I'll be right back," she said.

"All right, be careful," he cautioned.

Mae smiled. "I was *born* careful." She blew him a kiss. Then she slipped out the door.

Barry watched her go, then closed the door behind her, leaving it unbolted. He stood listening to her echoing footsteps for a moment, their taps fading as she moved down the hall. Barry realized that this was the first time they had been apart for more than a minute since they had arrived in Jamaica. Without Mae's company, the closed room felt oppressive to him. He almost wished he had gone along.

He returned to the table, picked up the bottle of liquor and headed for the balcony, to wait for his wife in the open air. He slid the glass panel back and walked outside. The tropical sun was still blazing, slipping slowly down the western sky. He felt better outside where at least there was a breeze than inside with the stillness and the tepid, half-hearted air conditioning. Barry could hear occasional laughter, snatches of conversation and the tinkle of glassware and ice, drifting up from the terrace below. He sat down and waited for Mae, feeling a little numb and disassociated from reality, wondering what surprises tomorrow would hold.

A noise from inside signaled Mae's return. She found him waiting on the balcony.

"Here you are. Good idea!"

She was proudly carrying three tumblers, two containing iced fountain Coke. "They didn't have any in cans or bottles," she explained. "Oh, I asked the bartender for these, too." The third glass held several small, fragrant slices of fresh lime.

Barry was impressed. "Super! This'll do fine. Thanks, Honey."

"You're welcome," she glowed, looking quite pleased with herself.

Her success shook him out of his lethargy, and he perked up and fixed the drinks. A squeeze of lime juice made them perfect, just enough to cut some of the heavy sweetness.

When he passed Mae her rum and Coke, she said, "Wait! We should drink to something."

"How about... Here's to a new start and a better day tomorrow."

"Cheers!" she replied.

They sat back and enjoyed the now pleasantly diluted potable. They finished those drinks in no time. Unused to drinking, Mae seemed both relaxed and emboldened by the strong liquor and volunteered to run back down to the bar. She did it two more times, going out and returning with glasses of Coke so they could enjoy their rum on their balcony.

For entertainment, they watched the setting sun — at no extra charge. The blazing red ball sank into the sea and the sky flared up in vivid oranges, pinks, and golds. While they watched, they listened to the tropical music from the band on the terrace, accompanied by the emerging rhythms of the wild reptile chorus. Twilight lingered a long time, but dusk eventually turned to darkness and the stars wheeled over their heads. The couple drank, got silly, and forgot their problems for a while.

CHAPTER EIGHT

Tuesday, Sept. 18 — Feeling spooked in the Blue Mountains

The spirits Barry and Mae invoked that Monday night had been fun. Of course, the rum had eventually worn them out until they could not keep their eyes open and had fallen into bed, spinning dizzily into deep, alcohol-induced slumber. Just about dawn the next morning, the Wrights awakened to the full enjoyment of their hangovers. Jackhammers pounded in their heads. Aches and throbs kept them in bed much longer than normal as they snuggled, moaning and comforting each other, feeling like staying in bed forever.

Something besides his headache nagged at Barry's consciousness. Just before the pounding in his head woke him up, he had been dreaming something important he recalled. He grasped after the evaporating fragments of the dream he had been having. It had something to do with Mae and what she thought she heard on the stairs, passing between the gossiping maids. But that was all he could remember. Thinking back, he could see how Mae might have mistaken a few whispered words of patois for something uttered in English, but why something so sinister.

Barry honestly did not know what to make of it, beyond adding one more item to his list of worries about Mae's excessive nervousness and increasingly frequent episodes of odd behavior. He let it go, at least for the time being. Oh, his head hurt too much to dwell on it.

Then Mae's tummy alarm went off, it suddenly made a noise like a grizzly bear. They laughed weakly, amused by the rude sound coming unexpectedly from Mae. But the jostling around that accompanied their laughter triggered more pangs of misery from the previous evening's spree.

Mae tried to lift herself up, groaning out loud with the effort, "Ow-w-w! I haven't felt this bad since that time I threw up all over the bushes," she complained, giving up and falling back into bed. "Remember, after the New Year's Eve party at Bill and Diane's?"

Mae wrapped her pillow around her head, futilely seeking a return to her anesthetic cocoon of sleep.

"I do," Barry chuckled, untangling himself from the hot, damp sheets and moving slowly to raise himself to a sitting position with both his feet on the floor.

He recalled how Mae had spent the whole time until midnight sitting in one spot, talking and drinking cheap champagne that went down way too easily. She had not been paying attention to how much she was drinking until the "Sneaky-Pete" factor kicked in. By then, it was too late.

"Kinda like last night," he suggested. "Except that time, you paid the price immediately."

All the way home from the party, Mae had been dizzy and nauseous with Barry offering to pull over repeatedly rather than risk having her mess up the car. Somehow, Mae had stoically managed to fight down her rising gorge; her husband had admired her stamina. She had finally upchucked in her own yard, just a few steps short of the front door. Still, Barry figured, including last night, he could count the number of times Mae had been drunk on one hand.

He sluggishly said, "I'm a little under the weather myself! Don't feel like the Lone Ranger, but I think I'll try and get up and go shave my tongue."

Barry still had a drum corps practice going on behind his eyes. Nevertheless, he stood up. As he straightened, his lower back pulsed with sudden, unexpected pain. He discovered he was achy and stiff from having been knocked to the ground Sunday night. Barry gingerly slipped on his light robe and walked to the balcony doorway. He opened the louvers slowly, prepared to defend his bleary eyes against the expected sun dazzle. He had no reason to be worried.

"Hey, looks like there's a storm brewing," he relayed the news to Mae.

Busy massaging her stomach for cramps with one hand and her eyes for persistent auras with the other, Mae grunted, acknowledging his report on the shift in the weather. It made no impression as she continued being shamelessly sorry for herself. Barry examined the threatening skies and realized this could be something new to see! That piqued his curiosity and woke him up considerably.

While watching the gloomy clouds, a sudden gust of wind came skirmishing up the beach, scattering sand, then blew away. The embattled sunrise in the eastern sky fired a golden volley through a momentary hole in the building rain clouds. The clouds closed ranks, but the sun found an occasional chink in the lofty gray configurations. Then the wind resumed its attack, this time with a vengeance, picking up steadily until the palm trees arched their backs and tossed their heads. It hit the bay with enough force to bully the water into raising a company of rowdy waves, crashing against the shore. The clouds continued to swell, and tongues of lightning flickered. The veil of darkening clouds forced the sunrise into mourning, and the skies burst loose with a heavy downpour.

"Honey, you should see the rain slashing down on the bay," marveled Barry, fascinated by the sudden fury of the tropical storm. He slid the door open a cautious couple of inches for a better look. "It's pretty cool! The raindrops are as big as…" he struggled to think of an appropriate comparison, "…those elephant aspirins at the zoo!"

Mae lamented, "I could use a couple of elephant aspirins. My head feels like a prize-winning melon."

The sweet, clean smell of the rain on the wind freshened the stuffy room, finally inducing Mae to open her eyes. She managed to sit up and swing her legs out of bed, then gradually found her slippers and robe. Slowly she managed to flip-flop over for a glimpse of the storm, joining him at the sliding door.

Barry noticed how cautiously she moved and equated it with the way he was feeling. He wished he had a cup of coffee, just to clear away some of the cobwebs.

"Good morning," he greeted with his arm outstretched. "I guess I didn't need to get you up, yet. There's no place we need to go. I mean, at least, not for a while."

Mae gave him a hug and said, "That's all right; it's... My head hurts. Ouch!"

She massaged her throbbing temples, then gently rubbed the sleep from her eyes.

"You can go back to sleep for a while, if..."

Mae interrupted, "I need to get up, so I can put my eye drops in. My corneas need time to dry out. Otherwise, I won't be able to see anything on the tour today." That is when Mae recalled, "Oh boy, I forgot to take my pill last night."

"Mae, that's not a good thing," Barry said, frowning.

"Should I take two this morning?"

"No, no. Get back to your routine," Barry advised. "One missed pill may not be too bad."

She remembered, "I'm supposed to take my pill with food. Are we going to breakfast?"

"Well... let's not," he said a little sheepishly, walking over to the table of fruit. "How hungry are you? Cause, if we skip breakfast, we could save a little more money."

"Barry, we skipped dinner last night! Besides, I need to take my pill with food!"

"I know, but can't you eat a banana or a mango?"

"Raw fruit on top of a hangover? Yuk! I was thinking of raisin toast and a cup of tea."

"Oh, sure, toast and tea, to the tune of about 15 dollars! You know, I'd like some coffee, myself," he said, unmoved by her desire. "But I think it would be a good idea if we could just wait. Today is Tuesday, so we're going on that tour of the bauxite mine, and we're supposed to have real, home-cooked Jamaican food for lunch, right? Why don't we save our appetites for that? We'll enjoy it more and really get our money's worth!"

"Oh, all right," Mae conceded. "I feel too sick to argue. But do you realize what time it is? It's a long time 'til lunch."

"Here, this should hold you," Barry said, tossing her a banana. "Ten o'clock will be here before you know it!"

*　*　*

It took Mae most of the next two-and-a-half hours to get her heart properly started.

While she showered, her movements were slow. She also felt like her blood creeping through her body. Her steps lacked their usual spring as she dried off and put on her clean underclothes. She puttered around, unhurriedly instilling her eye drops.

Standing back from the mirror, Mae watched her foggy reflection shift and blur each time she blinked. She wondered if it was her. It was hard to tell with her vision freshly blurred by medicine and moisture, but the familiar heart-shaped face that usually smiled back at her seemed oddly altered: too round, the eyelids puffy and swollen, and an unhappy mouth with quivering lips parted, corners pulling down. It was like looking at a stranger.

Next second, Mae's reflection spoke to her, *You know, they've been here, again.* Mae heard the voice that she had heard so many times already clearly inside her head. However, this time she heard the voice like a whisper in her left ear, too. She took a quick look around for Barry, then again turned to the mirror. Staring innocently back at herself from the glass but looking a bit wicked around the swollen eyes hid Stranger Danger, who said, *The Jamaicans have been in your room, again.*

Without a doubt, Mae *heard that*! But if she told Barry, he might not believe her. Stranger Danger prompted once more, whispering in her left ear, *The more you see, the blinder he gets.* Mae had no choice but to agree that it was true! She no longer found such dialogues odd. Rather, she had come to rely on them, to aid her in reasoning.

She finished getting dressed and picked her Afro to its full glory. By the time Mae came out of the bathroom, her hangover pulsed with a dull roar. Pleasantly surprised, she found that Barry had finished straightening up after their impromptu party; he had even made up the bed. He sat busy at the table, working carefully on the hard coconut with a tiny penknife from his shaving kit, making slow progress to carve chunks of white coconut flesh free of the shell and popping the occasional piece into his mouth.

"This coconut's very good." He offered, "Want some?"

Mae shook her head as she joined him at the little table.

He asked impishly, "So, *now* how are you feeling?"

"Better," she admitted. She took her medicine and reluctantly chomped on a banana. "I don't know why I ever drink. It's too high a price to pay for such a short bit of silly fun."

"I know," Barry chuckled. "We're just not used to it. I guess we got carried away."

Then she chuckled, too, finally admitting, "It *was* fun, though. But, never again," she vowed. "From now on, one drink is my limit. You know, I think the tour this morning will be fun. I'm looking forward to the serenity of the mountains."

"Me, too." Her husband leaned closer and nuzzled the back of her neck.

Mae giggled. "Barry, stop! Not now, it's time to meet the bus!"

"All right, all right! Better make it a quick kiss, and we'll get going!"

By 10 a.m., when the Wrights left the hotel for the cobblestone courtyard, the bright, sunny day showed no signs of the earlier drenching. The grounds had retained a clean, sparkling luster. The sky was clear and vividly blue, and the sun was already hot on their heads.

Mae and Barry joined the group of 10 other people boarding the modern, air-conditioned minibus. When it was their turn, Mae stepped up on the bus in front of Barry. She held onto the safety rail and watched her step while climbing. When she reached the top, Mae raised her head and, to her surprise, she found herself face-to-face with someone she had not expected to see, the tour rep Prudence Simpson."

Mae stuttered nervously, "Uh, hel-lo."

"Hello, Mrs. Wright," greeted Ms. Simpson, her face and mood as sunshiny as the beautifully restored day. "Don't you look nice!"

For a second, Ms. Simpson's smile revealed her very pointy teeth. As telling as her smile might have been, it was nothing like the man from Kingston's. Still, a shiver went down Mae's spine. Thrown off balance, she worried if the tour rep was a witch.

Finally, Mae responded, "Th-thank you."

"Are you surprised to see me," said Ms. Simpson, who quickly explained. "Sometimes I act as tour guide on our side trips, particularly our newer offerings."

"Well, that's nice." Mae babbled, "It's always nice to see you."

By that time, Mae had had a moment to recover. She glanced over at the bus driver and got another shock, as though the man had popped out of a Jack-in-the-box. In the driver's seat, looking a bit stiff in Hummingbird livery, sat Henry, the cab driver from the previous day.

Henry raised his driver's cap politely and the corners of his mouth made the little twitch he utilized as a smile.

That was all it took to make Mae flinch. It made the wrong sense to her. Her stomach knotted, followed by the familiar sinking feeling. Fear rose up within her, stole away her happiness and began to agitate her mind, stirring up suspicions.

Mae pasted a phony smile on her lips and waved familiarly to Henry as Stranger Danger reared up, *Now, what's this all about? What are these two doing here? Too much of a coincidence! These two can't possibly be up to any good!*

A nudge from Barry signaled to her that she was holding everyone up. Mae, who always made a point of sitting in the front of the bus, surprised her husband by hurrying all the way to the back, to secure a seat beside the emergency exit. Mae thought, just in case she and Barry needed to bail out of a bad situation, take no chances on winding up trapped.

Soon, in her most charming Jamaican accent, Ms. Simpson addressed her small captive audience over the PA system. "Good morning, ladies and gentlemen. We're off to the Blue Mountains to visit the bauxite mine. You should enjoy the ride. We'll have a change of scenery as we climb inland and cooler temperatures, too. When we arrive at the mine, the on-site tour will be conducted by the former plant manager. Afterward, we will accompany him to his home for a buffet luncheon of authentic Jamaican cuisine, prepared by his charming wife, who is quite an accomplished gourmet chef."

Ms. Simpson, seemingly as excited about the tour as any of the tourists, explained, "This is the first time Hummingbird Tropical Tours has offered this unique excursion. We hope you all enjoy this special opportunity to join in the home-life of a real Jamaican family."

The bus took off from the hotel headed for the uplands, first moving through downtown Ochi and passing the roundabout, then westward ascending into the Blue Mountains. Along the way, the road did a lot of zigzagging, which Ms. Simpson said more than doubled the actual distance. The terrain changed from lush vegetation to deep, flat-bottomed vales of red-clay soil and steep limestone ridges in extraordinary formations. They saw brown cattle with their piggy-backing egrets.

Now and then, when they reached a level stretch, they would pass an abandoned airplane.

"They don't appear to have crashed," noted Barry to Mae, as they passed the third plane they encountered along their journey. It was a small, single-engine job, just sitting in an upland meadow about 50 yards from the highway.

"I see you're all wondering about the airplanes," Ms. Simpson announced. "The planes belonged to drug smugglers who landed in these isolated fields to load up cargoes of ganja. When they were captured by the police, the planes were left where they landed to serve as warnings to others who might be tempted." She also explained the tall poles that were regularly placed along the roadside but carried no utility wires. "They are there to prevent straight stretches of the road from being used for landings."

Mae's mood was as bumpy as the mountain road. With a bump she would be at her heights, thrilled to see some new sight Barry pointed out. In that frame of mind, she recognized that what she had been feeling made no sense, that all her fears of their safety were groundless. Then Barry would grow quiet and left alone with her worrisome thoughts, Mae would soon bottom out, grow confused and wind up all troubled and anxious, again. She would be troubled, panic-stricken, thinking they were not safe on the bus with Henry and that Simpson woman!

She rode the bus and her mental seesaw, fighting hard to hide her cognitive teeter-totter from Barry, managing a not-very-secure grip on reality, fearful she might start hearing or seeing things. She tried to calm herself by focusing her scattered thoughts on the positive, reminding herself that there was no need to be afraid because Barry would not let anything happen to her.

Mae gazed at his familiar face, remembering the previous day. Unhesitatingly Barry had put himself between her and mortal danger, despite how he dreaded confrontations. That was love, she grasped with certainty. He truly loves me! That thought gave her strength and helped her sort out some confusion. But it did not last. Minutes later, as they entered the gate to the bauxite-mining site and left the lush green of the mountain countryside behind, they rolled across a landscape that turned harsh and alien, composed of high hills of red dirt and mysterious industrial structures of rusting iron.

Mae was swamped with misgivings, feeling regretful of being lured into this strange trip. Stranger Danger, the familiar voice in a grating whisper suggested, *It looks like the perfect place to dump a couple of unsightly dead bodies... Or a dozen of them!*

Unaware of Mae's mental state, Barry, holding out his hand companionably and kidding around, said, "Coming?"

When Mae took hold of his hand, her fears surged up with such force, her knees almost buckled. She felt too scared to get off the bus but told herself once more, "Maintain, be cool."

"Let's go," he urged cheerfully.

Swallowing hard, Mae put all her trust in the man she loved and followed him off the bus in the wake of their traveling companions. Henry stayed behind.

Mae worried about whether Henry was guarding the bus or cutting off their escape. She looked at the bizarre, man-made wasteland around her and conceded to thinking, Stranger Danger is right! She clung tightly to her husband's hand and gutted it out. As soon as she exited the bus, someone new joined the group.

Ms. Simpson welcomed the tall, handsome stranger dressed in a nicely tailored suit. After shaking hands with this new addition who had dark, wavy hair and a golden suntanned skin tone, Ms. Simpson introduced him to the group.

"This is our host, Mr. John Mitchell."

"Pleased to meet you," said Mr. Mitchell, who appeared to be a likable fellow, all smiles and executive confidence. With the look of a natural leader, he waved his arm in a broad gesture, beckoning, "Follow me, everybody!"

And everybody did. Mr. Mitchell led the tour group between the waste heaps of reddish minerals across a harsh Martian landscape toward the Space Age-looking, 1960s-style building that served as the plant's headquarters. Mae found it too weird and lagged behind Barry, dragging on him like a 10-pound fish on a 6-pound test line and slowing him down.

Her inner voice screamed, *This guy Mitchell is too perfect!*

Suddenly she made some sense of the situation: Ms. Simpson controlled Mr. Mitchell! Mae realized the tour rep was using him for his charisma to keep them all following him exactly where she wanted them to go! But her revelation came too late. They entered a building already. Inside the deserted building, where it was cool and a trifle dark, their steps rang on the tiled floor. Mr. Mitchell led the tour group to a conference room as Ms. Simpson counted heads.

Barry whispered, "She reminds me of elementary school."

* * *

In the conference room, Barry wondered why Mae insisted they sit close to the exit door. He noticed Mae acting awfully jumpy, again. He made a mental note to get to the bottom of all this nervousness soon. Also, he thought her breathing sounded fast and shallow, rationalizing that it was the altitude although realizing that would be a little odd since he doubted that they were more than a couple thousand feet above sea level, if that much. Still, he never knew with Mae, what with her asthma and sarcoidosis. He just wanted her to calm down and relax.

As soon as everyone was seated, Ms. Simpson announced, "Mr. Mitchell has prepared a short talk on bauxite mining and aluminum production. Mr. Mitchell…"

Barry could see that Mae was scanning the room, half-listening to Mr. Mitchell's remarks. He was underwhelmed, too.

"Hey," he whispered, leaning in close and speaking softly in Mae's ear, "Does this remind you of school or what?" When his humor got no reaction, he tried again. "You don't think there'll be a test, do you? No lunch unless we get a passing grade?"

Mae smiled that time, but she still seemed more distressed than amused. Barry held her lightly trembling hand, puzzled by her behavior, while Mr. Mitchell's no-doubt fascinating, educational discourse sailed over his head.

Once Mr. Mitchell had finished his brief presentation and fielded a few easy questions, he said, "Let's get on to the fun part, then. Shall we?"

The host led the group from the headquarters building to the mine itself, which was across the road. It amounted to an enormous pit gouged into the mountain with a fenced-in observation deck, cantilevered to jut out over the edge of the mine. Mae, who was never very good about high places (not even when she was at her best), did not want to go out on the deck. Barry tried to coax her on. She tried, tightly clutching his hand, but edged forward only close enough to sneak a peek at the mine, which looked to be a mile deep and as wide as the Grand Canyon. Worse than that, Jan Crows were soaring *beneath* her. That was enough to top off Mae's terrors with a breath-taking rush of vertigo and send her scrambling back to solid ground, tugging him along.

While the others gaped into the impressive cavity, Barry waited with Mae a dozen yards from the edge of the pit. "Sorry," she apologized breathlessly. "I just *can't…*"

"…It's okay, Honey. I know how you are about heights."

Suddenly, Mae looked like she wanted to share something with him. However, as she struggled to put her thoughts into words, Ms. Simpson walked up, too close for Mae's comfort.

When everyone had been properly impressed by the hole's magnitude, the host, along with Ms. Simpson, led the way back to the bus. All climbed aboard, including Mr. Mitchell who sat beside the tour rep, and they left the otherworldly landscape of the mine site behind. Henry headed for the Mitchell home, steering the minibus further into the magnificent mountains.

The vista was breathtaking. The temperature was at least 10 degrees cooler than sea level.

After 20 minutes of travel, Henry veered off the two-lane blacktop onto a steep dirt drive bordered by tall, waving ferns and huge festive, multi-hued crotons. The drive leveled off and the bus came to rest alongside a spacious, English-style cottage built atop a fertile plateau. The tour group had arrived at the mountaintop home of the former plant manager for luncheon at about half past twelve noon. There, an attractive, middle-aged White woman came out of the house to eager to greet everyone as they got off the bus. Dressed to deemphasize her bosomy figure in a tasteful outfit of muted heather tones, the lady had highlights in her sandy brown hair.

"Hello, John," she said sweetly and turned her cheek to accept his polite, aristocratic kiss.

Mr. Mitchell squeezed her hand as she greeted the emerging tour rep.

"Hello, Ms. Simpson. How nice to see you again."

Mr. Mitchell proudly stood beside the lady and introduced her in a polished manner as his wife. Pleasant and personable with a charming smile, Mrs. Mitchell graciously greeted each one, creating an ambience of warmth and congeniality. Soon host and hostess conducted the guests inside the elegant front door of their home.

*   *   *

Mae, having survived the potential dangers of the bauxite mine, should have felt relieved but no. Her anxiety and worries remained like a monkey on her back.

While waiting to be introduced to Mrs. Mitchell, Mae was intrigued by their color. Despite her alarm, a part of her was fascinated by Mr. Mitchell's skin. She decided, he was what her mother called "high yella." Mae suspected that Mrs. Mitchell had a tinge of African blood because she could have easily passed for White. She speculated that with their combined White blood and Mr. Mitchell's professional standing, they must hold a fairly prominent position in Jamaican society. She wondered how the Mitchell's would make out now that the mine was closed. Clearly, Mae saw their incentive to embrace the tourism industry to the point of throwing open the door of their home and extending hospitality to foreigners.

Despite her personal emotional challenge, Mae managed all these coherent thoughts and followed them through to a logical conclusion: Ms. Simpson is so eager to be here because she wants to check out these people's way of life! These thoughts helped nurture Mae's hope that the Mitchells were not part of the Jamaicans' scheme; they were just "folks." It also served to turn up the fire under her simmering suspicions regarding the duplicitous tour rep, Ms. Simpson.

The Wrights were the last ones to be introduced.

Mr. Mitchell said, "I'd like you to meet my wife, Martha Mitchell."

Barry replied, "Pleased to meet you. I'm Barry Wright and this is my wife, Mae."

"How do you do," said Mrs. Mitchell, shaking Mae's hand. If she noticed Mae's involuntary tremor, she gave no sign of it. "How nice to meet you! Where are you from?"

"Chicago," replied Mae. Her familiarity with etiquette and the social conventions helped her maintain her cool despite her mental maelstrom.

"Ah, the city with the skyscrapers! You must feel right at home in our mountains then." Mrs. Mitchell smiled and said, "Welcome."

"Thank you," said Mae, pretty sure her hometown and the Blue Mountains of Jamaica had almost nothing in common.

Yet, Martha Mitchell had instantly and effortlessly used her creativity to think of something to say to put her guest more at ease. Mae decided that Mrs. Mitchell was a caring person. Both the Mitchells had impressed her as a warm and genuine couple. They were unlikely to be part of a plot to hurt anyone.

Still, she could not discount the possibility that they were unwittingly being used as... ...*Judas goats,* prompted Stranger Danger, unleashing Mae's reptilian fears.

"We're so happy you could join us. Won't you come inside?" said Mrs. Mitchell, ignorant of Mae's distress.

She placed a light touch on her guest's arm and genteelly guided her up the walk. Barry and Mr. Mitchell followed, and the host and hostess conducted the last of their guests into their sweet home. The Mitchell house had appeared quaint and cozy from the outside. Inside, there were wall paintings, a piano and a few antique furnishings, including an Oriental rug — nice, but nothing extravagant. Every nook exhibited a refined taste in decor and the whole maintained immaculately. The picture windows presented a spectacular view of the Blue Mountains.

Guests accepted a rum punch or a soft drink from a pretty young girl stationed near the door. Then they mingled about admiring the splendid panorama of the mountain country from the comfort of the breezy living room.

Once again, Mae wrestled with her mood. Her irrational fear did a sit out and turn, got two points for the reversal, and left Mae feeling upside down. She was terrified, shut up in those strange Jamaicans' den where the rooms smelled funny and the sweating plaster walls closed in. And the pattern on the carpet crawled around her feet. She became increasingly frightened and agitated. Mae knew she was close to losing control. She did all she could to "maintain," acting as normal as she could while fighting down her panic. She scolded herself, "Stop being childish and get a grip on yourself!"

Mr. Mitchell introduced the Wrights to the vivacious young woman of college age, saying, "This is our daughter, Sally."

"Hello," said Sally Mitchell, smiling her mother's charming smile but not exactly pretty in the usual sense. Sally had an attractive exotic look: smooth, near-white complexion, cat eyes of light brown with flecks of amber, dark brown relaxed hair that needed a touch-up, and teeth set a wee bit far apart. Dressed simply in a pale green, sleeveless sundress, and fawn-colored sandals, Sally carried on hosting them.

"Would you like some rum punch, plain punch, or a soft drink?"

"A plain punch, please," said Mae, thinking that she could not imagine drinking any more rum anytime soon, not after the way she felt waking up that morning.

Stranger Danger asked quietly, so no one else could hear, *How about the way you're feeling right now?*

"Me, too," said Barry, seconding Mae's response to Sally's offer. "Thanks."

Sally walked them across the Oriental carpet to the antique mahogany bar, where she served them cups of fresh fruit punch from a silver bowl. Mae accepted and sipped her punch, which was unquestionably delicious.

Barry looked calm and happy, making small talk with Sally.

Mae's mind registered the existence of a café door behind the bar. Delicious smells emanated from beyond the door, which was extra wide with double action, swinging in and out. But Mae could not stop feeling all edgy and desperate. Her mind whirled with terrifying possibilities. Mae tried to convince herself to just relax.

Better not, warned Stranger Danger.

When Mae's attention returned to her immediate reality, Sally was saying, "...so if you'll excuse me, I'd better pop into the kitchen for a moment and get some more ice."

Sally took the silver bucket from the bar and pushed open the café door. The door swung wide and stuck open as Sally passed through the entrance and proceeded to a freezer to accomplish her task. Mae could not stop herself from looking through the doorway and into the busy kitchen.

The kitchen was literally a hotbed of activity with steam escaping from pots and pans and two dark-skinned Jamaican women and a dark-skinned Jamaican man hard at work, finishing preparations for the imminent luncheon. They were all chattering at one another softly, in patois. She saw Henry sitting at a kitchen table against the far wall, leaning over a glass of punch. The Black people in the kitchen all glanced up briefly at Sally, and their conversation abruptly ceased. They all turned to look toward the door she had inadvertently left standing open. Four pairs of dark eyes with expressionless faces descended on Mae and drilled straight into hers!

Mae froze. Her heart thumped into overdrive.

The unknown man left off what he was doing and walked slowly across the kitchen. He never broke eye contact with Mae until, with one hand, he rocked the door loose from its stopped position and slowly swung it closed.

The room where Mae stood closed in on her. It no longer smelled good. It smelled *funny.* She looked down into her cup. There were unidentifiable foreign objects floating in her punch, and it revolted her. She quickly put her cup down on the bar.

Barry, enjoying the last drops from his cup of punch, looked as if he were heading to help himself to another cup when he noticed her behavior. "Mae... what?"

The fact that Barry was speaking to her did not register. Mae was struggling not to break down in surrender to her anxiety attack as she fearfully gazed around the room while everything around her went out of control. The plaster walls seemed to sweat beads of sluggish moisture, something they had not been doing before. A small green lizard darted up the wall. She quickly dropped her eyes to the carpeted floor. The lurid pattern of the rug crawled towards her feet.

Her common sense tried to convince herself that what she saw was not happening. Her mind told her that it must be some trick of the light or have something to do with the damage in her eyes. But she clearly saw the furniture and walls moving and changing, looking abstract and dreamlike as though seen through a distorted lens or reflected in a funhouse mirror.

The other guests drank unconcernedly while they mingled and conversed, ignoring the lizards that fell from the ceiling like over-ripe fruit with a bloated plop! Then they skittered frenziedly over the tourists' shoes to disappear into the expanding cracks and darkening corners. Mae's gaze cut through the group to where an arch framed the entrance to the dining room. The Black manservant from the kitchen stood in that doorway, again staring directly into her eyes. Fully dressed, having donned a butler's black coat that, combined with his posture and baldhead, made him look like a Jan Crow. His thin hand dipped slowly into his jacket pocket then re-emerged with *something* gripped tightly between his bony thumb and forefinger. Mae could not believe her eyes! The man was holding a similar fetish to the one she had seen before, made from the severed leg and clawed foot of a chicken.

He shook the fetish rapidly from side to side. Only, in a split second, he held nothing more mysterious than a harmless silver bell. The small bell ringing got everyone's attention.

Mrs. Mitchell stood beside the servant in the entrance to the dining room and announced, "Everyone, luncheon is served. Please join us in the dining room."

There was a happy commotion as the guests moved into the adjoining room. Mae hung back in alarm. Barry seemed anxious to chow down, looking puzzled by her hesitation, he nudged her, "C'mon."

"Barry," Mae said softly, "I don't want to go in there. I...d-don't think I'm very hungry."

"Now, what's wrong?" Looking at her closely, his tone softened then worried, "Did I do something? Do you think I was flirting with Sally? I don't think so. I have a few questions for you but now is not the time or place." Barry shook his head rapidly like he was doing a mental warm boot. Then he took her hand and, again, urged her quietly, "Mae, you don't want to cause a scene, now. *Do you?*"

Of course, she did not want to bring any attention to herself, too scary. But Mae knew she did not want to go into the dining room either. She wanted to run or hide or scream for help. Or fight, if she had to — do anything but go meekly to her doom by playing straight into the hands of the evil Jamaicans. On the other hand, Mae refused to believe the Mitchells were part of the evil ones. She hoped they were what they appeared to be, a normal family, better off than many but still faced with challenges, still struggling to get along like them. And, as far as there being a conspiracy on anybody's part, her common sense could not help but keep raising the question: what if she was wrong? What if there was some other explanation? Mae decided she was just going to risk it. She could trust Barry to protect them if she judged things wrong.

"Of course not." Heart thudding, she pulled herself together and tried to go on, "It's just..." She was in a quandary about what to admit. Should she tell Barry that the carpet was moving? It continued to ripple, waving like kelp in an ocean current. Mae knew it could not be real but that did not stop it from being scary. She believed Barry would say something to the fearful Jamaicans if he saw what she observed.

So, Mae said, "Never mind." She swallowed hard. "All right, I'm ready. Let's go."

Mae started out, stepping gingerly across the crawling carpet. The floor felt solid and held still long enough for her to place each footstep. As they passed under the arch, she held onto Barry's arm, closed her eyes, feeling as if she were being swallowed alive.

The Wrights were the last ones to enter the dining room. Over the sound of the blood rushing in her ears, Mae heard Barry softly say, "Wow!"

Mae mustered her dwindling courage and opened her eyes. To her enormous relief, the carpet had ceased crawling. The Mitchells' dining room was behaving normally. Opened drapes in the large, high-ceiling room enhanced the tall windows that looked out on a charming garden. Bright, mountain sunlight suffused the entire scene, but the buffet was the most impressive sight.

The household "help" from the ranks of poor Black Jamaicans had prepared a lavish buffet table that stood perpendicular to a separate table with place settings for the guests. It was a lordly expanse of snow-white linen overlaid with ranks of gleaming silver bowls, trays and chafing dishes, all overflowing with savory, taste-tempting foods. The spaces in-between were filled with beautifully arranged tropical flowers. Everyone appeared pleased and put on their best behavior as they got in line and were served hot and cold dishes by the servants then took a seat at the separate dining table.

Barry whispered, "I've never seen so many scrumptious-looking dishes presented with so much artistry. I guess I'll have to mind my manners. In fact," he observed, "This gang that was loud talking and grab-assing all over the bauxite mine sure have settled down and hushed up."

But Mae's runaway anxiety would not let her relax. She soon viewed the scene in a different light. She saw that the two maids and the butler hovered over the food and thought there was no telling what poisons or noxious filth with which they might have doctored the goodies. She was not hungry *at all*, not anymore. She would not eat that food with a 10-foot pole. Yet, there was no graceful way to back out. She and Barry joined the serving line.

Despite her efforts to maintain her cool, Mae felt quite afraid, wondering if the Mitchell's knew what was happening to tourists like her and Barry. Did they know they were being robbed and swindled? She guessed not. But she also realized that their smiles and manners could be deceitful. So, Mae pretended to be having a good time, not wanting the Jamaicans to know how fearful she had become of them.

Barry gleefully said, "Everything looks wonderful!"

To Mae, it sounded like Barry shouted from the rooftops. Mae wondered why he chose this moment to start yelling, again.

She scolded very softly, "Please, Barry, not so loud." Her husband responded, "What?"

But as she thought about it, it *did* seem like *everybody* was keeping up an ill-mannered amount of noise. When a maid provided Mae with a plate, it lost its luster in her hand. What had appeared to be China turned out to be a common piece of heavy diner ware. This time, the Jamaican woman kept her eyes down, but Mae felt certain she heard the woman sniggering. When Barry received his plate, it was a lovely piece of delicate China.

Her feelings were hurt. But Stranger Danger cautioned, *Play along or they might hurt a lot more than your feelings.*

Mae swallowed her pride and fought to hide her terror. She feared the servants and Henry and Ms. Simpson, for sure. But she did not want to think so about the Mitchells, although still wondering how she could know for sure. Moving forward along the buffet table, Mae heard Mrs. Mitchell expounding on the various foods and dishes. The woman was practically shrieking to make herself heard over the uproar.

"This is jerk pork from an old family recipe," she explained. "It's a secret, don't you know, but I will share this much with you. The real secret to jerk cookery is pimento. Not pimiento, which is nothing but a sweet red pepper. Pimento is the tree that gives us allspice. Jerk is smoked slowly over pimento-wood fires, and allspice is a key ingredient in the sauce. I dare say, you Americans seem to smoke everything to death with hickory, don't you?"

Mrs. Mitchell moved further down the line, saying something informative about escovitch fish. Mae extended her plate to be served. The scavenger-bird manservant reached to put a piece of jerk pork onto her crockery plate. The steaming morsel went cold and gray as he placed it on her plate, oozing a slick of red grease.

Stranger Danger said, *Uh-uh, this dirty ol' buzzard dealt us off the bottom of the deck!*

Mae could see the rest of the jerk pork still in the chafing dish looked hot and appetizing. In the end, it did not matter since Mae had no plans to eat it, anyway, regardless of what it looked like. She clearly could not take the risk.

The old bird was staring at her. This time, he was barely capable of concealing his mirth.

It's nice to see the servants so happy in their work, sneered Stranger Danger, punctuating that cynical pronouncement with a sick chuckle. It was a nightmarish sound, and the little hairs rose on the back of Mae's neck.

Barry leaned in close and asked her, "What's so funny?"

Mae stiffened with the thought that Barry heard Stranger Danger, too. Or... She hated to think it, but did that scary sound come from... *her*?

"N-n-nothing," stuttered Mae, a basket case of nerves. She winced from fear. Then, trying to sound matter of fact, she asked, "How's your jerk pork?"

"Great! Glad she told us about the allspice; it'll save me a lot of experimenting at home."

The Wrights moved along the buffet. Mae could see that Barry's food looked much better than hers. She took a little of the salad and watched it wilt on her plate. That was enough for her. Her appetite was ruined. Afraid the food had been poisoned, Mae knew she was never going to be able to eat any of it. She abruptly left the serving line and moved to the dining table.

Mr. Mitchell stood beside his chair at the head of the table, holding the plate of food that Sally had fixed for him. He smiled toward Mae and indicated the waiting chairs. "Please sit anywhere you like," he said. "There's plenty of room."

Mae gave him a quick, nervous smile and sat down, then noticed her husband was watching her with a look of consternation flashing on his face like a neon sign. There was still a lot of enticing food waiting to be served between Barry and the far horizon of the buffet table. He hurried along to catch up with her as he paused to take helpings of a few more dishes before he went to sit down.

Mae, on pins and needles already, discovered the chair she had chosen did not help her. Although it had looked the same as all the others, when she sat down it wobbled alarmingly on a bad leg. So, she had to sit very still, hoping it would not break. Next, she noticed her place setting, discovering details that had not been immediately apparent. Her utensils were filmed and dull. What she first had taken for a lovely crystal water goblet turned out to be a chipped jelly glass. It was too late to move since all the places were taken, except for the empty place to her left, which was now being occupied by Barry. Mae was sure her husband had not noticed her predicament because he would have traded places with her.

"I thought you were hungry," Barry whispered. "Now's your big chance! Why aren't you having more to eat?"

Stranger Danger sighed, *He doesn't see things quite the same as you and me.*

"Seems like nobody does," Mae mumbled, close to tears.

She reached for her napkin. A blue-green lizard with orange feet tumbled out of the napkin's folds. The creature ran hotfooted over her lap then vanished beneath the tablecloth. Mae jumped, then regained control to cover her shock.

The American lady sitting beside her giggled.

Ignore the silly slut, recommended Stranger Danger. Mae dropped her eyes and stared at her hands.

Barry shouted, "I thought you wanted to try some authentic Jamaican food?"

Ignore Mr. Bluster, too. Try to live through this, advised Stranger Danger.

Mr. and Mrs. Mitchell smiled at their guests from either end of the table.

"Shall we begin?" said Mr. Mitchell.

No need to tell Barry twice. At first, he devoured the food on his plate like a ravenous wolf. Before long, though, he polished off the remainder slowly.

Mae watched how Barry ate and feared he was going to die and that, if she ate, she would die, too. Afraid that her husband was being poisoned, she could not watch. She could not eat her food, which looked no better than offal. Once again, Mae did her best to maintain her cool, pushing food around her plate, trying to hide her panic, and acting like everything was fine. She knew the servants were still watching her and so was that harpy Ms. Simpson. All around her, smiles turned into leers, eyes stared at her, and everyone seemed to be shouting. Mae hid her fear and hung on through the horrible meal, the whole time fighting a desire to stop struggling, give up and start screaming for help. Mae was on the verge of losing it totally when Mrs. Mitchell ended the luncheon by inviting people outside for a stroll in their private garden.

In the garden, strolling beside her husband, Mae prayed that things would return to normal. The lush horticultural plot, almost as large as the one at the Caw Park Beach Resort, encircled the rear and both sides of the home's rectangular layout. A great variety of vegetation grew abundantly, including pimento or allspice, palm and ferns, and limes. But the more Mae wanted things to be normal the more distorted reality turned.

Barry was the only person she could truly trust — her only link to reality. Yet, he was so easily duped. Mae believed the Jamaicans kept pulling the wool over his eyes. And it probably was not safe to discuss the Jamaicans with him anyway. She might put his life in greater danger, thinking, "Barry is likely to confront them with their lies... and then where would we be? Dead!"

Mae's nerves felt stretched, yanked, and twanged like a car antenna from second-guessing everyone and continuing her contrasting emotional duality: outwardly calm and inwardly panic-stricken. Her distress became so acute that she could not continue to act like things were normal. One glance at the smiling Prudence Simpson sent her rising tide of panic to a crest of fear.

She needed to get away from these horrible schemers. Using the excuse that she needed to use the bathroom, Mae hurried off to it and closed the door. She struggled to regain her composure, hyperventilating and questioning whether what she felt was real or unreal. Mae could not look in the mirror, too afraid of what she might see. She turned her back to it, rocking on the edge of insanity.

She wanted the Mitchells to be a normal family, making a living in the tourist trade now that the aluminum industry was pulling out. In this mental state, it made sense for her to scribble a note, using lipstick to write it on a sheet of toilet paper, begging them for rescue from the cutthroats in Ocho Rios. She slipped it into the hollow center of an extra roll of tissue paper on the side counter. Hiding the note calmed her down, as if she had taken some control over their fate. This spark of hope for their salvation helped Mae pull herself together. Having regained her composure, she returned to the party.

The tour group was ready to leave. Mae nervously boarded the bus. But a new surge of fear gripped her as she took her seat. Once more, she tussled with panic.

Barry kept asking, "Are you all right? Are you having a good time?"

"Yes, fine," she feigned a delightful smile.

But he looked at her with a mirthless smile and comfortingly snuggled next to her.

All the way back to Caw Park Beach Resort on the minibus, Mae heard the voices of their fellow passengers blathering loudly. She listened, terrified of the meaningless cacophony of sounds until, suddenly, she made out a whispering voice that said, "Too bad about the Americans, but they're doomed." Her heart pounded faster. She questioned if she heard that or maybe not. But in a Machiavellian defense, Mae acted like she did not. She did not want to give the Jamaicans the satisfaction of seeing her pathetic and unhinged. She had to keep her guard up.

Mae could not help wondering how these Jamaicans had managed to delude Barry so completely. She could hardly wait until they returned to their hotel room, thinking she must tell Barry what was happening and that he had to wise up!

* * *

On the bus, Barry tried to understand what was going on with Mae — he could not hear the voices like she could. He rode on the minibus getting angrier and angrier, concluding, "Talk about a bad trip, it's been a nightmare from start to finish!" He thought they should pack up and take the next flight out.

In the days to come, Barry would remember that thought and that moment. He would wish they had done just that.

* * *

Back at the hotel, the Wrights tried to relax and talk on their balcony. Barry wanted to find out what Mae was feeling. Unfortunately, Mae had lost her zeal to speak of the revelations she had felt so strongly in the mountains. Those feelings were gone. Mae felt all right and reluctant to put earlier thoughts into words; no longer sure her perceptions had been accurate.

Whenever her mood dropped, Mae felt her heart sink like a stone in a well of fear. She realized something was wrong with the emotions and perceptions she felt during those episodes. She truly wanted to tell Barry what was happening, but while it was going on she was freaked out. It was all she could do to hang on. Once her mood ascended, her heart came back up from the depths like a balloon. She came out of it and soon remembered her disturbing episode as little more than a fading nightmare... Or a more detached feeling, like someone told her the details of a disturbing dream. Or maybe she had a similar dream, or does it only seem like she did?

When Mae was at her most rational, she was in near-complete denial, only dimly aware of having had a problem. During moments of elation, Mae was filled with an overabundant sense of well-being and immediately forgot her fear and confusion. Her condition *only* troubled her *when* it troubled her.

An African American woman from the South Side of Chicago did not work herself up to be the head of PR/marketing at one of the world's largest zoos without a lot of self-confidence. But Mae was losing it, losing her self-assurance because she could not tell what was happening from what was without substance. She wanted to believe that her fear of the Jamaicans was her imagination but that frightened her in a whole new way. As always, she did not want to whine and complain. She fought to sort things out for herself and stewed in her juices of dread.

"I'm tired," she said moodily to Barry as if everything was fine. "It's been a long day."

In a last-ditch effort to cheer her up, Barry said, "We're already so far over budget, I'm not going to fight it anymore. How about going out to dinner, to one of those pricey restaurants?"

"Really?" Mae's eyes brightened. "Really!" She jumped up excitedly. "How about the one that Carl and Arlene told us about?"

Later that evening the Wrights went out for dinner at the restaurant that served the great sunshine (pumpkin) soup, The Lemon Tree. Mae dressed in her only dress, a pumpkin orange cotton sundress with a matching shawl by Pierre Cardin, which shimmered from interwoven threads of gold. Henry was at the cabstand and, with a surprised but approving smile, opened the door for Mae. When they arrived at the restaurant, located in a hotel on the main street in Ocho Rios, things looked better to Mae. They dined on a terrace high above the sea, surrounded by lush foliage and a huge lemon tree. It looked like a normal restaurant with normal people.

She was back in reality. Dining with her husband in a romantic ambience was so relaxing and enchanting. Mae was certain her troubles were over.

The Wrights, once more, enjoyed themselves. They returned to their hotel feeling upbeat and entered, they hoped, their inviolable room. Mae took her pill and instilled her eyedrops with no fuss. Out on the balcony, Barry and Mae watched a crescent moon glued to the black velvet sky, tasted the slight luminescent surf in the salty air, and listened to the crickets, frogs, and sudden unknown rustlings in the jungle nearby. Tired after a weary day, they turned in, fell asleep, and woke up on Wednesday morning.

CHAPTER NINE

Wednesday, Sept. 19 — Shopping and killing time in Paradise

Mae awakened that Wednesday morning with the hollow place inside her refilled with self-confidence and her nervousness gone. She would have stayed in bed if she had foreseen the emotional roller coaster she would be riding for the rest of the day. But perky and full of plans, she painstakingly assembled a house-of-cards sanity that depended on her constantly doing normal things in normal ways, one after another. She tried not to think too much about anything, otherwise her fragile house of cards might collapse. Mae resolved that no matter what, even if the world turned upside down, she would take it in stride.

"Honey," she said, lively stepping out of the shower and drying herself off. "I'm hungry. Let's go have breakfast."

Barry, who had just finished shaving, tossed his toiletries disgustedly in their case on the sink. He turned and stared at her, totally frustrated.

"Are you crazy? Honey, we have no money."

Mae felt hurt and shocked by his response. She knew he was the one who did not understand that they *had* to spend money. The Jamaicans expected it.

"How could he say they had no money? We can charge it!"

Barry's face and neck got red and blotchy. He spun around to look at himself in the mirror. After drawing in a slow, deep breath, he said softly, "Don't you get it? If we charge it, we still have to pay the money back."

Mae knew that, although Barry loved her, he was too big a fool to depend on. So, done doubting herself, she decided to take control of her fate.

"This is my vacation and you're not going to ruin it. I'm hungry, and I'm going to breakfast, with or without you. "

"Fine!" Barry sighed, "You're right. This is your vacation. If you want breakfast, fine. But I'm not going to spend 20 dollars that we don't have on a two-dollar breakfast! I'll go with you, but I'm not going to eat."

Mae could tell that Barry was in a mood, ready to explode with, "Let's go home!" He reluctantly accompanied her down to breakfast about 8 a.m., refusing anything but coffee.

Bruce and Cindy arrived and invariably joined them at breakfast. During their friendly chat, the Bennetts said that they planned to go into town. They invited the Wrights to join them.

"That's sounds great!" Mae said, "I'd like to go shopping."

"Mae, don't you think we should stay here? We could go swimming."

Knowing Barry was saying no to her plan because all her plans would cost money, Mae insisted, "No, let's go shopping."

"Not interested," Barry said. "I'd like to go snorkeling. Bruce, may I borrow your gear?"

* * *

Around 10:00 a.m., Barry went snorkeling at the hotel while Mae met the Bennetts in the lobby. They went to the cabstand. As Bruce gave the cab driver instructions, Cindy explained, "We need to go to the bank to exchange our money. That is where you get the best rates. Then we'll go shopping at the marketplace and later have lunch at a restaurant downtown."

Mae was agreeable to anything, if it kept her from recalling things that had happened to her recently and analyzing her perceptions. She spent money freely at the market on souvenirs, no haggling. She purchased an extra-large, multicolored straw tote, basically a woven rattan sack to put all her bargains in. She paid the vendors exactly what they asked for.

The Bennetts and Mae selected a cute continental restaurant, featuring seafood, to have lunch. While eating, Mae distinctly overheard other tourists who were seated at tables around them, whispering about her and her husband.

"That's the American woman from Caw Park," said one voice. "She won't eat; her husband won't let her shop." The voices said things like, "They are never going home!"

Mae no longer denied the delusions that assailed her. She knew with certainty that the voices were real. Her house of cards collapsed.

The waiter came over to serve them. Mae thought the man was staring at her in deep disappointment. He continued to stare at her while he spoke in patois to the other waiters, only this time Mae was surprised to find she understood most of what he was saying, Something like, "It's too bad but this big, stupid American and his troublesome wife have to die…"

Mae desperately wanted to scream in terror, "I heard you!"

Then she saw something that scared the hell out of her. She saw the coffee steward slip off his false face of resignation and stodginess for a couple of heartbeats. He showed her his true face, a Jamaican face with an angry, frowny look, and a hard glare. He had unusually sharp-looking teeth. Then he hid his face behind his mask again and got back to his job. Mae got the message: she was calling too much attention to herself, and they were all "in on it"!

The voice of Stranger Dander whispered in her head, *Of course, they're all in on it! They've got a real ugly unemployment problem on this island, you know that!*

Mae was convinced it was true. The Jamaicans were using their island paradise as a lure to trap Americans. They were doing it to survive, and they were dead serious about it, despite the big "come-back-to-Jamaica" smiles on their false faces. With that worked out, she thought about telling Barry. But her senses reeled, growing scared out of her wits until Mae's mind snapped.

Mae knew it but no longer cared. In the seconds following her losing touch with reality, she felt an enormous sense of relief. In her Stranger Danger mind, she thought, *If I had realized sooner how much better I was going to feel, I would have stopped struggling a long time ago!*

Mae was thoroughly convinced, *There is a conspiracy, a Jamaican conspiracy to victimize us!* She deduced, *Barry and I were "set up" by the Jamaicans right from the start! We've been singled out for the full treatment, and they won't be satisfied until they've robbed us blind, ruined our vacation, and run us off their island!*

Mae questioned whether she should bring Barry "in on" her conclusions. But, now absorbed by Stranger Danger, she decided, *Until I can get real proof, just play along!*

The delusions were no longer disturbing. They became Mae's reality. She grabbed control of herself, thinking *I know what I must do...* She began to play the Bennetts' game, knowing that they were "in on it," too.

Mae was certain that the schemers could kill her or Barry at any time. So, she planned to play along and buy as much time as she could. However, she determined that no one else was going to kill her. If she was going to die, she would choose the time and place by killing herself. That way, she would end these unbearable charades and deny the Jamaicans a victory.

Finished with lunch, she got into a cab with the Bennetts and returned to the hotel. Mae did not have to turn her head to know that the Bennetts were watching to make sure she went straight to her room. She felt eyes spying from behind every door. Mae expressed mirth because they were not fooling her anymore. In a few minutes, it would not matter anyway. She thought, *Too bad about poor Barry. I love him. But we'll be together again when we get to the other side.*

* * *

Barry thought Mae seemed quite perky when she came in their room around one o'clock that afternoon, swinging her "finds" from the market in the extra-large multicolored straw tote. He had been waiting for her and got mad as a trapped grizzly when he discovered she had spent money equivalent to more than $100 on a bag of junk!

Mae listened to his tirade, totally unconcerned. At one point she said, "What does it matter. It's only money! She told him, "Don't be such a grouch." In a flight of fantasy, she said, "You're like Italian bread: hard and crusty on the outside but soft and warm on the inside."

She voluntarily offered to give him a soothing backrub, something she almost never did. He gladly accepted that offer. The gentle massage and her hypnotic voice lulled him to the brink of sleep. Very relaxed, almost asleep, Barry said, "Mae, I'm glad you are having a good day. Maybe everything will be all right."

With that said, he floated into dreamland. But as he drifted off, he realized something was not quite right and...

Mae chose that moment to do what she planned, tiptoeing around so as not to disturb him.

...Barry snapped awake. His mind became completely alert as he listened... to the tiny sounds from the bathroom. He wondered what Mae was doing in there. Quietly Barry got up and walked to the bathroom door. The door was not quite closed. He pushed it slowly open...

Mae was in the bathroom, her back to Barry. Her hands were busy doing something he could not quite see, until... He saw that Mae was singing a little ditty softly to herself and swallowing all of her cortico-steroid pills.

"I'm... a little teapot," she sang with her mouth full of pills.

Mae had spotted his safety razor lying on the sink and tried to smash apart the safety razor to get at the thin, sharp stainless-steel blades. Harder than it looked, she fumbled ...

... Barry caught her from behind, grabbing her wrists and twisting a razor from her grasp. She screamed and struggled in his bear hug.

"Mae, what on earth are you trying to do?" Barry shouted, even though his eyes told him the answer.

There were little white pills on the counter and some on the floor. Barry held Mae very tightly until she quieted down. Mae's pill bottle was empty.

"Did you take all those pills, Honey?"

She would not answer, but her stubbornness made Barry sure the answer was yes.

Barry started to drag Mae out of the bathroom. He did not want to let her go, but he needed to reach for the telephone on the table beside the bed.

Mae struggled, raving at him, "Go back to sleep! Leave me alone!"

Barry pushed Mae onto the bed and used his superior size to press her back into the pillows while he grabbed for the phone. Then he wondered who he could call?

He called the hotel desk to ask for the location of the nearest poison-control center. The desk informed him that they were sure there was none of those in Jamaica. Mae grew quiet. Barry worried that he might be smothering her. He took a risk and sat up off Mae, continuing to hold her by the wrist.

"What about an Emergency Room,"

Yes, the desk was sure there was a hospital in St. Ann's Bay. He wanted to know if there was anything closer. No sir, that was the closest medical facility of any kind.

Mae was not struggling now. She was limp in his grasp.

Barry wanted to let her go, but wondered could he trust her to remain calm. He tossed her some clothes and told her to get dressed. Mae complied, grumbling about not wanting to go to the hospital. Barry watched her constantly while he got into his shirt, shorts, and shoes.

About 2:30 p.m., the Wrights made it down to the cabstand whereby a stroke of luck they found Henry waiting. Mae was becoming increasingly wild, again. She did not want to go with the Jamaican cabdriver. Barry stuffed her into the cab. He hurriedly explained to Henry that Mae had had an overdose of some very powerful medication and needed to get to a hospital right away. Henry knew St. Ann's Bay Hospital; his wife was the nurse there.

The Wrights were on their way to the hospital by 2:40 p.m. The Jamaican cabby drove very fast. Mae grew increasingly more distressed. She lunged for the door handle and managed to get the door part-way open to fling herself out the door. Barry held her tightly and prevented her from hurling herself from the racing van. He pulled her to safety, prying her fingers from the handles and closing the door. He knew he was hurting her, but he had no choice.

Henry focused on his break-neck driving.

* * *

Sept. 19, evening — Being the entertainment at St. Ann's Bay Hospital

They arrived at the hospital — if you could call it that — at 3:30 p.m. To Barry, it looked like a couple of prefab huts. Barry told Henry that he had very little cash with him but promised to take care of him when they returned to the hotel. Henry promised to wait.

Barry and Mae walked into the hospital, holding hands. She was quiescent by then.

Barry thought he was beginning to see a pattern to his wife's strange attacks. They were coming and going fitfully. For the next five or 10 minutes, she would be more-or-less herself, sick and frightened. Then an attack would come. Mae would no longer be herself but would become completely panicked, believing that "the Jamaicans" were all trying to kill her, and that Barry was completely duped by them. In this state of mind, she became suicidal, preferring to kill herself rather than give "the Jamaicans" the satisfaction of killing her.

Inside the hospital, no one appeared to be in charge. Barry, all sweaty, spotted a few Jamaicans about, presumably patients. He was hotter inside the hospital than he was outside because, in the hospital, Barry was denied the cooling effect of the breeze. He clung to Mae, who was growing disturbed at the sight of these Jamaicans. She had a couple of episodes while they waited and waited in the hallway, and the Jamaicans gathered to observe the spectacle of "the poor crazy American lady."

Barry realized that in their darkest hour he and his wife had become a few moments' entertainment in the lives of these childlike strangers. Finally, he heard footsteps coming down the corridor, a woman's heels. The crowd of curious onlookers pulled back some — but not too far since this was a pretty good show!

A Jamaican woman in a nurse's uniform and cap approached Barry and Mae. She looked to see a big, sweaty White man gripping a small struggling Black woman, taking it in stride.

Barry started, trying to explain. "This is my wife, Mae Wright. She took an overdose of her medication…"

The nurse took charge by questioning him. Barry answered her as well as he could, considering the difficulty he had in understanding her heavy Jamaican accent. While he talked to the nurse, Mae went from bawling and struggling to crying quietly.

The nurse, who noticed that she had calmed down but he had not let her go, said, "She has visible bruises up and down her arms."

The nurse looked at him with accusatory eyes. The nurse approached Mae, speaking to her soothingly, sister-to-sister, wanting to separate Mae from her brutish husband and giving her the chance to tell Nurse the "truth."

Barry was frustrated that the nurse did not believe him and that by her behavior she was implying he was an abusive husband. Barry allowed Nurse to walk Mae a foot or so beyond his grasp. She did appear calm and on the verge of speaking to Nurse. Nurse was "all ears" as she waited with a patient look on her face.

The crowd sucked in its breath. They had seen Mae in action!

And she did not disappoint them. Mae raised her eyes to the nurse, who started at the look of sheer hatred in her eyes. The sound that had trembled on Mae's lips became a snarl, and Mae lunged sideways, grabbing an IV bottle off a cart of medicines. She hurled the IV bottle to the floor, smashing it, and lurched after a large, jagged shard of glass. As her hand closed on the shard, Barry's big hands closed on Mae's wrists.

"No-o-o-o—!" wailed Mae, as Barry jerked her to her feet. She jerked and struggled in his grasp as he relieved her of her makeshift dagger.

Now, nurse knew why this big White man was so sweaty. Nurse saw the crowd of onlookers as if for the first time and yelled at them, "Go find something honest to do and leave these poor people alone!"

Nurse, having seen with her own eyes, was ready to listen to Barry. As Mae continued to heave and struggle in his body hug, Barry wanted to know if they could please get out of the hall.

Nurse nodded her assent and led the struggling couple to the doctor's office.

The doctor's office appeared to be doubling as a storeroom. Nurse cleared files from two chairs. Barry sat Mae down and looked to see that no potential weapons were within her reach. Then he seated himself beside her. Barry was wringing wet with perspiration, which ran into his eyes and down his neck. They both breathed heavily.

Nurse took her eyes away from the sweaty White man and saw the doctor's prize possession: a small desktop fan. She unplugged some diagnostic equipment to plug in the fan and aimed the insufficient result at Barry. The breeze it generated "didn't amount to a hill of beans," but it was an act of pure kindness for which Barry would always be grateful.

Mae was lapsing back into her quiescent, rational self. Nurse listened for a moment while Barry told his terrified bride where they were and what had been happening to her. When she was in her quiet mood, Mae seemed to understand. Barry knew they had only moments before his Mae would be swept away on an emotional tide beyond her power to resist, and all he would be able to do was prevent her from killing herself. Her life was in his hands.

He promised, "Honey, I will never let you go!"

Nurse excused herself to go and tell the doctor about Mae. She explained to the Wrights that it would be some time before the doctor would be able to see Mae, as he was currently performing an appendectomy. She had to push out past the curious onlookers who clogged the doorway the minute she opened it. Nurse berated them, again, and pulled the door shut.

Barry held Mae while she told him about all the things she had seen and heard ever since their arrival. Some of it, Barry had heard before; some of it was news to him. He filled in the blanks for Mae and explained to her that she was experiencing a reaction to her medication, especially now that she had swallowed so much of the stuff.

He wished someone were pumping her stomach right now, but probably already too late. Barry, the should-have-been doctor, could feel that her pulse was fast but strong. She breathed rapidly but appeared to be getting enough air. She felt cold to him, but that might be because he was so hot. She was coherent when she was herself. She was probably in no immediate physical danger from the drug. But then, what did he know?

Barry was in an agony of impatience, wondering, "How long will the doctor be?"

At that time, it was 3:51 p.m. Between then and half past 5 o'clock when the doctor finally arrived, Mae experienced eight or nine episodes of mood swings. Each time she started to slip away, Barry told her how much he loved her and how he would never let her go. Each time she grew wild and panic-stricken, she shrieked, cried, and bucked in his grip. Each time, he held on tightly and tried to soothe her until she finally relaxed, and he held his bride again.

The doctor arrived when Mae was in a lull. His name was Dr. Miller. He was the staff of this 30-bed facility, he and Nurse. Jamaica had one physician per 6,159 persons for a population of 2.55 million. He would now turn his full attention to the young lady, whom he understands is experiencing some problem.

"Oh, no. No problem here," said the beguiling Mae.

Dr. Miller started asking her questions to see what she remembered, engaging her in conversation to try and assess whether her behavior was irrational. Mae seemed so relaxed with the doctor that Barry let down his guard. He was aware of how it must look for him to sit there and grip this apparently rational woman by her wrists.

The doctor looked at Barry and indicated that he wanted him to let her go. Against his better judgement, Barry let go of Mae. Mae sat there smiling calmly at the doctor for a moment. Then she shrieked and lunged for the desk, arms outstretched. The doctor was caught completely by surprise but managed a frantic back-pedal on his stool, staying just beyond Mae's reach. He thought she was going for his throat, but Mae stretched her hands beyond the startled man and plunged her fingers into the electric fan!

Barry had recovered and was a half-heartbeat behind Mae, too late to prevent her straining fingers from contacting the spinning steel blades but able to jerk them back away a split second later. He pulled Mae to him, wrestled her into a full bear hug, holding her while she shrieked and spat and thrashed in front of the amazed doctor.

Gradually she quieted down. As soon as he dared, Barry sat her back down and held both her wrists tightly again.

Doctor Miller tore his eyes away from the spectacle and focused on his broken and now useless fan where it lay in the corner. He cleared his throat and, while he cleaned his eyeglasses, said helpful things like "Yes," "Well," and "I see." He checked to see that Barry had a good hold on Mae and asked a few questions about her medication, and how much she had taken.

He said, "In cases where corticosteroids are administered in large doses, as in Mae's case, sometimes the patient experiences a psychotic reaction." Mae seemed to be experiencing such a reaction. "Her vital signs are good, and she does not present any symptoms that put her in danger of immediate physical harm from her attempted overdose," he said. "However, her moods swing wildly from sane to insane as the psychosis comes and goes in waves."

Barry held Mae while Dr. Miller gave her an injection of Valium. Its result was almost immediate. Mae relaxed into a near stupor.

Dr. Miller said, "That should hold her for a while." He then gave Barry a small vial containing six pink tablets. "Give your wife one pill every four hours. It should be enough to help you get her to the United States."

He then told Barry that he must return Mae to the care of her physicians immediately, by the next available flight out. He felt she would need to be put through a period of detoxification while her physicians determined a more suitable dose that would control Mae's sarcoidosis without driving her out of her right mind. Dr. Miller told Barry that too much sunlight might be contributing to the severity of Mae's reaction. He was surprised that her physicians allowed her to visit a tropical country while taking such high doses of steroids.

He asked whether Mae had had any stressful experiences during her stay. Barry slowly nodded his head, thinking about all the unfair bullshit that had gone wrong with their vacation.

The tranquilizer had calmed Mae down. She now moved like she was very snoozy.

Barry had no money to pay the doctor. But Dr. Miller looked like it was an old story. He gave the doctor his address in the 'States and asked the doctor to please bill him whatever they owed. Barry thanked the doctor and Nurse and sleepwalked Mae out to the cab, where Henry had been faithfully waiting all this time.

The return trip that night was a quiet one. Mae slept. Barry worried. Henry drove.

*　*　*

When the Wrights returned to the hotel about 8 o'clock that night, Barry put Mae to bed. She went right back to sleep.

Now, challenged with how to get home from Jamaica, Barry had to confront the unknown world of travel arrangements. He knew nothing about the planning that went on for their trip. He had never booked an airplane flight in his life. He picked up the phone and called the desk to find out if it would be possible for him to reach his tour rep. They took a message for Ms. Simpson to call him at the start of business. Next, Barry called the airline. He wanted to get home at cosmic speed, but he was on Jamaica Time. He learned that the next flight departed from Montego Bay airport (code MBJ) on Thursday at 11:10 a.m.

Barry hung up the phone and watched over Mae as she slept. He felt so much stress that it was impossible for him to sleep. He gave Mae a tranquilizer at 10 p.m. and another at 2 a.m. She slept while he packed. Thursday morning, four pills remained.

By sunrise, Barry had packed all their things except for the clothes they would wear home. Mae woke up in a panic. Barry had to give her a tranquilizer, leaving him with three pills. While Mae was drug induced, Barry sleepwalked her through a shower. He dressed her as if she were a child and hastily made the bed so the sleepy Mae could lie back down.

Then he called room service for a pot of coffee. He next stowed their dirty clothes and made sure that they were ready for departure. When room service arrived with Barry's pot of coffee promptly that morning at 7 o'clock, Mae slept soundly.

Barry called the front desk and left a message for Mr. Dunbar to "please call." He sat and drank his coffee slowly, savoring the Jamaican Blue Mountain for its deep flavor and caffeine buzz. Paradoxically, the stimulating coffee calmed his nerves as he tried to focus on the immediate problems, one by one.

His short-term goal was to settle all their business in Jamaica: pay their hotel bill, cash-out his Jamaican currency for American dollars, and trade his tickets for two spaces on the 11:10 flight out. His ultimate goal was to put Mae in her own bed that night.

About 7:45 a.m., the tour rep returned Barry's call from the night before. He explained the problem and enlisted her aid in obtaining the tickets for their flight. Mr. Dunbar called at 8:10 a.m., responding to Barry's message. Barry asked him for a few minutes of his time to watch Mae while he took care of his business at 9 a.m. sharp. Mr. Dunbar agreed.

The tour rep called back at 8:20 a.m. to tell Barry she would meet him at the shuttle bus at 9:15 a.m. She would have the vouchers for their plane tickets and "something Barry would need to sign." The shuttle would leave for Montego Bay promptly at 9:30 a.m.

At 9 o'clock sharp, Mr. Dunbar arrived to watch Mae while Barry hurried through his business in the lobby. Barry returned and thanked Mr. Dunbar for his help.

Mae started stirring around 9:10 a.m. Barry quickly used the toilet and then roused Mae, insisting she do the same. All groggy, frightened, and growing belligerent, she did not want to cooperate. Looking at her panic-stricken face, Barry was not sure who she was. He was not looking forward to maneuvering a resistant Mae and all their luggage out to the shuttle bus. He decided to give her another tranquilizer, although it was a little soon after her last one, leaving him with two tranquilizers.

Mae went to the bathroom now, while Barry loaded up with the luggage. With his left hand, he put his arm through the shoulder straps of the two black soft-sided suitcases and hiked the straps as high on his shoulder as he could. Then, he stood there, patting his foot. Barry was about to barge in and get Mae when she came out looking disheveled and miffed about being rushed. He quickly pushed the multicolored tote of purchases in her arms. Next, he grabbed the black garment bag he would have to hold high to prevent it dragging. And finally, he grabbed Mae by the upper arm and forced her along despite her increasingly languid protests.

Good, thought Barry, the tranquilizer was kicking in. He headed Mae out the door, leaving the door ajar. Down at the bus stand at 9:15 a.m., Barry and Mae were the last to arrive. People were waiting in line to board the bus, and the luggage was still being stowed. Barry could feel the hot sun burning down on him and Mae, who was grouchy and yawning. Barry had to constantly hold her while passing their bags to the driver, who stowed them in the locker.

Standing in the line, waiting to board the bus, Barry wondered where their tour rep was. He wanted to get Mae out of the hot sun. Ms. Simpson arrived at last at 9:25 a.m. She presented some papers on a clipboard that Barry must sign. Barry did not want to sign these papers, which absolved Hummingbird Tropical Tours of all liability. But the pretty rep was all business now. Unless Barry signed the papers, he and his wife would not be allowed to board the bus.

Mae, with her sleepy eyes scrunched up against the blinding sun, was growing restive and alarmed. Her pretty brown face was beginning to shine with perspiration. Barry did not think about it for very long. He signed the papers and got Mae on board the air-conditioned bus. He made a mental note to call their lawyer when they got home. Barry put Mae against the window and seated himself beside the aisle, using his presence to keep Mae from going anywhere.

The bus started the trip back to MBJ at 9:30 a.m. It was an hour-long journey. As the bus roared over an ancient, steeply sloping stone bridge, it left the Parish of St. Ann behind and entered Trelawny Parish. To pass the time, the bus driver began to tell the passengers stories about the folklore of Jamaica.

His specialty seemed to be hauntings that had occurred in the countryside through which they traveled, as well as a few local legends about witchcraft and untimely death, usually resulting in more opportunities for hauntings.

The driver slowed for the fishing village of Rio Bueno where the A1 again hugged the coast, circling around a bay where the real fishermen were working at repairing their nets while a feral looking dog contested with several fat pelicans for discarded fish heads. The buildings here were of cut stone, but old and in poor repair. He noted that some folks believed this place to be the actual site of Columbus' landing in Jamaica on May 4, 1494. The place was so quaint and the seascape so picturesque it was easy to imagine several small caravels riding at anchor out on the blue swells.

* * *

While she traveled along, Mae lapsed in and out of a drugged sleep. Whenever she half-woke, she heard this Jamaican man going on and on with his weird tales. When she slept, his voice invaded her disturbing dreams, threatening to kill her and Barry while she struggled to move. But her legs would not go. Terrified, she tried to scream but no sound would come out. So, Mae struggled and moaned while her worried husband rode along beside her, clutching her warm hand.

At MBJ by 10:30 a.m., Mae "came to" in a panic. Barry held her by the arm while he got their luggage off the bus. He kept talking while pulling her toward the main entrance.

"Mae, it's important for you to cooperate so I can take you home to your doctor who will make everything all right," he pleaded, trying to "reach" her. But Mae did not want to go through the doors of Sangster International Airport because "the Jamaicans" would be waiting for them there. She struggled with Barry and managed to tear the pocket loose from his shirt. When she saw how surprised and hurt Barry was by her attack on his clothing, she stopped resisting and let him hustle her into the gateway to their return home.

* * *

Barry half-carried, half-dragged their belongings, as well as the balky Mae, all the way through the terminal to their departure gate. By 10:40 a.m., the Wrights had changed their tickets and turned over their baggage. Barry, forced to carry the stuffed extra-large multicolored tote on board as hand luggage, thought to pitch it. But it was too late. Mae simply did not want to get on board that plane, crying "the Jamaicans are waiting," as if monsters were at the top of the portable ramp. Barry just gripped her arm tightly and manhandled her up the steps, remembering her *Casablanca* fantasy from their much-different arrival. Now, as she was leaving, he reckoned her starring in *Gaslight*! He stuffed her on board the plane, past the startled flight attendants and down the aisle to their seats right in the middle of the damned plane, mercilessly no leg room for him. He deposited Mae beside the window, buckling her in good and tight before squeezing the extra-large tote in the overhead bin. Then he sat down in the cramped seat and buckled in.

The flight departed MBJ at 11:20 a.m. local time, taking to the air for Miami International Airport (code MIA), originally Wilcox Field. With Barry watching over her, Mae returned to an uneasy sleep. The flight to MIA took an hour and a half. But the plane circled the airport for 30 minutes before landing at 12:50 p.m.

Now, they were traveling on AT Time, Airport Travel Time. Holding on to Mae, Barry had to locate the checked baggage and report to U.S. Customs. Mae was a good deal of trouble since waking up. She did not want to go with him and had to be forced along by his strength and determination. MIA was a huge place. He was having a helluva time. It was 1:10 p.m. when they located the lines for customs and got in one.

Barry held Mae's arm tightly with one hand and used the other to manage the bags as they inched forward. An officer walked past Barry with a large German shepherd. The dog lunged at Mae and barked ferociously, barely controlled by its handler. Mae predictably freaked out, perhaps remembering the Big Bad Wolf she saw in her closet at home. Mae cried audibly and tried to convince Barry that they must alter their plans, flee in a new direction to outrun "the Jamaicans." The line moved up.

There was a young man, probably an American student, in front of the Wrights. It was that young guy's turn to heft his suitcase onto the counter for the inspector.

Barry watched him acting suspiciously. The customs inspector put one hand on his suitcase, and suddenly the young man bolted, running frantically away from customs into the vast Miami airport. The inspector was on his walkie-talkie immediately, notifying his fellow officers as to the description and last-known location of the runner. Another officer arrived and carried the runner's bag into a room beyond the inspection point. He used a key to unlock the door and carried the suitcase inside.

Barry, holding tight to his sobbing wife, watched with fascination another diversion. A second young man one counter over abandoned his bag to make a run for it, too. More communications, more activity, and another bag joined the first one in the locked room.

Soon, officers arrived with the first runner and into the locked room they went. Barry caught a glimpse of an officer hacking open one of the sealed plastic pipes he found in the suitcases. A spread-open newspaper, placed on the floor, caught the white powder that fell from the pipe. The door closed behind the officers who arrived with the second runner in custody.

The excitement was all over. It was Mae and Barry's turn to have their things inspected. Mae was crying a lot as the inspector poked through her things. The agent gave Barry a very strange look. Barry explained that Mae was in the midst of a medical emergency. The man said nothing. He completed his inspection and passed the Wrights through to the U.S.A. officially.

CHAPTER 10

Thursday, Sept. 20 — Dealing with flight delays home

At 1:22 p.m. EST, Barry realized they had a long way to go to reach the departure gate for the connecting flight to Atlanta Hartsfield (code ATL), originally Candler Field. He had the suitcases and garment bag while Mae's arms held the extra-large tote. Barry had seen airline employees driving electric carts, and he had seen handicapped people being transported on these carts. He wished he could arrange to have Mae transported, even if *he* had to walk and carry their luggage. He did not see anyone he could ask, so he kept walking, pulling a deeply terrified Mae along. Mae tried to run for it. She begged him to change their tickets. She tested his strength to keep moving and willpower to persist at every turn.

Mae strongly resisted going up the escalator and cried, "The Jamaicans are waiting up there. I know it!"

Curiously, no one in that busy international terminal paid much attention to them, the peculiar couple. Barry continued until he found the correct departure entrance and turned over all their luggage, except the darn tote. The Wrights passed through the metal detectors and arrived at their departure gate where Barry learned that the plane was now listed as delayed. They faced an estimated two-hour wait before they could board the flight to ATL. With the overstuffed tote at their feet at almost 1:40 p.m. EST, the Wrights sat and waited. Mae would not stop crying, so Barry administered a tranquilizer. Now, he had only one tranquilizer left. Mae calmed down and went to sleep. Barry sat, worrying about Mae. The AT Time extended to three hours with nothing he could do but wait.

Around 4:30 p.m. EST, the passengers going to ATL were called to board. Barry collected the dang tote, and, after a little trouble rousing her, the somnambulated Mae and headed onto the plane. Once on board, Mae returned to sleep. Barry returned to watching and worrying. The plane finally taxied onto the runway about 5 o'clock and soon they were airborne.

Mae was awake during the 5:55 p.m. EST landing at ATL. She was panicked and crying and constantly watching for "the Jamaicans" or any other strangers who approached since they could be hired by her tormentors. Barry had to grip her tightly to keep her in her seat.

Although Mae needed another tranquilizer, her husband needed her to be able to walk off this Miami flight and onto the one to Chicago. At least their baggage was being moved from plane to plane without Barry having to carry them through this airport. And, luckily, he was able to secure a little help at ATL.

As usual, people were slow to believe Barry's story about Mae's condition. But, on his insistence and ability to face another confrontation, the Wrights were given a cart-ride to their departure gate, and Barry got a chance to use the bathroom. He had not had the opportunity since early that morning, which was a long time for him.

At their departure gate by 6:10 p.m. EST, the Wrights faced the news of another long wait because it was storming in Atlanta. Their flight to Chicago had been rescheduled to depart at 8 p.m. Barry had virtually knocked himself out, trying to get to this point. With his hand tied by AT Time, he fought down a rising urge to cry, stuffed it back wherever it had come from before it could weaken his resolve.

"No one gives a damn about Mae, and, for sure, no one feels sorry for me!"

Thrust in a perilous situation, Barry was scared but did not panic. He knew that the Mae he loved was in there, and he swore to himself that he would go through hell to get her back! So, he had to stay strong no matter what.

Once again, Barry sat at a gate with Mae. She was in such obvious distress that he wanted to give her the one last precious tranquilizer he had left about 6:30 p.m. EST, but he waited. He had to tough it out. When they finally received the call to board, it was close to 9 o'clock. Barry had been unable to relieve himself for the simple reason that there was no one he could trust to hold on to his freaking wife for a couple of minutes!

While boarding the plane in Atlanta, he tried to explain his difficulty with Mae to the brunette flight attendant. He watched her fake eyelashes blinking as the first-puzzled expression ran the gamut through obvious skepticism and ended with fear, at which point she obviously decided that discretion was indeed the better part of valor. She pasted a stiff smile on her face and removed herself as far from their distress as her duties could take her. In any case, she made no effort to assist Barry with Mae, no effort at all.

On this last leg of their flight home, Barry's bladder felt like it was going to burst. He felt like any man badly needing to relieve himself: furious and ready to explode. The scratch on his throat burned, as did the matching red welts on the tender insides of his forearms. He smelled the BO from his damp, khaki camp shirt and shorts and found it almost unbearable. He detested being so filthy. He realized that he looked frightful. It occurred to him that he finally looked the part of the misnomer they teasingly had labeled him at work, Scary Barry.

His head ached so badly that he needed a bottle of elephant aspirins to cure it. If only he could take the Valium he had for Mae, but it was gone now. No more Valium. Barry stuffed the last pill in his wife's mouth after taking their seats on the plane to keep her in dreamland.

He grumpily refused any in-flight service. Who knew what jeopardy Mae could put herself in? Barry felt he had to keep Mae under his control. He held her hand constantly.

He had no way of knowing what the flight attendant had said to the rest of the crew. But he caught all three nervously glancing his way at one time or another during the flight. The older skinny blond woman glanced disapprovingly from afar, showing true fear in her eyes.

Barry yawned involuntarily and felt for a moment like he might pass out. In his chest, his heart flipped like a fish a few times, at least that is what it felt like. His pulse quickened. He wondered if he had been hyperventilating. Barry's insides felt all hollowed out. He had the oddest sensation that his stomach was a child's balloon being tugged and flexed by the tied string. He felt edgy and desperate, like anything could happen, like he could have a heart attack or explode or go blind or lose control of his bladder. Anything! He started to doubt that he could go on. Panic attack! Barry assured himself that if he could keep calm, he would be all right.

He unfastened his seatbelt and leaned forward, closing his eyes and lowering his head between his knees, trying to focus. He advised himself to think about something else. His mind's eye filled with an image of their 12-year-old son, Zachery, Barry hoped that he would be asleep when they got home, so he would not see his mother in her present condition.

Hidden in the shadows, Mae stirred and mumbled something in her sleep. His heartbeat quickened. He could not let her get away, which is when he invoked the power of *Clutch*. Barry sat up slowly, taking measured breaths. He willed himself to feel better, but, within a couple of heartbeats, his overtaxed mind was speeding again. He held tight to his stirring wife's hand as the plane began to drop through the clouds and rain, down through the dark, on the final approach to Chicago O'Hare International Airport (code ORD), originally Orchard Field.

Barry Moore Wright shook his head, finding it unbelievable that they had left their easy, comfortable home for the lifestyle of the rich and famous only to find themselves in this dangerous miserable condition of the impoverished and insignificant. At that moment, he contemplated thermonuclear warheads and tactical air strikes and calling down Armageddon on the island of Jamaica.

From his peripheral vision, Barry saw the brunette flight attendant march around to the opposite side of the cabin and over to the bulkhead seat to confront him, looking stern and officious. But when her gray eyes met his do-not-mess-with-me gaze, her stance changed. She took a more respectful approach, asking him to prepare for landing. Interrupted from his big payback fantasy and too cranky to speak, Barry never softened his expression as he rocked Mae into position for landing and then himself. He looked defiantly at the flight attendant, who had avoided helping him earlier.

When their plane finally landed at ORD around 11 p.m., CST, Barry was singing the "Hallelujah Chorus" from Handel's Messiah in his mind. He was so happy to be back in his hometown! The thought momentarily eased his mind but not for long because Mae awakened, and he had no more tranquilizers.

* * *

Sept. 20, evening — Nearing the end at the airport

Barry Moore Wright deplaned last, exiting from Gate C19 with a feisty Mae Bea Wright drowsily trying to squirm away from him. *Clutch* held her as they walked through the deserted airport terminal. Most of the restaurants and shops were closed at that late hour. Suddenly in another wave of jittery fear, Mae began struggling recklessly like a stressed gazelle, trying to escape his unrelenting grip. Barry felt like a six-foot-four-inch hulky European American male wrestler trying to hang on to an overstuffed, extra-large, multicolored woven straw tote with one hand while *Clutch* hung on to a five-foot-three-inch African American female featherweight boxer, constantly jabbing him with both hands.

Mae's natural coily hair, which reached Barry's heart, smooched upwards in messy peaks from laying so long against the airplane headrest. From the front, it looked like a burning bush as she struggled alongside her husband. From the rear, it laid flat, matted and nappy. Generally looking disheveled and devilish with her misapplied make-up smudged and her clothing as wrinkled as her forehead, Mae's unblinking wild-eyed stare looked spooky and cunning behind her lopsided aviator-style eyeglasses. Her eyes kept constantly scanning the crowd as if she were a soldier on reconnaissance. Now and then, she mightily mouthed something unintelligible.

"Keep walking," Barry ordered in a no-nonsense tone. "We need to get our luggage, take the shuttle bus to the car, and drive home."

Barry dragged Mae along, stepping like the seven-foot-tall silver robot Gort, programmed to walk straight ahead without stopping. Sporadically Mae lurched and twisted about like a squirrel in the road. He fantasized that if only he had a glove of Velcro, he could adhere it to her Afro and easily keep his wild and crazy wife in tow.

But all he could do was hold on. *Clutch* would not let her go.

No one asked Barry if he needed help. No one came near the Wrights, not even airline personnel. Passersby gave them plenty of room. A couple of people looked like they wanted to say something but did nothing — perhaps his size intimidated them.

Taking the escalator down to the baggage claim level, Barry kept hoping to find someone to assist them. In the distance, one member of the maintenance crew and a couple of passengers wandered around.

However, there was no help. To his surprise, one of the world's busiest airports was almost empty. Apprehensively Mae kept pace, taking three quick steps to each of his strides. Halfway across the floor of the echoing terminal, she really came alive, jerking and tugging to get away.

She demanded loudly, "Let me go!"

"Shush!" he barked, determined to keep right on moving.

With the escalator to the baggage level within sight, Barry pushed an actively resisting Mae towards the down escalator and pressed on.

"I'm not going down there!" Mae shrieked as she struggled, hardening her eyes and glaring at him while breathing heavily. "You can't make me!"

But Barry could, and he did. They descended. Mae sobbed, struggling alongside him constantly. Once they reached the bottom, he shoved her hard to get her feet moving. *Clutch* both prevented her from falling and kept her from getting away.

There was a good bit of activity when they reached the baggage area and more people around. The noisy baggage-handling machinery made it necessary for people to raise their voices. Their arrival attracted attention but not much. His treatment of her looked disturbing, but no one confronted him or showed interest in getting involved.

All in a dither, Mae pleaded, "Barry, we're in danger!" She grabbed a railing and held on tight, planting her feet. "Listen to me. They're following us! We should catch another flight; go somewhere they can't find us!" Jumping up and down, she implored, "Barry, *please.*"

Barry, showing stern determination, dropped the bothersome tote and patiently, deliberately but with sufficient force to hurt her, worked her fingers loose. As soon as her hands were free, he grabbed up the doggone tote and pushed it into her grasp, simultaneously resuming their forward motion toward the revolving belts to find the rest of their luggage.

"Mae, you have to help me," he yelled. "I can't carry everything by myself!"

She obeyed and stumbled along in his grasp, holding onto the damned tote. Suddenly she tried once more to pull free, unsuccessfully. She mumbled nervously, "Too many strangers, too much noise."

He soon located their checked luggage on the moving carousel. "Got 'em!"

With his left hand, he put his arm through the shoulder straps of the two black soft-sided suitcases and hiked the straps as high on his shoulder as he could, groaning from the too familiar aches. Next, he grabbed the black garment bag he would have to hold high to prevent it dragging, all without losing his right-hand grip on Mae. Then he headed for the up escalator to get back to the main floor and street level.

It was 11:50 p.m. by the time Barry and Mae got their luggage. Now, Mae carried the extra-large multicolored straw tote filled with gifts she had purchased over her shoulder, which accentuated her herky-jerky motions. Struggling to pick up his feet and sweating profusely, Barry carried two pieces of luggage slung over the same shoulder and held the black garment bag high with his left hand. *Clutch* tenaciously controlled Mae.

As Barry was Bogart-ing Mae onto the escalator, she exploded in another wave of panic. He managed to retain his grip and block her escape with his body, almost losing his balance and toppling backward. Mae banged into him. Barry propelled her forward.

The enormous terminal was almost empty. He tugged her toward the door to the outside world. A big sign above the door read CHICAGO. All at once, Mae fell to her knees, her lips almost touching the floor. Barry had no idea what Mae was trying to do. If he had known, he might have joined her.

Her actions, looking bizarre to him, caused him to yell, "Stop it!"

Clutch jerked her up in one rippling motion of force that went down her arm and bounced her back up on her feet before her lips quite touched the much trampled on floor. Embarrassed, frustrated, and angrier, Barry questioned whether this was happening.

"Jesus!" slipped out of his mouth. "Dammit, Mae, keep moving!" He blasted, "We've got to find the shuttle bus." He led the way, holding tight to his tremulous wife.

"Hold it!"

Stunned by the loud command, Barry turned to face an approaching cop in rain gear. He dropped his bags to the floor, straightening to his full height. But he never released his hold on Mae, still struggling to pull herself free.

"Yes, officer?"

"Just a minute there, you two! I'm Sergeant Mike Brannigan... I'm in charge of this section of the airport."

"*Please* help us!" pleaded Mae.

"Us?" The red-headed, leprechaun-faced police sergeant looked perplexed. "What's going on here? I've been watching you. Are you drunk?"

Sergeant Brannigan loosened his baton and stepped in real close to Barry. He looked him straight in the eye and sniffed for booze.

Barry did not give an inch. He stood his ground and met the cop's gaze, remembering his last close encounter with the police, not so many hours ago. At least, they were back in America where the law has limits, and a citizen still has a few rights. Barry willed himself to be calm. With as much patience as he could muster, he began, once again, to make his explanation to an authority figure with the power to make his life easy or make it hard.

"Sergeant, my name is Barry Wright. This is my wife, Mae. She's, uh... sick. We've just gotten back into town from Jamaica, and I'm trying to get her home. She's anxious and confused. I'm going to take her to the doctor as soon as I can."

Sergeant Brannigan deliberately broke eye contact with Barry. He turned to look closely at Mae. Obviously scared, Mae kept glancing around, as terrified of this policeman as she was of everyone else.

"You're not Jamaican," Mae said, and her wrinkled brow relaxed a tad. Still jittery, she wrung her hands while doing her best to explain. "You've got to help us. *Please*, we're not safe here!" More words tumbled out of her mouth. "Barry keeps on repeating the same tired lie, but here's the truth. The Jamaicans are trying to kill us!"

"I've been on the job for 17 years, lady. I've seen and heard about everything, but this is something new. There is no way you're in danger of being killed at *my* airport."

Obviously dealing with the public and the criminal element had made him cynical and quick to judge. Also, like a lot of people, he had some problem with the concept of mixed marriages. It was not so much racism, although there was some of that in him, but the Wrights were *unusual*, and consequently *undesirable*.

To Barry, he said, "She clearly needs help. What happens if you let her go?"

"She'll run. It comes and goes in waves," Barry explained.

Barry wished this cop would get off his case, wanting to gather up their luggage and anxious to keep moving. "Look Sergeant, I need to get my wife *home*. If you would like to see some I.D...."

"That's okay, buddy. Your story rings true to me." Sergeant Brannigan relaxed and took a step back, hooking his thumbs to his belt.

"Buddy?" grumbled Mae, "Just another smug, self-righteous idiot who won't listen to me." She stopped trying to out-explain Barry and settled down to quietly blubbering, "He's far more willing to believe another *White man* than a *Black woman*. Of course, *that* old story. Going along with Barry's lame plan, playing right into the hands of the Jamaicans. We're doomed!"

"She looks like she belongs in the hospital. I can call for an ambulance..."

"Oh, no!" Barry almost shouted with exasperation. An ambulance might look like an obvious solution, but Barry did not want to incur the expense. So tired of explaining, he remembered this cop was perfectly capable of impeding his progress and tried to put some patience into his voice. "We have an HMO plan. My wife needs help from the doctors who have been treating her. It's complicated, and they understand her problem," he sighed, wondering if they truly understood any of it, at all. "I want to get her home, for now."

Barry had an idea. There was something the police could do to help him. "If you want to help me out, there *is* something you can do..." Barry looked for signs of the man's reaction, "...Would you hold onto my wife, long enough for me to go to the men's room? I haven't had a chance to go in quite a while."

"No problem."

Sometimes, Sergeant Brannigan was still able to remember why he had joined the police force in the first place: he had wanted to help people in trouble. Every now and then, he got a chance "to serve and protect" like it said on the side of the squad car, and it made him feel good.

The sergeant smiled at the weeping Mae, who suddenly stopped crying and took an extreme interest in studying his *teeth*. "Young lady, it would be my pleasure."

He took Mae by the hand. With his other hand, he eased the multicolored woven tote full of souvenirs from her grasp and escorted her to a waiting area provided with chairs.

Barry quickly worked the cramp out of *Clutch* while gathering the rest of their luggage, leaving them near Mae.

Sergeant Brannigan sat a still sniffling Mae down and, continuing to gently hold her hand, nodded to him. "Your wife will be fine. We'll be right here waiting."

Barry made a beeline to the nearest men's room, before the cop could change his mind. He did not trust the police, and he knew better than to trust Mae. He rushed to take care of his business and returned in no time. Mae looked up when Barry approached. She smiled wanly.

The sergeant rose to his feet, as he put Mae's hand back in Barry's. "Are you sure that's all the help you need?"

"Yes, thank you, Sergeant..." Barry rapidly searched the cop's shirtfront for the name tag, "...Brannigan. You've been a big help already."

Barry promised himself that he would never say another bad word about a Chicago cop. He gathered their luggage and pressed the extra-large tote back into Mae's hands. Relieved and energized to tackle the last leg of their journey home.

There was an official-sounding babble from the police radio. Sergeant Brannigan listened for a moment, then answered back, responding with his "twenty." He returned his attention to Barry, "You *do* know it's pouring outside?"

"Yep, we landed in it." Barry led the way, holding his crying wife's hand tightly.

"All right, then. You folks be careful. And good luck!" The kind police sergeant watched him awkwardly manage their passage through the exit door. A powerful blast of wet September wind blew in. Barry overheard the sergeant mumbling, "Glad I'm not on traffic duty tonight."

* * *

The Wrights finally were outside waiting for transport to the parking lot when a stranger came out the door. Barry could see that the strange man's approach had triggered Mae's terror. He looked at the stranger, a slender, fashionably dressed Black man running for shelter, oblivious to them as they already waited inside the kiosk.

The man, ruining his shoes, made a dash for the kiosk. His eyes were on his feet as he avoided the bigger puddles. He raised his eyes, squinting out from under the soggy newspaper, looking as if he was aiming for the kiosk. Mae looked straight at the stranger then bucked in terror as the stranger began to run right in her direction. Suddenly a heart-rending scream tore loose from Mae's throat, "He's going to kill me!" Her eyes rolled right up in her head.

"Sweet Jesus!" The prayer came from the man's lips when he spotted Mae, struggling wildly in the grasp of big, scary Barry. He forgot all about his shoes and scrambled to avoid the kiosk. He looked back once to make sure nobody was chasing him and fled into the parking lot.

With his greatly depleted strength, Barry struggled to hold on to the wildly flailing Mae and begged her, "No! Stop!"

Mae shrieked, "I just wanted a *real* vacation."

His superior size and strength allowed him to outlast her. However, Barry was painfully aware that he was nearing the point of total exhaustion. He was dripping with sweat and might as well have been out in the storm. His lack of control over the situation broke his heart as he held on to her, crooning soothingly, "I know, I know. It's all right, Mae. It's all right."

Gradually Mae began to settle down. When she was still, at last, and her shrieks had subsided into steady, quiet sobbing, he noticed that the extra-large straw tote was lying in the wet street and her souvenirs were scattered about among the puddles. He held her close with one arm while awkwardly bending to collect the spilled "treasures," shaking them free of the dirty water and poking them back into the soggy sack. While doing this, Barry heard a diesel engine cutting through the noise of the wind and rain. He raised his head to see the shuttle bus coming at last.

Now, he knew the drill by heart. While holding Mae tightly, he collected their luggage. She seemed as quiescent as a child worn out from its tantrum, for the moment. But he knew better than to trust Mae. Barry held her tight.

* * *

When no bullets tore into her body, Mae gradually realized that she was still alive and unhurt, which cut through her panic. She risked opening her eyes, wondering where the attacker went. She tried to make sense of the disparity between what her senses told her one moment and what she found herself experiencing the next. She kept wobbling between alternate realities, and that in and of itself was troubling enough to keep her frightened and crying. In a detached way, Mae felt like a burden to Barry who was stooping and reaching around on the rain-soaked street. Wondering what he could be doing, through her tears she almost immediately saw the answer: Barry gathered up junk and put it in that tacky extra-large straw sack that he was forcing her to drag home from Jamaica.

With a squeal of wet brakes, the shuttle bus arrived. The door hissed open, and the bored-looking driver was treated to the entertaining spectacle of a big, seedy-looking White guy physically lifting a crazy-looking crying Black woman onto the bus, untucking her blouse in the process. Bags and suitcases landed in the aisle in a damp heap. Tripping on the steps, the guy had to drop the woman to catch hold of the rail. The driver caught the look on the big guy's face and decided to save the clever remark he had been about to make. He closed the door against the weather and put the bus back into gear.

Mae stumbled towards a seat, sobbing and trying to put her clothes back in order. There were plenty of empty seats to choose from; there could not have been more than half a dozen passengers on board. Ordinarily, she would never seek out the back of the bus as a matter of principle. But tonight, Mae wanted her back to the wall where nobody could sneak up behind her and she could keep her eyes on these strangers. She collapsed in the corner of the back seat, feeling like a sad little heap. Barry arrived, his last few steps gaining momentum as the bus accelerated. He let luggage fall wherever and collapsed wearily on the beat-up seat beside her, blocking her in.

At that moment in time, feeling subdued, Mae stopped crying although her cheeks still felt wet from the lines of her tears. She felt apologetic toward Barry for all he had endured.

"Bare-ree," she began and watched him tense up, the scowl that lately threatened to become a permanent fixture, ruining his attractive face. "Honey, don't be like that. Please, listen to me for a minute."

She fussed at his wet hair, and it hurt her when he flinched back from her touch. She almost started crying again.

"I'm listening, Mae," he said, looking doubtful that he wanted to hear what she had to say. "I wish this damned bus would move faster."

Mae sought her husband's hand and held it tenderly. She looked around the bus, wondering who among the passengers might be listening, and then spoke in a voice so low it was almost a whisper.

"I don't know what's happening to me. I'm not sure what's *real*, anymore."

She heard a nasty chuckle from somewhere on the bus and felt a surge of panic but fought it down. Little pinwheels of colored light spun insistently at the corners of her vision. She closed her eyes, but they were still there. She struggled to focus her mind on what she was trying to tell her husband. At first, the words would not form. But Mae tried once more, and the words tumbled out of her mouth in a soft rush.

"I want to say, I'm sorry, for getting you into this mess and for being so much trouble... and... I'll understand if you don't love me anymore." She raised her eyes to look at his face, ignoring the urgently spinning pinwheels as she read his expression.

A ripple of bewilderment played over his face. His hardened visage melted right before her eyes. She saw her husband's true look emerge, and, in that moment, he was the finest man she had ever seen.

*   *   *

Barry, expecting more nonsense, was completely blown away by Mae's apology and the expression of her doubts. He fought back tears that were flooding into his eyes and gathered Mae gently into his arms.

He held her tight, his breaking heart beating next to hers, and whispered into her ear, "I'll tell you what's *real*, Mae. I will *always* love you!"

In a tiny voice choked with grateful emotion, Mae responded, "And me, you."

They held each other close as the shuttle bus roared along through the storm, transporting them to the far side of the airport, to the remote parking lot where their little car waited.

Barry was glad for the breather but not sure how long it would last *this* time.

Mae nuzzled her face against his cheek, eyes closed. Barry did not want to let *this* Mae go. This Mae he could hold *tenderly*.

He hugged his wife, worrying that nothing would ever be normal again and wishing he could turn back time. He loved her so much. He could never do enough for her; he would have given her the sun, moon, and stars, if only he could. In this brown study, it came to him in a rush that giving Mae what she wanted was what landed them in this nightmare in the first place.

Off the bus and back in the rain and wind, the Wrights hurried down the row of parked cars to their VW Rabbit. Barry unlocked the passenger door so Mae could take shelter, locking her in, then braved the weather by himself for the time it took to unlock the hatch and load their bags. He rushed, not because of the rain, but to get himself back within arm's reach of Mae.

Barry knew from bitter experience that her mood could swing at any moment.

In the car, he checked to be sure that Mae had fastened her seatbelt. She sat with her head bowed down, one trembling hand over her eyes. Barry realized her teeth were chattering. He hoped she was not catching a cold, what with going from one weather extreme to another. He started the car and turned up the heater.

But Mae was not feeling cold. She was fighting a losing battle against a new wave of terror. She was desperately trying to keep one foot grounded in reality while being washed away into madness and spun out of control.

The digital clock in the dashboard told Barry it was 11:29 p.m. as he rocked the gearshift, putting the car in reverse. He let out the clutch expertly, backing rapidly out of the stall and, with a clutch and a shift, popped the sure-footed little car into first and zoomed through the standing water, heading for the exit.

Mae cringed in her seat, gripping the "oh, shit!" handle and breathing too rapidly.

Barry stopped at the booth and paid the pirate inside the blood money to ransom their car. Now that he was driving, he was champing at the bit to get going; he could see Mae was in trouble, again. It was a long minute before the gate lifted out of his way.

With a squeal of rubber on wet pavement, the Rabbit shot out of the lot. Barry took the entrance to the Tri-State Tollway, revving the engine and bringing the car up through the gears to highway speed. He drove as fast as he judged safe in the pouring rain. The trip to their hometown, Evanston, normally took under a half-hour in good weather, barring traffic jams. There would be no jams at this hour of the night, but there might well be storm-related accidents, and Barry did not want to be one of them.

Still, he held the speedometer at 65 m.p.h., 10 miles over the limit. He was grateful for the quartz-halogen headlights he had installed when the factory-issue sealed beams had burned out, and for the fact that unlike the older Beetles, the newer-model VWs with their radiators and water-cooled engines blew enough defrost to keep his windshield from fogging up.

Barry had to grip the wheel with a good deal of strength to hold the lightweight vehicle in its lane against the surges of wind that threatened to blow the car into another one. So enervated, he had to fight to keep his exhausted eyes from closing. He turned down the heater and risked a glance at Mae to see if she looked warm enough. Barry could hear her mumbling but could not make out the words.

He had the momentary notion that she was praying the rosary, but she was not Catholic.

Mae still maintained a white-knuckled grip on the handle. She stared through the streaming glass of her side window. She was apparently talking to herself.

Barry quickly returned his attention to the road ahead, bumping the wipers up to maximum speed. It did not make much difference. The brilliantly lit toll plaza swam out of the darkness ahead. Barry scrounged for change, which Mae normally would have sorted out and made ready for it.

The noise and vibration of the rumble strips made Mae jump in her seat. She looked around like she did not have the faintest idea where she was, alarm growing on her face.

Barry thought, dammit! He did not have enough change.

He would have gladly overpaid the automatic machine in the correct change lane, but he had a grand total of 15 cents in change. It took a minimum of 40 cents to pay the toll and raise the barrier gate. He checked his mirrors and rapidly crossed several lanes to reach a manned booth, braking to an abrupt halt.

Barry extended his hand with a $1 bill in it toward the brain-dead unfortunate in the booth. He frequently wondered if any amount of security and benefits could make a working lifetime of sucking in carbon monoxide worthwhile. The toll booth attendant took the proffered bill and dropped the change on the greasy pavement. The little green Rabbit was already speeding on its way. Barry worked back up through the gears and soon the speedometer indicated 65 m.p.h., again, as he took his position in the left lane.

Up ahead, in the breakdown lane, the emergency lights revolved atop a pair of State Police cruisers, flashing red and white into the darkness. Sure enough, an accident, thought Barry. He let his speed drop, downshifting, straining to see through the smeared windshield and hoping no other driver busy gawking at the carnage would rear-end the Rabbit. He saw a bright, orange sports car off the road, upside down, its underbelly obscenely displayed. Near a fire department ambulance, paramedics checked out a dazed-looking man. A trooper assisted a woman into one of the cruisers. The flares and flashing lights reflecting off the wet surfaces of the road lent a hellish illumination to the scene.

Barry heard Mae gasp.

The trooper from the other cruiser had finished igniting a flare and dropping it to the pavement, forming the last in a line to warn traffic over to the center lane. Barry dropped the car into first gear, and, as they crawled slowly past, he could see how absurdly young the trooper appeared. He wore a serious look on the fresh face of an Illinois farm boy. Water dripped from his plastic-covered "Smokey" hat and safety-yellow raincoat as he waved Barry onward with his flashlight. As he accelerated, Barry heard Mae gasp, again.

He shot her a worried glance. She had twisted toward the back seat and a tortured look of growing horror distorted her face as unintelligible, warbling sounds became far more frightening than actual screams or curses leaking out of her mouth.

Barry shouted, "Jesus Christ! What, right now?"

He realized his speed was almost 50 m.p.h. already, and he was powerless to divert his attention to his freaking wife. He needed to get over, get to the breakdown lane, knowing he needed to get there fast before there was another accident, and he was in it!

"Calm down, Mae. Please!" he begged, hoping to reach some still-rational portion of her brain. He shouted, knowing how useless it would be, "You're all right. Everything is fine!"

Mae tensed up and then spasmed against her seatbelt, as though she had received a massive jolt of electricity.

Barry felt his own surge of fresh panic. But at that exact moment there was nothing he could do but drive, and he needed both hands to do it. A semi-trailer truck thundered past, air horn blasting. The Rabbit was caught in the wash of rainwater thrown up by the truck. Barry found himself driving blind at the worst possible moment.

Mae let out a scream and began jerking frantically at the door latch.

Please God, prayed Barry, do not let her pull up the door lock!

That was precisely the next thing she did.

*   *   *

The maddening aura had not only frightened Mae but also the flashing and whirling had made her feel nauseous. She had not eaten breakfast since the previous day, so her stomach was empty of food and churning with the bitter acid she could taste in the back of her throat. Saliva flooded her mouth, and she swallowed, desperately fighting the urge to vomit. She held tight to the handy little handle in a futile attempt to hold on to her all-too-rapidly-dissolving reality.

When the little car hit the rumble strips at the toll plaza, the noise and vibration scared the hell out of Mae, shocking her into opening her eyes. The aura scattered and dissolved. Mae had no idea where she was. Her heart pounded. Mae realized that she was riding in the car with her husband at the wheel. They were at a toll booth. It was night... and it was storming. Barry was all wet, so she reasoned that he must have been out in the storm. But she was all wet, too, and could not remember why!

Growing in alarm, Mae wished Barry would slow down and drive sensibly. Nothing looked familiar to her; she wanted to ask Barry where they were. She wondered what was going on, but her confusion was too great to put into words. Mae felt the car slow down and gradually became aware of flashing, colored lights. It took her a minute to grasp that the colors were not inside her head but coming from police cars and emergency vehicles on the shoulder of the road.

While she watched, Mae gathered that the revolving emergency lights strobed in time to reggae music, wondering where *music* was coming from. She cut her eyes to the radio in the dash and could plainly see that the radio was not turned on. She looked at Barry, who was focused on his driving, wondering if he could hear the music, too. If he could, he kept it a secret. Her anxiety level climbed another notch. There was something about the pulsing, insistent music that sounded familiar... Mae pulled back from the memory; she surely did not want to go *there*.

Again, turning back to the scene outside her window, Mae looked around wondering where they were. She let out a gasp as she overlooked a scene from hell! Red flames spurted along the roadside, giving life to shadows that danced and frolicked like imps, seemingly as substantial as the human bodies that cast them. Pelted by the driving rain, humans and shadows mixed and milled in confusion or ecstasy around a furiously burning, upside-down car. Police officers with wicked grins dragged a struggling, bleeding man relentlessly towards a Black Maria. The man's feet slipped and skidded in the mud. Another policeman shoved the man's wife into the back seat of a police cruiser. While a stunned Mae watched, the police officer balled up a huge hand, drew back his fist, and viciously double-pumped the poor woman right square in the face! She toppled out of sight, and the officer of the law tossed back his head and laughed, then licked at his bloody knuckles.

Mae gave another gasp. She could not believe what she saw! She struggled to control her mounting panic, squeezing her eyes shut against the barbarous sight, wondering why Barry did not get them out of there. The second she closed her eyes she *knew* they were not alone in their car. She distinctly heard a low, dirty laugh coming from the back seat, right behind her! She could not stand it; she flopped and twisted in her seat, turned around and opened her eyes... and found herself staring at the empty seat!

To see *no one at all* was worse than anything Mae could imagine. Her horror was complete. She wanted to scream but had no control over her voice, and the helpless noises she heard herself making drove her right over the edge.

"Calm down, Mae. Please!" and "You're all right. Everything's fine!" she heard Barry say, his voice sounding faint, as if he called to her from a great distance.

She thought the poor, doomed fool had *no idea*. Then suddenly someone or something was *holding* her in her seat! Mae had to get out of the car!

* * *

Barry endeavored to shift the gears and control a writhing Mae with his right hand. His left hand handled the steering wheel. More than anything, he wanted to drive home or simply wake up from this dreadful nightmare. Barry was out of tranquilizers and ideas, and he was rapidly running out of stamina, too.

Barry seriously began to wonder if they were ever going to make it home. Instead, he decided then to head straight for Evanston General Hospital.

After a while, the car spun onto the expressway and reached a comfortable speed. Mae settled down and leaned back into her bucket seat. So much stuff raced through Barry's mind. How could he describe what happened to the doctors in the emergency room at the hospital? Where should he begin? Would anyone believe him? Perhaps he should stop and call Doc Mac. Although he disliked Mister Goody Two-shoes, Doc Mac knew him and would believe him. He had been Mae's doctor for years.

Barry decided, no. Mae might freak out again if he stopped. Again, he wondered why. Why did this happen to them? He believed someone must pay for this! Again, Barry thought about sending a missile to destroy an entire island of people. He did not notice that he turned onto Golf Road against the red light. Luckily, no one else drove by to get in his way. He reviewed the circumstances, again and again.

"Hon-*ey*! I don't feel like freezing my butt off on this vacation," he said aloud unconsciously mimicking his wife's high-pitched speech. "Now, look at you," he said harshly in his own voice. "We should've gone to Alaska!"

CHAPTER 11

Friday, Sept. 21 — Obtaining treatment in Evanston, Illinois

The Wrights arrived at Evanston General Hospital shortly after midnight that Friday. The trip had taken its toll on both of them.

Barry had been awake since the sun came up on Wednesday, about 43 hours, and he looked like it. He had the dark-rimmed eyes of a madman. His clothes were wrinkled and sweat-stained with one shirt pocket ripped off, one third of it hanging on by some threads. Mae, now wide-awake and in her quiescent phase, had bruised upper arms and rumpled clothes. A tear-stained face had ruined her make-up, and her once nicely picked natural Afro looked like a tangled bird's nest. Still, between the two, Mae looked better rested. She walked into the emergency ward under her own steam, annoyed that Barry continued to clutch her arm.

"May I help you?" asked the woman at the admitting desk, who looked surprised that between this man and this woman, the man was the one who gestured to speak.

Barry explained, "My wife and I just got back in town from Jamaica, where she began having a reaction to her prescribed medication. She has lapsed in and out of psychosis since Wednesday afternoon. It has taken me that long to get her to the States, here to the hospital."

It was a quiet night in the ER, so ER Time went unusually fast.

The triage nurse led the Wrights immediately to an open bay, where she instructed Mae to strip down to her underwear and put on a hospital gown. The on-duty interns were roused from wherever they were sleeping or studying and arrived soon. Mae was so calm and matter of fact, it was obvious that the interns were finding Barry's story hard to swallow. They made a preemptory examination of Mae, finding her general condition to be good.

Her attitude was one of disgust with all their foolishness.

The interns found both Mae's upper arms covered in bruises and sore to the touch. With this discovery, they shot Barry a "look." He had seen this look on many faces in many airports and on board several planes during the preceding hellish day.

Barry thought, "Let them think what they want, I did what I had to do to get Mae home.

He explained that Mae resisted his efforts to get her home during her psychotic episodes, which happened most of the time while she was awake. He explained about what the Jamaican doctor had said, about the tranquilizers he had been giving to Mae. Barry tried to make these interns understand that Mae's current placid behavior was temporary and that he had had to physically control her to get her there at all.

He could tell by the looks on their faces that they were doubtful. Further bruises on her hips and legs were exposed. Barry's heart broke to see how beat up Mae was, although he knew she sustained most of the lower bruises by thrashing around, trying to escape. The interns wanted to speak to Barry out of Mae's hearing, so they walked several steps away. They left Mae sitting on the gurney with no one holding onto her, and no one close enough to grab her if she made any sudden moves.

"Look, my wife cannot be trusted." Barry told them, "At any moment she could be swept away by another violent psychotic episode."

The interns looked at Mae, who had a look of disgust on her now placid face.

"You guys aren't listening!" Barry decided to shock the two into attentiveness. "She thinks I'm trying to leave her here so I can hurry home and fuck the babysitter! You must believe me. She looks calm, but she is paranoid and capable of hurting herself!"

The two interns, shocked by Barry's blunt language, were sizing him up, probably thinking that maybe he did want to fuck the babysitter. They were smart enough to know that the steroids Mae swallowed could and do cause psychotic reactions when given in high doses. And they had to admit the possibility that this rough-looking person might be telling the truth. So, they assigned a security guard to stand by Mae and watch her while they talked to Barry and arranged for someone in the Psych Department to come form an opinion about her condition.

Barry could see that Mae's behavior had altered since they arrived at the hospital. He knew that her mood would swing eventually, but he wondered if, deep down inside, Mae was gaining some control with the realization that they were in the hospital where she was going to get help from her doctors.

The security guard watched Mae, no doubt wondering what he was watching for. Mae took turns shooting looks of disgust, first at the guard and then at Barry. She shook her head at such foolishness and asked her husband, "Why won't you take me home?"

Barry left her in the guard's care and took a few personal minutes to go to the washroom, because he could. There he washed his face, combed his hair, and did what he could to repair his damaged appearance. He used the pay phone to call home. Julie answered the phone sleepily, quickly awakening to hear that the Wrights were now at the Evanston hospital and that Mae most likely would be admitted. Barry told her that he hoped to be home to see Zac before he left for school in the morning. Julie said she would be available to stay with Zac as long as needed. Barry thanked Julie and hung up the phone.

He returned to the ER bay, took Mae's hand, and they awaited the psychiatrist.

About 1 a.m., the psychologist arrived in the ER. Barry and Mae watched from the bay while the interns discussed what they knew with the older man. Barry could only wonder what they were telling him.

The psychologist came over to the bay and introduced himself as Dr. Keith. He said he understood they had traveled all the way from Ocho Rios with Mae in a psychotic state. He asked about her sarcoidosis and her medication. Barry answered his questions while Mae continued to act like she was above it all. Then Dr. Keith said he specifically wanted to talk to Mae by herself, asking Barry to go to the waiting area for a while. Barry acquiesced, but not before emphasizing that Mae had to be watched constantly to prevent her from harming herself.

Dr. Keith showed no sign of having heard what Barry said.

Barry removed himself to the waiting area out of earshot, but where he was able to observe the doctor and Mae. They talked, Dr. Keith examining the bruises on Mae's upper arms while he listened to the answers to his questions. He gave her some simple tests to determine whether her motor skills were impaired. He took note of the "steroid tremble" in her hands.

One of the young interns brought Dr. Keith Mae's hospital file, which he perused momentarily. Dr. Keith had a few more words with Mae before calling Barry to rejoin them. Evidently Dr. Keith had decided that Barry was telling the truth. He would be admitting Mae to the Internal Medicine ward where they would watch her overnight, and that her primary care physician would be in to see her in the morning.

Feeling like a broken record, Barry explained again that Mae should not be left unattended. Dr. Keith reassured Barry that Mae would be watched constantly, the hospital would provide a sitter. He now acted like Barry was genuinely concerned for Mae's wellbeing and regretted having doubted him as a devoted husband. Dr. Keith promised that someone would stay with Mae until they moved her to a room and then a sitter would be with her. He told Barry that this process could take time and suggested that, as an exhausted man, he had done all he could do and should go home and get some rest.

Not easily persuaded, Barry said nothing mattered to him but Mae's safety. He would stay with her for now. ER Time went by. Mae was fitted with a patient ID wrist band.

Called for another consultation, Dr. Keith soon had to leave. Once more, Barry stood guard over Mae alone. Finally, two orderlies came for Mae. Barry held her hand, gently now, the men moved her through the hallway to the elevator. She started crying, again, but softly.

In her room, the nurse had just finished preparing her bed. Mae wanted to use the bathroom. Barry felt alarmed until he saw that the nurse was going to stay with her. Afterward, the nurse helped Mae finish undressing and put her to bed with a sedative ordered by Dr. Keith. The nurse told Barry that the sitter was on her way, and that she would not leave Mae alone for a moment until the sitter arrived to take over. It was now time for him to go.

Barry leaned over and gently kissed Mae's cheek. After all they had been through, it was a hard thing for him to walk away and leave her now. Barry drove the short distance to their home in Evanston, feeling like some part of him was missing. Like a man who has lost a limb, he felt phantom pain. He felt her absence like a foreign presence.

Leaving the bags in the car, Barry let himself in the house, trying hard not to wake Zac or Julie. It was around 4 a.m., and Julie, asleep in the guest room, awakened when she heard him come in. She got up, put on her robe, and came out to the kitchen where she found Barry pouring several "fingers" of tequila into a tumbler.

Julie was a member of AA, but one look at Barry and she kept her own counsel.

"How's Mae?"

"They won't know anything more until her doctors come to see her later this morning," Barry told her. "I want to try and get a few hours' sleep and then return to the hospital. How's Zac doing?"

With sympathetic eyes, Julie told him about the past few days of school and activities. Barry sipped his drink while Julie talked but thought about how much he loved his wife and son and about how much he wanted Mae to get well so they could all get back to their normal lives.

Julie fixed a cup of tea, which she took with her as she returned to the guest room.

Barry Moore Wright sat a while longer, the one who made it home, almost too tired to move and yet too invigorated to expect much sleep. He hoped the alcohol would relax him, but his anxiety for Mae did not subside. After a while, he rose from his familiar chair, washed out his familiar glass, and left it on the familiar sink in the familiar kitchen. He walked softly down the familiar hall, stopping before the door to Zac's room where he eased open the door and quietly looked in on his son, careful not to awaken him.

Zac straddled the line between childhood and adolescence. Barry watched him as he slept and could still see the little boy in his face. He saw Mae there, too.

Barry wanted to wake him up and hold him; tell him his mom would be all right, everything would be all right. In telling his son, perhaps he could bolster his conviction. Instead, he softly closed the door and quietly crossed the hall into the bathroom, closing the bathroom door behind him. Barry began shedding his soiled clothes. He stood in the shower and let the steaming water wash over him as if to sluice away his anger and worry with the dirt and sweat. He stood in the stream of hot water, eyes closed, and something broke loose way down inside him. He began to cry. He cried for Mae — that it was she and not he who contracted the awful, life-threatening disease. He cried for all the horrors that she had been subjected to in seeking a cure — in the name of the "practice of medicine" by arrogant, self-serving doctors who thought they knew what they were doing. And he cried because Mae's desire for a vacation, which should have been fun, worked out so badly.

This big man who had held strong enough for Mae, to get her home, dissolved in huge wracking sobs of grief.

After a time — emotion spent, Barry realized that the shower had gone from near scalding to ice-cold and came back to himself and the awareness of where he was and what he must do. Barry turned off the tap and toweled himself dry. He wrapped the bath sheet around himself and gathered his dirty clothes, unsure whether to drop them into the hamper or the garbage since he never wanted to wear those clothes again. He carried them back to his and Mae's room and dropped them on the closet floor. Barry turned out the light, feeling less alone in the dark. He crawled into the too-empty bed and lay sleepless, blinking at the ceiling. Sometime before dawn, exhaustion won over anxiety and grief. He got a couple hours of troubled sleep.

* * *

Earlier, while Barry drove out of the hospital parking lot, Mae, under sedation, dozed in her room in the Internal Medicine ward. After a while, the nurse tapped her gently but insistently on the shoulder until Mae awakened. It was still dark outside the window. She wanted Mae to know that she was leaving and introduced Melody, a large, smiling Black woman who would stay and "sit" with her.

"Good morning, Mae," the woman said in the familiar lilt of an accent she had heard too much of late, immediately alerting Mae that the woman was Jamaican.

Mae filled with panic. She could taste her panic, smell her own fear, thinking, *The doctors are "in on it." First, they encourage us to go to Jamaica to be killed, and, when that doesn't work, they place an assassin at my bedside! Where is Barry? If he loves me so much, why isn't he here to rescue me? The Jamaicans must have tricked him, again, the way they've been doing for days! Any minute now this big bitch is going to stop pretending and kill me — unless I kill myself first!*

The nurse left and the sitter made herself comfortable while chatting soothingly to Mae about this and that. She started feeling around in a big woven purse, producing a bright ball of yarn and two very shiny, very sharp-looking knitting needles. Too scared to move, Mae cringed in her hospital bed, staring at Melody like a doomed rabbit hypnotized by a boa constrictor at feeding time in the Reptile House at the zoo. She wondered how the blow would come: a sudden flash of a long, silver needle or a pillow held over her face?

Mae tore her eyes away from the woman and looked frantically around the room. She gauged the distance from her bed to the window, considering how much force it would take to break the glass and whether or not she was far enough from the ground for a fall to kill herself. Her heart pounding, Mae spun her face back towards Melody. She caught Melody smiling at her again, and this time she was positive that the woman's teeth had been filed to points like a cannibal, the telltale sign of the conspirators!

Mae hallucinated while Melody knitted and yawned. As Melody's head wobbled, she began to snore softly. Mae watched an artery pulsing in the sleeping woman's neck. Unbelievably, her tormentor seemed to be falling asleep. *Unless she's pretending?* A knitting needle fell from her relaxing fingers and bounced first then rolled to within a few inches of Mae's bed.

Mae's eyes went from the pulsing artery to the needle, back to the pulse-point, and back to focus on the needle. She could not believe her good luck, that this over-confident assassin should doze off, believing that she could end Mae's life whenever she pleased.

But that's not what's going to happen, plotted Mae.

Slowly, resolutely, Mae arose from her bed and began to ease one bare foot toward the floor. Melody slept on, oblivious to her danger. Mae's foot touched the floor, and she began to transfer her weight to it, slipping from the bed to seize the needle. The vein in Melody's neck pulsed with urgency. *Like it wants it*, mused Mae with her fears melting and vanishing while homicidal impulses bloomed and grew in her brain like malignant tumors. Her fingers were about to close on the lethal length of steel...

"Ah, you're up!"

It was a cheery tone from the door. A young doctor stood there, holding a clipboard, and looking at Mae, not aware of the situation. Startled, Mae's foot slipped on some of her sheet that had puddled on the floor by the action of her rising. She had to drop her reaching hand to the floor to prevent herself from falling.

Melody came awake with a snort, blinking around at Mae and at the doctor, aware that she had been asleep on the job. She was relieved to see that the doctor apparently had not noticed her, his attention on Mae.

Mae, surprised in the middle of her murderous attempt, felt her heart filled with terror, again. She should have known that these Jamaicans would be looking out for each other. Mae pulled back into her bed and drew the covers up to her neck, shrinking as far from this "doctor" as she could get.

Melody, feeling around for her missing needle, eventually spotted it on the floor beside Mae's bed. She got up to retrieve it and, gathering her things, moved out to the hall to wait while the doctor interviewed Mae.

"Hello, I'm Dr. Perez." Mae cringed, and the doctor said," Don't be afraid."

Dr. Perez tried to present his absolute best bedside manner, hoping to relax Mae while he examined her and asked questions.

"Where is *my* doctor?" Mae wanted to know.

"Who is your doctor?" questioned Dr. Perez, who was interested in determining the extent and nature of Mae's psychosis.

Little did he know that if he had entered her room just a few seconds later, he would have had a very graphic demonstration presented in blood red.

"Dr. MacAreless," answered Mae, her mouth trembling. She was trembling all over, as if she were very cold.

Dr. Perez mused and made a notation. Then he said, "Dr. MacAreless is making his rounds now and should be here to see you very soon. Now, I get to ask you a question, Mae... What do you do for a living?"

Mae tried to stop her trembling. She gritted her teeth until they stopped chattering, wondering if she might be wrong about this young doctor, wondering if she could trust him.

"I-I'm in P-P-P. R.," she managed to say.

"P.R.? Me, too!" said Dr. Perez, seeking to earn the trust of this obviously frightened woman by presenting some common ground.

"I thought you were a doctor," Mae muttered suspiciously, gazing at him intently.

"Oh, I am," he told her, amiably. "But I'm originally from Puerto Rico."

Mae deduced, *Puerto Rico, way too close to Jamaica!* Her panic leaped to record high.

As she slipped out of the bed on the opposite side from the startled Dr. Perez and backed into the corner, Mae wailed, "Where's my husband?"

The doctor put down his clipboard and got up from his chair, watching Mae's eyes dart to the window. When she swallowed hard, Dr. Perez implored, "Jesus, Maria, y Joseph!"

He quickly rounded the foot of the bed to cut Mae off from the window in case she was thinking what he thought she was thinking. Mae, feeling doomed, slipped to the floor, covered her head with her hands and dissolved into tears.

Melody, aware of the commotion, had summoned the nurse. The nurse heard Mae let out a loud wail as Dr. Perez touched her. Mae's terror was complete: a pure, primitive emotion from the dawn of time.

She withdrew into herself as the doctor and nurse closed their hands on her. Surprisingly, they did not kill her. They lifted her back into bed and fussed the covers back around her with looks of deep concern on their faces.

"Restraints?" asked the nurse, exhibiting more common sense than the admitting doctors or Dr. Perez.

"Nonsense!" came a voice from the doorway. "She'll be fine."

Dr. MacAreless had arrived, broadcasting his usual golden boy self-confidence. He looked at Nurse, Melody, and Dr. Perez with bemusement in his blue eyes.

"How are you, Mae?" Dr. MacAreless oozed with comforting self-confidence. I hear you haven't been feeling so well. Is that right? Did you cut your vacation short?"

He visited with Mae in a soft voice. She began to settle, like a nervous thoroughbred horse with a good handler. The real Mae that had withdrawn deep inside began to respond to her doctor's gentle nature and gradually emerged, willing to trust this well-meaning bungler. The others watched with trepidation as the doctor smiled at them and took Mae's hand.

"Nurse, where's my patient's breakfast?" he wanted to know, turning to wink at Mae conspiratorially. Little did he realize that his wink triggered another wave of Mae's paranoia.

* * *

Mae's breakfast tray arrived a few minutes before Barry came through the door. Doc Mac was holding "court" before a trio of medical personnel that Barry had not met yet.

Barry went over to stand beside Mae, who was nervously picking at her breakfast. The last few hours without her had been longer to him than the entire nightmarish trip home. She looked glad to see him and kissed him with a nearly inappropriate passion.

Barry told her, "Eat your breakfast while I talk to the doctors."

Mae dutifully returned to picking at her food, examining it more than eating it. Then she tugged at her husband to lean closer and, when he did, she whispered, "This food is spoiled leftovers, and that sitter is one of 'the Jamaicans.'"

Barry looked at the sitter. He believed Mae might just be right and shook his head in disbelief at the stupid doctors. *Nobody* had been listening to him.

Doc Mac started telling Dr. Perez to get a blood work-up done on Mae. Barry, who had been looking around, tried to tell the doctors that Mae was not safe in the room, there were too many ways she could hurt herself. Doc Mac, who was pooh-poohing Barry's concern as unnecessary, glanced toward his patient and his blue eyes nearly popped out of his head.

* * *

Mae, who had been listening to the conversation about the blood testing to be done, was shocked when she heard this doctor whom she had trusted with her life telling the Puerto Rican to "drain all her blood; we'll make a good American tourist out of her, yet." It swept her away on a wave of psychosis. She would rather kill herself than let them do that. She grabbed the bread knife off her tray and began vigorously sawing away at the veins of her left wrist!

* * *

Barry was the first to reach Mae and wrestle the knife away from her. He was enormously grateful that Mae did not plunge the piece of cutlery into her eye, wasting its tapered point in favor of its dull edge. Barry held his crying wife and glared at the doctors, who were finally beginning to see that Barry, like Mae's knife, may have a point.

Dr. MacAreless recovered his composure when he saw that Barry had a good hold on Mae. Finally, he and Dr. Perez understood what Barry had been trying to tell them all along. They could see for themselves that Mae was out of control, a danger to herself and others. They prescribed a sedative and called in the day-shift psychiatrist, Dr. Sykes.

Dr. Sykes examined Mae then talked to Barry. "Your wife shows signs of paranoid schizophrenia, which appears to be the result of steroid-induced psychosis. It will take time to gradually taper her off from 100 mg of prednisone to about 40."

It seemed that the corticosteroid drug Prednisone which was prescribed to save her vision *and* her life put her into a state of drug-induced psychosis. This doctor realized the gravity of Mae's condition and wanted to move her immediately to the safe confines of the Psychiatric Intensive Care Unit (PICU). Dr. Sykes explained that it would be best for Mae to sign the necessary papers herself. Mae found it all very frightening but, with Barry's urging, bravely signed her name. She knew this meant she was not going home with her husband, and she would not see her son Zac for a while.

An orderly arrived with a wheelchair to take Mae to the Mental Health ward. Barry walked beside Mae, holding her hand, wanting to be with her for as long as they would let him. Mae knew it would be all right because she knew Barry truly loved her. She totally trusted him. He brought her home from Jamaica. He kept his promise to never let her go.

The Wrights followed Dr. Sykes, who led the way to the ICU. Barry and Mae realized that it was here where they would be forced to part. They held each other tightly and kissed. Barry promised to visit her as soon as they would let him and to take good care of Zac.

Dr. Sykes and the orderly took Mae behind the industrial green door. Barry stood there after the lock had snicked shut, watching for another few minutes before he went home, home to be with his son and to wait until he could be with Mae again.

* * *

Friday, Oct. 25 — Returning to real life and the real world

Five weeks went by before Mae detoxed off the high doses of corticosteroids and recovered from the diagnosis of steroid induced psychosis.

Mae received inpatient treatment for three weeks in the psychiatric intensive care unit, seeing a good therapist daily while she detoxed. Initially, she lost weight. At first, she thought the psych staff was punishing her because her room had no door, her shower only ran chilly water, and the food looked like garbage (all spoiled and wormy). All were hallucinations. It was too scary a challenge for her to water plants. One male technician kept sticking a scary skeleton ring in her face. Early on, Barry brought her a teddy bear, which she named Spitzer-Cohn.

As soon as Mae started feeling more like herself, she was transferred to care in the acute ward where she listened to reassuring love songs and thunderstorm tapes. Barry brought her yellow roses with a reassuring note, which read, "Mae, I love you. I always will, and nothing or no one can change that." Also, she had time to read a very good book that Julie sent by way of Barry, titled The Color Purple. Soon, on a smaller dose of steroids, Mae was quite sure of what was real and what was not.

When Barry came to see her on October 24, it was not for a visit. He had come to take her home. While in the acute ward, Mae had gained 30 pounds, unrecognizable behind the full-moon steroid mask. She no longer felt the same sense of self-confidence that she once had. But she glowed with the knowledge of one important fact: Barry had chosen to save her life.

Barry and Mae left the hospital very much in love, holding hands. Their companionship in the face of a life-threatening challenge made them feel very close. They became more than lovers. In a process experienced by only a fortunate few, they found in each other a true best friend. They freely shared their hopes and fears, and trusted one another to love, cherish and always *be there*. They had achieved a rewarding new plateau in their relationship.

When Mae got home, one dear person she was overjoyed to see again was Zac. Hugging him tightly, she wept and joked, "Oh, Pancho." He responded with a loving cry, "Oh, Cisco."

She found the gaudy, straw tote from Jamaica in the back of the bedroom closet. The only item worth keeping, including the bag, was a tie-dye tee shirt with green and gold ink for Zac.

Mae's battle with sarcoidosis went on for years. On a lower dose of the steroids, she was still edgy and paranoid. For a long time, Mae was too sick to go camping and fishing or hiking and climbing. And her career was stymied by the medical side effects. But Mae kept rebuilding her self-confidence and creative flair that she previously possessed and eventually rose to the position of director within the civil service.

Although her sarcoidosis warped and redefined the rest of their lives, Barry Moore Wright and Mae Bea Wright found real love during their *real* vacation. Love made Barry fight to understand and accept his wife. He kept the promise he made on the day they were married, and he kept the promise he made in Jamaica. Mae trusted Barry completely with all her heart, and her breakdown in Jamaica helped to solidify their bond. They figured out how to be faithful in sickness and in health.

Every so often, Mae enjoys a giant myrtle. But, most often, out of the blue she hugs Barry and whispers in his ear, "Honey, thanks for bringing me home alive from Jamaica."

In the Wright world, home is sublime. And they learned not to put the business of their lives on hold while they wait for the solution to their problems, but rather to see that solving those ever-present problems is the business of their lives.

Not long after leaving the hospital, Mae decided to write a novel, which would take decades to complete. She sat down at her Compaq portable computer and began the keystrokes, first writing a working title then Chapter One, followed by, "Thursday, Sept. 20, 1984..."

THE END

ABOUT THE AUTHORS

C. Jean Baker and Gary P. Baker are a writing team who live with their rescue dog in the northwest suburbs of Chicago. C. Jean Baker has worked in public relations, advertising, and marketing and founded a marketing agency, C. J. Baker & Associates, Inc. Gary P. Baker, formerly an animation artist and greeting card cartoonist, has primarily produced 35mm slides for business during his career. Jamaica Breakdown©, a fictionalized account of a loving couple challenged an unfamiliar sickness in 1984, is their first novel.